NOVA
DHALGREN
and now . . .
TALES OF NEVÈRYON

By ranking master of SF-Fantasy
Samuel R. Delany
Four-time winner of the Nebula Award

"Samuel R. Delany is the most interesting author of science fiction writing in English today."

—*The New York Times Book Review*

"A perfect example of what people ought to mean when they speak of a new wave of science fiction."

—*Science Fiction*

Tales of Nevèrÿon

Samuel R. Delany

For Joanna Russ, Luise White,
and Iva Hacker-Delany

TALES OF NEVÈRŸON
A Bantam Book / September 1979

The various epigraphs for *Tales of Nevèrÿon* come respective-
ly from:

Of Grammatology, by Jacques Derrida, translated and with
an introduction by Gayatri Chakravorty Spivak, The Johns
Hopkins University Press, Baltimore and London, 1976, p.
xviii.

Beginnings, Intention and Method, by Edward W. Said,
The Johns Hopkins University Press, Baltimore and London,
1975, p. 75.

*The Dissimulating Harmony, The Image of Interpretation in
Nietzsche, Rilke, Artaud, and Benjamin*, by Carol Jacobs, The
Johns Hopkins University Press, Baltimore and London, 1978,
p. xvi.

Reading the Cantos, A Study of Meaning in Ezra Pound, by
Noel Stock, Minerva Press, 1966, p. 34.

Anabasis, by St.-John Perse, translated and with a preface
by T. S. Eliot, Harcourt Brace Jovanovich, Inc., New York,
1949, p. 10.

The Archeology of Knowledge, by Michel Foucault, Pantheon
Books, New York, 1972, p. 21.

Desire and the Interpretation of Desire in Hamlet, by Jacques
Lacan, reprinted from a Lacan seminar in "Yale French
Studies," #55/56, edited by Shoshona Felman, Artes Gráficas
Soler, S.A.-Javea, 28-Valencia (7)-1978.

ISBN: 0-553-12333-5

Published simultaneously in the United States and Canada

*Bantam Books are published by Bantam Books, Inc. Its trade-
mark, consisting of the words "Bantam Books" and the por-
trayal of a bantam, is Registered in U.S. Patent and Trademark
Office and in other countries. Marca Registrada. Bantam
Books, Inc., 666 Fifth Avenue, New York, New York 10019.*

PRINTED IN THE UNITED STATES OF AMERICA

CONTENTS

And if the assumption of responsibility for one's own discourse leads to the conclusion that all conclusions are genuinely provisional and therefore inconclusive, that all origins are similarly unoriginal, that responsibility itself must cohabit with frivolity, this need not be a cause for gloom . . . Derrida, then, is asking us to change certain habits of mind: the authority of the text is provisional, the origin is a trace, contradicting logic, we must learn to use and erase our language at the same time . . . If one is always bound by one's perspective, one can at least deliberately reverse perspectives as often as possible, in the process undoing opposed perspectives, showing that the two terms of an opposition are merely accomplices of each other . . . : the notion that the setting up of unitary opposites is an instrument and a consequence of "making equal," and the dissolving of opposites is the philosopher's gesture against that will to power which would mystify her very self.

—Gayatri Chakravorty Spivak
Translator's Introduction
Of Grammatology

I

THE TALE OF GORGIK

Because we must deal with the unknown, whose nature is by definition speculative and outside the flowing chain of language, whatever we make of it will be no more than probability and no less than error. The awareness of possible error in speculation and of a continued speculation regardless of error is an event in the history of modern rationalism whose importance, I think, cannot be overemphasized . . . Nevertheless, the subject of how and when we become certain that what we are doing is quite possibly wrong *but at least a beginning* has to be studied in its full historical and intellectual richness.

—Edward Said
Beginnings, Intention and Method

1

His mother from time to time claimed eastern connections with one of the great families of fisherwomen in the Ulvayn Islands: she had the eyes, but not the hair. His father was a sailor who, after a hip injury at sea, had fixed himself to the port of Kolhari, where he worked as a waterfront dispatcher for a wealthier importer. So Gorgik grew up in the greatest of Nevèrÿon ports, his youth along the docks substantially rougher than his parents would have liked, and peppered with more trouble than they thought they could bear—though not so rough or troubled as some of his friends': he was neither killed by accidental deviltry nor arrested.

Childhood in Kolhari? Somehow, soldiers and sailors from the breadth of Nevèrÿon ambled and shouted all through it, up and down the Old Pavē; merchants and merchants' wives strolled on Black Avenue, so called for its topping that, on hot days, softened under the sandals; travelers and tradesmen met to chat in front of dockside inns—the Sump, the Kraken, the Dive; and among them all slipped the male and female slaves, those of aristocratic masters dressed more elegantly than many merchants while others were so ragged and dirty their sex was indistinguishable, yet all with the hinged iron collars above fine or frayed shirt-necks or boney shoulders, loose or tight around

2

stringy or fleshy necks, and sometimes even hidden under jeweled neckpieces of damasked cloth set with beryls and tourmalines. Frequently this double memory returned to Gorgik: leaving a room where a lot of coins, some stacked, some scattered, lay on sheets of written-over parchment, to enter the storage room at the back of the warehouse his father worked in—but instead of bolts of hide and bales of hemp, he saw some two dozen slaves, crosslegged on the gritty flooring, a few leaning against the earthen wall, three asleep in the corner and one making water a-straddle the trough that grooved the room's center. All were sullen, silent, naked—save the iron around their necks. As he walked through, none even looked at him. An hour, or two hours, or four hours later, he walked into that storage room again: empty. About the floor lay two dozen collars, hinged open. From each a chain coiled the pitted grit to hang from a plank set in the wall to which the last, oversized links were pegged. The air was cool and fetid. In another room coins clinked. Had he been six? Or seven? Or five . . . ? On the streets behind the dockside warehouses women made jewelry and men made baskets; for coppers boys sold baked potatoes that in winter were crunchy and cold on the outside with just a trace of warmth in the center and, in summer, hot on the first bite but with a hard wet knot in the middle; and mothers harangued their girls from rafia-curtained windows: "Get in the house, get in the house, get in the house this instant! There's work to do!"

With spring came the red and unmentionable ships from the south. And the balls. (Most things dubbed unmentionable have usually been mentioned quite fully in certain back alleys, at certain low dives, beside certain cisterns, by low men—and women—who do not shun low language. There have always been some phenomena, however, which are so baffling that neither high language nor low seems able to deal with them. The primitive response to such phenomena is terror and the sophisticated one, ignoral. These ships produced their share of both, sold their cargo, and were not talked of.) The balls were small enough for a big

man to hide one in his fist and made of some barely
pliable blackish matter that juvenile dissection revealed
hid a knuckle-sized bubble. With the balls came the
rhyme that you bounced to on the stone flags around
the neighborhood cistern:

> *I went out to Babàra's Pit*
> *At the crescent moon's first dawning.*
> *But the Thanes of Garth had covered it,*
> *And no one found a place to sit*
> *And Belham's key no longer fit,*
> *And all the soldiers fought a bit,*
> *And neither general cared a whit*
> *If any man of his was hit . . .*

The rhyme went on as long as you could keep the
little ball going, usually with a few repetitions, as many
improvisations; and when you wanted to stop, you
concluded:

> *. . . And the eagle sighed and the serpent cried*
> *For all my lady's warning!*

On *warning!* you slammed the ball hard as you could
into the cistern's salt-stained wall. The black ball
soared in sunlight. The boys and girls ran, pranced,
squinted. . . . Whoever caught it got next bounce.

Sometimes it was ". . . for all the Mad Witch's
warning . . . ," which didn't fit the rhythm; sometimes
it was ". . . for all Mad Olin's warning . . . ," which
did, but no one was sure what that meant. And anyone
with an amphibrachic name was always in for ribbing.
For one thing was certain: whoever'd done the warning
had meant no good by it.

A number of balls went into cisterns. A number of
others simply went wherever lost toys go. By autumn
they were gone. (He was sad for that, too, because
by many days practice on the abandoned cistern down
at the alley-end behind the warehouse, he had gotten
so he could bounce the ball higher than any but the
children half again his age.) The rhyme lingered in
the heaped-over corners of memory's store, turned up,

at longer and longer intervals, perhaps a moment before sleep on a winter evening, in a run along the
walled bank of the Big Khora on some next-summer's
afternoon.

A run in the streets of Kolhari? Those streets were
loud with the profanity of a dozen languages. At the
edges of the Spur, Gorgik learned that *voldreg* meant
"excrement-caked privates of a female camel," which
seemed to be the most common epithet in the glottal-
rich speech of the dark-robed northern men, but if
you used the word *ini,* which meant "a white gilley-
flower," with these same men, you could get a smack
for it. In the Alley of Gulls, inhabited mostly by southern folk, he heard the women, as they lugged their
daubed baskets of water, dripping over the triangular
flags, talk of *nivu* this and *nivu* that, in their sibilant,
lisping way, usually with a laugh. But when he asked
Miese, the southern barbarian girl who carried vegetables and fish to the back door of the Kraken, what
it meant, she told him, laughing, that it was not a word
a man would want to know.

"Then it must have something to do with what happens to women every month, yes?" he'd asked with all
the city-bred candor and sophistication of his (by
now) fourteen years.

Miese tugged her basket higher on her hip: "I should
think a man would want to know about *that!*" She
stepped up the stairs to shoulder through the leather
curtain that, when the boards were removed for the
day, became the Kraken's back door. "No, it has
nothing to do with a woman's monthly blood. You
city people have the strangest ideas." And she was
gone inside.

He never did learn the meaning.

The lower end of New Pavē (so called now for a
hundred years) was one with the dockside. Along the
upper end, male and female prostitutes loitered, or
drank in the streets, or solicited, many from exotic
places and many spawned by old Kolhari herself, all
with different dresses and personalities, all with stories
astonishingly alike. Kolhari port was home to any and

every adventurer. Adolescence spent roaming its boisterous backstreets, its bustling avenues, with its constant parade of strangers, taught Gorgik the double
lesson that is, finally, all civilization can know:

The breadth of the world is vasty and wide, nevertheless movement from place to place in it is possible;
the ways of humanity are various and complex, but
nevertheless negotiable.

Five weeks after Gorgik turned sixteen, the Child
Empress Ynelgo, whose coming was just and generous,
seized power. On that blustery afternoon in the month
of the Rat, soldiers shouted from every street corner
that the city's name was, now, in fact Kolhari, as every
beggar woman and ship's boy and tavern maid
and grain vendor on the waterfront had called it time
out of memory. (It was no longer Neveryóna—which
is what the last, dragon-bred residents of the High
Court of Eagles had officially but ineffectually renamed
it some twenty years back.) That night several wealthy
importers were assassinated, their homes sacked, the
employees murdered—among them Gorgik's father.
The employees' families were taken as slaves.

While in another room his mother's sobbing turned
suddenly into a scream, then abruptly ceased, Gorgik
was dragged naked into the freezing street. He spent
his next five years in a Nevèrÿon obsidian mine, a
hundred miles inland at the foot of the Faltha Mountains.

Gorgik was tall, strong, big-boned, good-natured,
and clever. Cleverness and good nature had kept him
from death and arrest on the docks. In the mines,
along with the fact that he had been taught enough
rudiments of writing to put down names and record
workloads, they eventually secured the slave a work-
gang foremanship: which meant that, with only a little
stealing, he could get enough food so that instead of
the wirey muscles that tightened along the boney
frames of most miners, his arms and thighs and neck
and chest swelled, high-veined and heavy, on his already heavy bones. At twenty-one he was a towering,
black-haired gorilla of a youth, eyes permanently
reddened from rockdust, a scar from a pickax flung in

a barracks brawl spilling over one brown cheekbone; his hands were huge and rough-palmed, his foot soles like cracked leather—he did not look a day more than fifteen years above his actual age.

2
___

The caravan of the Handmaid and Vizerine Myrgot, of the tan skin and tawny eyes, returning from the mountain Hold of fabled Ellamon to the High Court of Eagles at Kolhari, made camp half a mile from the mines, beneath the Falthas' ragged and piney escarpments. In her youth, Myrgot had been called "an interesting-looking girl"; today she was known as a bottomless well of cunning and vice.

It was spring and the Vizerine was bored.

She had volunteered for the Ellamon mission because life at the High Court, under the Child Empress Ynelgo, whose reign was peaceful and productive, had of late been also damnably dull. The journey itself had refreshed her. But within Ellamon's fabled walls, when one had spent the obligatory afternoon in the mountain sun, squinting up to watch the swoopings and turnings of the great, winged creatures (about which had gathered all the fables), she found herself, in the midst of her politicking with the mountain lairds and burghers, having to suffer the attentions of provincial bores —who were worse, she decided after a week, than their cosmopolitan counterparts.

But the mission was done. She sighed.

Myrgot stood in her tent door; she looked up at the black Falthas clawing through evening clouds, and wondered if she might see any of the dark and fabled creatures arch the sunset. But no, for when all the fables were over, the beasts were pretty well restricted to a few hundred yards of soaring and at a loss for launching anywhere other than their craggy perches. She watched the women in red scarves go off among other tents. She called, "Jahor . . . ?"

The eunuch steward with the large nose stepped from behind her, turbaned and breeched in blue wool.

"I have dismissed my maids for the night, Jahor. The mines are not far from here . . ." The Vizerine, known for her high-handed manners and low-minded pleasures, put her forearm across her breasts and kneaded her bare, boney elbow. "Go to the mines, Jahor. Bring me back the foulest, filthiest, wretchedest pit slave from the deepest and darkest hole. I wish to slake my passion in some vile, low way." Her tongue, only a pink bud, moved along the tight line of her lips.

Jahor touched the back of his fist to his forehead, nodded, bowed, backed away the three required steps, turned, and departed.

An hour later, the Vizerine was looking out through the seam in the canvas at the tent's corner.

The boy whom Jahor guided before him into the clearing limped a few steps forward, then turned his face up in the light drizzle which had begun minutes ago, opening and closing his mouth as if around a recently forgotten word. The pit slave's name was Noyeed. He was fourteen. He had lost an eye three weeks back: the wound had never been dressed and had not healed. He had a fever. He was shivering. Bleeding gums had left his mouth scabby. Dirt had made his flesh scaley. He had been at the mines one month and was not expected to last another. Seeing this as a reasonable excuse, seven miners two nights back had abused the boy cruelly and repeatedly— hence his limp.

Jahor let him stand there, mouthing tiny drops that glittered on his crusted lips, and went into the tent. "Madame, I—"

The Vizerine turned in the tent corner. "I have changed my mind." She frowned beneath the black hair (dyed now) braided in many loops across her forehead. From a tiny taboret, she picked up a thin-necked, copper cruet and reached up between the

brass chains to pour out half a cup more oil. The
lamp flared. She replaced the cruet on the low table.
"Oh, Jahor, there must be *someone* there . . . you
know what I like. Really, our tastes are not that different. Try again. Bring someone else."

Jahor touched the back of his fist to his forehead,
nodded his blue-bound head, and withdrew.

After returning Noyeed to his barracks, Jahor had
no trouble with his next selection. When he had first
come rattling the barred door of the overseer's cabin,
he had been testily sent in among the slat-walled barracks, with a sleepy guard for guide, to seek out one
of the gang foremen. In the foul sleeping quarters,
the great, burly slave whom Jahor had shaken awake
first cursed the steward like a dog; then, when he
heard the Vizerine's request, laughed. The tall fellow
had gotten up, taken Jahor to another even fouler
barracks, found Noyeed for him, and all in all seemed
a congenial sort. With his scarred and puggish face
and dirt-stiffened hair he was no one's handsome. But
he was animally strong, of a piece, and had enough
pit dirt ground into him to satisfy anyone's *naustalgie
de la boue,* thought Jahor as the foreman lumbered off
back to his own sleeping shack.

When, for the second time that night, the guard
unlocked the double catch at each side the plank across
the barrack entrance, Jahor pushed inside, stepping
from the rain and across the sill to flooring as muddy
within as without. The guard stepped in behind, holding up the spitting pine torch: smoke licked the damp
beams; vermin scurried in the light or dropped down,
glittering, to the dirt. Jahor picked his way across
muddy straw, went to the first heap curled away from
him in thatch and shadow. He stopped, pulled aside
frayed canvas.

The great head rolled up; red eyes blinked over a
heavy hairy arm. "Oh . . ." the slave grunted. "You
again?"

"Come with me," Jahor said. "She wants you now."

The reddened eyes narrowed; the slave pushed up
on one great arm. His face crinkled around its scar.

With his free hand he rubbed his massive neck, the skin stretched between thick thumb and horny forefinger cracked and gray. "She wants *me* to . . . ?" Again he frowned. Suddenly he went scrabbling in the straw beside him and a moment later turned back with the metal collar, hinged open, a semicircle of it in each huge hand. Once he shook his head, as if to rid it of sleep. Straw fell from his hair, slid across his bunched shoulders. Then he bent forward, raised the collar, and clacked it closed; matted hair caught in the clasp at the back of his neck. Digging with one thick finger, he pulled it loose. "There . . ." He rose from his pallet to stand among the sleeping slaves, looking twice his size in the barracks shadow. His eyes caught the big-nosed eunuch's. He grinned, rubbed the metal ring with three fingers. "Now they'll let me back in. Come on, then."

So Gorgik came, with Jahor, to the Vizerine's tent.

And passed the night with Myrgot—who was forty-five and, in the narrowly restricted area she allowed for personal life, rather a romantic. The most passionate, not to say the most perverse, lovemaking (we are not speaking of foreplay), though it run the night's course, seldom takes more than twenty minutes from the hour. As boredom was Myrgot's problem and lust only its emblem, here and there through the morning hours the pit slave found himself disposed in conversation with the Vizerine. Since there is very little entertainment for pit slaves in an obsidian mine *except* conversation and tall-tale telling, when Gorgik began to see her true dilemma, he obliged her with stories of his life before, and at, the mines—a few of which tales were lies appropriated from other slaves, a few of which were embroideries on his own childhood experiences. But since entertainment was the desired effect, and temporariness seemed the evening's hallmark, there was no reason to shun prevarication. Five times during the night, he made jokes the Vizerine thought wickedly funny. Three times he made observations on the working of the human heart she thought profound. For the rest, he was deferential, anecdotal, as honest about his feelings as

someone might be who sees no hope in his situation.
Gorgik's main interest in the encounter was the story
it would make at the next night's supper of gruel and
cold pig fat, though that interest was somewhat tem-
pered by the prospect of the ten-hour workday with
no sleep to come. Without illusion that more gain
than the tale would accrue, lying on his back on
sweaty silk his own body had soiled, and staring up
at the dead lamps swaying under the striped canvas,
sometimes dozing in the midst of his own ponderings
while the Vizerine beside him gave her own opinions
on this, that, or the other, he only hoped there would
be no higher price.

When the slits between the tent lacings turned
luminous, the Vizerine suddenly sat up in a rustle
of silks and a whisper of furs whose splendor had by
now become part of the glister of Gorgik's fatigue;
she called sharply for Jahor, then bade Gorgik rise
and stand outside.

Outside, Gorgik stood, tired, lightheaded, and
naked in the moist grass, already worn here and there
to the earth with the previous goings and comings
of the caravan personnel; he looked at the tents, at
the black mountains beyond them, at the cloudless
sky already coppered one side along the pinetops: I
could run, he thought; and if I ran, yes, I would
stumble into slavers' hands within the day; and I'm too
tired anyway. But I *could* run. I . . .

Inside, Myrgot, with sweaty silk bunched in her
fists beneath her chin, head bent and rocking slowly,
considered. "You know, Jahor," she said, her voice
quiet, because it was morning and if you have lived
most of your life in a castle with many other people
you are quiet in the morning; "that man is wasted
in the mines." The voice had been roughened by
excess. "I say man; he looks like a man; but he's
really just a boy—oh, I don't mean he's a genius or
anything. But he can speak two languages passably,
and can practically read in one of them. For him to
be sunk in an obsidian pit is ridiculous! And do you
know . . . I'm the only woman he's ever had?"

Outside, Gorgik, still standing, his eyes half closed,

was still thinking: Yes, perhaps I could . . . when Jahor came for him.

"Come with me."

"Back to the pit?" Gorgik snorted something that general good nature made come out half a laugh.

"No," Jahor said briskly and quietly in a way that made the slave frown. "To my tent."

Gorgik stayed in the large-nosed eunuch's tent all morning, on sheets and coverlets not so fine as the Vizerine's but fine enough; and the tent's furnishings —little chairs, low tables, shelves, compartmented chests, and numberless bronze and ceramic figurines set all over—were far more opulent than Myrgot's austere appointments. With forty minutes this hour and forty minutes that, Jahor found the slave gruff, friendly—and about as pleasant as an exhausted miner can be at four, five, or six in the morning. He corroborated the Vizerine's assessment—and Jahor had done things very much like this many, many times. At one point the eunuch rose from the bed, bound himself about with blue wool, turned to excuse himself a moment—unnecessarily, because Gorgik had fallen immediately to sleep—and went back to the Vizerine's tent.

Exactly what transpired there, Gorgik never learned. One subject, from time to time in the discussion, however, would no doubt have surprised, if not shocked, him. When the Vizerine had been much younger, she herself had been taken a slave for three weeks and forced to perform services arduous and demeaning for a provincial potentate—who bore such a resemblance to her present cook at Court that it all but kept her out of the kitchen. She had *only* been a slave for three weeks; an army had come, fire-arrows had lanced through the narrow stone windows, and the potentate's ill-shaven head was hacked off and tossed in the firelight from spear to spear by several incredibly dirty, incredibly tattooed soldiers so vicious and shrill that she finally decided (from what they later did to two women of the potentate's entourage in front of everyone) they were insane. The soldiers' chief, however, was in alliance with her uncle, and she had been returned to him comparatively unharmed. Still, the whole experience had been enough to make her decide that the institution of slavery was totally distasteful and so was the institution of war—that, indeed, the only excuse for the latter was the termination of the former. Such experiences, among an aristocracy deposed by the dragon for twenty years and only recently returned to power, were actually rather common, even if the ideas taken from them were not. The present government did not as an official policy oppose slavery, but it did not go out of its way to support it either; and the Child Empress herself, whose reign was proud and prudent, had set a tradition in which no slaves were used at court.

From dreams of hunger and pains in his gut and groin, where a one-eyed boy with clotted mouth and scaley hands tried to tell him something he could not understand, but which seemed desperately important that he know, Gorgik woke with the sun in his face. A blue-turbaned head blocked the light. "Oh, you *are* awake . . . ! Then you'd better come with me." With the noise of the decamping caravan around them Jahor took Gorgik to see the Vizerine; bluntly she informed him, while ox drivers, yellow-turbaned secretaries, red-scarved maids, and harnessed porters came in and out of the tent, lifting, carrying, unlacing throughout the interview, that she was taking him to Kolhari under her protection. He had been purchased from the mines—take off that collar and put it somewhere. At least by day. She would trust him never to speak to her unless she spoke to him first: he was to understand that if she suspected her decision were a mistake, she could and would make his life far more miserable than it had ever been in the mines. Gorgik was at first not so much astonished as uncomprehending; then, when astonishment, with comprehension, formed, he began to babble his inarticulate thanks—till, of a sudden, he became confused again and disbelieving and so, as suddenly, stopped. (Myrgot merely assumed he had realized that even gratitude is best displayed in moderation, which she took as another sign of his high character and her right choice.) Then men were taking the tent down from around them too. With narrowed eyes, Gorgik looked at the thin woman, in the green shift and sudden sun, sitting at a table from which women in red scarves were already removing caskets, things rolled and tied in ribbons, instruments of glass and bronze. Was she suddenly smaller? The thin braids, looped bright black about her head, looked artificial, almost like a wig (he knew they weren't). Her dress seemed made for a woman fleshier, broader. She looked at him, the skin near her eyes wrinkled in the bright morning, her neck a little loose, the veins on the back of her hands as high from age as those on his from labor. What he did realize, as she blinked in the full sunlight, was that he must suddenly look as different to her as she now looked to him.

Jahor touched Gorgik's arm, led him away.

Gorgik had at least ascertained that his new and precarious position meant keeping silent. The caravan master put him to work grooming oxen by day, which he liked. For the next two weeks he spent his nights in the Vizerine's tent. And dreams of the mutilated child only woke him with blocked throat and wide eyes perhaps half a dozen times. And Noyeed was probably dead by now anyway, as Gorgik had watched dozens of other slaves die in those suddenly fading years. Once Myrgot was assured that, during the day, Gorgik could keep himself to himself, she became quite lavish with gifts of clothing, jewels, and trinkets. (Though she herself never wore ornaments when traveling, she carried trunks of such things in her train.) Jahor—in whose tent from time to time Gorgik spent a morning or afternoon—advised him of the Vizerine's moods, of when he should come to her smelling of oxen and wearing the grimy leather-belted rag—with his slave collar—that was all he had taken from the mines. Or when, as happened more and more frequently over the second week, he should do better to arrive freshly washed, his beard shaved, disporting her various gifts; more important, he was advised when he should be prepared to make love, and when he should be ready simply to tell tales or, as it soon came, just to listen. And Gorgik began to learn that most valuable of lessons without which no social progress is possible: If you are to stay in the good graces of the powerful, you had best, however unobtrusively, please the servants of the powerful.

One morning the talk through the whole caravan was: "Kolhari by noon!"

By nine a silver thread, winding off between fields and cypress glades, had widened into a reed-bordered river down below the bank of the caravan road. The Kohra, one groom told him; which made Gorgik start. He had known the Big Kohra and the Kohra Spur as two walled and garbage-clotted canals, moving sluggishly into the harbor from beneath a big and a little rock-walled bridge at the lower end of New Pavē. The hovels and filthy alleys in the city between (also called the Spur) were home to thieves, pickpockets, murderers, and worse, he'd been told.

Here, on this stretch of the river, were great, high houses, of three and even four stories, widely spaced and frequently gated. Where were they now? Why, this *was* Kolhari—at least the precinct. They were passing through the suburb of Neveryòna (which so recently had named the entire port) where the oldest and richest of the city's aristocracy dwelt . . . not far in that direction was the suburb of Sellese, where the rich merchants and importers had their homes: though with less land and no prospect on the river, many of the actual houses there were far more elegant. This last was in conversation with a stocky woman—one of the red-scarved maids—who frequently took off her sandals, hiked up her skirts, and walked among the ox drivers, joking with them in the roughest language. In the midst of her description, Gorgik was surprised by a sudden and startling memory: playing at the edge of a statue-ringed rock-pool in the garden of his father's employer on some unique trip to Sellese as a child. With the memory came the realization that he had not the faintest idea how to get from these wealthy environs to the waterfront neighborhood that was *his* Kolhari. Minutes later, as the logical solution (follow the Khora) came, the caravan began to swing off the river road.

First in an overheard conversation among the caravan master and some grooms, then in another between the chief porter and the matron of attendant women, Gorgik heard: ". . . the High Court . . . ," ". . . the Court . . . ," and ". . . the High Court of Eagles . . . ," and one sweaty-armed black driver, whose beast was halted on the road with a cartwheel run into a ditch, wrestled and cursed his heavy-lidded charge as Gorgik passed: "By the Child Empress, whose reign is good and gracious, I'll break your flea-bitten neck! So close to home, and you run off the path!"

An hour on the new road, which wound back and forth between the glades of cypress, and Gorgik was not sure if the Kohra was to his right or left.

But ahead was a wall, with guard houses left and right of a gate over which a chipped and rough-carved eagle spread her man-length wings. Soldiers pulled back the massive planks (with their dozen barred insets), then stood back, joking with one another, as the carts rolled through.

Was *that* great building beside the lake the High Court?

No, merely one of the out buildings. Look there, above that hedge of trees . . . ?

"There . . . ?"

He hadn't seen it because it was too big. And when he did, rising and rising above the evergreens, for half a dozen seconds he tried to shake loose from his mind the idea that he was looking at some natural object, like the Falthas themselves—oh, yes, cut into here, leveled off there. But building upon building, wing upon wing, more like a city than a single edifice —that great pile (he kept trying to separate it into different buildings, but it all seemed, despite its many levels, and its outcroppings, and its abutments, one) could not have been *built . . . ?*

He kept wishing the caravan would halt so he could look at it all. But the road was carpeted with needles now, and evergreens swatted half-bare branches across the towers, the clouds, the sky. Then, for a few moments, a gray wall was coming toward him, was towering over him, was about to fall on him in some infinitely delayed topple—

Jahor was calling.

Gorgik looked down from the parapet.

The eunuch motioned him to follow the dozen women who had separated from the caravan—among them the Vizerine: a tiny door swallowed them one and another into the building. Gorgik had to duck.

As conversation babbled along the echoing corridor, past more soldiers standing in their separate niches (". . . home at last . . . ," ". . . what an exhausting trip . . . ," ". . . here at home in Kolhari . . . ," ". . . when one returns home to the High Court . . . ," ". . . only in Kolhari . . ."), Gorgik realized that, somehow, all along he had been expecting to come to his childhood home; and that, rather than coming home at all, he had no idea *where* he was.

Gorgik spent five months at the High Court of the Child Empress Ynelgo—the Vizerine put him in a small, low-ceilinged room, with a slit window (just behind her own suite); the stones of the floor and walls were out of line and missing mortar, as though pressure from the rock above, below, and around it had compacted the little chamber out of shape. By the end of the first month, both the Vizerine (and her steward) had all but lost interest in him. But several times before her interest waned, she had presented him at various private suppers (of seven to fourteen guests) in the several dining rooms of her suite, all with beamed ceilings and tapestried walls, some with wide windows opening out on sections of roof, some windowless with whole walls of numberless lamps and ingenious flues to suck off the fumes. Here he met some of her court friends, a number of whom found him interesting, and three of whom actually befriended him. At one such supper he talked too much; at two more he was too silent. At the other six, however, he acquitted himself well, for seven to fourteen is the

number a mine slave usually dines with, and he was
comfortable with the basic structures of communica-
tion by which such a group (whether seated on logs
and rocks, or cushions and couches) comports itself
at meals, if not with the forms of politeness this particular group's expression of those structures had settled on. But those could be learned. He learned them.

Gorgik had immediately seen there was no way to
compete with the aristocrats in sophistication: he in-
tuited that they would only be offended or, worse,
bored if he tried. What interested them in him was his
difference from them. And to their credit (or the
credit of the Vizerine's wise selection of supper guests)
for the sake of this interest (and affection for the
Vizerine) they made allowances (in ways he was only
to appreciate years later) when he drank too much,
or expressed like or dislike for one of their number
not present a little too freely, or when his language
became too hot on whatever topic was about—most
of the time to accuse them of nonsense or of playing
with him, coupled with good-natured but firm threats
of what he would do to them were they on his terri-
tory rather than he on theirs. *Their* language, polished
and mellifluous, flowed, between bouts of laughter in
which his indelicacies were generously absorbed and
forgiven (if not forgotten), over subjects ranging from
the scandalous to the scabrous: when Gorgik could
follow it, it often made his mouth drop, or at least
his teeth open behind his lips. *His* language, blunt
and blistered with scatalogs that frequently upped the
odd aristocratic eyebrow, adhered finally to a very
narrow range: the fights, feuds, and scrabblings for
tiny honors, petty dignities, and miniscule assertions
of rights among slaves and thieves, dock-beggars and
prostitutes, sailors and barmaids and more slaves—
people, in short, with no power beyond their voices,
fingers, or feet—a subject rendered acceptable to the
fine folk of the court only by his basic anecdotal talent
and the topic's novelty in a setting where boredom
was the greatest affliction.

Gorgik did not find the social strictures on his
relations with the Vizerine demeaning. The Vizerine

worked—the sort of work only those in art or government can really know, where the hours were seldom
defined and the real tasks were seldom put in simple
terms (while false tasks *always* were). Conferences
and consultations made up her day. At least two
meals out of every three were spent with some am-
bassador, governor, or petitioner, if not at some affair of state. To do her credit, in that first month, we
can thus account for all twenty-two evening meals
Myrgot did not share with her slave.

Had her slave, indeed, spent his past five years as,
say, a free, clever, and curious apprentice to a well-off
potter down in the port, he might have harbored some
image of a totally leisured and totally capricious aristocracy, for which there were certainly enough emblems around him now, but which emblems, had he
proceeded on them, as certainly would have gotten
him into trouble. Gorgik, however, had passed so
much of his life at drudgeries he knew would, foreman or no, probably kill him in another decade and
certainly in two, he was too dazzled by his own, unexpected freedom from such drudgeries to question how
others drudged. To pass the Vizerine's open door
and see Myrgot at her desk, head bent over a map,
a pair of compasses in one hand and a straight edge
in the other (which to that clever, curious, and ambitious apprentice would have signed work), and then
to pass the same door later and see her standing beside her desk, looking vacantly toward some cloud
passing by the high, beveled window (which, to the
same apprentice, would have signed a leisure that
could reasonably be intruded upon, thus making her
order never to intrude appear, for a lover at any rate,
patently unreasonable), were states he simply did not
distinguish: their textures were both so rich, so complex, and so unusual to him that he read no structure
of meaning in either, much less did he read the meaning of those structures somehow as opposition. In obey-
ing the Vizerine's restriction, and not intruding on
either situation, his reasons were closer to something
aesthetic than practical. Gorgik was acting on that
disposition for which the apprentice would have de-

spised him as the slave he was: he knew his place. Yet
that apprentice's valuation would have been too
coarse, for the truth is that in such society, Gorgik—
no more than a potter's boy—*had* no place . . . if
we use "to have" other than in that mythical (and
mystifying) sense in which both a slave *has* a master
and good people *have* certain rights, but rather in the
sense of possession that implies some way (either
through power or convention) of enforcing that possession, if not to the necessary extent, at least to a
visible one. Had Gorgik suddenly developed a disposition to intrude, from some rage grown either in whim
or reason, he *would* have intruded on either situation
—a disposition that his aristocratic supper companions would have found more sympathetic than the
apprentice's presumptions, assumptions, and distinctions all to no use. Our potter's boy would no doubt
have gotten himself turned out of the castle, thrown
into one of the High Court's lower dungeons, or killed
—for these were brutal and barbaric times, and the
Vizerine was frequently known to be both violent and
vicious. Had Gorgik intruded, yes, the aristocrats
would have been in far greater sympathy with him—
as they had him turned out, thrown in a dungeon, or
killed. No doubt this means the distinction is of
little use. But we are trying to map the borders of
the disposition that was, indeed, the case. Gorgik, who
had survived on the water-front and survived in the
mine, survived at the High Court of Eagles. To do it,
he had to learn a great deal.

Not allowed to approach the Vizerine and con-
strained to wait till she approached him, he learned,
among the first lessons, that there was hardly one
person at court who was not, practically speaking, in
a similar position with at least one other person—if
not whole groups. Thus the Suzeraine of Vanar (who
shared Jahor's tastes and gave Gorgik several large
rocks with gems embedded in them that lay in the
corners of his room, gathering dust) and the Baron
Inige (who did not, but who once took him hunting
in the royal preserves and talked endlessly about flowers throughout the breadth of the Nevèrÿon—and from

whom Gorgik now learned that an *ini,* which brought back a raft of memories from his dockside adolescence, was deadly poison) would never attend the same function, though both must always be invited. The Thane of Sallese could be invited to the same gathering as Lord Ekoris *unless* the Countess Esulla was to be present—however, in such cases Curly (the Baron Inige's nickname) would be excused. No one known as a friend of Lord Aldamir (who had not been at Court now for seven years, though everyone seemed to remember him with fondness) should be seated next to, or across from, any relative, unto the second cousins, of the Baronine Jeu-Forsi . . . Ah, but with perhaps half a dozen insistently minor exceptions, commented the young Princess Grutn, putting one arm back over the tasseled cushion and moving nuts about on her palm with her heavily ringed thumb.

But they were not minor at *all,* laughed Curly, sitting forward on his couch, joining his hands with a smile as excited as if he had just discovered a new toadstool.

But they *were* minor, insisted the Princess, letting the nuts fall back to the silver tray and picking up her chased-silver goblet to brood moodily on its wine: Why, several people had commented to her only within the last month that perhaps the Baron had regrettably lost sight of *just* how minor those exceptions were.

"Sometimes I wonder if the main sign of the power of our most charming cousin, whose reign is courteous and courageous, is that for her sake, all these amenities, both minor and major, are forgotten for a gathering she will attend!" Inige laughed.

And Gorgik, sitting on the floor, picked his teeth with a silver knife whose blade was shorter than his little finger and listened—not with the avidity of a social adventurer storing information for future dealings with the great, but with the relaxed attention of an aesthete hearing for the first time a difficult poem, which he already knows from the artist's previous work will require many exposures before its meaning truly clears.

Our young potter's boy would have brought with him to these same suppers a ready-made image of the pyramid of power, and no doubt in the light of these arcane informations tried to map the whole volume of that pyramid onto a single line, with every thane and duchess in place, each above this one and below that one, the whole forming a cord that could be negotiated knot by knot, a path that presumably ended at some *one*—perhaps the Child Empress Ynelgo herself. Gorgik, because he brought to the supper rooms no such preconceptions, soon learned, between evenings with the Vizerine, dawn rides with the Baron, afternoon gatherings in the Old Hall, arranged by the young earls Jue-Grutn (not to be confused with the two older men who bore the same title, the bearded one of which was said to be either insane, a sorcerer, or both), or simply from gatherings overseen and overheard in his wanderings through the chains of rooms which formed the Middle Style of the castle, that the hierarchy of prestige branched; that the branches interwove; and that the interweavings in several places formed perfectly closed, if inexplicable, loops; as well, he observed that the presence of this earl or that thane (not to mention this steward or that attendant maid) could throw a whole subsection of the system into a different linking altogether.

Jahor, especially during the first weeks, took many walks with Gorgik through the castle: the eunuch steward was hugely rich in information about the architecture itself; the building still mystified the ex-miner. The oldest wings, like the Old Hall, were vast, cavernous spaces, with open roofs and water conduits grooved into the floor: dozens of small, lightless cells opened off them, the upper ones reached by wooden ladders, stone steps, or sometimes mere mounds of earth heaped against the wall. Years ago, Jahor explained, these dusty, dank cavelets, smaller even than Gorgik's present room, had actually been the dwelling places of great kings, queens, and courtiers. From time to time they had housed officers of the army—and, during the several occupations, common soldiers. That little door up there, sealed over with stone and no steps to it? Why, that was where Mad Queen Olin had been walled up after she had presided at a banquet in this very hall, at which she served her own twin sons, their flesh roasted, their organs pickled. Halfway through the meal, a storm had burst over the castle, and rain had poured through the broad roof-opening, while lightning fluttered and flickered its pale whips; but Olin forbade her guests to rise from the table before the feast was consumed. It's still debatable, quipped the eunuch, whether they entombed her because of the supper or the soaking. (*Olin*, thought Gorgik. *Olin's warning . . . ?* But Jahor was both talking and walking on.) Today, except for the Old Hall that was kept in some use, these ancient echoing wells were deserted, the cells were empty, or at best used to store objects that had grown useless, if not meaningless, with rust, dust, and time. About fifty or a hundred years ago, some particularly clever artisan—the same who laid out the New Pavē down in the port, Jahor explained, waking Gorgik's wandering attention again—had come up with the idea of the corridor (as well as the coin-press). At least half the castle had been built since then (and most of Nevèrÿon's money minted); for at least half the castle had its meeting rooms and storerooms, its kitchens and its living quarters, laid out along corridors. There were six whole many-storied wings of them. In the third floor of one of the newest, the Vizerine had her suite; in the second and third floor of one of the oldest, most business of state was carried on around the throne room of the Child Empress. For the rest, the castle was built in that strange and disconcerting method known as the Middle Style, in which rooms, on two sides, three sides, four sides, and sometimes with steps going up or down, opened onto other rooms; which opened onto others—big rooms, little rooms, some empty, some lavishly appointed, many without windows, some incredibly musty; and frequently two or three perfectly dark ones, that had to be traversed with torch and taper, lying between two that were in current, active use, all like a vast and hopeless hive.

Did Jahor actually know his way around the entire edifice?

No one knew his way around the entire court. Indeed, though his mistress went occasionally, Jahor had never been anywhere near the Empress's suite or the throne room. He knew the location of the wing only by report.

What about the Child Empress herself? Did she know all of it?

Oh, especially not the Child Empress herself, Jahor explained, an irony which our potter's boy might have questioned, but which was just another strangeness to the ex-pit slave.

But it was after this conversation that Jahor's company too began to fall off.

Gorgik's aristocratic friends had a particularly upsetting habit: one day they would be perfectly friendly, if not downright intimate; the next afternoon, if they were walking with some companion unknown to Gorgik, they would pass him in some rocky corridor and not even deign recognition—even if he smiled, raised his hand, or started to speak. Such snubs and slights would have provoked our potter, however stoically he forebore, to who-knows-what final outburst, ultimate indelicacy, or denouncement of the whole, undemocratic sham. But though Gorgik saw quite well he was the butt of such behavior more than they, he saw too that they treated him thus not because he was different so much as because that was the way they treated each other. The social hierarchy and patterns of deference to be learned here were as complex as those that had to be mastered—even by a foreman—on moving into a new slave barracks in the mine. (Poor potter! With all his simplistic assumptions about the lives of aristocrats, he would have had just as many about the lives of slaves.) Indeed, among slaves Gorgik knew what generated such complexity: Servitude itself. The only question he could not answer here was: What were all *these* elegant lords and ladies slaves to? In this, of course, the potter would have had the advantage of knowledge. The answer was simple: Power, pure, raw, and obsessive. But in his ignorance, young Gorgik was again closer to the lords and ladies around him than an equally young potter's boy would have been. For it is precisely at its center that one loses the clear vision of what surrounds, what controls and contours every utterance, decides and develops every action, as the bird has no clear concept of air, though it supports her every turn, or the fish no true vision of water, though it blur all she sees. A goodly, if not frightening, number of these same lords and ladies dwelling at the court had as little idea of what shaped their every willed decision, conventional observance, and sheer, unthinking habit as did Gorgik—whereas the potter's boy Gorgik might have been, had the play of power five years before gone differently in these same halls and hives, would not even have had to ask.

For all the temperamental similarities we have drawn, Gorgik was not (nor should we be) under any illusion that either the lords, or their servants, accepted him as one of their own. But he had conversation; he had companionship—for some periods extremely warm companionship—from women and men who valued him for much the same reason as the Vizerine had. He was fed; he was given frequent gifts. From time to time people in rooms he was not in and never visited suggested to one another that they look out for the gruff youngster in the little room on the third floor, see that he was fed, or that he was not left too much alone. (And certainly a few times when such conversations might have helped, they never occurred.) But Gorgik, stripped to nothing but his history, began to learn that even such a history—on the docks and in the mines—as it set him apart in experience from these others, was in some small way the equivalent of an aristocracy in itself: those who met him here at Court either did not bother him about it, or they respected it and made allowances for his eccentricities because of it—which is, after all, all their own aristocratic privileges gained them from one another.

Once he went five days in the castle without eating. When Gorgik did not have an invitation to some

Countess's or Prince's dinner or luncheon, he went
to the Vizerine's kitchen to eat—Jahor had left standing instructions there that he was to be fed. But the
Vizerine, with most of her suite, was away on another
mission. And since the Vizerine's cooks had gone with
the caravan, her kitchen had been shut down.

One evening the little Princess Elyne took both
Gorgik's great hands in her small, brown ones and
exclaimed, as the other guests departed around them,
"But I have had to cancel the little get-together that
I'd asked you to tomorrow. It is too terrible! But I
must go visit my uncle, the Count, who will not be
put off another—" Here she stopped, pulled one of
her hands away and put it over her mouth. "But I *am*
too terrible. For I'm lying dreadfully, and you probably know it! Tomorrow I must go home to my own
horrid old castle, and I loathe it, loathe it there! Ah,
you *did* know it, but you're too polite to say anything." Gorgik, who'd known no such thing, laughed.
"So," went on the little Princess, "that is why I must
cancel the party. You see, I have reasons. You *do*
understand . . . ?" Gorgik, who was vaguely drunk,
laughed again, shook his head, raised his hand when
the Princess began to make more excuses, and, still
laughing, turned, and found his way back to his room.

The next day, as had happened before, no other
invitations came; and because the Vizerine's kitchen
was closed, he did not eat. The next day there were
still no invitations. He scoured as much of the castle
as he dared for Curly; and became suddenly aware
how little of the castle he felt comfortable wandering
in. The third day? Well, the first two days of a fast
are the most difficult, though Gorgik had no thoughts
of fasting. He was not above begging, but he could
not see how to beg here from someone he hadn't
been introduced to. Steal? Yes, there were other
suites, other kitchens. (Ah, it was now the fourth
day; and other than a little lightheaded, his actual
appetite seemed to have died somewhere inside him.)
Steal food . . . ? He sat on the edge of his raised pallet, his fists a great, horny knot of interlocked knuckle
and thickened nail, pendant between his knees. How

many times had these lords and ladies praised his straightforwardness, his honesty? He had been stripped to nothing but his history, and now that history included their evaluations of him. Though, both on the docks and in the mines no month had gone by since age six when he had not pilfered *some*thing, he'd stolen nothing here, and somehow he knew that to steal—here—meant losing part of this new history: and, in this mildly euphoric state, that new history seemed much too valuable—because it was associated with real learning (rather than with ill-applied judgments, which is what it would have meant for our young potter; and our young potter, though he had never stolen more than the odd cup from his master's shelf of seconds, would certainly have stolen now).

Gorgik had no idea how long it took to starve to death. But he had seen ill-fed men, worked fourteen hours a day, thrown into solitary confinement without food for three days, only to die within a week after their release. (And had once, in his first six months at the mines, been so confined himself; and had survived.) That a well-fed woman or man of total leisure (and leisure is all Gorgik had known now for close to half a year) might go more than a month with astonishing ease on nothing but water never occurred to him. On the fifth day he was still lightheaded, not hungry, and extremely worried over the possibility that this sensation itself was the beginning of starvation.

In his sandals with the brass buckles, and a red smock which hung to midthigh (it should have been worn with an ornamental collar he did not bother to put on, and should have been belted with a woven sash of scarlet and gold, wrapped three times around the waist with the tassels hanging to the floor, but absently he had wrapped round it the old leather strap he'd used to girdle his loin-rag in the mines), he left his room on the evening of the fifth day and again began to wander the castle. This time, perhaps because of the lightheadedness, he entered a hallway he had never entered before, and immediately found himself in a circular stone stairwell; on a whim, he went up

instead of down; after two circuits the stairwell opened
on another hallway—no, it was a roofed colonnade:
through the arches, the further crenellations and par-
apets of the castle interrupted a night misted by moonlight while the moon itself was somewhere out of sight.

At the colonnade's end, another stairwell took him
back down among cool rocks. About to leave the
stairwell at one exit because there was a faint glim-
mer of lamps somewhere off in the distance, he realized that what he'd taken for a buzzing in his own
ears was really—blurred by echoing stones—conversation and music from further below. Wondering if
perhaps some catered gathering large enough to absorb him were going on, with one hand on the wall,
he descended the spiral of stone.

In the vestibule at the bottom hung a bronze lamp.
But the vestibule's hangings were so drear the tiny
chamber still looked black. The attention of the guard
in the archway was all on the sumptuous bright
crowds within. When, after half a dozen heartbeats'
hesitation, Gorgik walked out into the crowded hall,
he was not detained.

Were there a hundred people in this brilliant room?
Passing among them, he saw the Baron Curly; and
the Countess Esulla; and over there the elderly Princess Grutn was talking with a dour, older gentleman
(the Earl of Jue-Grutn); and that was the Suzeraine
of Vanar! On the great table running the whole side
of the room sat tall decanters of wine, wide bowls of
fruit, platters of jellied welkin, circular loaves of hard
bread and rounds of soft cheese. Gorgik knew that if
he gorged himself he would be ill; and that, even if
he ate prudently, within an hour of his first bite, his
bowels would void themselves of five days' bile—in
short, knew what a man who had lived near hunger
for five years needed to know of hunger to survive.
Nevertheless, he made slow circuit after slow circuit
of the hall; each time he passed the table, he took a
fruit or a piece of bread. On the seventh round, because the food whipped up an astonishing thirst, he
poured himself a goblet of wine: three sips and it
went to his head like a torrent reversing itself to crash

back up the rocks. He wondered if he would be sick.
The music was reeds and drums. The musicians, in
great headdresses of gilded feathers and little else,
wandered through the crowd, somehow managing to
keep their insistent rhythms and reedy whines together. It was on the ninth round, with the goblet
still in his hand and his stomach like a small, swollen
bag swinging back and forth uneasily inside him, that
a thin girl with a brown, wide face and a sleeveless
white shift, high on her neck and down to the floor,
said, "Sir, you are not dressed for this party!" Which
was true.

Her rough hair was braided around her head, so
tight you could see her scalp between the spiralling
tiers.

Gorgik smiled and dropped his head just a little,
because that was usually the way to talk to aristocrats: "I'm not really a guest. I am a most presumptuous interloper here—a hungry man." While he kept
his smile, his stomach suddenly cramped, then, very
slowly, unknotted.

The girl's sleeves, high off her bare, brown shoulders, were circled with tiny diamonds. Around her
forehead ran the thinnest of silver wires, set every
inch with small, bright stones. "You are from the
mines, aren't you—the Vizerine's favorite and the pet
of Lord Aldamir's circle."

"I have never met Lord Aldamir," Gorgik said.
"Though everyone I have met here at the Court
speaks of him with regard."

To which the girl looked absolutely blank for
another moment; then she laughed, a high and childish laugh that had in it a hysteric edge he had not
heard before in any of his courtier acquaintance's
merriment. "The Empress Ynelgo would certainly
not have you put out just because your clothes are
poor—though, really, if you were going to come, you
might have shown *some* consideration."

"The Empress's reign is just and generous," Gorgik said, because that's what people always said at
any mention of the Empress. "This will probably
sound strange to such a well-bred little slip of thing

like yourself, but do you know that for the last five days I have not—" Someone touched his arm.

He glanced back to see Curly beside him.

"Your Highness," said the Baron, "have you been introduced to Gorgik yet? May I have the honor of presenting him to you? Gorgik, I present you to Her Majesty, the Child Empress Ynelgo."

Gorgik just remembered to press the back of his fist to his forehead. "Your Highness, I didn't know . . ."

"Curly," the Child Empress said, "really, we've already met. But then, I can't really call you Curly in front of him, now, can I?"

"You might as well, Your Highness. He does."

"Ah, I see. Of course. I've heard a great deal about Gorgik already. Is it presumptuous to assume that you—" Her large eyes, close to the surface of her dark brown face (like so many of the Nevèrÿon aristocrats), came to Gorgik's—"have heard a great deal about me?" And then she laughed again, emerging from it with: "Curly . . . !" with a sharpness that surprised the Baron as well.

"Your Highness." The Baron touched his fist to his forehead, and to Gorgik's distress, backed away.

The Empress looked again at Gorgik with an expression intense enough to make him start back himself. She said: "Let me tell you what the most beautiful and distressing section of Nevèrÿon's empire is, Gorgik. It is the province of Garth—especially the forests around the Vygernangx Monastery. I was kept there as a child, before I was made Empress. They say the elder gods dwell somewhere in the ruins on which it is built—and they are much older than the monastery." She began to talk of Nevèrÿon's craftsmenlike gods and general religion, a conversation which need not be recounted, both because Gorgik did not understand the fine points of such theological distinctions, and also because the true religion, or metaphysics, of a culture is another surround, both of that culture's slaves and of its lords: to specify it, even here, as different from our own would be to suggest, however much we tried to avoid it, that it occupied a different relation to its culture than ours does to ours—if only by those specified differences. (We are never out of metaphysics, even when we think we are critiquing someone else's.) Therefore it is a topic about which, by and large, we may be silent. After a while of such talk, she said: "The lands there in the Garth are lush and lovely. I long to visit them again. But even today, there is more trouble from that little spit of land than any corner of the empire."

"I will remember what you have told me, Your Highness," Gorgik said, because he could think of no other rejoinder.

"It would be very well if you did." The Child Empress blinked. Suddenly she looked left, then right, bit her lip in a most unimperial way, and walked quickly across the room. Threads of silver in the white shift glimmered.

"Isn't the Empress charming," Curly said, at Gorgik's shoulder once more; with his hand on Gorgik's arm, he was leading the way.

"Eh . . . yes. She . . . the Empress is charming," Gorgik said, because he had learned in the last months that when something must be said to fill the silence, but no one knows what, repetition of something said before will usually at least effect a delay.

"The Empress is perfectly charming," Curly went on as they walked. "The Empress is more charming than I've ever seen her before. Really, she is the most charming person in the entire court . . ."

Somewhere in the middle of this, Gorgik realized the Baron had no more idea what to say than Gorgik. They reached the door. The Baron lowered his voice and his largish larynx rose behind his embroidered collar. "You have received the Empress's favor. Anything else the evening might offer you would undoubtedly be an anticlimax. Gorgik, you would be wise to retire from the party . . ." Then, in an even lower voice: "When I tell you, look to your left: you will see a gentleman in red look away from you just as you look at him . . . All right: Now."

Gorgik looked: across the hall, talking to a glittering group, an older man with a brown, boney face,

grizzled white hair, a red cloak, and a heavy copper
chestpiece over his tunic, turned back to his conversation with two bejeweled women.

"Do you know who that is?"

Gorgik shook his head.

"That is Krodar. Please. Look away from him now.
I should not need to tell you that Nevèrÿon is *his*
Empire; his soldiers put the Empress on the throne;
his forces have kept her there. More to the point,
his forces threw down the previous and unmentionable residents of the High Court of Eagles. The Power of the Child Empress Ynelgo is Krodar's power.
While the Child Empress favored you with a moment's conversation, Krodar cast in your direction a
frown which few in this company failed to notice."
The Baron sighed. "So you see, your position here
has completely changed."

"But how——? Of course I shall leave, but . . ." Feeling a sudden ominousness, Gorgik frowned, lightheaded and bewildered. "I mean, I don't want anything from the Empress."

"There is no one in this room who does not want
*some*thing from the Empress—including myself. For
that reason alone, no one here would believe you—
including myself."

"But——"

"You came to court with the favor of the Vizerine.
Everyone knows—or thinks they know—that such
favor from Myrgot is only favor of the flesh, which
they can gossip about, find amusing, and therefore
tolerate. Most do not realize that Myrgot decides
when to let such news of her favor enter the circuit
of gossip—and that, in your case, such decision was
made after your flesh ceased to interest her; and in
such ways the rumor can be, and has been, put to
use." The Baron's larynx bounded in his neck. "But
no one ever knows precisely what the Empress's favor means. No one is ever quite sure what use either
she or you will make of it. Therefore, it is much more
dangerous to have. And there is Krodar's disfavor
to consider. For Krodar is the Empress's minister—
her chief steward if you will. Can you imagine how

difficult your life would have been here at court if you had, say, the Vizerine's favor but Jahor's enmity?"

Gorgik nodded, now lightheaded and ill. "Should I go to Krodar then and show him he has nothing to fear from——"

"Krodar holds all the power of this Empire in his hands. He is not 'afraid' of anyone. My friend——" the Baron put his pale hand up on Gorgik's thick shoulder and leaned close——"when you entered this game, you entered on the next to the highest level possible and under the tutelage of one of its best players. You know that the Vizerine is not at court and is not expected till tomorrow. Remember: so do the people who planned this party. There are many individual men and women in this very room, wearing enough jewelry tonight to buy a year's produce of the mine you once worked in, who have struggled half their lives or more to arrive at a level in the play far below the one you began at. You were allowed to stay on that level because you had nothing and convinced those of us who met you that you wanted nothing. Indeed, for us, you were a relief from such murderous games."

"I was a miner, working sixteen hours a day in a pit that would have killed me in ten years; I am now . . . favored at the High Court of Eagles. What else *could* I want?"

"But you see, you have just moved from the next-to-highest level of play to the *very* highest. You come into a party to which you—and your protectoress—were specifically not invited, dressed like a barbarian; and in five minutes you won a word from the Empress herself. Do you know that with fifteen minutes proper conversation with the proper people who are here tonight you could parley that into a governorship of a fairly valuable, if outlying, province—more, if you were skillful. I do not intend to introduce you to those people, because just as easily you could win your death from someone both desperate for, and deserving of, the same position who merely lacked that all-important credential: a word from Her Maj-

esty. The Empress knows all this; so does Krodar—
that indeed may be why he frowned."

"But *you* spoke with—"

"Friend, I may speak with the Empress any time
I wish. She is my second cousin once removed. When
she was nine and I was twenty-three, we spent eight
months together in the same dungeon cell, while our
execution was put off day by day by day—but that
was when she was still a princess. The Empress may
not speak to me any time she wishes, or she risks
endangering the subtle balance of power between my
forces at Yenla'h and hers at Egelt'on—should the
wrong thane or princeling misconstrue her friendliness as a sign of military weakness and move his
forces accordingly. My approaches to her, you see,
are only considered nepotistic fawning. Hers to me
are considered something else again. Gorgik, you
have amused me. You have even tolerated my enthusiasm for botany. I don't want to hear that your corpse
was pulled out of a sewage trough, or worse, was
found floating somewhere in the Korha down in the
port. And the excuse for such an outrage need easily
be no more than Krodar's frown—if not the Empress's smile."

Gorgik stepped back, because his gut suddenly
knotted. He began to sweat. But the Baron's thin
fingers dug his shoulder, pulling him forward:

"Do you understand? Do you understand that,
minutes ago, you had nothing anyone here *could*
have wanted? Do you understand that now you have
what a third of us in this room have at least once
committed murder for and the other two thirds done
far worse to obtain: an unsolicited word from the
Empress."

Gorgik swayed. "Curly, I'm sick. I want a loaf of
bread and a bottle of wine . . ."

The Baron frowned. He looked around. They were
standing by the table end. "There is a decanter; there
is a loaf. And there is the door." The Baron shrugged.
"Take the first two and use the third."

Gorgik took a breath which made the cloth of
his tunic slide on his wet back. With a lurching mo-

tion, he picked up a loaf in one hand and a decanter in the other and lumbered through the arch.

A young duchess, who had been standing only a few feet away, turned to Inige: "Do you know, if I'm not mistaken, I believe I just saw your inelegantly dressed companion who, only a moment ago, was conferring with Her Highness, do the *strangest* thing—"

"And do *you* know," said the Baron, taking her arm, "that two months by, when I was in the Zenari provinces, I saw the most remarkable species of schist moss with a most uncharacteristic blossom. Let me tell you . . ." and he led her across the room.

Gorgik lurched through the drear vestibule, once more unhindered by the guard; once he stopped to grasp the hangings, which released dust dragons to coil down about the decanter hooked to his thumb and his dribbling arm; he plunged into the stairwell.

He climbed.

Each time he came around the narrow circle, a sharp breeze caught him on the right side. Suddenly he stopped, dropped his head, and, still holding the decanter by his thumb, leaned his forearm high on the wall (the decanter clicked the stone) and vomited. And vomited again. And once again. Then, while his belly clamped once more, suddenly and surprisingly, his gut gave up its runny freight, which slid down both legs to puddle around his heels. Splattered and befouled, his inner thighs wet, his chin dripping, he began to shiver; the breeze scoured his right flank. Bread and bottle away from his sides, he climbed, pausing now and again to scrape off his sandal soles on the bowed steps' edges, his skin crinkling with gooseflesh, teeth clattering.

The wide brass basin clattered and clinked in its ring. He finished washing himself, let the rag drop on the basin edge (weighted on one side, it ceased its tiny rocking), turned on the wet stones, stepped to his pallet, and stretched naked. The fur throw dampened beneath his hair, his cheek, his heavy legs, his shoulders. Each knob of bone on each other knob felt awash at his body's joints. Belly and gut were still liquefactious. Any movement might restart the shivering and the teeth chattering for ten, twenty seconds, a minute, or more. He turned on his back.

And shivered a while.

From time to time he reached from the bed to tear off a small piece from the loaf on the floor, sometimes dipping its edge in the chased silver beaker of wine that, with every third dip, he threatened to overturn on the flags. While he lay, listening to the nighthawks cooing beyond the hangings at his narrow window, he thought: about where he'd first learned what happened to the body during days without food. After the fight that had gained him his scar, he'd been put in the solitary cell, foodless, for three days. Afterward, an old slave whose name, for the life of him, he could not remember, had taken him back to the barracks, told him the symptoms to expect, and snored by his side for the first night. Only a rich man who had no experience of the prison at all could have seriously considered his current situation at the palace its equal. Still, minutes at a time, Gorgik could entertain the notion that the only difference between then and now was that—now—he was a little sicker, a little lonelier, and was in a situation where he had been forced, for reasons that baffled him, to pretend to be well and happy. Also, for five years he had done ten to eighteen hours a day hard labor; for almost five months now he had done nothing. In some ways his present illness merely seemed an extension of a feeling he'd had frequently of late: that his entire body was in a singular state of confusion about how to react to anything and that this confusion had nothing to do with his mind. And yet his mind found the situation confusing enough. For a while Gorgik thought about his parents. His father was dead—he'd watched the murder happen. His mother was . . . dead. He had heard enough to know any other assumption was as improbable as his arrival here at the High Court. These crimes had been committed at the ascent of the Child Empress, and her entourage, including the Vizerine, Curly, the princesses Elyne and Grutn, and Jahor; that was why he, Gorgik, had been taken a slave. Perhaps, here at court, he had even met the person who had given some order that, in the carrying out, had caused Gorgik's own life to veer as sharply from waterfront dock rat as it had recently veered away from pit slave.

Gorgik—he had not shivered for the last few minutes now—smiled wryly in the dark. Curly? The Vizerine? Krodar? The Child Empress herself? It was not a new thought; had he been insensitive enough never to have entertained it before, it might have infused him, in his weakness, with some new sense now of power or purpose; he might even have experienced in his sickness an urge to revenge. But months ago he had, for good or bad, dismissed it as a useless one. Now, when it might, in its awkward way, have been some bitter solace, he found he could not keep it in the foreground of consciousness; it simply fragmented, the fragments dissolving into myriad flickers. But he was, for all his unfocused thought, learning—still learning. He was learning that power—the great power that shattered lives and twisted the course of nations—was like a fog over a meadow at evening. From any distance, it seemed to have a shape, a substance, a color, an edge, yet as you approached it, it seemed to recede before you. Finally, when common sense said you were at its very center, it still seemed just as far away, only by this time it was on all sides, obscuring any vision of the world beyond it. He lay on damp fur and remembered walking through such a foggy field in a line with other slaves, chains heavy from his neck before and behind. Wet grass had whipped his legs; twigs and pebbles had bit through the mud caking his feet; then the vision flickered, fragmented, drifted. Lord Aldamir . . . ? Surfacing among all the names and titles with which his last months had been filled, this one now: Was this phenomenon he had noted the reason why such men, who were truly concerned with the workings of pow-

er, chose to stay away from its center, so that they
might never lose sight of power's contours? Then
that thought fragmented in a sudden bout of chills.

Toward dawn, footsteps in the corridor outside
woke him; there, people were grunting with heavy
trunks. People were passing, were talking less quietly than they might. He lay, feeling much better than
when he had drifted to sleep, listening to the return
of the Vizerine's suite. To date Gorgik had not vio-
lated the Vizerine's stricture on their intercourse. But
shortly he rose, dressed, and went to Jahor's rooms to
request an audience. Why? the eunuch asked, looking
stern.

Gorgik told him, and told him also his plan.

The large-nosed eunuch nodded. Yes, that was
probably very wise. But why didn't Gorgik go first to
the Vizerine's kitchen and take a reasonable breakfast?

Gorgik was sitting on the corner of a large wood
table, eating a bowl of gruel from the fat cook, whose
hairy belly pushed over the top of his stained apron
(already sweat-blotched at the thighs from stoking
the week-cold hearth), and joking with the sleepy
kitchen girl, when Jahor stepped through the door:
"The Vizerine will see you now."

"So," said Myrgot, one elbow on the parchment
strewn desk, running a thumb, on which she had already replaced the heavy rings of court, over her
forehead—a gesture Gorgik knew meant she was
tired, "you had a word last night with our most grave
and gracious Empress."

Which took Gorgik aback; he had not even mentioned that to Jahor. "Curly left a message that greeted
me at the door," the Vizerine explained. "Tell me
what she said: everything. If you can remember it
word for word, so much the better."

"She said she had heard of me. And that she would
not have me put out of the party because my clothes
were poor—"

Myrgot grunted. "Well, it's true. I have not been
as munificent with you of late as I might have been—"

"My Lady, I make no accusation. I only tell you what she—"

The Vizerine reached across the desk, took Gorgik's great wrist. "I know you don't." She stood, still holding his arm, and came around to the side, where, as he had done in the kitchen a little while before, she sat down on the desk's corner. "Though any six of my former lovers—not to mention the present one—would have meant it as an accusation in the same situation. No, the accusation comes from our just and generous ruler herself." She patted his hand, then dropped it. "Go on."

"She nodded Curly—the Baron Inige, I mean— away. She spoke of religion. Then she said that the most beautiful and distressing section of Nevèrÿon's empire is the province of Garth, especially the forests around some monastery—"

"The Vygernangx."

"Yes. She said she was kept there as a girl before she was Empress. Curly told me later about when the two of them were in prison—"

"I know all about that time. I was in a cell only two away from theirs. Go on with what she said."

"She said that the elder gods dwell there, and that they are even older than the monastery. She said that the lands were lush and lovely and that she longed to revisit them. But that even today there was more trouble from that little bit of land than from any other place in the Empire."

"And while she spoke with you thus, Krodar cast you a dark look . . . ?" The Vizerine dropped both hands to the desk. She sighed. "Do you know the Garth Peninsula?"

Gorgik shook his head.

"A brutish, uncivilized place—though the scenery is pretty enough. Every other old hovel one comes across houses a witch or a wizard; not to mention the occasional mad priest. And then, a few miles to the south, it is no longer forest but jungle; and there are nothing but barbarian tribes. And the amount of worry it causes is absolutely staggering!" She sighed again. "Of course you know, Gorgik, that the Empress associates you with me. So any word spoken to you—or even a look cast your way—may be read in some way as a message intended for Myrgot."

"Then I hope I have not brought Myrgot an unhappy one."

"It's not a good one." The Vizerine sighed, leaned back a little on the desk, placing one fingertip on the shale of parchment. "For the Empress to declare the elder gods are older than the monastery is to concede me a theological point that I support and that, till now, she has opposed; over this point, many people have died. For her to say she wishes to go there is tantamount to declaring war on Lord Aldamir, in whose circle you and I both move, and who keeps his center of power there. For her to choose *you* to deliver this message is . . . But I shouldn't trouble you with the details of that meaning."

"Yes, My Lady. There is no need. My Lady—?"

The Vizerine raised her eyebrow.

"I *asked* to come and speak to you. Because I cannot stay here at Court any longer. What can I do to serve you in the outside world? Can I be a messenger for you? Can I work some bit of your land? Within the castle here there is nothing for me."

The Vizerine was silent long enough for Gorgik to suspect she disapproved of his request. "Of course you're right," she said at last, so that he was surprised and relieved. "No, you can't stay on here. Especially after last night. I suppose I could always return you to the mine . . . no, that is a tasteless joke. Forgive me."

"There is nothing to forgive, my lady," though Gorgik's heart had suddenly started. While it slowed, he ventured: "Any post you can put me to, I would most happily fill."

After another few moments, the Vizerine said: "Go now. I will send for you in an hour. By then we shall have decided what to do with you."

"You know, Jahor—" The Vizerine stood by the window, looking between the bars at the rain, at further battlements beyond the veils of water, the dripping mansards and streaming crenellations. "—he really is an exceptional man. After five months, he wishes to leave the castle. Think of many many of the finest sons and daughters of provincial noblemen who, once presented here, become parasites and hangers-on for five *years* or more—before they finally reach such a propitious decision as he has." Rain gathered on the bars and dripped, wetting inches of the beveled sill.

Jahor sat in the Vizerine's great, curved-back chair, rather slump-shouldered, and for all his greater bulk, filling it noticeably less well than she. "He was wasted in the mines, My Lady. He is wasted at the castle. Only consider, My Lady, what *is* such a man fit for? First, childhood as a portside ragamuffin, then his youth as a mine slave, followed by a few months' skulking in the shadows at the Court of Eagles—where, apparently, he still was not able to keep completely out of sight. That is an erratic education to say the least. I can think of no place where he could put it to use. Return him to the mines now, My Lady. Not as a slave, if that troubles you. Make him a free overseer. That is still more than he might ever have hoped for six months ago."

The bars dripped.

Myrgot pondered.

Jahor picked up a carefully crafted astrolabe from the desk, ran a long forenail over its calibrations, then rubbed his thumb across the curlicues of the rhet.

The Vizerine said: "No. I do not think that I will do that, Jahor. It is too close to slavery." She turned from the window and thought about her cook. "I shall do something else with him."

"*I* would put him back in the mines without his freedom," Jahor said sullenly. "But then, My Lady is almost as generous as the Empress herself. And as just."

The Vizerine raised an eyebrow at what she considered an ill-put compliment. But then, of course, Jahor did not know the Empress's most recent message that Gorgik had so dutifully delivered. "No. I have another idea for him. . . ."

"To the mines with him, My Lady, and you will save yourself much trouble, if not grief."

Had Gorgik known of the argument that was progressing in the Vizerine's chamber, he would most probably have misassigned the positions of the respective advocates—perhaps the strongest sign of his unfitness for court life.

Though it does not explain the actual assignment of the positions themselves, there was a simple reason for the tones of voice in which the respective positions were argued: For the last three weeks the Vizerine's lover had been a lithe, seventeen-year-old with bitten nails and mad blue eyes, who would, someday, inherit the title of Suzeraine of Strethi—though the land his parents owned, near the marshy Avila, was little more than a sizeable farm. And the youth, for all his coming title, was—in his manners and bearing—little more than a farmer's son. His passion was for horses, which he rode superbly. Indeed, he had careered, naked, on a black mount, about the Vizerine's caravan for an hour one moonlit night when, two months before, she had been to visit the Avila province to meet with its reigning families anent taxes. She had sent Jahor to ascertain how she might meet this fiery youth. A guest of his parents one evening, she discovered that they were quite anxious for him to go to court and that for one so young he had an impressive list of illegitimate children throughout the surrounding neighborhoods and was something of a bane to his kin. She had agreed to take him with her; and had kept her agreement. But the relationship was of the volatile and explosive sort that made her, from time to time, look back with fondness on the weeks with Gorgik. Four times now the suzeraine-apparent had run up atrocious debts gambling with the servants, twice he had tried to blackmail her, and had been unfaithful to her with at least three palace serving women, and what's more they were *not* of Lord Aldamir's circle. The night before the Vizerine had departed on this her most recent mission—to get away from the child? but no—they had gotten into an incredible argument over a white gold chain which had ended with his declaring he would never let her withered lips and wrinkled paws defile his strong, lithe body again. But just last night, however, hours before her return, he had ridden out to meet her caravan, charged into her tent, and declared he could not live without her caress another moment. In short, that small sector of Myrgot's life she set aside for personal involvement was currently full to overflowing. (Jahor, currently, had no lover at all, nor was he overfond of the Vizerine's.)

The Vizerine, in deference to the vaguest of promises to his parents, had been desultorily attempting to secure a small commission for the blond youth with some garrison in a safer part of the Empire. She knew he was too young for such a post, and of an impossible temperament to fulfill it, even were he half a dozen years older; also, there was really no way, in those days, to ascertain if any part of the Empire would remain safe. In any open combat, the little fool—for he was a fool, she did not delude herself to that—would probably be killed, and more than likely get any man under him killed as well—if his men did not turn and kill him first. (She had known such things to happen.) This young, unlettered nobleman was the sort who, for all his good looks, fiery temperament, and coming inheritance, one either loved or despised. And she had discovered, upon making inquiries into the gambling affair, much to her surprise, that no one in court other than herself seemed to love him in the least. Well, she still did not want him to leave the court . . . not just now. She had only put any effort toward obtaining his commission at those moments when she had been most aware that soon she must want him as far away as possible.

The commission had arrived while she had been away; it was on her desk now.

No, after his marvelous ride last night to meet

her, she did *not* want him to leave . . . *just* yet. But
she was experienced enough to know the wishes that
he would, with such as he, must come again. As would
other commissions.

"Gorgik," she said, when Jahor had led him in
and retired, "I am going to put you for six weeks
with Master Narbu: he trains all of Curly's personal
guards and has instructed many of the finest generals
of this Empire in the arts of war. Most of the young
men there will be two or three years younger than
you, but that may easily, at your age, be as much
an advantage as a hinderance. At the end of that
time, you will be put in charge of a small garrison
near the edge of the K'haki desert—north of the
Faltha's. At the termination of your commission you
will have the freedom in fact that, as of this morning,
you now have on paper. I hope you will distinguish
yourself in the name of the Empress, who is wise
and wondrous." She smiled. "Will you agree that
this now terminates any and all of our mutual obli-
gations?"

"You are very generous, My Lady," Gorgik said,
almost as flabbergasted as when he'd discovered himself purchased from the mines.

"Our Empress is just and generous," the Vizerine said, almost as if correcting him. "I am merely
soft-hearted." Her hand had strayed to the astrolabe.
Suddenly she picked up the verdigrised disk, turned
it over, frowned at it. "Here, take this. Go on. Take
it, keep it; and take with it one final piece of advice.
It's heartfelt advice, my young friend. I want you
always to remember the Empress's words to you last
night. *Do* you promise? Good—and as you value
your freedom and your life, never set foot on the
Garth peninsula. And if the Vygernangx Monastery
ever thrusts so much as the tiny tip of one tower over
the tree-tops within the circle of your vision, you will
turn yourself directly around and ride, run, crawl
away as fast and as far as you can go. Now take it—
take it, go on. And go."

With the Vizerine's verdigrised astrolabe in his

hand, Gorgik touched his forehead and backed, frowning, from the chamber.

"My Lady, his education is already erratic enough. By making him an officer, you do not bring it to heel. It will only give him presumptions, which will bring him grief and you embarrassment."

"Perhaps, Jahor. Then again, perhaps not. We shall see."

Outside the window, the rains, which, after having let up for the space of an hour's sunlight, blew violently again, clouding the far towers and splattering all the way in to the edge of the stone sill, running down the inner wall to the floor.

"My Lady, wasn't there an astrolabe here on your desk earlier this morning . . . ?"

"Was there now . . . ? Ah yes. My pesky, little blue-eyed devil was in here only moments ago, picking at it. No doubt he pocketed it on his way down to the stables. Really, Jahor, I *must* do something about that gold-haired, little tyrant. He has become the bane of my life!"

Six weeks is long enough for a man to learn to enjoy himself on a horse; it is not long enough to learn to ride.

Six weeks is long enough for a man to learn the rules and forms of fencing; it is not long enough to become a swordsman.

Master Narbu, born a slave himself to a high household in the eastern hills of the Falthas not far from fabled Ellamon, had as a child shown some animal grace that his baronial owner thought best turned to weapon wielding—from a sort of retrograde, baronial caprice. Naturally slaves were not encouraged to excel in arms. Narbu had taken the opportunity to practice —from a retrograde despair at servitude—constantly, continuously, dawn, noon, night, and any spare moment between. At first the hope had been, naturally and secretly and obviously to any but such a capricious master, for escape. Skill had become craft and craft had become art; and developing along was an impassioned love for weaponry itself. The Baron displayed the young slave's skill to friends; mock contests were arranged; then real contests—with other slaves, with freemen. Lords of the realm proud of their own skills challenged him; two lords of the realm died. And Narbu found himself in this paradoxical position: his license to sink sword blade into an aristocratic gut was only vouchsafed by the protection of an aristocrat. During several provincial skirmishes, Narbu fought valiantly beside his master. In several others, his master rented him out as a mercenary—by now his reputation (though he was not out of his twenties) was such that he was being urged, pressed, forced to learn the larger organizational skills and strategies that make war possible. One cannot truly trace the course of a life in a thousand pages. Let us have the reticence here not to attempt it in a thousand words. Twenty years later, during one of the many battles that resulted in the ascension of the present Child Empress Ynelgo to the Throne of Eagles, Narbu (now forty-four) and his master had been lucky enough to be on the winning side—though his master was killed. But Narbu had distinguished himself. As a reward—for the Empress was brave and benevolent—Narbu was given his freedom and offered a position as instructor of the Empress's own guard, a job which involved training the sons of favored aristocrats in the finer (and grosser) points of battle. (Two of Narbu's earliest instructors had been daughters of the mysterious Western Crevasse, and much of his early finesse had been gained from these masked women with their strange and strangely sinister blades. Twice he had fought with such women; and once against them. But they did not usually venture in large groups too far from their own lands. Still, he had always suspected that Nevèrÿon, with its strictly male armies, was overcompensating for something.) In his position as royal master at arms, he found himself developing a rich and ritual tirade against his new pupils: They were soft, or when they were hard they had no discipline, or, when they had discipline, had no heart. What training they'd gotten must all be undone before they could really begin; aristocrats could never make good soldiers anyway; what was needed was good, common stock. Though master Narbu *was* common stock, had fought common stock, and been taught by common stock, Gorgik was the first man of common stock Master Narbu, in six years, had ever been paid to teach. And the good master now discovered that, as a teacher, somehow he had never developed a language to instruct any other than aristocrats—however badly trained, undisciplined, or heartless they were. As well, he found himself actually resenting this great-muscled, affable, quiet, giant of a youth. First, Gorgik's physique was not the sort (as Narbu was quick to point out to him) that naturally lent itself to horsemanship or any but gross combative skills. Besides, the rumor had gone the rounds that the youth had been put under Narbu's tutelage not even because of his exceptional strength, but because he was some high Court lady's catamite. But one morning, Master Narbu woke, frowned at some sound outside, and sat up on his pallet: through the bars on his window, he looked out across the yard where the training dummies and exercise forms stood in moonlight—it was over an hour to sunup. On the porch of the student barracks, beneath the frayed thatch, a great form, naked and crossed with shadow from the nearest porch poles, moved and turned and moved.

The new pupil was practicing. First he would try a few swings with the light wooden sword to develop form, moving slowly, returning to starting position, hefting the blade again. And going through the swing, parry, recovery . . . a little too self-consciously; and the arm not fully extended at the peak of the swing, the blade a little too high. . . . Narbu frowned. The new student put down the wooden blade against the barrack wall, picked up the treble-weight iron blade used to improve strength: swing, parry, recovery; again, swing, parry—the student halted, stepped back, began again. Good. He'd remembered the extension this time. Better, Narbu reflected. Better . . . but not excellent. Of course, for the weighted blade, it was

better than most of the youths—with those great sacks
of muscle about his bones, really not so surprising . . .
No, he didn't let the blade sag. But what was he
doing up this early anyway . . . ?

Then Narbu saw something.

Narbu squinted a little to make sure he saw it.

What he saw was something he could not have
named himself, either to baron or commoner. Indeed,
we may have trouble describing it: He saw a concentration in this extremely strong, naked, young
man's practicing that, by so many little twists and
sets of the body, flicks of the eye, bearings of the
arms and hips, signed its origins in inspiration. He
saw something that much resembled not a younger
Narbu, but something that had been part of the
younger Narbu and which, when he recognized it
now, he realized was all-important. The others, Narbu thought (and his lips, set about with gray stubble,
shaped the words), were too pampered, too soft . . .
how many hours before sunrise? Not those others, no,
not on your . . . that one, yes, *was* good common
stock.

Narbu lay back down.

No, this common, one-time mercenary slave still
did not know how to speak to a common, one-time
pit slave as a teacher; and no, six weeks were *not*
enough. But now, in the practice sessions, and sometimes in the rest periods during and after them,
Narbu began to say things to the tall, scar-faced
youth: "In rocky terrain, look for a rider who holds
one rein up near his beast's ear, with his thumb tucked
well down; he'll be a Narnisman and the one to show
you how to coax most from your mount in the mountains. Stick by him and watch him fast. . . ." And:
"The best men with throwing weapons I've ever seen
are the desert Adami: shy men, with little brass wires
sewn up around the backs of their ears. You'll be
lucky if you have a few in your garrison. Get one of
them to practice with you, and you might learn something. . . ." Or: "When you requisition cart oxen in
the Avila swamplands, if you get them from the Men
of the Hide Shields, you must get one of them to

drive, for it will be a good beast, but nervous. If you get a beast from the Men of the Palm Fiber Shields, then anyone in your garrison can drive it—they train them differently, but just how I am not sure." Narbu said these things and many others. His saws cut through to where and how and what one might need to learn beyond those six weeks. They came out in no organized manner. But there were many of them. Gorgik remembered many; and he forgot many. Some of those he forgot would have saved him much time and trouble in the coming years. Some that he remembered he never got an opportunity to use. But even more than the practice and the instruction (and because Gorgik practiced most, at the end of the six weeks he was easily the best in his class), this was the education he took with him. And Myrgot was away from the castle when his commission began . . .

3

There was an oxcart ride along a narrow road with mountains looking over the trees to the left; with six other young officers, he forded an icy stream, up to his waist in foam; a horse ride over bare rocks, around steep slopes of slate . . . ahead were the little tongues of army campfires, alick on the blue, with the desert below, white as milk in quarterlight.

Gorgik took over his garrison with an advantage over most: five years' experience in the mines as a foreman over fifty slaves.

His garrison contained only twenty-nine.

Nor were they despairing, unskilled, and purchased for life. Though, over the next few years, from time to time Gorgik wondered just how much difference that made in the daily texture of their lives, for guards' lives were rough in those days. Over those same years, Gorgik became a good officer. He gained the affection of his men, mainly by keeping them alive in an epoch in which one of the horrors of war was that every time more than ten garrisons were brought together, twenty percent were lost through communicable diseases having nothing to do with battle (and much of the knowledge for this could be traced back to some of Master Narbu's more eccentric saw concerning various herbs, moldy fruit rinds, and moss—and not a few of Baron Curly's observations on botany that Gorgik found himself now and again recalling to great effect). As regards the army itself, Gorgik was a man recently enough blessed with an unexpected hope of life that all the human energy expended to create an institution solely bent on smashing that hope seemed arbitrary and absurd enough to marshal all his intelligence toward surviving it. He saw battle as a test to be endured, with true freedom as prize. He had experienced leading of a sort before, and he led well. But the personalities of his men—both their blustering camaraderie (which seemed a pale and farcical shadow of the brutal and destructive mayhem that, from time to time, had broken out in the slave quarters at the mines, always leaving three or four dead), and the constant resignation to danger and death (that any sane slave would have been trying his utmost to avoid) both confused him (and confusion he had traditionally dealt with by silence) and depressed him (and depression, frankly, he had never really had time to deal with, nor did he really here, so that its effects, finally, were basically just more anecdotes for later years on the stupidity of the military mind).

He knew all his men, and had a far easier relationship with them than most officers of that day. But only a very few did he ever consider friends, and then not for long. A frequent occurrence: some young recruit would take the easiness of some late-night campfire talk, or the revelations that occurred on a foggy morning hike, as a sign of lasting intimacy, only to find himself reprimanded (and, in three cases over the two years, struck to the ground for the presumption: for these were barbaric and brutal times), in a manner that recalled nothing so much (at least to Gorgik, eternally frustrated by having to give out these reprimands) as the snubs he had received in the halls of the High Court of Eagles the mornings after some particularly revelatory exchange with some count or princess.

Couldn't these imbeciles learn?

He had.

The ones who stayed in his garrison did. And respected him for the lesson—loved him, some of them would even have said in the drunken evenings that, during some rare, lax period, now at a village tavern, now at a mountain campsite where wine had been impounded from a passing caravan, still punctuated a guard's life. Gorgik laughed at this. His own silent appraisal of the situation had been, from the beginning: I may die; they may die; but if there is any way their death can delay mine, let theirs come down.

Yet within this strictly selfish ethical matrix, he was able to display enough lineaments both of reason and bravery to satisfy those above him in rank and those below—till, from time to time, especially in the face of rank cowardness (which he always tried to construe—and usually succeeded—as rank stupidity) in others, he could convince himself there might be something to the whole idea. "Might"—for survival's sake he never allowed it to go any further.

He survived.

But such survival was a lonely business. After six months, out of loneliness, he hired a scribe to help him compose a long letter to the Vizerine: inelegant, rambling, uncomfortable with its own discourse, wisely it touched neither on his affection for her nor his debt to her, but rather turned about what he had learned, had seen, had felt: the oddly depressed atmosphere of the marketplace in the town they had passed through the day before; the hectic nature of the smuggling in that small port where, for two weeks now, they had been garrisoned; the anxious gossip of the soldiers and prostitutes about the proposed public building scheduled to replace a section of slumlike huts in a city to the north; the brazen look to the sky from a southern mountain path that he and his men had wandered on for two hours in the evening before stopping to camp.

At the High Court the Vizerine read his letter—several times, and with a fondness that, now all pretence at the erotic was gone, grew, rather than diminished, in directions it would have been harder for grosser souls to follow, much less appreciate. His letter contained this paragraph:

"Rumors came down among the lieutenants last week that all the garrisons hereabout were to be gone south for the Garth in a month. I drank wine with the Major, diced him for his bone-handled knives and won. Two garrisons were to go the Able-aini, in the swamps east of the Faltha—a thankless position, putting down small squabbles for ungrateful lords, he assured me, more dangerous and less interesting than the south. I gave him back his knives. He scratched his gray beard in which one or two rough red hairs still twist, and gave me his promise of the Faltha post, thinking me mad."

The Vizerine read it, at dawn, standing by the barred windows (dripping with light rain as they had dripped on the morning of her last interview with Gorgik, half a year before), remembered him, looked back toward her desk where once a bronze astrolabe had lain among the parchment. A lamp flame wavered, threatened to go out, and steadied. She smiled.

Toward the end of Gorgik's three years (the occasional, unmistakably royal messenger and scribe who came to his tent to deliver Myrgot's brief and very formal acknowledgments and take back other messages from him did not hurt his reputation among his troops), when his garrison was moving back and forth at biweekly intervals, from the desert skirmishes near the Venarra canyon to the comparatively calm hold of Fabled Ellamon high in the Faltha range (where, like all tourists, Gorgik and his men went out to observe, from the white lime slopes, across the crags to the far corrals of the fabled, flying beasts that scarred the evening sky with their exercises), he discovered that some of his men had been smuggling purses of salt from the desert to the mountains. He made no great issue of it; but he called in the man whom he suspected to be second in charge of the smuggling operation and told him he wished a share— a modest share—of the profits. With that share, he purchased three extra carts, and four oxen to pull them; and with a daring that astonished his men (for the Empress's royal inspectors were neither easy nor forgiving) on his last trek back, a week before his discharge, he brought three whole cartfuls of contraband salt, which he got through by turning off the main road, whereupon they were shortly met by what was obviously a ragged, private guard at the edge of private lands.

"Common soldiers may not trespass on the Hold of the Princess Elyne—!"

"Conduct me to her Highness!" Gorgik announced, holding his hand up to halt his men.

After dark, he returned to them (with a memory of high fires in the dank, roofless hall; and the happy princess with her heavy, jeweled robes and her hair greasy and her fingers thin [and grubbier than his], taking his hard, cracked hands in hers and saying: "Oh, but you see what I've come home to? A bunch of hereditary heathens who think I am a goddess, and cannot make proper conversation for five minutes. No, no, tell me again of the Vizerine's last letter. I don't care if you've told me twice before. Tell me *again,* for it's been over a year since I've heard anything at all from Court. And I long for their company, I long for it. All my stay there taught me was to be dissatisfied with *this* ancient, moldy pile. No, sit there, on that bench, and I will sit beside you. And have them bring us more mead and bread and meat. And you shall simply tell me again, friend Gorgik . . .") with leave for his men and his carts to pass through the lands; and thus he avoided the Empress's customs inspectors.

A month after he left the army, some friendlier
men of an intricately tattooed and scarred desert tribe
gave him some intricately worked copper vases. Provincial burghers in Arganini bought them from him
for a price five times what he recalled, from his youth
in the ports, such work was worth in civilized lands.
From the mountain women of Ka'hesh (well below
Ellamon) he purchased a load of the brown berry
leaves which, when smoked, put one in a state more
relaxed than wine—he was now almost a year beyond
his release from the army—and transported it all the
way to the Port of Serness, where, in small quantities,
he sold it to sailors on outgoing merchant ships. While
he was there, a man who he had paid to help him
told him of a warehouse whose back window was
loose in which were stored great numbers of . . .
But we could fill pages; let us compress both time
and the word.

The basic education of Gorgik had been laid. All
that followed—the months he reentered a private service as a mercenary officer again, then as a game-
keeper to a provincial count's lands, then as paid
slave-overseer to the same count's tree-cutters, then
as bargeman on the river that ran through that count's
land, again as a smuggler in Vinelet, the port at the
estuary of that river, then as a mercenary again, then
as a private caravan guard—all of these merely developed motifs we have already sounded. Gorgik, at
thirty-six, was tall and great-muscled, with rough,
thinning hair and a face (with its great scar) that
looked no more than half a dozen years older than
it had at twenty-one, a man comfortable with horses
and sword, at home with slaves, thieves, soldiers,
prostitutes, merchants, counts, and princesses; a man
who was—in his way and for his epoch—the optimum
product of his civilization. The slave mine, the court,
the army, the great ports and mountain holds, desert,
field, and forest: each of his civilization's institutions
had contributed to creating this scar-faced giant, who
wore thick furs in cold weather and in the heat went
naked (save for a layered disk of metal, with arcane
etchings and cut-outs upon it—an astrolabe—chained

around his veined and heavy neck, whatever the month), an easy man in company yet able to hold his silence. For the civilization in which he lived he was a civilized man.

II

THE TALE OF
OLD VENN

The chain of deconstructions cannot, of course, be contained here: for if the image functions as a violent displacement from the origin, life, or meaning to which it apparently refers, there is a second fundamental question raised more or less explicitly in each of these essays. What about my text as the image of the image: what about the possibility of reading . . . ?

—Carol Jacobs
The Dissimulating Harmony

1

The Ulvayn islands lay well east of port Kolhari; known on the Nevèrÿon shore for the fisherwomen who occasionally appeared at the mainland docks, these islands had—had anyone bothered to count—probably four fishermen to every fisherwoman. Alas, its particular fame on the Nevèrÿon coast was more a projection of the over-masculinization of that culture (empress and all) than a true reflection of the island culture so famed.

Nevertheless Norema's mother had been for a time firstmate on a fishingboat (captained by an older cousin, a rough-skinned and wrinkled woman after whom Norema had been named—for fishing tended to run in families); the child spent her first two years more or less bound to her mother's back, as Quema swayed on the boat's pitched and pitching deck. Snar, her father, was a boat builder; and after the second girl was born, Quema left the fishingboat to work in Snar's island boat yard. The second girl died, but Quema stayed on at the yard, where the boat skeletons rose, more and more of them each year, their high ribs, yellow for the first week, gray thereafter. She sorted bundles of pitch-backed bark, went into the village to harangue the smith to finish a shipment of brads made from a combination of metals and magic that her husband (with Venn's help) had discovered did not rust; she stirred at great cauldrons of glue, while her daughter tagged along and stared, or ran off and giggled. And she felt unhappy with life and proud of her husband and girl and wished she were back at sea.

Another daughter came, who lived. Both Snar and Quema spent more time directing other workers who labored in the yard; and Norema ran after her younger sister now, more than her mother did.

Snar was a tall, sullen man with a rough beard and tool-scarred hands, who loved his family and his work with breath-stopping intensity—and was frequently and frankly impossible with anyone he did not think of as a friend; indeed, he made a rather bad salesman in a prospering business that soon had to deal with many more people from other islands and even Nevèryon herself, rather than just the small circle who had bought his boats or brought him boats to repair in the early years. Quema, on the other hand, had the personality called in the inns and drinking places along the island's docks (and in that language the term applied equally to men and women) a good sailor, which meant someone who could live easily in close quarters with others under swaying conditions. So Quema actually did much of the selling and bargaining over materials from their suppliers and over finished boats with their customers; and she frequently took the girls to other islands, rimmed with blue and silver sand, when she went out on business.

Coming back from such a trip, at night, with moonlight on the deck of the boat they'd built themselves (at any rate, twelve-year-old Norema had carried bark and driven dowels and caulked seams and mixed glue; and three-year-old Jori had once stepped in a bowl of that same glue), the three sat on the deck with the fire box glowing through its grillwork, fish grilling on its tines, and the rocks of the Lesser Ulvayns thrusting high and sheer at the sea's edge like the broken flanks of some shattered, petrified beast. Quema sat across from the fire box; the flattened copper circles she wore in her ears ran with light (her hair, in that moonlight, had lost the last of its reds to some color like the gray shrubs that grew on the island hills); the rings and her hair quavered in the gusts. And she told her daughters stories about sea monsters and sunken cities and water witches and wind wizards; sometimes she told of sailing lore and fishing routes; and sometimes just the lazy, late-night woman-talk of people and places mother and daughters could discuss here in a detail so much more exact, insightful, and intense because—here—moonlight and the dark mirror circling them put the subjects at a distance that had precisely the proper illumination and focal length for such marine investigation. (Venn had a curved mirror that she had once shown to Norema; and had made up a term in that language which might as well be translated "focal length.") Sometimes they just sat and didn't talk at all, their backs wedged against the rail of the boat, feeling the sea's sibilances under them and the rocking night over them and the probing chills around them (usually, by now, Jori was asleep, curled against her mother's leggings). Norema stared across the seven feet of damp, varnished decking to where her mother sat, arms across her knees, looking as contented as Norema ever saw her; and Norema sometimes wondered, too, if her mother hadn't been somewhat cheated by her father's near fanatical absorption in his craft and trade. For wasn't it here that an eminently sea-worthy and seasoned woman really belonged, under the wind and the moon, with her own good boat rocking on the belly of the Great Mother, like a woman half dreaming on her back with her own sea-daughter a-straddle her?

And they would sail; and sail; and sometimes Norema would sleep; and when she would wake up, it was always curious which would come first: the flares set out on the docks of the island's harbor, or the red dawn—the old scar of the horizon broke open and bleeding again, cut by the sun like a copper coin with its rim knife-sharpened.

Then Quema was hauling dock rope through the wooden cleats, one bare foot on the deck, one on the deck rail, the ligaments along her brown ankle shifting as the boat shifted; Norema pulled cloth bags from under the leanto that served them as cabin; and Jori strolled up the dock, humming. It was day.

Venn?

Norema first knew her as a woman who had been a close friend of her parents. Later, through anecdotes (and both Quema and Snar were still fond of the elderly woman), Norema realized that the closeness with each parent dated from different times. As a child, her father had built boats with Venn, and together they had invented all sorts of tools and tackling devices that her father still used; even before then Venn had figured out, by herself, a system for telling where you were by the stars. That was even before her father was born. From time to time, rumor had it, Venn disappeared. One such disappearance was a trip to Nevèrÿon, where she met (the adults still talked of it) with an aged and great inventor of that country who himself had actually invented the lock and key; he'd also taken her navigation system and used it for a series of metal disks—rhet, scales, and map, which, today, sailors and travelers called an astrolabe. The great man, it was said, from time to time even came to the island to meet with her, for he knew a wise woman when he met one. It was after returning from one such disappearance that Venn and her mother had shared a hut (long since torn down) out of which Quema had gone every morning to work on the fishing boat with Old Norema and from which Venn went, apparently, to study the woods and the waterfalls that plummeted from the high rocks.

Her mother had married her father; and somehow contact with the woman who was eighteen years older than both of them faltered and all but ceased. Yet both swore that Venn was the wisest woman on the island.

Norema suspected Venn was perfectly crazy.

Nevertheless, Norema was sent, with the daughters and sons of most of the other families in the harbor village—some thirty-five in all—to be with Venn every morning. Some of the young men and women of the village when they'd been children had built a shelter, under Venn's instruction, with ingenious traps in its roof so you could climb up on top and look down from the hill across the huts to the harbor; and Norema and the children who sat with Venn under the thatched awning every morning made a cage for small animals they caught; and they learned the marks Venn could make on pieces of dried vegetable fiber (that you could unroll from the reeds that grew in the swamps across the hill): some marks were for animals, some for fish, some for numbers, and some for ideas; and some were for words (Norema's own contribution to the system, with which Venn was appropriately impressed)—there was a great spate of secret-message sending that autumn. Marks in red clay meant one thing. The same mark in black charcoal meant something else. You could use Venn's system, or make up a new one with your friends. They nearly used up all the reeds, and Venn made them plant many more and go hunting for seedlings to be carefully nursed in especially nice mud. The whole enterprise came to a stop when someone got the idea of assigning special marks for everyone's name, so you could tell at a glance (rather than having to figure it out from what it was about) just whom the message came from. Venn apparently intercepted one of these; someone apparently deciphered it for her.

"We must stop this," she told them, holding her walking stick tight with both hands up near the head, while an autumn rain fell from the edge of the thatch to make a curtain at her back, fraying the great oak tree, sheeting the broken slope that rose beside it, dulling the foot path that cut across the grass beneath it. "Or we must curtail it severely. I did not invent this system. I only learned it—when I was in Nevèrÿon. And I modified it, even as you have done. And do you know what it was invented for, and still is largely used for there? The control of slaves. If you can write down a woman's or a man's name, you can write down all sorts of things *next* to that name, about the amount of work they do, the time it takes for them to do it, about their methods, their attitudes, and you can compare all this very carefully with what you have written about others. If you do this, you can maneuver your own dealings with them in ways that will soon control them; and very soon you will have the control over your fellows that is slavery. Civilized people are very careful about who they let write down their names, and who they do not. Since we, here, do not aspire to civilization, it is perhaps best we halt the entire process." Venn separated her hands on the gnarled stick. And Norema thought about her father's ship yard, where there was an old man who came to work some days and not others and about whom her father always complained: If I wrote down his name, Norema thought, and made one mark for every day he came to work and another for every day he failed to come, if after a month I showed it to my father, and said, yes, here, my father's grumbling *would* turn to open anger, and he would tell him to go away, not to come back, that he was not worth the time, the food, the shelter, and the man would go away and perhaps die. . . . And Norema felt strange and powerful and frightened.

But Venn had started to tell them a story. Venn's stories were very much like her mother's; indeed, some were the same. Norema loved her mother; but Venn told tales better. Most were scarey. Sitting under the thatch, on the ground, shoulder to shoulder with the others, with Venn seated on the heavy log across the end, the sunlight now bursting through the rain, a glitter in the grass, on the tree trunks, runneling down the slate scarp, here in the little space of shadow ("We are sitting in the shadow of knowledge; knowledge is written all around us, in the trees and on the rocks, as clearly as my marks on reed paper," Venn often told them) Norema would suddenly feel her shoulders and the back of her neck prickle at tales of some lone man's approach to some ancient pile of rough-cut masonry, at some intrepid twin sisters' boat foundering closer and closer to the weedy rocks.

Venn taught them the stories (as she must once have taught her mother, Norema surmised): the chil-

dren would tell them back, and Venn would get angry
if they got the names of various giants, queens, and
the distances between imaginary islands wrong, or
misdescribed various landscapes at various times of
year; other things in the tales she urged them to
elaborate on and invent for themselves—the kinds
of beasts found guarding some treasure that stood
behind two tall white stones, one of which, on the
last day of summer, cast a shadow, an hour after sunrise, three times the length of the other ("that," said
Venn, "you'd best not forget."), or the family names
of the hero's and heroine's maternal uncle who provided a train of twenty-three servants ("That you
must remember."), each of which tried to betray
them in any way the children could think of.

For a while, Venn spent much time with a particular half a dozen youngsters, going for walks with
them after the others were dismissed, exploring the
edges of the forest, or the sea, sometimes summoning
them up to her small, wonder-filled shack at dawn,
sometimes turning up at any one of theirs down in
the village at sunset. The group included Norema, and
for a while Norema thought (as did the rest) Venn
favored them because they were cleverer. Later, she
realized that, though none of them were backward,
they were just more astutely sociable than most ado-
lescents—more tolerant of a crippled, old woman's
oddities. Though Venn commanded an almost awed
respect from the village adults, her friends were more
or less the children. And this particular group was
finally not all that clever, or wonderful, or talented.
They were just her friends.

One afternoon, Norema and two others of the
favored few rambled with the old woman alongside
the Neum Stream. For a while, above the sound of
Venn's stick shushing through the leaves, Norema had
been talking on about the trials of working in her
parents' boat yard—indeed, had been talking on for
quite some time, and had just begun to wonder if for
the last few minutes Venn had really heard. (Dell
was arguing softly and intently with Enin, who wasn't

listening.) Venn stopped at a wide rock tabling into the water.

Gnats thrashed in the sun beyond.

Venn, tapping her stick—rather nervously—said, suddenly and hoarsely: "I know something. I know how to tell you *about* it, but I don't know how to tell you *what* it is. I can show you what it does, but I cannot show you the 'what' itself. Come here, children. Out in the sun."

Dell stopped talking; Enin started listening.

And Norema felt embarrassed at her own prattling and smiled alertly to show she didn't.

Venn, her stick leaning in the crook of her arm, reached around in her many-pocketed, orange robe. The shoulders were threadbare. The hem was stained with leaf dirt. "Come here." She beckoned Norema onto the stone with a sharp, brown chin. "What is this?"

A piece of reed paper? Venn's brown fingers pecked in it and prodded it open. She held it up. The red marks across the paper, left to right, were Venn's special signs for: a three-horned beetle, three horned lizards, and two crested parrots. Red meant she had observed them before noon.

"You saw a three-horned beetle, three horned lizards, and two crested parrots in the morning—probably you were at the estuary, on the far bank; because the parrots never come over on this side. And it was probably yesterday morning, because it was raining the night before last and the lizards usually come out in the mornings after rain."

"That's a very good reading." Venn smiled. "Now, Enin. Come out here, on the rock, and stand just so." The tall, short-haired boy stepped out, blinking. The mirror he wore strapped across his stomach flashed light down on Venn's stained hem. (All the boys, for the last month, had taken to wearing the mirrored stomach plates.) "Norema," Venn said. "Come here and look at this now."

Norema stepped up beside her old teacher.

"Here," Venn said. "Here, girl. Hold the paper up

beside your face, crouch down, and look at it in Enin's belly."

Norema took the paper and held it open beside her face; she had to stoop to a half-squat to see.

"Now what is it?"

In the shiny, irregular shaped plate, topped by Enin's first chest hair and below which ran his shell belt, she saw her concentrating face and, beside it, in her fingers . . . "Of course, it's backward," Norema said. When they painted the prow designs on her father's boats, frequently for the more delicate work that could not be done with the cut-out stencils, the painters checked their outlines in mirrors. The reversal of the image made irregularities more apparent. "It goes wrong way forward."

"Read it," Venn said.

"Um . . . crested parrots two, horned lizards . . . four . . . eh . . . no, three . . . a green . . . *fish!*" Norema laughed. "But that's because the sign for green fish is just the sign for horned beetle written reversed. That's why I hesitated over the others . . . I think." She started to stand.

"No," Venn said. "Keep looking. Dell, now you come stand here."

Dell, who was short and wore his hair in three long braids, stepped up beside Norema on the rock.

"No," Venn said. "You stand over here behind Norema. Yes, that's right. Here . . . Now, Norema, turn around and look at Dell's mirror, until you can see in it the reflection in Enin's."

Norema, in her uncomfortable squat, turned to face the other boy's stomach, with the bright plate thonged across it. "Wait a moment. No, there . . . Come on, Dell, move your hand . . ." She squat-walked to the right, leaned to the left. "Enin, you move around that—no, the *other* way. No, not so much! There . . ."

"Read what you see," Venn said.

"But I . . ." Norema, of course, had expected to see the message put back left to right, its signs in the proper order. But what, in the frame within a frame, she looked at was the back of her own head.

And on the paper, held up beside it, written in black charcoal:

"The great star clears the horizon two cups of water after the eighth hour." Norema stood up, laughed, and turned the paper over. What she had read in the second mirror had been written on the paper's back. "I didn't even know that was there," she said.

"Which is the point," Venn said.

Then, of course, there was much unstrapping and restrapping of mirror thongs and repositioning on the rocks, so that Enin and Dell could see the phenomenon of the changing words. When they had, and everyone had on their own clothes again, Venn said: "And of course I haven't told you what I am trying to tell you *about*. No, not at all. I have just given you an example of it." As they walked from the rock, Venn beat in fallen leaves with her stick. "Let me give you another." She frowned at the ground, and for a few steps, her stick was still. "Years ago, when I was about your age, girl—oh, maybe a year or two older—I had a fight with a sea monster. To this day I have no idea what *kind* of monster it was. I mean I'd never heard of it or seen one like it before; nor have I since. It was a moonlit night. I was seventeen, alone on my boat. It rose up between the rocks by which I was sailing from some uninhabited island's deserted harbor and flung an arm across the boat, taking away the railing and rocking that side of the deck below water. It had as many eyes as arms, and on stalks just as long and as strong; and when one stalk wrapped around my leg, I hacked it off with my fishing knife. The beast slid back into the sea and the boat foundered away from it. The five feet of it just lay there on the deck, wriggling and twisting and coiling and uncoiling—for an hour.

"I wanted to cut it up and see how its muscles worked once it calmed itself, but I just wasn't up to catching it and tying it down. And when I came down from tying up part of the rigging that had been torn, it had wriggled between the rail break and fallen into the calm." Venn stepped gingerly and unsteadily among the large rocks and small branches fallen by the stream. "All through the experience, however, from the moment it hove up between the rocks, till . . . well, really, dawn next morning, when I was miles away, I did not know if I would live or die . . . for all I knew, it was following along after me to rise again. Even through all my curiosity about the tentacle, I lived those hours like someone who might be obliterated from the surface of the sea as a patch of foam is dispersed by a passing dolphin's fluke. Does such fear make everything brighter, more intense, more vivid? I suppose so. It also makes everything exhausting—an exhaustion which, when I had got my boat back to the port here, ached to be filled with . . . words." Venn walked a few more silent steps. "So I told about it—at the inn (that used to stand where the current one does before that building was blown down in the hurricane two summers before you were born, girl) over a bowl of hot fish broth. I was still getting gooseflesh. I told it to half a dozen, who, as I started to talk, gathered a dozen more around them, all their eyes wide and all their mouths gaping, and all their heads shaking, amazed. I told them how, as my boat passed among these certain rocks, a creature, all wriggling arms and eyes, rose up and flung itself toward me. I told of my broken rail and my flooded deck and my terror and my curiosity. But as I told them, as I watched them, I realized: While for me, the value of the experience I had lived through was that, for its duration, I had not known from moment to moment if I would live or die, for them, the value of the telling was that, indeed, I *had* lived through it, that I *had* survived it, that here I was, safe and alive, confirmed as much by my solid presence as my stuttering voice and half incoherent account, running on and on about an experience during which *I* just happened not to have known the outcome." Venn laughed. "And what did I *do* with my sudden realization? I went on talking, and they went on listening. The more I tried to remember the details, remember the moonlight a-slither on freckled scales, remember the fetid smell of cut muscle, remember the trail of bubbled mucus glistening, the sea water dripping from the splintered rail-end, gray outside with weathering, white splinters within, each detail recounted to convince them of *what* I had lived through—an experience in which my survival as a fact of it was outside any possible consideration—the more evidence they had, by my onrush of living talk, that I *had* lived through it, the more certain they were that I had survived *some*thing, though the 'what' of it, just because of that certainty, was quite beyond them.

"The innkeeper's wife gave me blankets and I slept under the stairs that night with a bag of cedar chips for a pillow. And what did I think of, on and off between edgy dozings, till the window above me began to go blue? Another time I would have said I thought about what had happened to me. But it wasn't that. I thought about what I *said* had happened to me. And slowly, remembering all my listeners' reactions, I began to pick pieces from my own ramblings that they had seemed to recognize as true or accurate. And I began to put them in order so that these reactions would build as my reactions to the remembered experience had built. I mortared my descriptions together with explanations and directions for the experience of my listeners. And in the morning, when another group of wide-eyed men and women, who had heard of my adventures from those I had told the previous night, came and asked me what had happened, I told them . . . well, I told them essentially the story I told you. No stuttering, now; no suddenly remembered details. For now it *was* a story, like any other tale I have ever amused or frightened you with. And I was now much happier with the reaction of my listeners, for now that it was a story, the telling grew and directed their responses with a certain precision that at least followed the same form as my own experience on that two-days-previous terrifying night. But I will tell you here: For all her fleshy scales and eyes and slime, for all I use the same words to tell you of her as I first used to babble of her in fear, but ordered and recalled in calmness, she is an entirely different monster." Venn narrowed her eyes in a way that was a smile. "Do you understand?"

Norema frowned. "I . . . I think so."

"What happened to you," Dell said, "was like the signs on the paper."

"And what you told the first night," said Enin, "was like what we saw in the first mirror, with its meaning all backward."

"And what you told again the next morning," Norema said, feeling rather like it was expected of her and terribly uncomfortable with the expectation, "was like what we saw in the second mirror. Something else entirely, with its own meaning."

"As much as mirrors and monsters can be alike," mused Venn, whose sudden distraction seemed one with Norema's discomfort. "Which brings me, girl, to what you were saying about your father."

Norema blinked; she'd thought the subject abandoned.

"What came to mind when you were talking about your father, and working in your father's boat yard, was . . . well, another example, and perhaps the least illustrative: when we were young—Ah, I used to make plans for beautiful, marvelous, impossible boats. Your father would build models of them, when we were children. And once he told me that many of the things he learned from making those models were very important to the success of the real boats he builds today. My plans, his models, and his later boats, you see, are merely another example of what I am talking about. And then, you see, something else came to mind—which may finally tell you something about your father's business as well as what I am trying to tell you. For it is yet another example: I was thinking about the Rulvyn tribes, back in the island's hills. They are a very shy, very proud people, and they almost never come down to the shore villages. The men hunt geese and wild goats; the women provide the bulk of the food by growing turnips and other roots, fruits, and a few leaf vegetables—and when one considers the amount of hours actually spent at the various tasks—if one marked down names

and made marks for the hours each actually spends
working (for I did that once when I was there), the
women do far and above more work than the men
toward keeping the tribe alive. But because they do
not come much to the sea and they have no fish,
meat is an important food to them. Because it is an
important food, the hunting men are looked upon as
rather prestigious creatures. Groups of women share
a single hunter, who goes out with a group of hunters
and brings back meat for the women. The women
make pots and baskets and clothes and jewelry, which
they trade with each other; they build the houses,
grow and cook the food; indeed—except for very
circumscribed, prestige decisions—the women control
the tribe. Or at least they used to. You all have heard
the tales of those who have recently gone up into the
hills to spend time among the Rulvyn; our shore people come back and shake their heads, look dour, and
say things are not well with the mountain folk. When
I was last there, not three years ago, I walked and
looked and listened and made my signs on reed paper in order to mark and remember what I heard and
saw. Up till a few years ago, the Rulvyn were tribes
who lived entirely by their women exchanging goods
and work with other women for whatever goods and
work they needed. Even if meat were part of the
exchange, the men would bring it to the women who
would then do the actual bartering. From time to
time men would exchange weapons, but this was still
part of a prestigious ritual, not the basis of daily life.
The Rulvyn were simple, proud, insular—like an island within our island.

"But our people, here at the shore, with our bigger
and bigger boats, for three generations now have been
using the coins that come from Nevèrÿon to make our
exchanges with. And as more and more of us went
back into the hills to trade with the Rulvyn, the Rulvyn began to acquire money; and finally began to use
money among themselves in order to make their exchanges. Now one of the prestige tasks of the men is
to make trades with strangers to the tribe—whereas
the women do all the trading and exchanging within

the tribe. Three generations ago, such trading with out-
siders might occur once a year, or even once in five.
And it was a sumptuous tribal event. But now, perhaps
once a month someone from the village travels up into the hills, and once a year at least a small party of
Rulvyn men, in their colorful shoulder furs and chin
feathers, come down to the port; you have all gathered
at the edge of net houses to peek at them strolling the
docks. Because money was exotic as well as part of
the prestige process of trading with foreigners, money
went primarily to the men of the society; and indeed
both the men and women of the tribe at first agreed
that money *ought* to be the providence of men, just as
hunting was. And the Rulvyn began to use money
among themselves.

"Now money, when it moves into a new tribe, very
quickly creates an image of the food, craft, and work
there: it gathers around them, molds to them, stays
away from the places where none are to be found, and
clots near the positions where much wealth occurs.
Yet, like a mirror image, it is reversed just as surely
as the writing on a piece of paper is reversed when
you read its reflection on a boy's belly. For both in
time and space, where money is, food, work, and
craft are not: where money is, food, work, and craft
either will shortly be, or in the recent past were. But
the actual place where the coin sits, fills a place where
wealth may just have passed from, or may soon pass
into, but where it cannot be now—by the whole purpose of money as an exchange object. When money
came among the Rulvyn, something very strange happened: Before money came, a woman with strength,
skills, or goods could exchange them directly with
another woman for whatever she needed. She who did
the most work and did it the best was the most powerful woman. Now, the same woman had to go to someone with money, frequently a man, exchange her
goods for money, and then exchange the money for
what she needed. But if there was no money available,
all her strength and skill and goods gave her no power
at all—and she might as well not have had them.
Among the Rulvyn before money, a strong woman

married a prestigious hunter; then another strong woman would join them in marriage—frequently her friend—and the family would grow. Now that money has come, a prestigious hunter must first amass money —for what woman would marry a man in such a system who did *not* have money—and then go looking for good, strong workers to marry . . . for that is the only way *he* can amass more money. The women are unhappy, for now the men *make* them work, pit them against each other, blatantly and subtly chide them with the work of their co-wives. In the Rulvyn before money, the prestige granted the hunter was a compensation for his lack of social power. Now that money has come, prestige has become a sign of social power, as surely as the double stroke I made on a clay jar means that it contains forked ginger roots. And are the men happy? The Rulvyn men are strong, beautiful, proud, and their concerns were the concerns of hunters, the concerns of prestige. But since they have taken over the handling of money—with great diligence and responsibility, I might add, for they *are* proud men—now, even though the women still do all the work, the men are suddenly responsible for the livelihood of all their wives—rather than several wives sharing the responsibility for the care and feeding of a single hunter. The simple job of supplying their wives with a triweekly piece of prestigious food has become much more complex. And another sad truth is simply that the temperament needed to be a good handler of money is frequently the very opposite of the temperament needed to be a good hunter. When I went up into the hills last to talk to my Rulvyn friends, I found that since money has come, the young women are afraid of the men. The women *want* good hunters; but because they understand real power, they know that they must have good money masters.

"In the Rulvyn before money, there were always many more unmarried males than unmarried females. Frequently the unmarried men were the not-so-skilled hunters. Outside every Rulvyn tribal ground, there is a Men's House, rather like the thatched-over place we meet to talk every morning. The unmarried men

can go there, meet there, stay there for days at a time
if they like. Many of these men were connected by
friendship or family ties to some large family group,
with which they ate, slept, sometimes even formed informal sexual ties with one of the wives. But such
men tended to become far closer with each other—if
only because they did not have even the social use the
fine hunters had. Because they had the Men's House
to go to, they began to figure out money-gathering
schemes there, and there plan the business ideas, and
arranged their plans among themselves and one another. Very soon, *these* were the men who could afford
to get married, who could take women for themselves
—while the fine hunters could not. Groups of women
found themselves married to and working for these
new husbands who basically preferred to spend their
time with one another, rather than living as the single,
valued male in a communal woman's work group. The
sign of the family was no longer a fine, proud hunter
content to be made much of by the women who con-
stituted the family itself. Now the center of the family
itself *was* a man, harrassed and harried by the worries
of uncomfortable and competing working women,
women who were now the signs of *his* power, a man
who would prefer to spend his time with other men in
the same situation who could at least be sympathetic to
his problems.

"In the Rulvyn before money, large, old families
with many wives and a single hunter—sometimes even
two or three—were the glories of the tribe. Now that
money has come, even the men who are involved in
businesses together cannot afford families of more
than three of four women. Women are afraid to join
families too large, just as the men are afraid of enlarg-
ing them. The feel and flow of life among the Rulvyn
is very different from what it was before.

"When last I was there, a woman still married a man
with the same rituals and prayers, feast-foods, and
flowers, but the look in her eyes has changed. So has
the look in his. There are still men in the Men's House
gossiping or polishing their spears' heads, but what
they gossip about is not the same. Hunters still rise

before dawn and stand in front of their huts to chant a ritual supplication, but the tone they chant in has a very different timbre. And the women, at their turnip gardens and their basket making and the child chasing and their pot painting and their pig feeding, still pause and lean together and talk. But what they talk of is different, and the tones are shriller, their whispers quieter, and their faces show a different sort of strain; and the children, running and laughing or crying between their legs, seem to point this change in their mothers, rather than seem to express the tribe's full and complex life." They walked a few more steps, Venn's stick threshing, Venn's face furrowed. "You know, I first began to realize how powerful this thing is that I am telling you about—which, you must realize, is not money any more than it is mirrors or boat models or monsters, or even the telling of tales—when an old and very intelligent friend of mine came to see me. We became friends a long time ago, once when I was in Nevèrÿon. This friend has only twice visited me here on my home island; and that was the time I took my last visit, with my friend, up to visit the Rulvyn. Now Nevèrÿon is where money comes from, and indeed they have used it there for at least four generations now—far longer than we. In Nevèrÿon, all things, they say, can be bought with it, and—so I finally discovered through my friend—everyone thinks in the colorings and shadings it seems to cast, even when that is not their true colors. When we went up into the hills, we visited two Rulvyn tribes—one that had been using money for a while now, and another, much further back, that had not yet really adapted the custom of coin. We visited families in both, played with children in both, were given a great dinner in both, watched a wedding in one and a funeral in the other. And do you know . . . ? My friend could not see the difference. At least not the differences I saw. Even when I explained them, tried to point out the specific changes, my friend simply put a hand on my shoulder and said, 'Venn, if you've got a big, strong, lazy hunting man, with five or six wives who do all the child rearing and the food gathering and the gardening and the housekeeping and the water carrying, of *course* he's exploiting them; I don't care whether there's money around or not! As far as a new kind of man getting married, or families not being quite so large, you are just observing the social turnover that must occur in even the most fixed social system if it is indeed to remain stable and not simply collapse. The shrinking family size is much more likely from either a desire to imitate their more prospering cousins living monogamously down at the harbor, or a reflection of poor rainfalls and reduced turnip yields. No, my dear girl—' and why my friend calls me that I shall never know, since I am three years the elder—'you are as much an inventor of fancies as you are an observer of facts—though without a few fancies, I know, the facts never really make sense. Still, the only difference *I* can see between your two Rulvyn tribes is that the one which uses money seems a little more active, a little more anxious. And that, Venn, is the *way* of money. All *you* are seeing is your own nostalgia for your girlhood trips up here into the hills, which were no doubt colored with the pleasantries of youth and idealism, which is—won't you admit it?—finally just a form of ignorance.' " Venn made a snorting sound and struck at a low branch. "Nostalgia! When I was twenty-two I lived with the Rulvyn for nearly three years. I married into the family of a woman named Ii, a large, heavy woman with small, green eyes, whom I thought was the wittiest person I had ever met. There were two younger wives in the family also, Ydit and Acia, who thought the world of me because I'd shown them how to make irrigation ditches through their turnip gardens. There was a crevass which we all had to climb down and climb up again every time we wanted to get across to the tribal meeting ground. I designed a bridge and we built it out of great stones we four levered down from the hills and with trees we cut down and tugged out of the forest—it's still standing. And three years ago, when my friend saw it—oh, what exclamations about the marvelous cleverness of native knowledge, once that tall, proud people put down their spears and cleaned off their hunting paint! No, I gave my Nevèr-

ÿon friend no enlightenment—that, indeed, it was a
much better example of what that tall, proud people
could do once they put down their babies and their
water baskets and their turnip rakes. Nor did I mention the design was mine . . . Living there, those three
years, was a wonderful experience for me. I made
some of the best friends of my life. Yet, when I *had*
spent three years there, I had quite decided that I *must*
get out by *any* effort. Spending practically every minute of your day on pure survival is an absolutely involving and absolutely boring life. Our hunter was a
great-shouldered, beetle-browed creature with a chest
like a shaggy red rug, named Arkvid. Oh, I remember
when they married me to him—flowers in his hair,
feathers and daubs of yellow clay in mine; and, Oh!
the feast we had, of wild turtle meat and stuffed
goose, all of which the poor man had had to hunt
down the previous day because turtle meat spoils so
fast in that heat; and then, he had been up with ritual
chantings and what have you, purifying himself on the
steps of the Men's House half the night—but pride
wouldn't let him show for a moment how exhausted
he was. And it was his third marriage that year, poor
thing. When I decided to leave, three years later, Ii
and Ydit and Acia argued with me for days. They
liked me and they needed me, and in the savage mind
that's an unbeatable combination. And certainly I
loved them . . . After Ii had exhausted all her wit and
good humor to make me stay, Ydit took me for a long,
sad walk in the woods to see how the new arrangement
of fire bricks I had suggested for her mother's kiln
was working out, and recounted in a perfectly heart-
wrenching way everything we had ever done together,
said together, and how much it had meant to her,
while her little two-year-old Kell galloped about us,
beating in the leaves with her stick and bringing back
the names of every plant and flower and saying it
dutifully three times—what a marvelous child. By
herself, she might have made me stay. And then, when
we got back from Ydit's mother's, Acia had raked my
turnip garden for me; and, as I stood there, quite astonished, she stepped up to me and silently handed me

a clay bowl she had painted herself with green birds and green flowers—about a month before, I had invented green paint and now the whole tribe was using it on *everything*. When I told them I *still* had to leave, they got Arkvid to come to me.

"We were in the house, I recall; and it was evening. He came in wearing all his ceremonial hunting gear—only used for holiday and show—his fur shoulder pieces, his feathered chin strap, his bark penis sheath (green), feathers stuck all behind the thongs binding his rult to his belly, and a flint-headed spear over his shoulder, hung with shells and colored stones. He walked slowly and regally around the floor mat, displaying himself to me—he really was magnificent! Then he stood up before me, opened his feather-rimmed sack, and presented me with a turtle—the shell had already been cracked and the carcass bound back together with bark-twine.

"He asked me most humbly would I put a little turtle meat in with the turnips and the millet and the mushrooms and the palm hearts and the dyll nuts that I had been grinding, cutting, shelling, mashing, stewing, and what-have-you all day. And when I took off the twine, and opened the shell, I found that he had gutted it and cleaned it already and packed the carefully sliced meat with pungent leaves for flavor. Meanwhile Ii and Ydit and Acia were, one by one, finding things to do outside the hut—though one could hear them hovering beyond the walls.

"Arkvid was not what you would call an articulate man. But he was a good hunter, and he had a certain . . . one can only call it an affinity, with trees, turtles, rivers, geese, gazelles, and rocks. I don't think he *thought* like them, actually. But I think he *felt* like them—if you know what I mean? And in the same way, I think he had a perfectly nonverbal understanding of women. While I was taking out the spiced turtle meat and arranging it on the hot stones along the side of the fire, he did the most natural and wonderful and unpremeditated thing in the world: he began to play with my baby. There on the floor mat the two of them were poking at each other and laughing at each other and prodding each other. Now his spear rolled off, rattling its string of shells against the wall. There went his chin feathers; his penis sheath was somewhere back under the edge of the sleeping platform; and the next thing you know, the two of them were naked as eggs, and giggling all over the cabin floor. And as babies will, mine finally curled up in the crook of Arkvid's knee and went to sleep. And Arkvid lay still on the floor, watching me, and breathing as hard from his bout of baby wrestling as if he had just placed first in one of the hunting games the men staged for our entertainment once a month on the morning after the moon pared itself down to the smallest whittling. Then he asked me to come to him . . . oh, it was marvelous, and marvelously sad; and in a life where there was so little time for emotions, such things become so intense. After we made love, he put his great, shaggy head on my stomach and cried softly and implored me to stay. I cried too, stroking the back of his neck which was my favorite spot on him, where the red hair made little soft curls—and left next morning at dawn." Venn was silent the next few steps. "My little baby son, just a year-and-a-half old . . . I left him with the Rulvyn. It has always struck me as strange the rapidity with which we absorb the values of people we share food with. If my child had been a daughter, I might have stayed. Or brought her back here to the shore with me. The Rulvyn value daughters much more than sons —Oh, to a stranger like my friend, it seems just the opposite: that they make much more fuss over sons. They pamper them, show them off, dress them up in ridiculous and unwearable little hunting costumes and scold them unmercifully should any of it get broken or soiled—all of which seems eminently unfair to the child and which, frankly, I simply could not be bothered with, though the others thought I was the stranger for it. They let the little girls run around and do more or less as they want. But while all this showing off and pampering is going on, the demands made on the male children—to be good and independent at the same time, to be well behaved and brave at once, all a dozen times an hour, is all so contradictory that you finally begin to understand why the men turn out the way they do: high on emotions, defenses, pride; low on logic, domestic—sometimes called 'common'—and aesthetic sense. No one pays anything other than expectational attention to the boys until they're at least six or seven; and nobody teaches them a thing. Girl children, on the other hand, get taught, talked to, treated more or less like real people from the time they start to act like real people—which, as I recall, is at about six weeks, when babies smile for the first time. Sometimes they're dealt with more harshly, true; but they're loved the more deeply for it." Venn sighed. "Yes, a daughter . . . and it would have all gone differently. I didn't see my son for sixteen years . . . afraid, I suspect, that if I went back he might hate me. That was when I went away from the islands, finally, to Nevèrÿon, and the mountains and deserts beyond her." Venn hit the leaves again, laughing. "And when I finally did come back, here to my island and up into the hills? He was a handsome young man, astonishingly like his father. A great, strong boy, a good hunter, quick to laugh, quick to cry, and with a river of sweetness running throughout his personality one kept threatening to fall down into and drown in." Another sigh broke through, though the smile stayed. "Alas, he's not what you'd call bright. Not like a daughter would have been, raised in that family. He was desperately pleased to see me, and everyone in the village knew that his mother was the foreign lady who had built the bridge. Oh, he was proud of that! Ydit's Kell was a wonderful young woman—I told you I had invented green paint? Kell took me and showed me all the pigments she had recently made herself—reds, browns, purples—and as soon as she got me alone, she seized my arm and asked me whether I thought it would be a good idea for her to move down from the hills to the harbor here at the island's edge, for with her gray eyes and her black braids and freckles, she was curious about the world . . . a marvelous young woman! She finally did come here for a while, took a husband from another island, left him two years later, and came back . . . and *that* was all twenty years ago, before money really came to the Rulvyn." The stick shushed again in walking rhythms. "And how many years later is it, and my Nevèrÿon friend is saying all my observations are nostalgia? I *know* what I'm nostalgic about! And I know what changes in the Rulvyn society money has brought. If you don't look closely at what's in the mirror, you might not even notice it's any different from the thing in front of it. And now, of course, you're wondering what all this has to do with your father's boat yard, 'ey, girl?" Venn's smile turned on Norema. "Because it does." Venn's hand came up to take Norema's shoulder. "We here on the island's shore haven't always had money either. It came from Nevèrÿon with the trade our parents established. And you can be sure that since it came, the values we live with now are a reversal of those we had before, even if the forms that express those values are not terribly far from what they were. We at the shore have always lived by the sea, so our society was never organized like the Rulvyn. More than likely—on the shore—social power was always more equally divided between men and women. On the shore, women tend only to have one husband, and husbands tend only to have one wife. If you reverse a sign already symmetrical, you do not distort its value—at least quite so much. Yet I think we all retain some suspicion of a time when things carried about with them and bore their own powers—baskets, heaps of fruit, piles of clams, the smell of cooking eel, a goose egg, a pot, or even a cast of a fishing line or a chop with a stone axe at a tree. Though if growing old has taught me anything, it is that knowledge begins precisely as we begin to suspect such suspicions. Your parents pay me to talk to you every morning; I am happy they do. But they pay the same money to Blen's and Holi's father and uncle who are so skilled with stone they can build a stone wall in a day: and the same money goes to Crey, who is a hulking halfwit, but is lucky enough to have a back and arm strong enough to dig shit-ditches. The same money goes to your mother for a string of her seatrout as goes to your father for a boat to go catch sea trout of one's own from. So much

time and thought goes into trying to figure out what
the comparative worth of all these skills and labors
are. But the problem begins with trying to reduce them
all to the same measure of coin in the first place: skilled
time, unskilled time, the talk of a clever woman, nature's gifts of fish and fruit, the invention of a craftsman, the strength of a laboring woman—one simply
cannot measure weight, coldness, the passage of time,
and the brightness of fire all on the same scale."

"The image in the mirror," Dell said, "it *looks* real,
and deep, and as full of space as the real. But it's
flat—really. There's nothing *behind* the mirror—but
my belly." He pulled one of his three braids over his
shoulder, and let his fist hang on it. "And if you tried
to store a basket of oysters in it, you'd certainly spill
shells."

"You mean," said Enin, "that money, like a mirror,
flattens everything out, even though it looks, at first,
like a perfect copy, moving when things move, holding
shape when they're still."

"I certainly mean something like that. Your father's
a craftsman, Norema. To be a craftsman is to be a
little dazzled by the magic of things—wood, rock, clay,
metal, flesh, bone, muscle: and it is also to be a little
awed by the change each can work on the other under
the twin lamps of application and dedication. But at
the same time, he can sense the flatness in the mirror
of money that claims to give him for all his work a
perfect and accurate copy. Yet money is a faithful
mirror—for the more he works, the more he is paid;
the better he works, the better he is paid . . . except
that more and better, *in* the mirror, flatten to the same
thing. But I suspect this may be why he tries to bury
himself *in* his work, not so much to make the money
that allows him to go on working, more and better
both, but to get away from it: only it surrounds him
on all sides, and the only way to escape from such a
situation is inward. So he retreats from everything,
even you, and your sister, and your mother." Venn
sighed, and dropped her hand from the girl's shoulder.

"So therefore," Dell said, coming to beside Norema,

"you should try and learn the dedication and application from him and forgive the coldness."

"And you should learn the old values from him," Enin said, stepping up between her and Venn on her other side, "and understand and forgive him for being befuddled by the new ones."

Both boys looked at Venn for approval.

"There are certain thoughts," Venn said, dryly, "which, reflected by language in the mirror of speech, flatten out entirely, lose all depth, and though they may have begun as rich and complex feelings, become, when flattened by speech, the most shallow and pompous self-righteousness. Tell me, why do *all* the boys on this island have such shallow, pompous, self-satisfied little souls—for, though I love him like a brother, Norema, your father suffers from that *quite* as much as he does from the situation we have been discussing. Yes, I suppose it does make one nostalgic for the silent, inland hunters. There at least one can *imagine* the depths . . . for a year or two."

"Venn?" Norema felt relief enough from the uncomfortable things she'd felt at Venn's turning her attention to the boys to ask for that attention back: "From what you say, in a society like ours, or the Rulvyn, money is only the first mirror, or the first telling of the sea monster tale. What is the second mirror, or the second telling, the one that doesn't reverse, but changes it all into something else?"

"Ah!" Venn dropped the tip of her stick in more leaves. "Now that is something to speculate on." She laughed her old woman's laugh. "Who knows what that would be now . . . ? A method of exchange that would be a reflection of money and a model of money without being money. Well, perhaps you could get everybody to count what money each had, give each a sheet of reed paper and a piece of charcoal, then take all the money itself and collect it in a central money house, where it could be used for works the village really needs, and for dealings with foreign traders; and each person would conduct her or his business with the other members of the tribe on paper, subtracting six coins from this one's paper and adding it on that one's sheet, and the like . . ." Venn fell to musing.

"I see how that would cut out the middle person," Dell said. He was a boy forever fascinated by the impossible, and would no doubt be suggesting such a scheme to the class within the week, as if the idea were completely his. "But the reflection of the reflection is not supposed to reverse the values back; it's supposed to change them into something completely new!"

"But I can see how it would do that," said Enin. He was always taking clever ideas and running them into the ground. "People would have to trust each other even *more* than they did just trading goods. And that trust would probably be a new value in our tribe. And suppose you wanted to get together a business. You could go to a lot of people and get each one to pledge just a little bit of their money on paper, and then go right off and act just as though you had it. It's like Venn said: money always is where goods and work aren't. Well, this way, it's not that you have your goods and work in the *same* place as the money, but you have a kind of money that can be in a lot of places at once, doing lots of different things. That's got to make everything completely different. I mean, who knows how far the differences would go. Anything you could figure out how to make, if you could just tell people about it, you could probably get enough of this new kind of money to make it. Instead of boats that sailed from island to island, you could make boats—"

"—that flew from land to land," suggested Dell, "by digging with their wings and tunneling under the floor of the sea. Instead of a woman having a turnip garden of her own, you could have one *big* turnip garden—"

"—that floated on the ocean and was worked by specially trained fish that had been raised for the purpose," chimed in Enin, "trained the way one trains dogs or parrots."

The two boys laughed.

Then Enin shouted and started running.

The stream had fanned; the first dock stood above

its quivering reflection, and there was Dell's cousin's boat pulling in to it.

Dell was off after.

Then the two boys were out on the boards and halloing Fevin (who was hairy-shouldered, and with a touch of red in his beard that spoke of Rulvyn forebears), who hallooed back. The boat's prow cut into a splash of sun that left a black pearl pulsing in Norema's eyes. The light had been a reflection from one or the other boy's mirror.

"The things that would come. . . ."

Norema looked at the old woman beside her.

Leaves about them rustled, chattered, stilled.

". . . burrowing boats and floating turnip gardens —no, the things that would come would be far stranger than that, I'm sure. Far stranger. Perhaps your father does well to stay away from whatever he avoids by doing whatever he does."

Norema laughed.

The boys were on the boat, rushing back and forth to aid Fevin with his unloading. Norema watched and wondered why she had not run out with them. She had yesterday; she probably would tomorrow. When her father's business was slow, sometimes Fevin worked for her mother when they would take a boat out to fish some of the nearer beds. Other times, if irregularly, the young man worked in her father's yards—indeed, Snar had often said he would like to have him as a permanent woodcrafter; but Fevin liked to get out on the water. Norema had gone out with him on his boat a dozen times, as had most of the children in the village.

The boat-rim rocked above a reflected, rocking rim. The boys' bellies flashed; here and there water flared.

Venn started walking again.

Norema came with her.

The water widened, ceased as estuary and became sea.

More docks now; and they were out of the trees and onto the waterfront. As they walked through tall masts' shadows, raddled across the small stones, Norema asked: "Venn, would another example of

this idea you're talking about be men and women? I
mean, suppose somewhere there was a plan—
like a design for a boat—of the ideal human being:
and this ideal human being was the true original of
everybody? Suppose men were made first, in the image
of this original. But because they were only an image,
they reversed all its values—I mean men are petty,
greedy, and they fight with each other. So then women
were made, after men; and so they were an image of
an image, and took on an *entirely* new pattern of
values; they—"

"Who?" Venn asked.

"They . . . the women."

Venn leaned nearer to her. " 'We,' girl. Not 'they'—
we are the women."

"Well," Norema said. "Of course. I meant 'we.'
Anyway. Of course it's possible the women . . . eh,
we were made first. And we reversed the values of
the original ideal plan. And men, after us, embody the
completely different values." She frowned, because this
last idea felt distinctly uncomfortable.

Venn slowed her steps, her staff grinding among
small stones more and more slowly. At last she stopped.
"That is the most horrendous notion I've ever heard."
Then she began to walk again, so quickly Norema had
to ignore her own surprise to catch up—fortunate, because it did not give the surprise time to become hurt.
"What I've observed—the pattern behind what I've
observed—explains why what happens happens the
way it does. It makes the whole process easier to see.
Your idea is a possible explanation not of observations
but of a set of speculations, which, if you accepted
them along with the explanation, would then only make
you start seeing things and half-things where no things
are. Suppose people with green eyes were the image
of your ideal human plan, which completely reversed
the plan's value. And people with gray eyes were an
image of the image, with a completely different value.
Or people who liked to hunt, as opposed to people
who liked to fish. Or people who were fat as opposed
to people who were thin. Just consider how monstrous—" Venn stopped talking, kept walking. Then

she stopped walking, sighed, and said: "And of course that is the problem with all truly powerful ideas. And what we have been talking of is certainly that. What it produces is illuminated by it. But applied where it does not pertain, it produces distortions as terrifying as the idea was powerful. And it doesn't help that we cannot express the idea itself, but only give examples —situations which can evoke the idea in some strong way. Look, girl: Where *is* your 'ideal' plan? Floating in the clouds somewhere? *I* start with a real thing, like barter, words written on reed paper, an experience at sea, and discuss what happens to their value when series of reflections occur. *You* start with a value—an ideal human being—that is the result of so many real people and imagined people's real and imagined actions, and then try to say the people are a result of this value . . . I mean . . . well: let me tell you another tale of my time with the Rulvyn. Oh yes, let me tell you *this* tale."

2

There is no point in referring back to all of this unless it permits us to shed some light on what Freud must leave out.

—Jacques Lacan
Desire and the Interpretation of Desire in HAMLET

"I was in the house cooking, with the children. It was raining—a light, warm rain. Ii, Ydit, and Acia were outside tying down hides over some of the farm equip-

ment. Arkvid was inside, sitting on the bench and
carving a rult. Two-year-old Kell was teaching my boy,
who had just begun to walk at his first year, where to
urinate. With one hand she would grasp her genitals
and say proudly, 'Gorgi!' and then she would pat the
boy's genitals and say, with an explanatory inflection,
'Gorgi!' and he would do the same, and laugh. There
was a latrine trough, that ran under the wall and out
of the house, in the corner; Kell stood in front of it
with her legs pressed together and peed at the plank on
the back. She had just learned, as every little girl does,
that the more you open your legs, the lower the angle
of the water. At the same time, she was trying to
demonstrate to my boy that he, less economically
constructed than she, had best use his hands to guide
himself, otherwise things tended to flap and splatter,
and that he did not aim naturally straight forward as
she did. He, of course, wanted to do it like his big
sister. But if you're a boy, simply standing with your
legs together is no guarantee that your urine will spurt
straight out. And the idea of using your hand to guide,
rather than just to make yourself feel good, had not
penetrated his one-and-a-half-year-old mind. At any
rate, being a two-and-a-half-year-old of high origin-
ality and wide interest, Kell suddenly turned around,
saw her father on the bench, dashed across the floor
mat, flung herself between his knees, and, holding onto
his thigh with one arm, seized his penis, lifted it up,
and crowed, with a look of perfect delight, 'Gorgi!'
And of course the boy was there, right behind her,
reaching over her shoulder to hold it too. Now Arkvid
was a patient man. He glanced down, surprised, over
his carving; then his surprise became a laugh. 'If you
two keep that up,' he announced to them, 'you'll have
it as big as it is when I get up in the morning.' Which
made me laugh, over where I was stirring a stew pot
at the fire. Kell, however, had made her point; she
released her father's penis and now came over to
where I was—Arkvid went back to picking his knife
point at the rult—and put her arms around my knee
and, as I had just started to put my apron on, said,
' 'Bye-'bye, gorgi,' which, that week, was what she

had been saying when she saw any Rulvyn adult cover their genitals with an apron, penis sheath, or what have you. And of course, there was the boy, right at her shoulder, gazing at me, equally rapt.

" 'Hey, you,' Arkvid called to the boy, as he had just finished his carving. 'I've something here for you, son.'

" 'Bye-'bye, gorgi.' My son waved at my vagina and turned to his father.

" 'Here now, boy. This is your rult.' And Arkvid took the leather thongs that threaded through the carving to tie it around the boy's belly—just the way our boys have taken to wearing their mirrors . . . I am sure it is really just a form of the same custom, though what drew it down from the hills to the shore I'm sure I don't know. But you must know about the rults—you've seen the Rulvyn men wearing theirs when they come to our village here. It is a special, wooden carving that Rulvyn fathers make and give to their infant sons. They are considered very strong hunting magic. Girls do not get them. Indeed, girls are not even supposed to touch them; and the part of the carving the boy wears against his flesh girls are not even supposed to see. Now the Rulvyn, besides being a proud people, are also a fairly sensible one. And except in very old, strict, formal families, don't try to run the privileges of the rult into the ground. Mothers can loosen their sons' rults, in order to wash beneath them, but the first thing you try to teach a boy is to wash under his own rult. And unless it's absolutely necessary, you *don't* refer to it in public—though the Rulvyn language abounds in euphemisms for the rult, especially among the men; and all of these euphemisms are considered more or less impolite. Naturally, as with any such taboo, within the home such strictures are relaxed in the face of practical considerations. Also, our family considered itself particularly forward thinking—indeed, I could never have married into them had they been in the least conservative. At any rate, there was Arkvid, tying the carving to the boy's stomach. Suddenly Kell ran over to him to see what he was doing. Arkvid shifted his knee to shield her view. 'No, no,' he said, in a perfectly affectionate way, 'this is none of your affair, little girl.'

"She tried to step around his knee to see.

" 'No,' he repeated, more firmly, and turned the boy away from her eyes.

"And Kell, like any two-year-old denied access to a nut, or a stick, or a rock, or a shell, began to cry and pull at his knee.

" 'Come on,' Arkvid said, a bit testily. 'Now I shouldn't even be doing this with you in the house, but—here . . . hey, Venn. Come take her away, will you. She keeps trying to touch his' and here he laughed and used one of the more childish euphemisms for that most sacred object.

"I came over and lifted her. She rose with an ear-piercing squeal and for the next two hours there was a battle—renewed every thirty seconds to five minutes —to touch, tug, or examine the carving now tied to her brother's stomach, with Arkvid patiently getting between them when I began to lose patience, and sometimes saying, 'I mean, I suppose there's nothing really *wrong* with it, but suppose she were to do it outside.' Somewhere near the end of this, Kell made the connection that the carving tied to her father's stomach, which she had till now never paid much attention to, was the same species of object now on her brother's, and for minutes stood, her eyes going back and forth between them, looking perfectly forlorn. Finally she resolved the whole thing by taking a small, clay pot top, holding it to her stomach, and walking back and forth with it, giving both her father and me surly-eyed little glances; and of course she would have nothing to do with her brother, who, having gotten over the thrill of having something his sister didn't, now wanted someone to play with. Arkvid stood by the door, tugging on his penis, which Rulvyn men tend to do when nervous, and finally said to me: 'I just hope you women can break her of that, and not let it turn into a habit.' He sighed. To a Rulvyn of either sex, a girl wearing a rult is a perfectly incongruous image. And a girl *pretending* to wear one borders on the obscene. And as every Rulvyn knows, though most of them seldom talk about it, the giving of the rult from father to son can sometimes occasion months of such hostility in little girls, what with keeping the girls from touching it and not letting them examine it and generally inculcating the respect necessary for it to retain its magic. Indeed, discussions of the various ways the rult should be given in a family with girls—informally as an ordinary part of an ordinary day, as Arkvid had done, or formally before the whole clan with the little girls held safe in their mothers' arms, or whether the father should take the boy off and make the exchange in private out in the forest—form a major subject of conversation on the porch of the Men's House or across the borders between turnip yards. Kell got by, I remember, with only a couple of weeks' annoyance over the whole business before she found other things to absorb her. But it was a few nights later, when we were all getting ready to celebrate a naven on the completion of the house of a new young family across the road that Arkvid, after we had fed him, lingered squatting by the hearth till we had set up plates for our own meal. 'I have been thinking,' he said as Ydit passed turnips to Ii, and I took barley from Acia's bowl, 'and I have an idea,' in that pontifical way Rulvyn men take on when they are talking to all their wives together. 'An idea about why women's ways are so different from men's.'

" 'Are you still hungry?' Ii asked him. 'You can take some nuts and butter wrapped in a fava leaf to the Men's House and eat it while you dress for tonight.'

" 'Now that's exactly what I mean,' Arkvid said. 'Here I have a perfectly fascinating *idea,* and all *you* want to talk about is appeasing hunger, building houses, and tilling the soil,' which are considered the classical concerns of Rulvyn women. 'Listen to me. I have discovered why women behave so differently from men. It has to do with rults.' Now there's a very strange thing. If a grown boy or a man were to visit a friend or relative's home *without* his rult, everyone would feel extremely uncomfortable. At the same time, rults are *not* a subject you *talk* about—especially at dinner. But Arkvid was our husband and hunter. 'This is my idea: The little girl sees that her brother and her father have rults,' Arkvid explained in a clear, precise voice which let us know he had been thinking about this a long time, 'and she is jealous and envious of the rult —as she does not possess one. It is right that she should be jealous, for the rult is strong, full of powerful magic, and a man would be hardpressed to kill a wild goat, or a mountain cat, or a rock turtle without one—that is certainly clear. Now even though in a week or a year the little girl seems to forget this jealousy, my idea is that she does not. My idea is that the little girl will put this jealousy down in the dark places below memory where things eat and gnaw at one all through a life, in silence, without ever saying their names. My idea is that the reason women like to have babies is that they think of the new child as a little rult growing inside them, and if the child is a male, they are particularly happy because they know that soon the little boy will be given a rult by his father and, in effect, while the boy is still a baby, they will now have one. My idea is that those women who fail to pay the proper respect to their hunters for bringing meat to add to their yams and mullet and turnips and apricots and palm hearts are simply suffering from the jealousy over the rult, even stronger than most, though they do not realize it.' Arkvid folded his arms and looked extremely pleased with himself.

"After a while, Ydit ventured, in the most respectful form of address, 'My most prestigious hunter, speaking as a woman who was once a little girl in these tribes, your idea does not quite correspond to my experience of things.'

" 'Well, remember now,' Arkvid said quickly, 'this is all happening deep down in the dark places of the mind, below memory. So you wouldn't necessarily *feel* this jealousy. But you can't deny—I mean everyone knows about it, though one *doesn't* usually discuss it, I'll admit—that little girls *are* jealous of the strength and the magic in their father's and brother's rults. We have all seen it, even in this hut.'

"Acia looked as if she was going to say something,

so I waited. When she didn't, I suddenly felt all uncomfortable.

" 'Arkvid,' I said, 'that's the most ridiculous idea I've ever heard. I mean, if you carried on about your . . . well, your gorgi,' which he was tugging at again, 'the way you carry on about your rult, you'd have the little girls jealous of *that* in a minute.'

" 'Now *that* is *truly* ridiculous,' Arkvid said. 'Why would a little girl be jealous of a little boy's gorgi when she has a perfectly good gorgi of her own, and more compactly built at that? In fact, I'm sure that what you're expressing now, whether you are aware of it or not, is just this deep-down rult-jealousy left over from your own babyhood.' And he let go of his penis, looked very proud, and folded his arms once more.

" 'Arkvid,' I said, 'until two years ago, when I came up here into the hills, I had never even seen a rult.' "

" 'Well, you must have *heard* of them. Besides, I'm not so much talking about the rult itself, but the power, strength, and magic that the rult embodies. The rult is not just a piece of wood, you know. It's the whole concept of distinction, of difference itself. Come on now, Venn,' for he was always a little placating toward my foreign ways, 'even if my idea isn't exactly right —though I'm sure it is—you must admit it has, as an idea, great beauty.' "

"When I'd been working on the bridge, the Rulvyn had all been impressed with some of the principles of the lever and lifts I had showed them, and they found them to be, as indeed they are, beautiful. From then on there had been a mad spate of 'beautiful' ideas about practically everything that, alas, applied—practically—to nothing.

" 'Besides,' Arkvid added, no doubt thinking along the lines I had been, 'here, in this tribe, little girls just aren't jealous of little boys' gorgis, nor are little boys jealous of little girls', for that matter—curiosity is not jealousy. But girls *are* jealous of rults—and that's just a fact, whether the idea is beautiful or not.' For, if only upon my own family, I had been impressing ever since the importance of facts.

" 'Arkvid,' said Ii, who knew how to humor hunters, 'you are a strong, handsome man, with four wives who have between them the best-irrigated, if not the largest, turnip gardens in the village. Your daughters will grow up strong and clever and your sons, handsome and brave. Your catch this week could probably have fed twice the number of wives you have. And Acia here has roasted a haunch of the goat you caught the day before yesterday to take to the naven tonight, and you should get many admiring glances for that. Why do you bother your handsome head with these things that should only be the concern of women anyway. Now give us a smile and take yourself off to the Men's House and dress yourself for the naven tonight in honor of our neighbors' new dwelling.'

"Arkvid stood up, stalked to the door, then turned. And gave a sudden, great, and generous laugh, which was what Rulvyn men used to do when they were crossed by women—though since the coming of money, that laugh is no longer so generous, but is shot through with contempt. And he left, still laughing, for the Men's House.

" 'Now you mustn't mind him,' Ydit said, as Ii and Acia turned to me. 'The fact that he even tries to have such ideas is a compliment to you. For didn't *you* first tell us about the great, dark places below memory where stories and numbers come from?' (Where *do* you get your crazy ideas, one of them had asked me not a week ago. What was I supposed to say? Well, then, they wanted to know why didn't *everybody* come up with stories and numbers? For the Rulvyn are persistent. Well, I explained, in some people the things in the deep, dark places are so deep and so dark that they cannot say their names. I don't know . . . it had a sort of beauty when I said it.) 'You let yourself get too upset about the babbling of hunters,' Ydit went on. 'You always have, too.' And she looked at me wryly and passed me one of the clay bowls Acia's mother had made, full of tamerind juice whose amber was still a-quiver from where Ii had just sipped. I took it. I sipped. I said:

" 'But don't you see, Ydit. This rult-jealousy of

Arkvid's is all out of his own overvaluation of the rult, and nothing more. Let me describe exactly what happened while you were out a few days back.' When I had, they all laughed.

" 'Though, even so,' Ii said through her laughter, 'you must admit that a raised knee to shield a naughty child's prying eyes or simply to turn a boy a modest-so-much for the same effect is not a lot in the line of overvaluation. There are some men, of this tribe too, who carry on about their rults as if they *were* indeed their gorgis—and what's more as if their gorgi had just been kicked there by a mountain goat!'

" 'And to give our prestigious husband credit, there *are* women who sometimes act with their hunter as if they would like to snatch their rults away. After all,' Acia went on, wiping her mouth of barley flakes, 'would you really want to go to bed with your husband *without* one? One could *do* it, probably: but you must admit it would be bizarre!' And they all laughed.

" 'Seriously,' Ydit said; she was toying with a fruit rind. 'You and Ii are not being honest with our most prestigious husband's newest wife.' She looked down at the bowls among us, dropped the rind on a pile of rinds. 'There are more things than you suggest behind his idea. And you know it.'

"The others were suddenly very quiet. I looked at Ydit, who—suddenly and startlingly, looked up at me. 'Many, many years before you came, Venn, a terrible thing happened in the tribe. And while we laugh and joke here, we are all thinking about it. And I am sure Arkvid was thinking about it when he got his idea. What happened, all those years ago, is that the Great Hunter Mallik went mad. But it was a slow, evil madness. First he brought home no meat, but ate all his catch, raw, alone in the woods. Then he befouled with urine and feces the rest and left it to rot in the forest. He refused to sleep with any of his six wives, and finally he took to bringing home sand in his feathered hunting sack, and scattering it on his wives' turnip gardens. Several nights he left his house and tore up the turnip fields of the women who lived in the thatched house next door so that his wives were

obliged to replant them; and, in general, he made his
wives' lives miserable. There are many stories of the
awful things that occurred within that sad, unfortunate
home. Once, in a rage, he beat his oldest son to death,
and another time he broke his littlest daughter's wrist
with a turnip rake. He disgraced his wives in every
way; he even walked around the village with his rult
all undone, hanging down with its inner carving showing like a careless, baby boy whose mother has ne-
glected to retie the thongs after washing—and when
there was a naven, he refused to dress himself in the
Men's House, but would run off instead into the woods
and spend four or five days in the forest, from which
he would return half starved and ranting like some old
holy woman, only without any holy words. And within
the house he made his wives' lives an endless and
terrible dream by mockings and by violences of the
sort that the sane can hardly imagine. Several times he
put poisonous herbs into the cooking pots and sat
laughing and singing while his wives and children lay
sick and vomiting in their front yard. This is when he
did not take to threatening and beating them all outright—I have spoken of the murder of his son . . . ?
One night, after what particular outrage no one can
be sure, his wives, driven half to madness themselves
no doubt, with the help of Mallik's mother and an aunt,
killed him when he lay sleeping. They cut off his hands
and his gorgi and his feet; these they buried at the
four corners and the center of the oldest wife's turnip
garden. Then they . . .' Her eyes moved away from
mine. 'They took his rult, broke it, dipped the pieces
in blood and hung them by the thongs from the door-
posts. Then they slit the throats of their children; and
then their own throats. All were found dead the next
morning. You can't imagine what it was like, Venn, for
twelve-year-old Arkvid to come upon that obscene,
bloody carving dangling from the door of his mother's
brother's home; and then to walk in upon the car-
nage—' and she stopped for the look that crossed my
face; for once more I had been brought up by how
small a tribe my beloved Rulvyn were, how quickly
they grew up, how young they married, how soon they

died—with everyone related to everyone in at least three directions, and where 'many, many years ago' can be three as easily as thirty, and where a seventeen-year-old wife, with a child at her feet, telling you of something that happened in her great grandmother's time might just mean six years ago when her fifty-year-old great grandmother was, indeed, alive. For as well as farming and cooking and baby-caring with Ydit and Acia and Ii, somehow I had managed to learn how Acia had got lost in the forest for three days when she was seven, and how she had slept next to a suckling mother goat; and how Ii had stolen a big jar of honey when she was ten and was beaten for it till she couldn't walk for three days; or how Acia used to run off at night as a girl and sit by the stream for hours in the moonlight—and myriad other things that made up who these women were—in the same way I suppose I tended to forget that one's prestigious hunter ever had a childhood, or that anything had ever happened in it worth remembering. 'You see, something *is* going on down in the places below memory you so easily speak of.' Ydit looked at me again. 'The rult has always been too much here associated with death: for it is what empowers the hunter to kill his goats and his geese and his turtles. And on that day, hanging bloody and broken from that profaned doorpost, it was a sign of the death for all who lay inside.' She took my wrist in her hand and dropped her head to the side. 'So if our most prestigious hunter has devised a way to make the rult a sign of life—if he wants to see the child growing in my womb as me growing a little rult, then I think there is a beauty, a necessary beauty there.' Her smile formed and became that strangely private and at once public smile that I always envied in the Rulvyn women and have always missed so in the women of the shore; 'I have the best-irrigated turnip fields in the village. So I can certainly allow our hunter his little idea.'

" 'Yes,' I said. And I took the wrist of her hand with my other hand and held it tightly; for I felt she was stronger than I, I did. And I wanted to hold on to someone strong when I said this: 'There *is* a beauty

there. And Arkvid is a good hunter, as well as a very
nice man; I am truly fond of him. But his idea is *still*
wrong. The story of Mallik is a terrible story, but it
says, sadly, far more about the overvaluation I spoke
of than about women's jealousy of rults. You are the
wives of our most prestigious hunter and I love you
more than sisters. Yet ignorance is ignorance, no matter where you find it—even in our most prestigious
hunter himself. And I would betray the love I bear
you, as well as dishonor his own prestige, if I said
otherwise.' And while I held her wrist and she held
mine, I was actually afraid that she would pull her
hand away and strike me, for the Rulvyn women were
proud, powerful, and honorable women, and it was a
point of honor with them that no one dishonor their
hunter.

"But Ii said: 'We are all betraying the spirit of the
evening.' And she laughed and pushed away the tamerind bowl. 'At least we are if we go on talking about
such weighty matters as Mallik and rults and right.
Women, there's a naven tonight! And we shall never
be dressed for it by the horn's fifth bleat if we do not
hurry up.'

" 'All right,' I said; and Acia let go of my wrist. I
let go of hers. We put away the dishes and pots and
the palm fronds, and all was back to a normal that can
only be achieved in a place where work is so steady
and constant. Nevertheless, I think they had all begun
to sense that I was growing dissatisfied with life there."
Venn sighed. "Yes, ignorance is ignorance—and there
is as much here at the shore as there is among the
Rulvyn in the hills. But our life is easier here, and I
can spend my mornings with you children, dispelling
what little part of that ignorance I can, and your
parents will keep me alive with their gifts while I do—
whereas with the Rulvyn there was only turnips,
bridges, paints, pots, and babies. So I would rather live
here. But in a sense, Norema, Arkvid's idea was very
like yours. I don't mean just that I feel they are both
wrong; rather, they are alike in the way in which they
both strive toward rightness and the way in which they
manage to take what is real and what might be right,

put them in each other's places, then draw lines between that simply cross no space." Venn mulled for a few more steps. "I wonder if the Rulvyn men still have ideas like that now that money has come and power has shifted. Today, if a woman crosses a man, it is the woman who must laugh. But they do it with little chuckles, embarrassed snickers, and pleading smiles. They cannot do it openly and generously. They no longer have it in them."

Again she was silent.

"Venn," Norema asked, "what's a naven?"

Venn raised an eyebrow. "Ah, yes. The naven." She smiled. "It is a celebration ceremony performed when almost any act of social importance is done in the village: when a girl harvests her first turnip crop, when a boy kills his first wild goose, when a house is built, when a yellow deer is sighted wandering through the village, or when a honey tree is found in the forest. Then the men go to the Men's House and take two long, fat calabash melons, tuck their gorgis up behind them, and tie the melons between their legs long way, with tufts of dry grass all around them, so that it looks as if they have great, outsized, women's gorgis, and they put on women's aprons and headdresses and take up old, broken turnip rakes—meanwhile the women, in their homes, tie a long brown gourd, with two big, hairy, dyll-nut husks behind them, up between their legs, so that it hangs down, and tuck dried grass all around them; and they put a man's old, split penis sheath around the gourd, and they paint themselves with hunting paint, and put on chin feathers, and they take old, broken and cracked spears, and mangy shoulder furs and put them on; and the older women —though the younger ones may not—tie an old piece of burnt wood to their bellies like a rult. At the sound of five bleats on the sacred gourd—and sometimes it's only blown two or three times, and everybody starts to the door and, when it stops short of five, all laugh and go back in again—at the sound of five bleats, everybody rushes outside into the square to dance as hard as they can. Uncles get down on all fours and rub their heads on their niece's knee. People take leafy switches

and beat up as much dust into the air as possible. Fires
are set blazing and drums are pounded and rattles
shaken. There are lots of comic songs and skits performed in which wives refuse to cook for their husbands, who then starve to death, and in which husbands
are unfaithful to their wives, who then run about the
village pretending to be mountain wolves. The whole
thing climaxes in a village feast. And through it all the
children, who have woken up with the noise by now,
run around pointing and squealing at their mothers
and fathers and aunts and uncles who are all cavorting
in each other's clothes as though it was the funniest
thing in the world." And from the particular look on
Venn's face, though there was no laughter in it, Norema thought that it might indeed be.

Norema said: "It's like a reflection—"

"—of a reflection," Venn said. "It doesn't reverse
values. It makes new values that the whole tribe bene-
fits from. Now there's a custom I wish would work
its way down to the shore. Here, girl—" Venn once
more took Norema's shoulder. "I want you to think
about what I said before, about reflections, and what
you said about men and women, until you see how
they aren't the same. I want you to think about my
idea until you see what's wrong with yours—and indeed you may find out in the process things wrong
with mine as well. If, when you finish, you can tell me
about them, I will be very grateful. Will you do this for
me?" The horny hand tightened. "Will you?"

Norema, who loved wonders (and who had been
given many by this woman) said, "Yes, I . . . all right.
I'll try . . ." And wondered how one even began such
a task. And in the midst of wondering, realized that
Venn, whom she really wanted to talk to some more,
was wandering away across the docks.

On a boat an old sailor with a bald, freckled scalp,
was laughing and telling a very involved story to a
younger man who was scrubbing doggedly at a deck
railing, not listening. Was this, she wondered, an image
of Venn and herself? On the dock, crumpled against
the piling, was Mad Marga, in a man's ragged jerkin,
snoring through loose lips. Sores speckled her large,

loose arms, her scaly ankles. Hip flesh pushed through a tear in her rags. Food or something had dried on her chin. Was Marga, wondered Norema, in some way an image of Norema's own strong, inquiring mind? Or of the naven? Or of all women; or of all women and men? And how to find out?

Along the dock sounded the chang-chang-chang of one of the new metal hammers recently from Nevèrÿon that her mother thought so ill of and her father found "interesting." What was the relation of the wooden mallet and dowels with which Big Inek fixed down deckboards in her parents' boat yards and this new, metal-headed engine and the iron spikes it could hold wood together with—as long as you did not use them near water.

And more important, how to tell? And what relation would whatever method she devised to tell bear to the method through which Venn had arrived at her inexpressible principle?

In the boat yards that afternoon, Norema wandered about aimlessly for an hour; then, when Inek made a comment, prepared a cauldron of glue inefficiently for another hour, so that at least it looked as if she were doing something. Thinking: the value of real work and the value of work-just-for-show: couldn't those be the first two terms in an example of Venn's principle? And what would the third term be . . . ? But she also began to think of things to do, ways to examine.

That evening she took out a sheaf of reed paper on which were the carefully drawn plans for a boat that already stood half finished in the yard, its ribs rising naked and supported by cut treetrunks, which, over the years of their use, had lost much of their bark but still dangled some, like sea weed. She stood with her weight mostly on one foot and studied the plans. She climbed up through the thick struts, bearing cuts of the smoothing blades like inverted fish scales up their curves; and she studied the boat—not so much to see how one followed the other, but to see what each, as two things that did so follow, was in itself, how each was different.

Soon she got another piece of reed paper and one of the styluses (which you hung around your neck on a leather thong, and a horn with an inch of berry juice in the bottom that you dipped your stylus into) and began making notes, sketches, more plans.

Next morning she was at the yard early, had gotten out paint jars, artist's mirrors, stencils, trimming patterns, and examined them under the porch roof which, as the sun warmed the storage hut, began to buzz with insects that lived in the thatching. Then she left the yard and walked toward the forest. She looked at flowers and seeds. She looked at dead leaves and live ones, holding them close to examine how the pale veins branched through the flat, tough green or the frail, brittle brown, and squinted up at the dark, brown branches, an expanding net in the flakes of green that massed about them. In the midst of all this, various idealike images, model, example, expression, representation, symbol, and reflection began to separate themselves for her. Her thoughts went back to what Venn had said, as Norema walked back to the boat yard. Inside the gate, she told a quickly made-up story to little Jori, who stared at her through the tale with wide, incredulous eyes, pawing at the sawdust with her bare toes, and twisting at a piece of vine, her pale hair matted for all the world like a clutch of pine splinters. Then Norema asked Jori to tell the story to Big Inek. Then she got Big Inek to tell it back to her. He grunted between sentences each time his mallet fell on the thumb-thick dowel which sank more each stroke, its head splintering a little more each hit: at which point she remembered the old and the young sailor she had seen on the docks with Venn, and realized, not as two connected ideas, but as a single idea for which there were no words to express it as a unity: while any situation could be *used* as an image of any other, no thing could *be* an image of another—especially two things as complicated as two people. And to use them as such was to abuse them and delude oneself—that it was the coherence and ability of things (especially people) to be their unique and individual selves that allowed the malleability and richness of images to occur at all.

Such was her concentration on Venn's idea that the only thing she took away from Venn's morning class next day was a patch of sunlight through a hole in the trap above in the thatch, falling to shape itself to the brown shoulder of the girl who sat in front of her, and the rustle of Venn's stick in the straw with which the class floor was covered.

Meals at home, where she pondered all Venn had said of the matrix of money and material in which her parents' business was fixed and which bounded her parents' so diverse personalities, sometimes approached disaster: her father frowned across the wooden table with its clay and brass settings. The woman who helped her mother with the house and the cooking, clicked her teeth and said Norema must not have put her head on when she'd gotten up that morning. Jori laughed. And Quema asked—so many times that her father told her to stop—if there were anything the matter. Through it all, their words were images of illogic and incomprehension; her soup was the sea and her bread was the island a-float in it. The smell of apples in batter recalled the orchards where she had picked them last week, or run with others to steal them last year. Every sensation led to the memory of myriad others. Any pattern perceived could be set beside any other, the relation between the patterns becoming a pattern of its own, itself to be set beside another and related. . . .

She went to the waterfront and looked at nets and trees. She looked at women and men with rough hands and rags tied around their heads, working on their boat rigs. She looked at fish scales and bird feathers and at a broken length of boat ribbing, just washed ashore, whose smoothing-blade cuts were invisible on the grainy gray. She looked at three women and a man carrying baskets of fish, roped around their shoulders, up the sand, which clung to their feet high as their ankles, an image of glittering shoes. The baskets were woven from tree branches. She drew on her paper the curve of sand around the water, and beside it, the curve of water up to the sand. Behind a beached snaggle of wood, she heard a sound like a baby, and looked behind it to find Marga, asleep and crying to herself. Later she heard a gull shriek like a mad woman, wailing. And a day later, when she was coming down a narrow alley toward the docks, from the window beside her she heard a baby—for the world like a mewing gull.

In a blade of sunlight a-slant the dust between the shadows of two stone huts, she stopped. While she listened, she remembered, for the first time in a while, the actual walk with Venn down the stream when the idea she had been examining these last days had been first presented to her. She recalled her absurd attempt to construct an example—an image that, because it was constructed of things it simply did not fit, reversed the idea into an idea silly by itself, ridiculous in application—a ridiculousness that could easily, she saw, have strayed into the pernicious, the odious, or the destructive, depending how widely one had insisted on applying it. There was Venn's idea (the baby had stopped crying); there was her image of it, formed of all possible misunderstanding; and there . . .

Something happened: it happened inside her head; it happened to her mind, and its effect spread her body like a chill, or a warmth, and was realer than either. She gasped and blinked, looking at the sun, dust, shadow, tried to apprehend what had just changed, and felt a stray thread on her sleeve tickle her arm in the breeze, a leather crease across her instep from her soft leather shoe, the air passing in through the rims of her nostrils breathing, the moisture at the corners of her eyes.

It's a *new* thought, she thought. But immediately knew that was only because she had been thinking in words so insistently for the past few days that words came easily to cling about everything in her head; she quickly shook them away to look at the idea more clearly. It was at least as inexpressible as Venn's so highly inexpressible idea, which, image before image ago, had been its content. She opened her mouth, feeling her tongue's weight on the floor of her mouth, the spots of dryness spreading it, and tasting the air's differences, that marked not the air's but the tongue's itself. Words fell away, leaving only the relations they had set up between the sensual and the sensory, which was not words but which had been organized—without any of it ever leaving its place on the reed paper of her perception—by words: that organization was the way in which the stretch of sand between the house walls beside her and the stretch of sky between the house roofs above her could reflect one another; the thrum of a wasp worrying at its gray, flaking home under the thatched eaves up there could recall the thrum of water worrying the root-tangled spit at the beach's far end, leaving the sand, leaves, wings, waves, wasps . . .

What a glorious and useless thing to know, she thought, yet recognizing that every joy she had ever felt before had merely been some fragment of the pattern sensed dim and distant, which now, in plurality, was too great for laughter—it hardly allowed for breath, much less awe! What she had sensed, she realized as the words she could not hold away any longer finally moved in, was that the world in which images occurred was opaque, complete, and closed, though what gave it its weight and meaning was that this was not true of the space of examples, samples, symbols, models, expressions, reasons, representations and the rest—yet that everything and anything could be an image of everything and anything—the true of the false, the imaginary of the real, the useful of the useless, the helpful of the hurtful—was what gave such strength to the particular types of images that went by all those other names; that it was the organized coherence of them all which made distinguishing them possible.

But of course that was *not* what she had known . . . only an expression of it, one sort of image. And yes, she thought, remembering Venn again, to express it was to reverse much of its value. To express it was to call it containable: and it was its uncontainableness she had known.

Some flash caught her eye; she turned and saw Fevin coming down the side street. Rolls of net hung

over his shoulder; net dragged behind him in the dust.
Her sister Jori and two little boys were trying to step
on it. The flash had come from a mirror tied to one
boy's—no, not to a little boy, she realized; it was Nari,
her sister's friend. Norema thought of rults and Rulvyn, mirrors and models; and smiled.

Fevin hailed her: "Have you heard what happened
to old Venn?"

Norema looked perplexed. "What?"

"While she was off last night, on one of her exploring trips, she fell down from a tree and—"

Norema's eyes widened.

"—and sprained her hip. She just got home this
morning; some youngsters found her hobbling through
the swamp."

"Is she all right?" Norema demanded.

"As right as one can be at seventy with a sprained
hip—when you were already crippled at thirty-five."

Norema turned and dashed up the street while
Fevin suddenly bellowed: "Hey, you little ones. Cut
that out! You tear my nets and I'll tear off your toes!"

Norema ran through sun, over shells, under shadow.
On wooden, leaf-littered stairs, she tugged at the rail,
taking three steps at a time, while the breeze dipped
branches almost to her head and, from the bare earth
banked on the other side, roots wriggled free and
stuck there, under thin dust. She leaped rocks she
had helped position in the stream for stepping, jumped
to the bank (which broke open under her feet between
grass blades) and, with grass flailing her calves, reached
the rut that wound the high rock on her left (the great
oak on her right) to the thatched school shelter.

In front of the shack, she demanded of Dell, who
had one hand on the corner post, squinting after some
bird who beat away between the leaves, "Is she all
right?"

"Uh-hm," Dell said, not looking down. "But she'd
like to see you."

Norema dashed to the door, pushed inside. Thatch
that has been rained on and sun-dried and rained on
and sun-dried enough ceases to have much smell of
its own, but it begins to do something to the other

smells around it, underlining some, muting others, adding to others an accent missing in stone or wooden dwellings. On the shelves along one wall: rocks, small skeletons, butterflies, rolls of reed paper tied with rubbed vine. On the other wall: a cooking fire's mudded stones, with a series of wooden baffles for the smoke that Venn had been experimenting with a year ago but had never gotten to the efficiency of your average kitchen hearth. A half charred potato lay on the ashes against the stone.

The bed had been pulled over to the table (instead of pulling the table to the bed, which was typically Venn). Three scrolled, metal lamps hung from the ceiling. Chains for a fourth angled near them. On the table among sheets of reed paper, were brass rules, compasses, calipers, astrolabes, and a paint-box finer than the ones her father kept his blueprints in. Venn sat on the bed, her naked back full of sharp bones and small muscles—still the hard back of a sea woman, a turnip hoer, a bridge builder. The skin at the crease of her armpits was wrinkled, that across her bony shoulders thin.

Norema said: "I heard about . . ."

Venn turned slowly (painfully?) on the raddled furs. And grinned. "I was wondering if you'd come to see me."

Then the young woman and the old woman laughed, at their different pitches in the close room, but with a shared, insistent relief.

"The boys have been hanging around being *helpful* all morning. The trouble is I don't *like* boys—I suppose that's why I spend so much energy being pleasant and patient with them. Then patience wears through, and I get snappish and send them off. Where were you, girl? Have you ever noticed about the men on this coast? It's the strangest thing: they will cook for one another at the drop of a leaf—on fishing trips, out overnight in the hills, or visiting one another in some bachelor hut full of litter and squalor. But the only time it would even enter their heads to cook for a woman—even if she's crippled and in bed with a sprained hip—is if they want to bed her. And I, fortunately, am past that. Come around here, woman. Under the shelf there is a basket: most of the things in it would make a nice salad—and I assume you're clever enough to recognize the things that wouldn't. (If you're dubious, just ask.) You'll find a knife under there; and a bowl. That's right. I'd do it myself, but my better judgment tells me not to even try to walk for at least three days. Did I ever tell you about my Nevèrÿon friend—who once went with me up to visit the Rulvyn? Yes, of course, I was telling you only a week or so ago. Well, you know we haven't seen each other for years. My friend is from an old and complicated Nevèrÿon family, half of which, so I have been told, are always in dungeons somewhere and the other half of which are always fighting to avoid dungeons—with perhaps still another half fighting to keep them there. Well, only a night ago, my friend came to see me. All the way from Nevèrÿon. And in a beautiful boat, the richest I've ever seen, with its rowing slaves dressed finer than the members of our best families, I tell you. And we talked—oh, how we talked! Till the sun rose and I had heard of the most amazing and dire marvels, all of which my friend asked my opinion on—as if I were some Rulvyn holy woman, fresh from a spate of meditation in the mountains! Ha! And when the first waterfront sounds drifted up from the blue between the trees, my friend left." Venn sighed. "What a *marvelous* boat! And I shall probably never see my friend or the boat again. But that's the way of the world. Ah, of course I'm sure you would rather hear about what happened to me last night. Has it ever occurred to you—and it did to me, last night, when I got to overhear two hill women who passed under me in the swamp where I was relaxing in a rough-barked tree: paddling along on their raft, they each spoke slightly different dialects, and were having trouble understanding each other, I realized—but at any rate, it occurred to me that language always has the choice of developing two ways. Consider: you're inventing language and you come on an object for the first time, so you name it 'tree.' Then you go on and you find another object.

You have the choice of calling it a tree-only-with-special-properties, such as squat, hard, gray, leafless, and branchless, for instance—or you can name it a completely different object, say: 'rock.' And then the next object you encounter you may decide is a 'big rock,' *or* a 'boulder,' *or* a 'bush,' *or* 'a small, squat tree,' and so on. Now two languages will not only have different words for the same things, but they will end up having divided those same things up into categories and properties along completely different lines. And that division, as much or more than the different words themselves, will naturally mold all the thinking of the people who use that language. We say 'vagina' and 'penis' for a man's and woman's genitals, while the Rulvyn say 'gorgi' for both, for which 'male' and 'female' are just two different properties that a gorgi can exhibit, and believe me it makes all the difference! Still, the initial division, as one goes about on the first, new, bright trip through a world without names is, for all practical purposes, arbitrary. (That was when I fell out of the tree and sprained my cursed hip! That salad looks good, woman. There are two bowls.) Now consider, for instance, even the word for word . . ."

Two years later, Venn died.

She had apparently gone up through the trap of the teaching station to lay under the winter stars, with a few instruments, a few sheets of reed paper, and there, probably just after dawn—for her body was not yet stiff—with what thoughts a-dash through her mind like the shooting stars of which she had logged seven, she died: and Norema and Jori and the others, with oddly dry throats, blinking a lot, and opening and closing their hands, stood in the grass, looking up, while Fevin, at the roof's edge, lowered (with a rope around the chest and under the arms) the thin woman with the stained hem and flapping, bony ankles.

Three months after that, the red ship came.

3

"Have you *seen* it?" Jori demanded, bursting into the kitchen from the back garden. "It's so big!" and ran through the kitchen, banging her hip against the plank table hard enough to make the bowls and the pans clatter. Quema scowled at a pot of something bubbling on the firehook. Norema put the shell, whose pale, inner lip she had been polishing with a piece of worn, wild kid's skin, on the table, and wondered if she should go to the docks or not.

She didn't—that afternoon.

And the stories began to come back:

The boat had stayed at the waterfront dock not more than an hour; only three women had come down the plank to squint around—their hair was dusty, braided, brown. Then they had gone back up. The boat had weighed anchor again and was now up in the middle of the sounds, the reflection of its high, scarlet, scroll-worked rim wrinkling over and running on the water.

All its crew were women or girls, came back the story now. They had sent out a small skiff for the port: the women had gone to the inn and sat and told stories and drank: tall ones, short ones, brown ones, black ones, fat ones, blond ones—every kind of woman you could think of! (Norema began to look askance at Enin who was recounting this. A *small* skiff? *How* many women were in it all together? Twenty! Thirty! exclaimed Enin, then frowned: Well, maybe six . . . or seven. Norema shook her head.)

All the crew were women or girls *except* the captain, came back next morning's revision. He was a great, tall, black man with brass rings in his ears, a

110

leopard skin over one shoulder, wooden-soled sandals with fur straps, broad bands of tooled leather around his thick calves and forearms, six small knives in finger-long scabbards on the heavy chain around his short kilt, and a cloth made all of interlocked metal rings that jingled when he ambled the dock.

Norema's father stood by the yard's plank fence (it was shaggy with bark) and listened to Big Inek recount this, and frowned, rolling an awl handle between his thumb and forefinger.

Norema watched her father frown and watched her mother, with an arm full of boards, pause behind him, hear also, frown harder, and walk on.

Jori, behind one of the net houses, told her that evening, in a slather of blue shadows with the water down between the dock-boards flashing copper, about Morin (the girl who had once sat in front of Norema with sunlight on her shoulder beneath Venn's thatched teaching porch). Morin was a tall, bony girl, slow to understand, quick to laugh, who worked a boat that had been her uncle's but was now good as her own —or so she said. She had come to Venn's classes infrequently, and only this, really, because for a while Venn had taken a special interest in her that seemed to have more to do with her talents as a fisherman than her wit: her likes ran toward late evenings in the tavern where she hung on the edge of boisterous gatherings, with bright eyes, drinking nothing herself for hours, saying little for the same—till all at once she would get up and leave: two- and three-day trips alone in her boat, fishing only to eat, which trips would end with her sudden return to dock, loud and boisterous as if drunk herself, generally cursing out the village for the backwater sumphole that it was, and treating this group or that group to a round of drinks at the tavern, trying for all the world to start a boisterous evening, upon which, if it got going, she would fall silent and watch, again, bright eyed, and only water in her mug. At any rate, Jori went on, Morin's dislike for village life was well known. So no one could have been too surprised when she fell in to talking with a bunch of the ship's sailors, or that they offered her a job; or that she had accepted.

Well:

Her father and her uncle, whom she lived with, had a fit! They forbade her to go. When she refused to stay, they beat her up and locked her in the house and now refused to let her out until the boat left the shore. And that's not all, Jori went on, for that afternoon, three older girls had come back from swimming (with Imek's little daughter tagging along), and had met the Captain and two of the sailors, one of whom was a fat, yellow-haired woman, who, at the inn the night before, had drunk amazing amounts and slapped her scarred, fleshy hands on the counter and told shrill stories that had kept everyone laughing for hours; the Captain and the two sailors had taken the girls out to the boat! An hour later, when one of the sailors rowed the girls back, parents and relatives had gathered on the shore to snatch up their offspring. The sailor had not docked because she had seen the angry group, and had made the children swim in the last few feet —at which point someone had jumped in and tried to upset her skiff and gotten his knuckles pounded with an oarhandle for his pains. The sailor had rowed back to the ship.

And no more sailors had come in from the boat that evening to explore the waterfront or eat in the inn. But the boat still sat on its maroon reflection in the sounds—waiting, apparently, for a party of women to return from the Rulvyn, where they had gone to trade.

Norema and Jori walked back on the irregularly cobbled lane that sided the backs of the poorer houses; nets and laundry and ropes and bird cages hung in the trees between black, daub-and-wattle huts. The thick, sandy grass that would grow anywhere save on the salt beach had pushed aside stones Norema had watched men and women set in place when she was younger than Jori.

As they reached the shaggy bark fence that was the back of her father's yard, the gate ahead swung forward on its wide, leather hinges and half a dozen men tromped out, leaving her father looking after them, one hand on the log bolt he had just pushed back to let them leave. His cheeks were wrinkled in concentration above his beard. He rubbed the curly red hair on his jaw with two sap-stained fingers.

"Father, what did they want?" Jori demanded with more boldness than Norema dared (it signified less real curiosity, at least that's what the older girl had always thought).

The wrinkles fell. But he still stared after the men.

"Father . . . !" Jori insisted.

"Nothing. Nothing you need worry yourself about." Behind him, across the yard, between the high and half-hulled ribs, a horizontal thread of light blistered with silver, and was the sea.

"Does it have to do with the red ship?"

Their father frowned down at the two girls. "They asked me for my word that I would sell the ship no supplies nor offer them any services should any of its wicked women or its accursed captain sneak in to shore after sunset."

"What did you say?" Jori demanded.

"Well, I couldn't very well refuse." Her father's smile spoke vaguely of indulgence. "Big Inek's daughter is one of the girls they took out to their boat; and he works for me."

"What did they do to her?" Jori demanded on.

"Nothing." But the vague smile became a vague frown. "Or so I hear—and we should all be thankful for it. It's not what they did do, but what they could do."

Norema asked, "What could they do, Father?"

"Look, I'm not going to stand here in the road and be interrogated by my own children about things I have no wish to discuss." The frown hardened. "If girls want to talk about such unpleasant things—and I can't see any reason for it, myself—they must do so with their mothers. Not me. Now run home and stop dawdling here on the road. Go on now, run."

And Norema, who was distinctly too old to go dashing home before an irrational father, felt uncomfortable and embarrassed—and walked quickly after Jori, who was indeed now sprinting down the dusty highway.

Childhood is that time in which we never question the fact that every adult act is not only an autonomous occurrence in the universe, but that it is also filled, packed, overflowing with meaning, whether that meaning works for ill or good, whether the ill or good is or is not comprehended.

Adulthood is that time in which we see that all human actions follow forms, whether well or badly, and it is the perseverance of the forms that is, whether for better or worse, their meaning.

Various cultures make the transition at various ages, which transition period lasts for varying lengths of time, one accomplishing it in a week with careful dances, ancient prayers, and isolate and specified rituals; another, letting it take its own course, offering no help for it, and allowing it to run on frequently for years. But at the center of the changeover there is a period—whether it be a moment's vision or a yearlong suspicion—where the maturing youth sees all adult behavior as *merely* formal and *totally* meaningless.

Norema was at such a point that afternoon. "Talk to your mother, indeed," she thought, and started off to do so. (It was because she was at that point that she chose to talk to her mother about it in the particular way she did.)

Tadeem was going out the door when Norema barged in. Her mother, alone now in the kitchen, was pulling at the ropes that came through the wooden collar in the sandy wall beside the fire. Somewhere, baffles creaked and scraped.

Norema went to the table, and with her fingernail pried at a dark line on the plank that she thought might be a loose splinter. "Mother?" It wasn't. "You know the red ship anchored up in the sounds?"

Her mother tugged; baffles clashed.

"What would you do—" She ran her nail again along what she now knew was just a particularly deep grain—"if I said I had shipped aboard as a sailor?"

"What?" Clashing ceased. "No—you're not *that*

thick-skulled. But why would you even want to suggest such an awful thing?"

"Why is it awful? What have they done, and why is everyone so upset about them?"

Her mother stood up. "Upset? A boatload of women, half of them girls hardly older than you, with a strange man for captain, combing the port for more girls to take off from our island—and you ask *why* people are upset?"

"Yes," Norema said. "I want to know why."

Her mother raised her eyes, then turned back to the baffles. ". . . this fireplace. Really!" Baffles clashed again.

"Two summers ago—" Norema leaned against the thick table plank—"Fevin was the only man working on Beaio's boat. I went out with them for three days and you didn't complain."

"Fevin was not a foreign, black captain combing our port for women to snatch away forever. Norema, suppose this captain sells these women for slaves. And who knows what he does with those girls at night, when the day's watch is ended."

"It couldn't be too unpleasant," Norema said. "There're more of them than there are of him."

Her mother's *humpf* mixed contempt with frustration. "You just don't understand anything, do you? We try to bring up our children so that they are protected from the world's evils, only to find we've raised a pack of innocents who seem to be about to stumble into them at every turn just from sheer stupidity! Girl, when you *look* at that scarlet hulk, floating out there in the sounds, can't you just *feel* how strange, unnatural, and dangerous it is?"

"Oh, Mother!" Norema said. "Really!"

Then, because she saw her mother start to tug at the baffle ropes again—which, by now, were perfectly well set—she realized just *how* upset her mother was. So she sat down at the table and hulled the speckled nuts in the clay bowl that Jori had collected the previous afternoon.

Then she went back to the waterfront.

Wandering between the docks and the storage sheds,

the net houses and the small boats pulled up and upturned on the roped logs, she felt the oddest quality to
the lazy, evening dockside. Was it, she wondered, the
red boat which, from here, was not even visible?

Strolling the violet evening, she suddenly realized
that the strange air in the little waterfront streets was
simply emptiness. The sailors from the strange boat
were, of course, no longer frequenting the inns and
docks. And the local waterfronters, though not exactly
scared off by the prospect of these same sailors, were
still keeping away.

It was too amusing!

She turned toward the door around the side of
the inn, when Enin came charging down the steps,
saw her, stopped, and whispered (though there was
no one else in the gravel-covered alley): "Did you
hear, they're going to do it tonight!"

Norema frowned.

"The ship! The red ship! They're going to burn it!"
He turned, running, and she saw part of her reflection
whiz across his stomach mirror. "Burn it to the water
line!" he shouted back toward her—she turned to
watch him—and ran down the street.

On the deserted gravel, before the sandy docks,
where masts bent together and swayed apart, Norema
felt a sudden chill along her left side, under her shift;
it was horror—not the complete and stifling horror
that encases the body in a paralysis of inaction, but a
simple and slight horror whose only physical sign was
a tingling, all on one side, that someone else could
have as easily put to the breeze that had cooled the
dock some few degrees over the previous minutes.

Certain storytelling conventions would have us here,
to point and personalize Norema's response to Enin's
news, go back and insert some fictive encounter between the girl and one or more of the sailor women: a
sunny afternoon on the docks, Norema sharing a
watermelon and inner secrets with a coarse-haired,
wide-eyed twenty-year-old; Norema and a fourteen-
year-old whose dirty blond hair was bound with beaded
thongs, sitting knee to knee on a weathered log, talking of journeys taken and journeys desired; or a dawn

encounter at a beached dinghy between Norema and
some heavy-armed redhead falling to silent communion
at some task of mending, bailing, or caulking. Certainly the addition of such a scene, somewhere previous
to this in our text, would make what happens next con-
form more closely to the general run of tales. The only
trouble with such fictive encounters is, first, they frequently do not occur, and second, frequently when
they do, rather than leading to the action fiction uses
them to impel, they make us feel that, somehow, we
have already acted, already done our part to deploy a
few good feelings—especially when the action required
goes against the general will.

Norema, as we have seen, was a young woman who
knew the passions of analysis: today we say such people are more likely to place their energies behind an
abstract cause than to work at untangling the every-
day snarl of things. And though it would not have
been all that difficult to say the same in Norema's time,
she was, nevertheless, not that different from you and
me.

On the street, before the inn, Norema resolved to
do something about the burning—or at least see what
the burners were doing and do something about it if
there was anything to be done.

She turned away and walked from the inn, spreading
her toes wide in her loose, soft shoes, each step. A mo-
mentary memory of a morning walk with Venn, with
the shadows of the masts across the gravel . . . Those
shadows now lay out on the water, shattered by little
waves: and the memory shattered before feet scrabbling on the docks.

A man hallooed.

A younger man hallooed back.

Ahead, two boys jumped off the deck of a boat, ran
to the dock's foot, and peered across the street. From
around the corner came a dozen men, Big Inek and
Fevin among them.

Norema hooked two fingers on the cord around the
high, canvas-covered bale beside her, moved halfway
behind it, then moved out again so she could see the
ropes tossed back to the dock, see the one mast among

the others, swaying and swaying, stalk out on the blue-black water.

Between two houses, Norema could see sunset's copper smear. Above, the sky was the darkening indigo the calmest ocean can never quite reflect. Children's voices snarled in the street.

Norema looked down. Three grubby children had run out between the huts:

"Let's play red ship!"

"I'll be the captain!"

"You can't be the captain. You're a girl!"

"Are we going to sneak up on it and burn it?"

"Yeah!"

"All right. You be the captain. We'll sneak up and we'll burn *you!*"

"No, come on. You can't do that, either. Didn't you see? Only men go out to do that."

"Then you go on and play by yourself, then. I'm not going to play with you!"

"No, come on . . ."

"Yeah, come on. You have to play."

"You have to have girls to play red ship."

"That's what the game is all about."

"Come on, now. You play."

The mast moved beyond the clutch of masts. A sail, jerking and flapping, rose, filled, and pulled around toward the sound.

The two boys were running up the dock.

The little girl ran behind. "Hey, wait for me! All right, I *said* I'll play . . ."

Norema stepped from behind the bale, frowning, uncomfortable, sure she had just seen something very important and totally unable to say why—a situation which, for someone like Norema, *was* discomfort.

The children were gone.

The boat was away.

The docks were empty.

She strolled to the center of the gravel and started forward.

The urge to move nearer to the buildings along the street—or to keep closer to the bales and upturned dinghies along the dock—was almost overpowering.

Ambling down the center, she smiled at the discomfort and thought: The threat of the red ship . . .

And watched, while she walked, the threatened streets.

Half the tangled roots had pulled from the bank. The leafless tree leaned over the twelve-foot semicircle of sand. Norema and Venn had sat there for an hour once and argued whether the little beach, like a giant copper coin tilted half into the water, was growing or shrinking . . . how many years ago now? And the beach was the same. Norema sat wedged between the two well-anchored trees, looking out through the branches of the leaning third.

The ship, a-top its reflection, made her think of leaves, stacked one on the other, a breeze making the whole leaf column shiver, dance, but never quite topple.

The ship, dark now on dark water, held it down.

She had been sitting there almost two hours. The sky was blue-black; a few stars scattered the east. One twig of the slant tree lay like a shatter-line across the distant hull (Venn had once taken her to see a puddle of lava high in the mountains, broken by cooling— Venn's theory—or the mountain goats' hooves—Dell's —some slaggy scar from the fires burning beneath the sea's floor, whose eruptions—Venn's theory again— had thrown up all the islands around.) Fire . . . !

It spurted up the stern. Then it rushed across the waterline. What had happened was that men from the island's boat (hidden on the opposite bank) had swum up with bladders of oil and smeared the base of the ship (with light oil to the height of an arm), then ringed the ship with a lace (*not* a single wide ribbon) of heavy oil out to fifteen feet from the hull. (Where had she learned to fire a free-anchored ship? From Venn's old tale of the Three Beetles and the White Bird; which was probably where the men had learned it, too . . .) Then you took the cover off a floating tinder-dish in which a lighted rag, rolled in sand and soaked in oil, would smolder for an hour—light the ship at the downwind end, and the lace at the upwind end, then swim away for all you're worth.

Bark bit her hand. Her jaw began to throb. She pushed back against the trunk as leaf after leaf down the column caught, all the way to the base of sand below her.

A story . . . she thought. The Three Beetles and the White Bird was a tale she had hugged her knees at, leaned forward to hear of its hill-skirmishes and sea-chases, its burnings and battles, its brave feats and betrayals. Reflected there on the flickering waters, it all seemed somehow reversed to . . . not something horrible. The reason she held the branch so tightly, pressed herself back against the tree, was not from any active fear, but rather from a sort of terrible expectation of emotion, waiting for the sound (amidst the faint crackling she could just make out) of screams, waiting to see figures leaping or falling into the ring of flaming waters. All she actually felt (she loosed her hand from the branch beside her) was numb anticipation.

There are people in there, she thought, almost to see the result of such thought, *dying.* Nothing. *There are women dying in there,* she tried again (and could hear Venn making the correction): still it was just a curious phrase. Suddenly she raised her chin a little, closed her eyes, and this time tried moving her lips to the words: "There are women in there dying and our men are killing them . . ." and felt a tickling of terror; because for a moment she was watching two boys and a little girl playing on the docks. And all the waters before her and the forest behind her was a-glitter and a-glimmer with threat.

She opened her eyes: because something moved in the water . . . twenty feet away? Fifteen? (In the bay's center, fire fell back to the water's surface, with things floating in it aflame.) Several largish pieces of flotsam were drifting inland.

The one just in front of the beach stalled on submerged sands: charred and wet, it was some kind of carton, which, as she watched it, suddenly came apart. For a moment, the dozens of things floating out of it actually seemed alive. Taking up the same current, they continued, tiny and dark, into the shore.

After a while she got up and walked down to the sands' wet edge, stooped, and picked up . . . a ball of some sort, perhaps as big as her father's curled-up forefinger. Wet, black, it wasn't exactly soft. Many, many of them, she saw, were bobbing in the dark water.

Squeezing it, frowning at it (the boat was craggy, dark, blotched with fading embers), she turned back and walked back up into the woods.

She walked away on her soft-soled shoes in the loud underbrush, pondering an unresolvable troubling— till finally, after climbing into the window of her room, and lying on her bed, looking at the shadows on her bare, narrow walls—she slept. The rubber ball was under her pillow.

4
___

Shortly after that began a period of some five years, which, were one to have asked her after it was over, she would have no doubt said was the most important of her life. Certainly it obliterated the clear memory of much of what we have recounted. We, however, shall all but omit it—at least we shall condense it mightily: four weeks after the burning she met an affable red-haired man from another island who worked (indeed who was the leader of) a twelve-boat fishing cooperative of ten men and two women. Three months after meeting him she married him and moved to his island. Their first child was a son; then, in what seemed to her much less than eighteen months, she had two daughters. Through those years there were moments which, when they occurred, she thought to remember for the rest of her life (in much the same way that the firelight on the night beach she had thought to drop from her memory forever): sitting on the deck with her husband and her children at dawn the way she had sat with her mother and her sister; moonlit evenings on Willow Scarp—her favorite spot on her new island —looking out over the nets of foam that rippled round the rocky point; the afternoons when her husband would be working on his nets, perched on one of the pilings that stuck up about the rush-matted docks, and she would come up silently behind him and look up to see his sunburned back, the curls of coppery hair clawing at the translucent shell that was his ear. She had already begun to do some of the things with her own children that Venn, years ago, had done with her and the children of her island; and was both amused and a little proud that she quickly developed, on her new island, the reputation for being both odd and wise—a reputation which she could never quite understand why her husband so disapproved of.

In the fifth year of her marriage came the plague.

It killed her son, five years old now, and had she not been so involved in nursing the island's ill with one of Venn's herbal remedies that at least lessened the pains if it did not curb the disease, she would have taken one of the overturned dinghies and put to sea in it until land was out of sight, then sunk it and herself with a knife jammed through the sapped-over rushes.

The plague killed seven fishers in her husband's fleet.

Then, at the height of the sickness, when the wailing of the children and the coughing of the aged hacked at the walls of her hut from the huts both sides of hers, her husband came in early one afternoon—the time he would have normally returned from a morning with his fishing fleet, though he had told her earlier he was not taking his boat to water that day. For five minutes he paced around the house, picking at the loose staves of a half finished basket, rubbing his big toe in the dirt by the side of the hearthflags: suddenly he turned to her and announced to her he was taking a second wife.

She was astonished, and she protested—more from that simple astonishment than from any real desire to actually rebut him. He argued, and while he argued, memories of Venn's account of the Rulvyn returned to her—the second wife was apparently the daughter of a wealthy fisherman who had recently moved to their island, a very beautiful seventeen-year-old girl who had developed a reputation in the village as a spoiled and impossible person. Somewhere in the midst of her arguing, it suddenly struck her what she must do.

So she agreed.

Her husband looked at her with utmost surprise, seemed about to say several things, then turned and stalked out of the hut.

Two hours later he returned—she was squatting by the cradle of her younger daughter whose breathing was becoming strangely rough over the last hour and was trying to ignore the three-year-old who was asking, "But why can the fishes swim, Mommy? Why can fishes swim? What do they do under the water when they're *not* swimming? Mommy, you're not listening to me. Why do they—"

Her husband grabbed her up by the shoulder, whirled her around, and shoved her back against the support pole so that the thatch shook between the ceiling sticks across the hut's whole roof. The three-year-old's chatter cut off with an astonished silence into which her husband began to pour the most incredible vituperation:

Did she know that she was a vile woman and a horrible mother? That she had ruined his business, soul, and reputation? That she was in every way a plague to him and all who came near her far worse than the one that wracked the island? That she had murdered his son and was no doubt poisoning his daughters against him even now? And how *dare* she (the while, he was striking her in the chest with the flat of first one hand then the other) think she were fit to share the same hut with the beautiful and sensitive and compassionate woman he was now determined to leave her for? Even her suggesting they might all share one house was such an obscenity that—

Suddenly he backed away, and pushed through the door's vine hangings. Seven hours later Norema, her eyes closed, her arms locked across her belly, a shrill and strangled sound seeping from her pursed lips (somehow she had managed to get the three-year-old to an older cousin's when the infant's blood-laced, greenish phlegm and raw choking had assured her exactly what it was), sat on the floor of her hut with her baby girl dead and stiff on the dirt at her knees.

Two weeks later some boats came to take her to Nevèrÿon's Kolhari, with the fifty others, who, from the island village whose population had been close to eight hundred, were the only ones left. ("In the name of the Child Empress Ynelgo, whose reign is kind and compassionate, all those who can pass before our three physicians and show no stain of plague may have free passage to Her chief port city in Nevèrÿon, there to begin a new life for Her honor and glory." The captain was a small, hairy man with a verdigrised helmet, a fur jerkin, bloodshot eyes, and tarry hands, with a dumb goodwill that in him had now become a sort of fury about every detail of the evacuation, as his ship plied from stricken island to stricken island.) Once more she looked for some great feeling when she saw that two among the dozen who had been turned away from the boat by the physicians, with their poking at groins and armpits and their pulling back of eyelids and staring down into ears and throats, were her husband and his new woman. No, it had never been anger she'd felt—hurt, once, but grief had obliterated that. (Her remaining daughter had been taken away to a neighboring island a week before on the very day her phlegm had gone green—Norema did not know if her child was alive or dead. . . . No, she knew.) Rather, it was the exhausted sympathy for the misfortunes of someone who, a long time ago, had been a difficult friend. And so, as she came into Kolhari port, numbed by an experience of rejection and death, she kept telling herself that whomever she might now become, it was *this* experience that would be responsible for anything bad or good that ever befell her again; yet while she was trying to rehearse all the awfulness of the past months, sort it all out in memory as the portscape drew nearer and nearer through the dawn, fragments of it were constantly slipping from memory, and her imagination kept retreating through the years to afternoon walks with Venn, to the night on the tiny beach with flames out on the waters.

III

THE TALE OF
SMALL SARG

And if, tomorrow, all the history on which it
is based is found to be defective, the clay
tablets wrongly interpreted, or the whole
formed out of a mistaken identification of
several periods and places, our reading of it
will not be affected in the slightest, for the
Stranger, the City, the sights, smells and
sounds, formed by the poet out of history and
human activity, are real now at another level
of being.

—Noel Stock
Reading the Cantos

In that brutal and barbaric time he was a real barbarian prince—which meant that his mother's brother wore women's jewelry and was consulted about animals and sickness. It meant at fourteen his feet were rough from scurrying up rough-barked palms, and his palms were hard from pulling off the little nodules of sap from the places where new shoots had broken away. Every three or four years the strangers came to trade for them colored stones and a few metal cutting tools; as a prince, he was expected to have collected the most. It meant his hair was matted and that hunger was a permanent condition relieved every two or three days when someone brought in a piece of arduously tracked and killed game, or a new fruit tree was (so rarely) found; for his tribe did not have even the most primitive of agricultural knowledge.

Everyone said fruit and game were getting scarcer.

To be a barbarian prince meant that when his mother yelled and shrieked and threatened death or tribal expulsion, people did what she said with dispatch—which included stoning Crazy Nargit to death. Crazy Nargit, within the space of a moon's coming and going, had gotten into an argument with a woman called Blin and killed her. Everyone said that Blin had been in the wrong, but still. Then Nargit got into another fight with Arini and broke the young hunter's

leg so that Arini would be unable to walk for a year
and would limp for the rest of his life. Also, Crazy
Nargit had killed a black, female rat (which was
sacred) and for two days wandered around the village
holding it by the tail and singing an obscene song about
a tree spirit and a moth. The rat, small Sarg's mother
insisted, made it obvious that Nargit wished for death.

His uncle, shaking his blue-stone strings of women's
ear-bangles, had suggested simply driving Nargit from
the tribe.

Sarg's mother said her brother was almost as crazy
as Nargit; the tribe wasn't strong enough to keep Nargit
out if he really wanted to come in and just kill people,
which is what, from time to time, with clenched teeth
and sweating forehead, shivering like a man just pulled
out of the stream after being tied there all night (which
several times they had had to do with Nargit when he
was much younger), Nargit hissed and hissed and
hissed was exactly what he wanted above all things to
do. Nargit, his mother explained, was bound to get
worse.

So they did it.

Stoning someone to death, he discovered, takes a
long time. For the first hour of it, Nargit merely clung
to a tree and sang another obscene song. After two
more hours, because Sarg was a barbarian prince (and
because he was feeling rather ill), he went and found
a large rock and came back to the tree at the foot of
which Nargit was now curled up, bloody and gasping
—two small stones hit Sarg's shoulder and he barked
back for the others to cease. Then he smashed Nargit's
skull. To be a barbarian prince meant that, if he
wanted to, he could put on women's jewelry and go
off in the woods for long fasting periods and come
back and be consulted himself. But he preferred men's
jewelry; there was more of it, it was more colorful, and
(because he was a prince) he had a better collection of
it than most. His older sister, who had very red, curly
hair, and whose reign, therefore, as barbarian queen
was expected to be quite spectacular, was already practicing the imperial ways of his mother.

Small Sarg was left pretty much alone.

The stretch of woods that went from just beyond the fork of the little river and the big stream (where many weasels lived) up to the first fissure in the rocky shelves (two days' walk all told) he knew to practically every tree, to every man-path and deer-path, almost every rock and nearly every pebble; indeed, most of the animals that lived there he could identify individually as well as he could recognize all the human members of the Seven Clans, which, together, formed his principality. Outside that boundary, there was nothing: and nothing was part of darkness, night, sleep, and death, all of which were mysterious and powerful and rightly the providence of terror—all outside his principality was unknown, ignored, and monstrous. The Seven Clans consisted of the Rabbit Clan, the Dog Clan, the Green Bird Clan, and the Crow Clan —this last of which was his.

It was only after the strangers came and took him away that it occurred to him there really were just four to the Seven Clans, and that therefore his tribe had probably once been much larger. Suddenly Small Sarg began to conceptualize something that fitted very closely to a particular idea of history—which, because we have never truly been without it, is ultimately incomprehensible to the likes of you and me—only one of the many ideas he had been learning in the rough, brutal, and inhuman place they called civilization. Once that had happened, of course, he could never be a true barbarian again.

2

Beneath the thatched canopy that covered half the square, the market of Ellamon was closing down for the evening. Light slanted across dust scaled like some reptile, with myriad lapping footprints; a spilled tomato basket, a pile of hay, trampled vegetable leaves . . . a man with a wicker hamper roped around his shoulders stopped shouting, took a deep breath, and turned to amble away from under the canopy, off down an alley. A woman with a broom trailed a swirling pattern as she backed across the dust, erasing her own bare footprints among a dozen others. Another man pulled a toppling, overturning an evergrowing pile of garbage across the ground with a rake.

In one corner, by a supporting post, a fat man stopped wiping sweat from his bald head to brush at a bushy mustache in which, despite his pullings and pluckings, were still some bread flakes, and a bit of apple skin; also something stuck the corner hairs together at the left. His furry belly lapped a broad belt set with studs. A ring with a key a double forefinger's length hung at the hip of his red, ragged skirt.

Beside him on the ground, chained in iron collars, sat: an old man, knees, elbows, and vertebrae irregular knobs in parchment skin otherwise as wrinkled as many times crushed and straightened velum; a woman who might have just seen twenty, in gray rags, a strip of cloth tied around her head, with an ugly scab showing from under the bandage. Her short hair above and below the dirty cloth was yellow-white as goat's butter, her eyes were narrow and blue. She sat and held her cracked feet and rocked a little. The third was a boy, his skin burned to a gold darker than his matted hair; there was a bruise on his arm and another on his boney hip. He squatted, holding his chain in one hand, intently rubbing the links in his rough fingers with a leaf.

A shadow moved across the dust to fall over the single heavy plank to which all their chains were peglocked.

The slaver and the woman looked up. The old man, one shoulder against the support pole, slept.

The boy rubbed.

The man whose shadow it was was very tall; on the blocky muscles of arm, chest, and shin the veins sat high in thin, sunbrowned skin. He was thick legged;

his face bore a six-inch scar; his genitals were pouched in a leather web through which pushed hair and scrotal flesh. Rings of brass clinked each step about one wide ankle; his bare feet were broad, flat, and cracked on their hard edges. A fur bag hung on his hip from a thin chain that slanted his waist; a fur knife-sheath hung from a second chain that slanted the other way. Around his upper arm, chased with strange designs, was a brass bracelet so tight it bit into the muscle. From his neck, on a thong, hung a bronze disk, blurred with verdigris. His dusty hair had been braided to one side with another leather strip, but, with the business of the day, braid and leather had come half unraveled. The leather dangled over the multiple heads of his ridged and rigid shoulder. He stopped before the plank, looked down at the chained three, and ground one foreknuckle around in his right nostril. (Black on one thumbnail told of a recent injury; the nails were thick, broad through heredity, short from labor, and scimitared at cuticle and crown with labor's more ineradicable grime.) His palms were almost as cracked and horny as his soles. He snuffled hugely, then spat.

Dust drew in to his mucus, graying the edge.

"So. This is the lousy lot left from the morning?" The man's voice was naturally hoarse; bits of a grin scattered among general facial signs of contempt.

"The girl is sound and cooks in the western style, though she's strong enough for labor—or would be with some fattening. And she's comely." The slaver spread one hand on his belly, as if to keep it from tearing away with its own doughy weight; he squinted. "You were here this morning, and I was speaking to you about a price . . . ?"

"I was here," the man said, "passing in the crowd. We didn't speak."

"Ah, just looking then. Take the girl. She's pretty; she knows how to keep herself clean. She's of a good temper—"

"You're a liar," the tall man said.

The slaver went on as though he had not been interrupted: "But you *are* interested in buying . . . ? In this high and loathsome hold, they seem to think slaves are too good for them. Believe me, it's not as if they were concerned with the fates of the wretches for sale. I want you to know I take care of my wares. I feed them once a day and put them through a bathhouse, where-ever we happen to be, once every new moon. That's more than I can say for some. No—" He wiped again at his trickling forehead with a fleshy thumb. "No, they think here that such luxuries as I have out are namby-pamby and not suited for the austere mountain life."

A child with a near-bald head, breasts small as two handfuls of sand, and rags wrapped around her middle, ran up clutching something in leaves. "A dragon's egg!" she panted and, blinking, opened her hands. "A dragon's egg, fertile and ready to hatch, from the cor-ral of the flying beasts not two miles above in the rocks. Only a bit of silver. Only a—"

"Go on with you," said the slaver. "What do you think, I've never been in the high hold of fabled Ella-mon before? Last time I was here, someone tried to sell me a whole trayful of these things, swore I could raise the beasts into a prime flock and make my fortune." He *humphed*, making to push the child, who merely turned to the tall man.

"A dragon's egg . . . ?"

"A dragon's egg would be a good bargain at only a bit of silver." The man prodded the leathery thing in the leaves with a rough forefinger. "But this—I spent a week here, once, picking these off the trees that grow down near the Faltha Falls. Lay them in the sun for a week, turning them every day, and you have something that looks a pretty passable version of one of the winged wonder's spores."

"Is *that* how they do it?" The slaver flapped both hands on his stomach.

"—only you forgot to pull the stem off this one," the tall man said. "Now go away."

The girl, still blinking, ran off a few steps, looked back—not at the two men standing, but at the tow-headed woman, whose hair was short as (if lighter than) her own, who was still sitting, who was still rock-ing, who was whispering something to herself now.

"So, you know the lay of the rocks 'round Ellamon." The slaver moved his hands up and down over his stomach, moving his stomach up and down. "What's your name?"

"Gorgik—unless I have need for another. When I do, I take another for a while. But I've stopped in many mountain holds over the years, fabled or unfabled, to spend a day, or a week, or a month. That makes Ellamon no different for me from any hundred other towns on the desert, among the peaks, or in the jungles." Gorgik inclined his scarred face toward the slaves, gesturing with his blunt, stubbled chin. "Where are they from?"

"The old man? Who knows. He's the one I couldn't sell in the last lot—a bunch of house slaves, and him all the time asleep anyway. The boy's new-captured from some raid in the south. A barbarian from the jungles just below the Vygernangx . . ." One hand left the slaver's gut to prod at Gorgik's chest—"where your astrolabe comes from."

Gorgik raised a bushy eyebrow.

"The stars, set so on the rhet, must be from a southern latitude. And the design around the edge—it's the same as one the boy had on a band around his ankle before we took it off him and sold it."

"What's he doing?" Gorgik frowned. "Trying to wear his chains through by rubbing them with a leaf?"

The slaver frowned too. "I've kicked him a couple of times. But he won't stop. And he certainly won't rub it through in his lifetime!"

With his knee, Gorgik nudged the boy's shoulder. "What are you doing?"

The boy did not even look up, but kept on rubbing the leaf against the link.

"He's simpleminded?" Gorgik asked.

"Now the woman," said the slaver, not answering, "is from a little farming province in the west. Apparently she was once captured by raiders from the desert. I guess she escaped, made it all the way to the port of Kolhari, where she was working as a prostitute on the waterfronts; but without guild protection. Got taken by slavers again. Thus it goes. She's a fine piece, the pick of the lot as far as I can see. But no one wants to buy her."

The woman's eyes suddenly widened. She turned her head just a little, and a faint shivering took her. She spoke suddenly, in a sharp and shrill voice, that seemed addressed not to Gorgik but to some one who might have stood six inches behind him and seven inches to the side: "Buy me, lord! You will take me, please, away from him! We go to the desert tribes and I'll be sold there again. Do you know what they do to women slaves in the desert? I was there before. I don't want to go back. Please, take me, lord. Please—"

Gorgik asked: "How much for the boy?"

The woman stopped, her mouth still open around a word. Her eyes narrowed, she shivered again, and her eyes moved on to stare somewhere else. (The girl with the false egg, who had been standing fifteen feet off, turned now and ran.) Once more the woman began to rock.

"For him? Twenty bits of silver and your astrolabe there—I like the quality of its work."

"Ten bits of silver and I keep my astrolabe. You want to get rid of them before you have to waste more on their food—and bathhouses. The Empress's slave-tax falls due within the next full moon on all who would take slaves across province lines. If you're going with these to the desert—"

"Twenty-five and you can have the lot of them. The boy's the best of the three, certainly. In Kolhari I could get twenty-five for him alone."

"This isn't Kolhari. This is a mountainhold where they pay mountain prices. And I don't need three slaves. I'll give you twelve for the boy just to shut you up."

"Thirteen and your astrolabe there. You see I couldn't take the thirteen by itself because certain gods that I respect consider that a highly dangerous number—"

"I'll keep my astrolabe and give you fourteen, which is twice seven—which certain other gods regard as highly propitious. Now stop this back-country squabbling and . . ."

But the slaver was already squatting by the heavy plank, twisting one of his thick keys in the peg lock while sweat beaded the creases on his neck. "Well, get it out. Get your money out. Let's see it."

Gorgik fingered apart his fur sack and shook out a palmful of coins, pushing off some with his thumb to clink back in. "There's your money." He poured the palmful into the slaver's cupped hands, then took the proffered key and bent to grab up the loosened chain. "The iron coin is desert money and worth two and a half silver bits to the Empress's tax collectors." Gorgik tugged the boy up by the shoulder, wound the chain high on the boy's arm, pulled it tight across the narrow, boney back, and wound it high on the other arm: pigeoning the shoulders made running at any speed impossible.

"I know the desert money." The slaver fingered through, translating the various coinage into imperials and adding them with silent tongue and moving lips. "And you know too, apparently, the way they bind slaves in the mines down at the Faltha's feet." (Gorgik finished tying the boy's wrist; the boy was still looking down at where his leaf had fallen.) "Were you once an overseer there? Or a gang foreman?"

"You have your money," Gorgik said. "Let me be on my way. You be on yours." Gorgik pushed the boy forward and pulled the end of the chain tight. "Go on, and keep out to the very end." The boy started walking. Gorgik followed. "If you run," Gorgik said, matter of factly, "in a single tug I can break both your arms. And if I have to do that, then I'll break your legs too and leave you in a ditch somewhere. Because you'll be no use to me at all."

From behind, the slaver called: "Are you sure I can't buy your astrolabe? Two silver bits! It's a nice piece, and I have a yearning for it!"

Gorgik walked on.

As they passed from under the scraggly market awning, the boy twisted back to look at Gorgik with a serious frown.

He wasn't a good-looking boy, Gorgik reflected. His shoulders were burned brown as river mud. His hair, bleached in bronze streaks, was matted low on his forehead. His green eyes were bright, small, and set too close. His chin was wide and weak, his nose was broad and flat—in short, he looked like any other dirty and unmannered barbarian (they had lived in their own, filthy neighborhoods along Alley of Gulls at the north side of the Spur whenever any of them had ended up in Kolhari). The boy said: "You should have take the woman. You get her work in the day, her body at night."

Gorgik tugged the chain. "You think I'll get any less from you?"

3
———

Gorgik ate heartily from a heavily laden table. He joined in an army song and beat a mug of mead on the boards in unison with the mugs of the soldiers; half his spilled the horny knot of his fist. With the fifteen-year-old barmaid on his knee, he told a story to three soldiers that made the girl shriek and the soldiers roar. A very drunk man challenged him to dice; Gorgik lost three rounds and suspected that the dice were loaded by an old and fallible system; his next bet, which he won, confirmed it. But the man's drunkenness seemed real, for Gorgik had been watching him drink. In a long, long swallow, Gorgik finished his mug and staggered away from the table looking far drunker than he was. Two women who had come to the mountains from the plains and, having eaten behind a screen, had come out to watch the game, laughed shrilly. The soldiers laughed gruffly. And, at least, the barmaid was gone. One of the soldiers wanted the older of the women to gamble with the drunken dice man.

Gorgik found the inn owner's wife in the kitchen. Outside, a few moments later, furs piled high as his chin, furs swinging against his ankles (as it was too warm for furs inside the house, she hadn't even charged him), Gorgik edged between the ox-rail and the cistern wall and out of the light on the packed dirt behind the pantry window.

The inn, frequent in provincial middle-class cities, had once been a great house; the house had been closed up, ruined, parts of it pulled down, parts of it rebuilt. For more than a century only a third of it had stood at any one time; seldom for twenty years had it been the same third.

Gorgik carried the furs across what might have once been a great hall, or perhaps an open court. He stepped over stones that had, centuries or decades ago, been a wall. He walked by a wall still standing, and up a stand of rocks. Earlier, when he had asked the innkeeper's wife where to house his slave, she had told him to put the boy in one of the "outrooms."

Out of the three, one had been filled with benches, branches, broken three-legged pots no one had gotten 'round to mending, and a cart with a shattered axle; the other two were fairly empty, but one had an unpleasant smell. The "outrooms" had probably once been quite as "inside" the house as the pantry in which the heavy, spotty-cheeked woman had paused, on her way from kitchen to common room, with a basket of roots on her hip, to instruct Gorgik the way here to them. The rooms sat alone on a rag of granite that crumbled away behind the inn itself, a single wall from one winding down (here and there fallen down), to join with the wall of the standing wing.

This was Gorgik's third trip to the outrooms.

The first trip, just before sunset, had been to chain up his young barbarian to the post that supported what was still left of the room's sagging ceiling (the straw was sticking out of the cracked daub): more than half the ceiling was down and most of two walls had fallen, so that the room was missing one corner.

The second trip, before his own dinner, had been to bring the barbarian his supper—a pan of the same roots the woman had been carrying, skinned and boiled with a little olive oil. In taste, texture, and color they were between sweet potatoes and turnips. Also, in the pan, were pieces of fried fat that, if still hot and served with salt and mustard, were fairly tasty. It was standard fare for a laboring slave, and substantially better than the boy would have gotten with his slaver. Gorgik had paid the extravagant price for salt, and, in the smokey kitchen, stolen a handful of ground mustard and another of chopped green pepper from two crocks on the table, scattered them about the pan, then, brushing his hands against his leg, ducked under the slant beam of the kitchen's transom, with a yellow mustard flower on his thigh.

The third trip—this one—was to bring out the blankets—not that it was particularly chill tonight. As he reached the room, a black cloud dropped its silvered edge from the moon (one of the rugs, up under his chin, tickling the side of his nose in the pulsing breeze, was white); as the leaf-rush up about the thick trunks stilled, Gorgik heard the sound that had begun before the end of his first visit, had continued all through his second, and was whispering on into this, his third.

Gorgik stepped over the broken wall.

The boy, squatting away from him, so that only one knee was in direct moonlight, rubbed and rubbed his chain with a leaf.

The food in the pan was gone.

Gorgik dropped two of the furs on the rock floor, and began to spread the third, black one.

The boy kept rubbing.

"I bought you—" Gorgik kicked a corner straight—"because I thought you were simple. You're not. You're crazy. Stop that. And tell me why you're doing it." He shook out the second, white fur, dropped it to lap the black, and flung out the brown on top of both.

The barbarian stopped, then squat-walked around and squinted at his owner, dropping both forearms over his knees; the chain hung down from his neck (a length sagged between his two fists) to coil on the ground before snaking away to its pole back in the dark. The boy said: "I am dead, yes? So I do my death task."

"You're crazy is what you are. That scraping and rubbing, it gets on my nerves." Gorgik stepped onto the blanket edge and sat down. "Come over here."

The boy, without rising, squat-walked onto the white fur. (Behind him, the chain lifted an inch from the ground, swung.) "I am not crazy. I am dead. Nargit was crazy, but not . . ." The boy lowered his eyes, moving his heavy upper lip around over his teeth—one of which, Gorgik had noticed by now, lapped the tooth beside, giving all his barbaric expressions still another imperfection. "Crazy Nargit is dead too . . . now. Because I kill him . . . I wonder if I would meet him here."

Gorgik frowned, waited.

The mark of the truly civilized is their (truly baffling to the likes of you and me) patience with what truly baffles.

The boy said: "I have as many lifetimes as there are leaves on a catalpa tree three times the height of a man in which to go at my task. So I must get back to work." He brought leaf and link together; then he dropped his eyes again. "But already I am very tired of it."

Gorgik pursed his lips. "You look very much alive to me." He grunted. "Had I thought you were dead, I never would have purchased you. A dead slave is not much use."

"Oh, I am already dead, all right!" The boy looked up. "I figure it out, at the beginning. It is almost exactly like the tales of my uncle. I am chain in a place where there is no night and there is no day; and if I rub a single leaf against my chain for a length of time equal to as many lifetimes as there are leaves on a catalpa tree three times the height of a man, my chain will wear away, I shall be free, and I can go to the fork in the river where there will always be full fruit trees and easy game . . . But you know?" The barbarian cocked his head. "When they took me from the forest, they chain me right away. And right away I begin my task. But after a week, a whole *week* into this death of mine, when they gave me to the man from which you took me, they took away my old chain and gave me a new one. And it wasn't fair. Because I had already work at my task for a week. Work hard. And do it faithfully every waking hour. A week, I know, is not so much out of a length of time equal to as many lifetimes as there are leaves on a catalpa tree three times the height of a man. Still, I *had* work hard. I had do my task. And it make me very discouraged. So discouraged I almost cry."

"Let me tell you something about being a slave," Gorgik said, quietly. "Even if you work at your task a length of time equal to the number of lifetimes as there are leaves in an entire catalpa forest, as soon as your master sees that you are one leaf's thickness nearer freedom, he will promptly put you in another chain." There was a length of silence. Then Gorgik said: "If I take that chain off, will you run?"

The boy frowned. "I do not even know which way I should go to find the fork in the river from here. And I am very tired."

"How long have you been captured now?"

The barbarian shrugged. "A moon, a moon-and-a-half . . . But it feel like a man's lifetime."

Gorgik fingered for the pouch dangling beside his buttock, took out the key, went forward on his knees, and reached for the boy's neck. The boy raised his chin sharply. The key went into the lock; the chain fell—soft on fur, a-clink on rock.

Gorgik went back to sitting, rolling the key between his fingers.

The boy reached up and felt his neck. "Will you take the collar off too?"

"No," Gorgik said. "I won't take the collar off."

Slave and owner squatted and sat at opposite edges of the blanket, one frowning, fingering his collar, the other watching, turning the key.

Then the moonlight in the boy's matted hair darkened.

Both looked up.

"What are those?" the barbarian asked.

"The giant flying lizards which these mountains are

fabled for. They raise them in the corrals further up among the rocks." Gorgik suddenly lay back on the fur. "They are the special wards of the Child Empress, groomed and trained with special riders. There—" Gorgik pointed up through the broken roof. "Another one. And another."

The boy went forward on all fours and craned his head up to see. "I saw some out earlier. But not as many as now." Now the barbarian sat, crossing his legs. One knee bumped Gorgik's.

Dark wings interrupted the moonlight; and more wings; and more. Then the wings were away.

"Strange to see so many out," Gorgik said. "When I was last through Ellamon, I only saw one my whole stay—and that might have been a mountain vulture, off between the crags."

"No vulture has a tail—or a neck—like that."

Grunting his agreement, Gorgik stretched on the rug. His ankle hit the food pan; it scraped over rock. He drew his foot back from stone to fur. "There, the whole flock is coming back again. Move over here, and you can see."

"Why are they all over—no, they're turning." The barbarian moved nearer Gorgik and leaned back on his elbows. "They have riders? What must it be to fly so high, even above the mountains?"

Gorgik grunted again. He put one hand under his head and stretched out the other—just as the barbarian lay down. The metal collar hit Gorgik's horny palm; the matted head started to lift, but Gorgik's horny fingers locked the nape. The barbarian looked over.

Gorgik, eyes on the careening shapes aloft, said: "Do you know what we are going to do together here?"

Suddenly the barbarian's frown changed again. "We are?" He pushed himself up on an elbow and looked at the scarred, stubbled face, the rough, dark hair. "But that's silly. You're a man. That is what boys do, away from the village huts, off in the forest. You become a man, you take a woman and you do it in your house with her. You don't do it with boys in the woods any more."

Gorgik gave a snort that may have had laughter in it. "I'm glad you have done it before, then. It is better that way." He glanced at the barbarian. "Yes . . . ?"

The barbarian, still frowning, put his head back down on the fur. Gorgik's fingers relaxed.

Suddenly the slave sat up and looked down at his owner. "All right. We do it. But you take this off me." He hooked a finger under the collar. "You take this off . . . please. Because . . ." He shook his head. "Because, if I wear this, I don't know if I can do anything."

"No," Gorgik said. "You keep it on." Looking up at the barbarian, he snorted again. "You see . . . if one of us does not wear it, *I* will not be able to do anything." At the barbarian's puzzled look, Gorgik raised one bushy eyebrow and gave a small nod. "And right now, *I* do not feel like wearing it . . . at least tonight. Some other night I will take it off you and put it on myself. Then we will do it that way. But not now." Gorgik's eyes had again gone to the sky; what darkened the moon now were cloud wisps. He looked back at the boy. "Does it seem so strange to you, barbarian? You must understand; it is just part of the price one pays for civilization. Fire, slavery, cloth, coin, and stone—these are the basis of civilized life. Sometimes it happens that one or another of them gets hopelessly involved in the most basic appetites of a woman or a man. There are people I have met in my travels who cannot eat food unless it has been held long over fire; and there are others, like me, who cannot love without some mark of possession. Both, no doubt, seem equally strange and incomprehensible to you, 'ey, barbarian?"

The boy, his expression changed yet again, lowered himself to his elbow. "You people, here in the land of death, you really are crazy, yes?" He put his head down on the crook of Gorgik's arm. Gorgik's hand came up to close on the barbarian's shoulder. The barbarian said: "Every time I think I am wearing one chain, I only find that you have changed it for another." Gorgik's fingers on the barbarian's shoulders tightened.

4

Small Sarg woke smelling beasts too near. But his next breath told him the beasts were long dead. He turned his face on the fur, relaxed his fingers around the rug's edge (fur one side, leather the other). Beside him, Gorgik's great shoulder jerked in darkness and the rough voice mumbled: ". . . get away from me . . . get away you little one-eyed devil . . ." Gorgik flopped over on his back, one hand flinging up above his head. His eyes were closed, his mouth opened. His breathing, irregular for three, then four, then five breaths, returned to its normal, soundless rhythm. Stubbled overlip and wet underlip moved about some final, silent word: through none of it, Sarg saw, had sleep been broken.

The boy pushed up on his elbow to regard the man. The chain was coiled away on the rock. The collar, wide open, lay half on brown fur near Gorgik's cracked and horny foot.

Getting to his knees, Sarg reached down and picked it up. He drew his legs beneath him on the rug, and held the half-circles in each fist, working the whispering hinge. He looked back at his owner. On that tree-trunk of a neck, the collar—closed—would cut into the windpipe and pull in the flanking ligaments. On Sarg it had hung loosely, rubbing the knobs of his collarbone.

"Why would you wear this?" the barbarian asked the sleeping man. "It does not fit you. It does not fit me."

Gorgik rolled back on his side; and for a moment the barbarian wondered if the man were really sleeping.

A sound that might have been a leaf against a leaf came from somewhere. The barbarian noted it, because that too had always been his way. With a disgusted grimace, he put down the collar, rose to his feet in a motion, stepped to the rock, grabbed the broken wall, leaped (outside that sound again) and came down facing a moon, shattered by a lace of leaves and four times as large as any moon should be, as it fell toward the obscured horizon.

He looked around at the fallen rocks, at the trees, at the walls of the inn, and the flakes of light, laid out over it all. Then, because not only was he a barbarian but a barbarian prince as well—which meant that a number of his naturally barbaric talents had been refined by training even beyond the impressive level of your ordinary forest dweller—he said to the little girl hiding behind the bushes in back of the fallen wall (she would have been completely invisible to the likes of you and me): "So, you have got rid of your false dragon's egg now." For he could detect such things on the night breath of the forest. "Why are you crouching back there and watching us?"

What had been the sound of a leaf against a leaf became the sound of a foot moving on leaves. The girl pushed back the brush, stood up, climbed up on the wall, and jumped down. She was all over a dapple of moonlight, short hair, bare breasts, and bony knees. From her breathing, that for the barbarian played through the sound of leaves, Sarg could tell she was frightened.

The boy felt very superior to the girl and rather proud of his talent for detecting the unseeable. To show his pride, he squatted down, without lifting his heels from the rock, and folded his arms on his knees. He smiled.

The girl said: "You're not a slave now."

The barbarian, who had thought very little to date about what a slave exactly was (and therefore had thought even less about what it was not to be one) cocked his head, frowned, and grunted questioningly.

"You no longer wear the collar. So you are not a

slave any more." Then she took a breath. "The woman is."

"What woman?" the barbarian asked.

"The woman you were bound with down at the market today. And the old man. I went down earlier tonight to the campsite where the slaver kept his cart. Then I came here where your new master had taken you. The woman still wears her collar."

"And who did you finally sell your egg to?" the boy asked.

"I threw it away—" The girl, in a welter of moon-dapplings, squatted too, folded her arms on her own knees. (The barbarian heard the change in her breathing that told him that she was both lying and no longer afraid.) She said: "Did you see the dragons, earlier tonight, flying against the moon? I climbed up the rocks to the corrals, to watch the riders go through their full-moon maneuvers. You know the fabled flying dragons are cousins to the tiny night-lizards that scurry about the rocks on spring evenings. There's a trainer there who showed me how the great flying beasts and the little night crawlers have the same pattern of scales in black and green on the undersides of their hind claws."

"And who is this trainer? Is he some aged local who has trained the great dragons and their riders to darken the moon in your parents' time and your parents' parents'?"

"Oh, no." She took a little breath. "She comes from far away, in the Western Crevasse. She has a two-pronged sword and she is not a very old woman—she has no more years than your master. But she wears a mask and is the only dragon trainer who will take time off to talk to me or the other children who creep up to the corrals. The other trainers chase us away. For the other trainers, yes, are local women who have trained dragons and their riders all their lives. But she has only worked here since last winter. The other trainers only talk among themselves or to the riders —usually to curse them."

The barbarian cocked his head the other way. "So

here in this mountain hold, the training of dragons is a woman's rite?"

"The riders are all girls," the girl explained. "That's because if the dragons are to fly, the riders must be small and light . . . But the girls who are impressed to be riders are all bad girls—ones who are caught stealing, or fighting, or those who have babies out of wedlock and kill them or sell them; or those who are disrespectful to their fathers. To groom and ride the dragons is dangerous work. The riders ride bareback, with only a halter; and if a dragon turns sharply in the sky, or mounts a glide-current too suddenly, a girl can be thrown and fall down to the rocks a thousand feet below. And since the dragons can only glide a few hundred yards, if they come down in rough and unclimbable terrain, and the dragons cannot take off again, then dragon and rider are left to die there. They say no girl has ever escaped . . . though sometimes I think they say that only to frighten the riders from trying."

"And would you ride dragons?" the barbarian asked.

"I am not a bad girl," the little girl said. "When I go home, if my aunt discovers I have been out, she will beat me. And she will call me the curse left on her from her sister's womb."

The barbarian snorted. "If I were to return to my home now, contaminated by this death I am living, my uncle would no doubt beat me too—to drive away the demons I would bring back with me. Though no one would call me a curse."

The girl snorted now (hearing it, the barbarian realized whom he had been imitating when he'd first made the sound. Are these the ways that civilization passed on? he wondered); the girl apparently did not think much of, or possibly understand, such demons. She said: "I would like to ride a dragon. I would like to mount the great humped and scaly back, and grip the halter close in to my sides. I'd obey all the trainers' instructions and not be lazy or foolish like the riders who endanger their lives in their uncaring mischief and devilment . . . do you know that the riders *killed* a man two months ago? He was a stranger

who had heard of the fabled band of little girls kept
up in the rocks and stole up to see them. The girls
caught him, tied him to a tree upside down by one
ankle, then cut him to pieces. And the trainers just
looked the other way. Because even though they are
only the lowest mountain girls, from bad families
every one, all of them criminals and thieves, they
are wards of the Child Empress, whose reign is marvelous and miraculous. Oh, they are horribly bad
girls! And I am not. You cannot fly, and I cannot fly.
Because you are not a girl—and I am not bad."

"But you still try to sell strangers false dragon
eggs . . ." said the boy with gravity.

"The woman is still a slave," said the girl, with
equal gravity—though to the barbarian the connection
seemed rather unclear. "And you are a slave no longer.
I snuck down to the camp and watched the slaver feed
the woman and the old man—only a handful of
yellow mush, not even on a plate but just dumped on
the board where they were chained. Then, when the
moon was high, he roused them and drove them before
him into the night. They will journey through the
darkness, toward the desert. He wants to reach the
desert soon and sell the woman before the Empress's
slave tax falls due. If the old man cannot travel fast
enough, he will break both his legs and heave him
over the side of the road. I heard him say it to a salt
smuggler who had made camp on the other side of
the same clearing." Then she added: "It was the salt
smuggler to whom I sold my egg. So I had to hide
well so they would not see me . . . they will do terrible
things to the woman in the desert. You may have once
been a slave. But you are not a slave any more."

The barbarian was puzzled by the girl's urgency,
which, from her breathing, was moving again toward
fear. Because he was a barbarian, the boy sought an
explanation in religion: "Well, perhaps if she had
done her task as faithfully as I had done mine, instead
of calling to passersby to buy her, wailing and rocking
like a mad woman, and getting herself beaten for her
troubles, her scar showing her to have a nasty temper
anyway, she too might have gotten a kind master who

would have taken off her collar and her chain for the night."

The girl suddenly rose: "You are a fool, you dirty barbarian slave!" Then she was only a moon-flicker, a leafy crash of feet.

The barbarian, who really knew very little about slavery, but knew nevertheless that the moon was powerful magic, whether the branches of mountain catalpas or the wings of soaring dragons shattered its light, shivered slightly. He rose, turned, and climbed back over the outroom's wall.

Seated again on the blanket, he looked at sleeping Gorgik for a while; the broad back was toward him. The tight bronze band high on the arm caught the moon's faint breath in its chased edge. After a while, the boy again picked up the hinged collar.

He started to put it around his own neck, then returned it to his lap, frowning. He looked again at his sleeping owner. The barbarian moved up the blanket. "If I try to close it, he will wake up . . . though if I only *place* it around his neck" Again on his knees, he laid the collar on the thick neck—and was settling back down when the great chest heaved, heaved again; Gorgik rolled over. His eyes opened in his scarred, sleep-laden face. Gorgik shoved himself up on one elbow; his free hand swept across his chest to his chin. The collar flew (landing, Small Sarg could not help noting despite his startlement, near the foot of the blanket only inches away from where he had first picked it up by Gorgik's foot); for a drawn-out breath, owner and property looked at each other, at the collar, and at each other again.

True wakefulness came to Gorgik's eyes; the eyes narrowed. A certain handsomeness that, by day, overrode the scar, the heavy features, the reddened eyes, and the unshaven jaw, had vanished in the shadow. Though it did not upset Sarg the way it might have someone less barbaric, the boy saw a combination of strength, violence, and ugliness in Gorgik's face which, till now, had not struck him.

"What is it . . . ?" Gorgik asked. "What is it, barbarian?"

"That," the boy said, who only in the instant that he actually spoke saw what he now pointed to. "The man who sold me to you said that come from the south —from the part of the country which is my home. Do you know my home country . . . I mean, have you ever go there?"

Gorgik dropped his chin to stare down at the astrolabe hanging against his hairy chest. He snorted. "I don't know your home, boy; and I don't want to know it. Now lie down and go to sleep, or the collar goes back on. We have to move early tomorrow when we quit this mountain sumphole for Kolhari." Gorgik lay down again and twisted around on the blanket, pulling a corner over his shoulder that immediately fell off, kicking at a fur fold that seemed to have worked its way permanently beneath his shin. His eyes were closed.

The barbarian lay beside him, very still. After a few minutes Gorgik's heavy, braceleted arm fell over Small Sarg's shoulder. The barbarian, feeling more or less awake yet drifting off to sleep far more often than he realized, and Gorgik, wide awake but lying perfectly still with his eyes closed and hoping to be thought sleeping, lay together till sunrise, for by now it was only an hour or two till morning.

IV

THE TALE OF POTTERS AND DRAGONS

The justification of such abbreviation of method is that the sequence of images coincides and concentrates into one intense impression of barbaric civilization. The reader has to allow the images to fall into his memory successively without questioning the reasonableness of each at the moment; so that, at the end, a total effect is produced.

—T. S. Eliot
Preface to 'Anabase'

1

". . . entirely a good idea, my boy." The old man with
the clay-ey hands sat back on the split-log bench to
rest his knuckles, rouged with terracotta, on rough
knees. "Think of the people it connects! It makes all
of us one, as if we were fingers a-jut off a single palm:
myself, a common pot spinner, a drudger forty years
in this poor waterfront shop in this poor port city; a
noble gentleman like Lord Aldamir, once an intimate,
you may be sure, of the Child Empress herself (whose
reign—" The knuckles came up from knee to forehead, and the wrinkled eyes dropped to the shards
about the floor—"is fine and fecund); and even that
taciturn giant of a messenger who approached me with
that distant lord's ingenuous plan; and the children
who will buy the little treasures, bounce them, prattle
over them, trade and treasure them. It is as though we
are all rendered heart, bone, liver, and lights of a
single creature. Money—" and his eyes rose as high
at the name of the exchange commodity as they had
dropped low at the mention of the Empress— "is what
allows it all to be. Yes, though others argue, I'm convinced it's an entirely good thing. Ah, my boy, I can
remember back when it was all trade. A pot went out;
eggs came in. Another pot: barley this time. Another
pot: goat's milk. But suppose I wanted cheese when
there was only butter available? Suppose someone with

butter needed grain but had more than enough pots? Oh, those were perilous times—and perilous in ways that money, which can be saved, stored, spent wisely or foolishly, and doesn't go bad like eggs or butter, has abolished. But that was fifty years ago and need not worry a young head like yours . . . All of us, a lord, a lord's man, an enterprising and successful artisan with a will to expand his business, and the little children whose joyous laughter guilds the city from the alleys of the Spur to the gardens of Sellese—the web of money makes us all one!"

"And the one who sells these little rubber balls you would import from Lord Aldamir in the Garth Peninsula, here to Kolhari." The young man smiled.

"Well, of course, that's where you come in, Bayle. I am a common potter and you are a common potter's boy: but though I am as near sixty as you are near twenty, believe me, it is only a beginning for us both. And I shall need you to do a great deal more than simply sell. We are still a little business and must do everything ourselves, you and I . . ."

Bayle grinned at the thought of incorporation into this creature whose blood was coin.

"Yes," said old Zwon, for perhaps the seventh time that morning, "as far as I can see, money is an *entirely* good idea! As fine an idea as writing and public drainage systems, I'll be bound. As fine as fibrous rope and woven fabric—indeed, as the stone chisel and the potter's wheel itself. And I remember, boy, when every single one of those marvels—save the potter's wheel —entered my life, or my father's life, or my grandfather's. You sit there, and they surround you. You don't know what the world was like without them. Levers and fulcrums, levers and fulcrums—that's all there was and they raised stone walls and made cities look like cities. But for the common woman or common man going about a common day's business, give me a piece of rope or a clay drainpipe any day. Well—" Zwon's hands made claws over his knees—"it will mean a bit of travel for you, Bayle. For Lord Aldamir wants someone whom I trust to visit him in the south and survey the actual orchards—I wonder how exten-

sive those orchards must be if he intends to harvest
so many of the little toys—to oversee the shipment
personally. Now that, my boy, is the true aristocratic
style filtering down to us urban scufflers. Well—"
Between the old knees, clay-ey claws meshed—"you
better get down to the docks, Bayle. You have your
bedroll packed, your letter of introduction to his
Lordship. The boat sails this afternoon, but I want
you to be at least an hour early, since we have yet
to invent an accurate timetable for shipping traffic in
and out of Kolhari harbor. Go on, now, boy!"

Bayle, the potter's boy, with all the delight proper
to an eighteen-year-old launched on a journey involving adventure and responsibility, stood up still grinning
(was he nervous? Yes!), hoisted his bundle by its
woven strap and heaved it over his shoulder. "Zwon,
I'll make you proud! I will! Thank you!"

"Ah," said Zwon, "these are brutal and barbaric
times, and you are journeying into the brutal and barbaric south. You may well have to do any number of
things on this trip that are not so prideful—I'll mark
that clearly on the clay," which was an adage long
used by Kolhari potters. "What *I* want you to do is
any and all of those things that will make me rich!"

Bayle was a strong, stocky lad, with an inch of
yellow beard—mostly beneath his chin (no real mustache), with broad shoulders from cutting firewood
to fit the open pine fires for the rough rhaku wear,
and the elm and hickory kilns for the figured, three-
legged pots and glazed animals; his forearms were
heavy from holding clay to shape on the turning wheel.
A comfortably thick body made him look like a young
bear—a thickness that twenty years hence would be
fat, but for now simply made him look affable.
He stood in the middle of the shadowed shop and
laughed his most affable laugh, for he was a well-liked
youth and knew it. (And to do well when you are
well-liked is usually easy.) Laughing, he turned on soft
sandals, their broad straps laced to his knees. He strode
over shards to the door, ducked his curly head at the
slant lintel. He did not need to; but a year ago an
extraordinarily tall and handsome black had worked

for a month in the shop, who *had* needed to duck in order to enter and leave: and Bayle, impressed with the black's carriage, had taken up the gesture, though the top of his own curly head—and Bayle's father, a fat man with remnants of the same bronze curls, had been bald at twenty-five—barely brushed the wide-grained plank. With a thumb under his belt, Bayle adjusted the cloth, bound once between his legs and twice around his hips, and stepped to the pitted street.

Half a dozen potter's shops squeezed between fish stalls, wine sellers, cheap taverns and cramped dwellings—a third the shops that had been there fifty years ago, which had given the waterfront end of the alley its name: Potters' Lane. An irony: three blocks over, port Kolhari supported some seventeen more potters in a street named, incongruously enough, Netmenders' Row.

Lugging his roll on his back, grown quickly sweaty beneath it, Bayle went down the curving alley, its right side a-blaze with white sun (bright, warn-wood buildings), the left a-swim in blue shadows (garbage-clotted puddles still drying about the uneven road). Ships usually departed in the morning or the evening—now it was no more than three hours after noon. The little street emptied him out on Old Pavē, five times as wide, a third as crowded: oxcarts trundled, merchants strolled by with heads hooded or parasols raised against the heat. Bayle's bundle slid on his back with his striding; the strap was wet on his dribbling shoulder. Fifty yards ahead, the cobbled road shivered before the docks and warehouses, almost deserted now at the hottest part of the day.

There was his ship!

And the tavern across from it, with scattered oyster shells before it, had colored stuffs hung out on the poles set in the ground for awnings. Three sailors and a porter sat on their stools, leaning together over the split-log benches, laughing quietly and continuously at some endless round-robin account.

Bayle walked in under the awning, set his bundle on broken shells, and sat at an empty table, only vaguely aware of the voices of two women that came from the curtained alcove in the back: he did not pay attention to any of their quiet conversation, that had begun before he'd come in, that continued through his three mugs of cool cider, that was still going on after he got up to wander over to the boat to take a look at his berth.

"Come now, dear girl: don't mind the heat. There's your ship. Who knows how many hours before it puts out for the Garth. And a tavern, right across from it! Let's set out under one of those awnings in the front and drink a toast to your coming adventure and my coming wealth. Who'd have thought, when I struck up a conversation with you in the public garden only a day after you'd arrived in Kolhari, that, a year later, you'd be my most trusted secretary and my missionary to the south to petition Lord Aldamir! Oh, it's an enterprise we are well bound up in, and rest assured the result will be wealth for us both. Mark it, Norema —for it is inked like writing on velum that has soaked clear through and will not come off for all your scraping with a writing knife—" which was an old adage among Kolhari merchants—"money draws to money. And we start from a very good position. Ah, ten years ago, when I took over my dear, dead brother's foundering business—nothing but a mass of papers, names of ships, lists of captains and sailors, and the key to several warehouses in which I found the most terrifying things—I'm sure I felt all the fears that a childless woman of forty-five, with only the memory of a husband gone out my life before I was thirty, could possibly feel in those hectic and heartless times. But now that I am fifty-five and have made a go of it for a decade, I have learned some of that fear is actually what men call the thrill of adventure; and I have come to enjoy it, in reasonable doses. Besides, what's in my warehouses no longer frightens me. Oh, yes, Norema, let us sit here out in the sunlight and drink something heady and hearty!"

"Madame Keyne," said the serious-looking young woman with the short red hair, "they have a curtained women's alcove inside . . . ?"

"Would *you* be more comfortable inside?" the older woman asked in a swirl of diaphanous blues and greens, bracelets and finger chains and anklets and ear bangles a-clatter—for veils and bangles were the rich and conservative attire in that time and place for a rich and conservative matron. "But then—" blues and greens settled—"you really *were* asking on my behalf, weren't you?" She sighed, and her hands disappeared in the folds of her dress. "Here I am—here *we* are—on the threshold of an adventure, nautical for you and economic for us both: I certainly don't wish to be bothered now by obstreperous men, neither the well-off who, if we sat out under the awnings, will think their attentions flatter us, nor the not so well-off whose attentions would annoy us though they have no other aim than to make us put up a pleased smile before that annoyance, nor the completely destitute—the mad or crippled ones who live in such pathetic incompetence they cannot tell us from their mothers and expect any woman to hand out food and sympathy and money from sheer constitutional maternalism."

Norema smiled. "But *you* would be unhappy in the shadowed and curtained women's alcove, where we could escape such annoyances—"

"—because I *wish* to sit out in the air and light. Which is precisely where we would *not* escape them. Well, it is no surprise to you, having worked for me a year. I do not like woman's place in this society, and that place is nothing so simple as a curtained alcove in the back corner of a waterfront tavern, or a split-log table in the front of one: that place, you know, is neither my walled garden in Sellese that makes the world bearable for me, nor my warehouses at the back of the Spur, which makes the bearable possible. And while we stand here brooding over why we can be happy neither in the sun nor in the shadow, give a thought too to the brilliant notions on art, economics, or philosophy we are not now having because we are concerned instead with *this!*" She beat her hand through her skirts: the blues and greens flew up from layers of indigo and chartreuse. "Come, Norema, let us go back into our alcove and enjoy a pitcher of

cider!" The older woman started in among the tables
and benches, a faint smile on her face—because she
thought the younger woman behind was no doubt
smiling too at what that young woman would certainly
take to be excessive. The young woman followed, with
a perfectly serious expression—because, although she
felt an almost obsessive compulsion to be honest with
her employer, which compulsion grew from the twin
motivations that, first, very few other people were, and,
second, she had an astute awareness of her employer's
rather astonishing business acumen in a world where
business was an enterprise not more than five generations old, Norema felt an awe before this woman that
had, months ago, decided her that the lightest of
Madame Keyne's pronouncements were worthy of the
heaviest consideration—a decision she'd already had
many reasons to approve in herself.

"Norema," Madame Keyne said, when they had
seated themselves behind the frayed drapery of a particularly glum red and black weave (and before they
had let themselves become too annoyed that, after
having been seated for five whole minutes, the waiter,
who was joking with three men in the front, had not
yet served them), "something intrigues me—if you'll
allow me to harp on a subject. Now you hail from the
Ulvayns. There, so the stories that come to Kolhari
would have it, we hear of nothing except the women
who captain those fishing boats like men. We doubtless
idealize your freedom, here in the midst of civilization's
repressive toils. Nevertheless, I know that were we
sitting outside, and some man *did* come to importune
us, you would *not* be that bothered . . . ?"

"Nor," said Norema, "am I particularly annoyed by
sitting here in our alcove." Then she pulled her hands
back into her lap and her serious expression for a
moment became a frown. "I would be annoyed by the
bothersome men; and I could ignore the simply trivial
ones—which I suspect would be most of those that
actually approached us, Madame Keyne."

"But for you to ignore, for you to not be bothered,
there must be one of two explanations. And, my dear,
I am not sure which of them applies. Either you are

so content, so superior to me as a woman, so sure
of yourself—thanks to your far better upbringing in
a far better land than this—that you truly are above
such annoyances, such bothers: which means that art,
economics, philosophy, and adventure are not in the
least closed to you, but are things you can explore
from behind the drapes of our alcove just as easily
as you might explore them out in the sun and air. But
the other explanation is this: to avoid being bothered,
to avoid being annoyed, you have shut down one whole
section of your mind, that most sensitive section, the
section that responds to even the faintest ugliness precisely because it is what also responds to the faintest
nuance of sensible or logical beauty—you must shut
it down tight, board it up, and hide the key. And,
Norema, if this is what we must do to ourselves to
'enjoy' our seat in the sun, then we sit in the shadow
not as explorers after art or adventure, but as self-
maimed cripples. For those store-chambers of the
mind are not opened up and shut down so easily
as all that—that is one of the things I *have* learned
in fifty-five years." The waiter pushed back the drape,
took Madame Keyne's curt order for cider with an
expressionless nod and a half-hearted swipe of his
cloth over the varnished grain, that was certainly (if
only because it was less used) cleaner already than
any of the tables out in the common room. "I do not
know which applies to you—to us. I don't think any
woman can be sure." (The waiter left.) "That's why
I choose to worry and gnaw the question like a can-
tankerous bitch who will not give up what may well
be a very worn-out bit of rug—nevertheless, it suits
me to worry it. Even if it doesn't suit you."

Norema let herself ponder. "Well, Madame, even
if I'm not out for art or economics, this journey to
the south to negotiate for you with Lord Aldimir is
certainly an adventure."

Madame Keyne laughed—a throaty sound that made
Norema suspect, more than anything else, that this
childless, widowed woman, whose life seemed so circumscribed by the exacting business of the waterfront
and the equally exacting social pleasures of Sellese's

monied residents, had truly lived—though, equally true, neither Sellese nor the waterfront seemed, separately, a life that could have totally satisfied Norema, though both had fascinated her now for a year.

"I remember when I was a girl, the little balls would wend their way, somehow, every summer, into Kolhari —in my family, we actually called it Nèveryòna, back then. (My dear, there are days when I'm surprised I'm still alive!) Rich children in the fountained gardens of Sellese (and I remember, my dear, when the first fountain was invented: all of a sudden there it was— in the back yard of an obnoxious little neighbor whose parents were ever so much more wealthy than mine were; then, the next thing you know, everybody had to have one, or two, or a dozen, and the young barbarian who had invented them grew very wealthy and, later I heard, went quite mad and drank himself to death in some other city, or so the rumor came back), urchins by the fetid cisterns of the Spur, it made no difference: We all bounced our balls and shouted our rhyme—how did it go?

> *I went down to Babàra's pit,*
> *for all my Lady's warning . . .*

"At any rate, the summer sale of those little balls in the ports along the Nevèrÿon coast are as much a part of our life as the rule of the Child Empress herself, whose reign is marvelous and miraculous."

"I'm just surprised—" Some memory deviled the edge of Norema's pensive expression—"that nobody ever decided to import them before. I mean in large quantities. Or, else, how did they get here?"

"Well, there must be a first time for everything. And stranger things than that are happening in our time. Money—" and here the red ceramic pitcher arrived in the waiter's hand, along with two mugs on a wet tray, all cooled in the tavern's ice pit from the great blocks hauled down from the Falthas in winter and stored beneath mounds of sawdust through the hot months—"I have my serious doubts, Norema, about whether money is a good thing. I heard the other day, from a woman who, though she is not at court, is a confidante of Lord Ekoris (who is) that a man approached Her Highness not a month back with a scheme for making money of velum. The Empress would hold in store all the gold and silver and tin from which we now make coins; the velum, on which patterns would be embossed in rare inks and of a cleverness so surprising in their design that they could not be imitated by unauthorized means, would be issued to stand for specific amounts of metal, and would be used in place of coins . . ." Madame Keyne shook her head, though she noted that expression on her young secretary's face which had always made her feel that somewhere in Norema's past the most ingenious of Madame Keyne's mercantile ideas had been encountered in some other form and that complex comparisons were being made. (But then, Madame Keyne would remind herself, we civilized peoples are always romanticizing the barbaric, and she is really little different from a sensitive, extremely clever, and eager-to-learn barbarian.) "The Empress, apparently, discouraged him, quipping that such a plan would be for her unborn granddaughter's reign. Nevertheless, I still wonder. Each of us, with money, gets further and further away from those moments where the hand pulls the beet root from the soil, shakes the fish from the net into the basket—not to mention the way it separates us from one another, so that when enough money comes between people, they lie apart like parts of a chicken hacked up for stewing . . . More cider? This barrel must be from Baron Inige's apple orchards. That fine, cool tartness—I would know it anywhere, my dear. He has a way of making his apples sweet, that he used to tell my father about when we would visit him in the north, involving cow dung and minerals mined in the southern mountains, that, really, verged on sorcery . . ."

Bayle stepped around barrels and over coiled rope. The slender woman with the short red hair, strangely costumed (from her brass-linked belt, to her open-work boots; and pants. Of soft leather—Bayle had never seen *anyone* in pants before), rubbed her bare breast absently with a rough hand. (She was probably a little secretary somewhere: secretarying in those days meant mostly the whitening of reed and animal parchments with pumice, the melting of hot wax for wax pads, the sharpening of styluses and the mashing and boiling of berries for juice and the crushing of stones for pigments—it was hard on the hands.) "Those boxes," she said, frowning. "The porters were supposed to have taken those boxes onto the ship this morning. Now the Captain says we're leaving in ten minutes. And I just see them here now. If they don't go with me, Madame Keyne will have a fit!"

"Well, then," said Bayle, who had just taken his own bundle aboard and had wandered back down on the dock for a last look at the shore, "I'll carry this one on for you." As he squatted to hoist up the little crate to his shoulder, someone else said:

"—and I'll take these two. There, woman, grab up the fourth and we'll have them all aboard before they get their sails tied."

Bayle looked up at the sailor—? No, it was a woman, though those brown arms were knotted as any woodcutting man's. There were metal and colored stones in the woman's lank black hair. A shaggy scabbard was belted about the dark cloth she wore around her loins. She hoisted up one crate by its binding rope, and—at the redhead's confirming nod— swung up the duffle sack on her shoulder. Her hands were broad and worn as any farmwoman's (a very different kind of wear from a secretary's), and her bare feet were hard around the rims. She had the lithe, hard back of an active woman not quite thirty. Halfway up the gangplank, when she glanced behind to see if Bayle and the redhead were following her (her skin was red-brown as the darkest terracotta before drying), he saw the black rag mask tied across her face: through frayed holes her eyes were blue as some manganese glaze.

"All passengers go below to their cabins," the mate repeated for something like the fifth time, between orders bawled to the sailors rushing about the deck. "Please, all passengers to their cabins. Now *couldn't* you have brought those things on an hour ago when there was less confusion—or simply had the porter bring them on with the regular stores this morning? Never mind. Just get that stuff stowed fast. Once we're off, you can come up any time you want. But for now, would you please . . ."

2

"Cider on shore, wine on the water. Isn't that what they say?" asked the redhead, turning from the cabin table. "No, please stay—the both of you—and have a cup with me. My name is Norema and I'm secretary to Madame Keyne, of Kolhari port, and bound southward on this ship." From the duffle sack she'd already unstrapped, she took out a wax-stoppered wine jar and set it beside some rough-ware cups (low-fired with softwoods, thought Bayle) on the table against the wall. As she began to pick at the wax with a small knife, Bayle sat down on the box he'd carried in and noted again how sumptuous this so-fashionably garbed secretary's cabin was. (His berth, the cheapest on the ship, was a storage locker in the forepeak, in which he could just sit up; indeed, he had visited it twice during the afternoon, the first time to see it, the second time to see if, with its smell of old tar, its shavings in the corner, its chips of resin loosening between the boards, it was as grim as his first look had told him —may the Great Craftsman help him if he were ever ill in it from heaving seas!) The dark woman with the rag mask and the light eyes climbed a few steps up a ladder to some storage cabinet high in the wall, turned, and sat. She looked like some black cousin to the worst waterfront ruffian in the Spur. Her smile, like her eyes, was preternaturally bright as she looked down at the cozily appointed cabin. (Bayle wondered where *she* slept, or if she were even a passenger.) "My name is Raven," the masked woman suddenly announced (almost in answer to Bayle's thought). "I hail from the Western Crevasse. And I have been traveling three years in your strange and terrible lands!" From her perch, she barked a sharp, shrill laugh. "Strange and terrible, yes. I am on a mission for the royal family, and—alas—I can tell you no more about it." And she leaned, most unceremoniously, down between her boney knees and took the cup Norema had just filled.

This Raven, thought Bayle, has neither the air of a Kolhari woman, who expects to be served before men, nor the air of a provincial woman who expects to be served after. He looked at the redhead.

Norema, pouring two more cups, had the quiet smile of someone who has just been told a rather obscure joke and is not sure whether she truly understands it. (An island woman, Bayle thought: that hair and those eyes . . . the moment he placed her foreignness, he also felt a sudden liking for her, despite her odd dress.)

"Of course there are those," said Raven, sitting up and directing her glazed grin (a crescent of small, stained teeth) at the cup she turned in her fingers, "who would say I have said too much already. Well," and her bright eyes came up again, "I can speak three languages passably, two badly, and can write numbers and do the calculations that the Mentats invented in the Western Hills for building houses. Him," which was addressed directly down to Bayle, "who is he and what does he do?"

Bayle took the cup Norema offered, smiled up at Raven and decided he did not like her. "I'm Bayle, the Potter—or at any rate, I am a potter's assistant, and I go to the south on a journey for my master's profit."

Norema, her back to the table, lifted her hip to it and sipped at her own cup. (Bayle looked into his red-black disk to see the wax chips bump the brim.) What had been the gentlest rolling beneath them became a deep-breasted lurch. The timbre of voices from the deck above filled, deepened—

"We've launched." Raven drained half her cup.

—and quieted, after count-ten. "Perhaps," said Bayle, when, through the portal, something unrecognizable passed in the distance (a far building? a further mountain?), "we can go up now? It sounds quieter; we won't be in the way."

"Very well, pretty man. Let's go up with him," which was Raven, of course. She stood and stalked down the ladder on her broad, cracked feet.

Emerging on deck, Raven before him, Norema behind, Bayle (still holding his cup beneath his chin) saw that the confusion of departure had only abated, not stopped. Should he suggest to the women that they return below? And how to do it tactfully? But Norema and Raven were both already out among the bustling sailors (most of the men naked, all of them sweating) with what Bayle took to be their respective modes of female obliviousness: the redhead seemed certain she couldn't possibly be in the way (Bayle flinched when she sidestepped a sailor handling a barrel across the deck by its rim, and was surprised a moment later when she stooped down to pick up a four-legged metal box lying on the deck and set it in a broad capstan rail in which there were, apparently, four little cutouts for its legs to sit in: "Thank you, ma'am," called a naked sailor climbing down a rat line, who now started up again as though his job had been done). The black-haired woman with the dull stones in her hair, the rag mask, and her bright smile, turned here and there about the deck, looking for the world as if she were trying to decide which task to lend a hand with (which reminded Bayle, more than anything, of the wealthy provincials who had wandered into Zwon's shops three days before and, in their enthusiasm for the wares, had actually volunteered to return and stoke the kilns later that afternoon, much to Bayle's and Zwon's embarrassment).

The first mate walked up, a winejug on his shoulder: "The Captain wishes me to greet all our passengers and offer them a glass of our best, burnt brandy—ah, there you are. Oh, but you've already got your glasses . . . ?" (Rushing up behind the mate, in a stained apron of woven grass, a wall-eyed sailor with

a tray of cups stopped, looking confused.) "But there
. . . has someone poured you a drink already?" (Raven,
Bayle saw, was grinning at the sailor with the tray; but,
thanks to that wall-eye, one couldn't be sure what *he*
was looking at.) "Well, perhaps . . ."

Raven solved the dilemma by downing her wine,
dashing the dregs over the rail, and proffering her cup.
"Now we shall have a tasty drink . . . !"

Bayle and Norema followed suit; and somehow, as
the mate poured, it emerged that all three of them
were debarking at the Vygernangx at Garth. The mate
had already excused himself to see after some activity
involving three sailors and the try-net at the stern,
when Norema said, a little drunkenly, with a pleased
and embarrassed smile, "I am going to the south with
an import petition for Lord Aldamir."

"Are you now?" asked Bayle, one hand on the rail,
a second helping of brandy swaying in his cup, a smile
on his face and a queasy feel in his gut. "I too have
business with that southern Lord." And while Norema
raised a questioning eyebrow, Raven laughed like a
barking banshee, clutching her brandy in one hand,
holding her neck in the other, and bending back and
forth. As the deck tilted and reversed its tilts, the
horizon tilted opposite; the roofs of Kolhari receded
north.

"There." Norema rose from her knees among the
sailors squatting around the grilling box (for that was
what Norema had set upright on the capstan rail
earlier). "See if the heat doesn't spread more evenly
and your fish cook through faster and more regularly,
now it's stoked all proper."

"Ay, that's the way they do it out among the Ulvayns," one sailor assured others, who nodded among
themselves. Coals glowed through the wires, black
between bronzing fish. On the night deck, save for a
lantern hung back at the ladder to the upper deck, there
was only the grilling box's red glow and starlight. Bayle
stood against a dorry post, beside a half dozen squatting
men who were patiently grilling their sea trout and
flounders, six at a time.

Bayle's queasiness had not turned to full seasickness, but neither had it ceased. When the first mate had again brought them a message from the Captain—he'd asked to be excused from the customary first dinner out with his passengers and might they make do with their own stores for the evening—Bayle had felt relief more than anything. Minutes ago, at a sudden toss of the deck, he'd dropped the (empty) wine cup he'd been holding all this time (sailors had laughed) and was still getting his self-composure back together: the pieces of it had shattered across the deck with the ceramic shards.

Against the post, uneasy and discomforted, he watched Raven amble beneath the lantern, her arms crossed under her small, flat-hanging breasts with their black-brown nipples, her ominous mask and awkward smile.

Movement in the shadow behind her—two crouching sailors, the one pushing at the other, reached toward the woman's hip: Raven suddenly whirled to snatch away the handle of the sword one of the sailors had half drawn from her shaggy scabbard. Her laugh crossed the deck for all the night like a seal's bark. She held the blade up out of the sailor's reach. The two men cowered back, the one whispering to the other: "See, there! I told you, I told you! Look at it! I told you so . . . !"

"Watch out, men! You are not so pretty that you can handle a woman's blade!" But as Raven turned the blade by the lantern (Bayle squinted because two threads of light lanced from the gnarly hilt), she was still grinning. "Ah, you men would take everything away from a woman—I've been in your strange and terrible land long enough to know that. But you won't have this. See it, and know that it will never be yours!" She laughed. (It wasn't one blade on the hilt, Bayle realized, but two, running parallel, perhaps an inch apart: as she brandished it, the lantern flashed between and either side.) Other sailors had turned; the answering laughter near Bayle had an expectant edge.

"Will you tell the story, Western Woman?" one sailor called.

"Can she tell the story?" asked another.

And another: "She is a daughter of the Western Crevasse. She knows the story . . ."

Bayle frowned. Raven laughed again: she seemed familiar with all this, though it baffled Bayle.

"Ah," called Raven, sliding her double blade back into its hairy scabbard, "it is not your sword, and it is not your story."

"Woman, won't you tell us the tale—of how your western god made the world and the trees and the flowers and men and women," a sailor cajoled.

"But you have your own craft gods in this strange and terrible country, no? Why should you want mine, unless you wished to steal her from me as you would steal my double-bladed sword?" (To Bayle, Raven seemed to relish the attention.) "I am an adventurer, not a storyteller."

"Tell it! Tell it! Go on . . ." they cried.

"Also," said Raven, turning now to lean against the capstan rail, "it is not a man's story. It is for women."

Which made Bayle, as well as some of the other sailors, glance at Norema. She stood quietly at the edge of the squatting men, her hands in the slits at the hips of her strange leg-coverings—internal storage pouches, apparently, which Bayle found himself insistently thinking of as little extra wombs that Norema, for some reason, had decided to carry about, an amusing thought that had added to his liking of her at the same time as his dislike of the Western Raven had grown.

"If you, Island Woman, would hear a tale of my god, then I will tell it," the masked woman said. "But for them, there is no need." Red fire-spots in Raven's blue eyes glittered from frayed cloth.

Norema glanced at Bayle with an embarrassed smile, at the sailors. "Well, if the others want—"

"Ah, no." Raven raised her hand. With her dark hair and her black rag mask, she was practically a head shorter than Norema—a fact which had somehow escaped Bayle till now. "It is not for them to decide."

Norema suddenly took her hands from her pockets

and folded them behind her. "Very well, then. Tell me the story."

And the sailors, with much shoulder nudging, fell so silent the only sound was the bubbling of fish grease on hot wires.

"Very well, I will." Raven gave her raucous laugh. "But know that they will try to take it away from us, as men take everything from women in this strange and terrible land—for isn't that why it is so strange and terrible? At any rate. Listen to me, heathen woman. In the beginning was the act—"

One sailor coughed. Another shushed him.

"—and the act was within the womb of god. But there was neither flesh nor fiber, neither soil nor stone, neither clear air nor cloudy mists, neither rivers nor rain, to make the act manifest. So god reached into her womb with her own hand and delivered herself of the act, which, outside god's being, became a handful of fire. And god scattered fire across the night, making stars and—from the bulk of it—the sun itself. Then she breathed the winds from her nostrils and voided her bowels and bladder to make the bitter soil and the salt seas. And she vomited her bile, green and brown, out upon the water and the land, and the shapes in which it fell became models for the animals and trees and fish and flying and crawling insects and birds and worms and mollusks that live about the earth and water and air. And god modeled the animals all from the flesh of her body. And the fingers of god became the ten, great female deities of matter and process; and the toes of god became the ten, minor male deities of emotion and illusion—"

"But that's much later!" called a sailor who had unsheathed her sword. "You haven't told how your god made women and men."

Raven looked at Norema, who, after a moment, smiled and said: "Well, tell me how god made men and women."

"Very well." Raven's smile suggested she was playing a game. Yet Bayle already sensed stakes far beyond what such a tale might win in either laughter or awe. "When god had made her a world of sweet winds and fierce storms, gentle showers and lashing rains, fierce animals and songful birds, she said to her two companions—the great worm and the great eagle— let me make a woman of my own shape, to praise me, to adore me, to hear my words, and to ascertain by inspection and reflection the wonder of the act. And the worm raised her green head and hissed, 'Yes, god, that is good. And I will give her left hand and her right hand and her left foot and her right foot dominion over my home, the earth.' And the eagle beat her red wings and screeched: 'Yes, god, that is good. And I will give her left eye and her right eye and her left ear and her right ear and her left nostril and her right nostril dominion over the sights and sounds and scents that drift through my home, the air.' And so god took of her own flesh and made Jevim, the first woman. And god loved Jevim and suckled her at both breasts—and when Jevim suckled at god's right breast, the milk dropped from god's left with love, and that milk became a circle of light that today we call the moon. And Jevim was beloved of both the worm and the eagle. And as Jevim grew in beauty and strength, god gave Jevim the world for her pleasure, and commanded all the animals to obey her and the weather to warm her, and for this Jevim praised and adored god, and heard god's words, and by inspection and reflection discerned the wonder of the act; and Jevim prospered; and the daughters of Jevim prospered; and the tribes of Jevim filled the world and praised the wonder of god and the act. And there was soil and rock, fiber and flesh, rain and river, clear winds and cloudy mists to manifest the act; and all this Jevim praised and god was happy.

"Now Jevim asked god, 'God, will you make me a companion, that we may praise you in harmony and antiphony. For have you not told me, and have I not ascertained, both by inspection and reflection, that the nature of the act is diversity and difference?' And god was pleased and said: 'Go in your loneliness to sleep on nettles spread on burning sand. And when you wake, you will have a companion.' And because Jevim loved god, she could sleep as easily on hot sand

and sharp nettles as she could on soft grass under sweet winds. And while Jevim slept, god made Eif'h. And god loved Eif'h, and suckled her at both breasts, and when Eif'h suckled at god's left breast, the milk flowed from god's right breast with love, and that milk became the misty river of light that crosses the night and which, today, we call the milky way. And the daughters of Eif'h prospered; and the tribes of Eif'h spread. And when Eif'h, like Jevim, had been blessed by both the eagle and the worm, god lay Eif'h down to sleep on the sand and nettles next to Jevim. And when Jevim woke, she saw Eif'h, and said of her: 'God, you have given me a companion. Praise be to you,' and then Jevim said to Eif'h: 'Come, my companion, let us sing and praise god together.'

"But Eif'h was of a different mind than Jevim, and she raised up on her elbows and looked around, frowning, and said: 'Why have we waked on sand and nettles rather than on soft grass and under sweet winds?'

"And Jevim, who had never heard the act discerned by this particular distinction before, said: 'Sand and nettles, grass and breeze, it is all one of the garden of god. We must sing the praise of god.'—which is, of course, not the way to praise the act at all—for the act is always manifest in difference, diversity, and distinction. But Jevim could not see, yet, that this was merely the distinction between herself and her companion: for the act must be praised with and by distinction.

"One day, Eif'h was walking from the mountain to the woods, and as she crossed a large orchard of many fruit trees that lay between them, she came across the worm and the eagle. And Eif'h said: 'I wish to sing the wonder of the act. You are god's privileged beasts. Tell me where I can find the pure and unpolluted essence of the act?'

"The worm raised her head and hissed: 'When god reached her hand into her own womb and delivered herself of the act, it became a handful of fire that she scattered across the night, which became the stars.'

"The eagle stretched her wings and screeched: 'When god reached her hand into her own womb and delivered herself of the act, it became a handful of fire, the bulk of which became the sun.'

" 'Very well,' said Eif'h, 'I shall praise only the sun and the stars, the one and the many, the manifestations of the act in its purest form. Come, worm; come, eagle! Let us do as we were set here to do, and praise god and the act, as inspection and reflection have shown it to be manifested in its purest form. And we shall praise no other, impure thing, no obstreperous plurality, no false unity.' And Eif'h, with the eagle and the worm, all day praised the unity of the sun and all night praised the plurality of the stars.

"One day Jevim came by and asked: 'My companion, what do you do here day and night with the worm and the eagle?'

"And Eif'h answered: 'I am using the worm and the eagle to my purpose, to praise the purest manifestation of the act, as I have discerned it through inspection and reflection, as I was put here to do. And you must also.'

"And because Jevim wished to do her duty, there in the orchard between the mountain and the woods, she joined with Eif'h and the eagle and the worm. Now the orchard about them bore a great variety of fruit: pomegranates, peaches, apples, and mangoes. And Jevim said to Eif'h, 'I will praise the variety of god's works by tasting of each fruit.' And she picked an apple and tasted it.

"But Eif'h said: 'Eat not of the apple nor the pomegranate nor the mango nor the peach. Rather, worship the act only in its purest manifestation.'

"And so, for a day and a night, Jevim and Eif'h, with the worm and the eagle, praised only the sun and the stars. And the beaver and the otter and the lion and the fox came by the orchard; and the fish and the crab and the snail and the dolphin swam through the river that flowed by the orchard; and the sparrow and the moth and the dragonfly and the bat flew through the air above the orchard. And Eif'h said: 'We shall neither inspect, nor reflect on, the variety of the sky or the earth or the water. For we are here to praise, with the eagle and the worm, the act only in its purest form: the one that is the sun, and the many that is the stars.'

"And the animals and insects crawled or flitted away into the woods and the mountains; and the fish and swimming beasts slithered away in the water; and the birds and butterflies flew off through the air. And the fruit rotted on the trees and fell, uneaten, to the ground.

"Then god came unto this desolate field that had once been a rich and lovely orchard. And she said: 'Where are Jevim and Eif'h, whom I placed in my world to adore me and to praise the act?'

"And Jevim and Eif'h stood and said: 'We are here, god. We are praising the act in its purest form, the one and the many, the sun's fire and the stars' light.'

"And god said: 'I hear no harmony, only a single melody, sung by two voices, the one prideful in its pretention, the other shameful in its knowledge of sin. Know that I am angry. And I shall punish you, for you have not praised me in the diversity of my works. Eif'h, I shall punish you, unless any of my other creatures can speak for you and say that, during this day and night, you have praised me with and within diversity.'

"And there was no answer among the beasts, birds, fish, and insects. And god said: 'Eagle, you are a privileged beast. Can you not say anything for Eif'h?'

"And the Eagle bowed her head and said: 'I can not say anything for Eif'h.'

"So god pulled two trees from the ground, one of lithe, live green wood and one of hard, near-dry wood, and she struck Eif'h across the loins; and across the breasts; and across the face. And she beat Eif'h with the trunks of those two trees. And Eif'h screamed and cowered and clutched at herself and called for mercy; but god beat her bloody about the face and breasts and loins. And where god beat her on the face, coarse hairs sprouted; and where god beat her on her throat, her voice roughened and went deep; and where god beat her about the breasts, the very flesh and organs were torn away so that she could no longer suckle her daughters; and where god beat her about the groin, her womb was broken and collapsed on itself, and rags of flesh fell, dangling, from her loins, so that when they healed, her womb was forever sealed and useless, and the rags of flesh hanging between her legs were forever sore and sensitive, so that Eif'h was forever touching and ministering to them, where upon they would leak their infectious pus.

"Then god said: 'Eif'h, I have beaten you until you are no longer a woman. For you can no longer bear, nor any longer suckle. You have praised neither me nor the act well.' And so Eif'h bowed her hairy face and covered her poor, ropey genitals, and was called no longer woman, but 'man, which means broken woman. And she was called no longer she, but 'he, as a mark of her pretention, ignorance, and shame.

"Then god said: 'Jevim, I must punish you.'

"And Jevim stood with her head bowed before her god, for she too knew shame in that she had not praised the difference and the diversity of god by which the act is manifest.

"And god said, 'Jevim, I shall punish you, unless any of my other creatures can speak for you and say that, during this day and night, you have praised me with and within diversity.'

"And there was no answer among the beasts, birds, fish, and insects. And so god raised her two trees and struck Jevin across the groin: and she drew blood, as the daughters of Jevim had bled, every month, ever since. But here Jevim fell to her knees and cried out: 'God, your blows are just and right, but will you not ask your privileged beasts if they can speak for me, as you asked them for Eif'h?'

"And god halted her blows and said: 'Worm, you are a privileged beast. Can you say anything for Jevim?'

"And the worm raised her head and hissed: 'Only that when Jevim first joined with Eif'h, she tasted an apple in order to praise you in your diversity.'

"And god's anger against Jevim abated. And she said: 'Go, Jevim, and Eif'h,' which, in my language, means both 'Jevim's companion' and 'Jevim's shame' —'go woman and 'man, and roam the earth, the hills, the forests, and the seas. Go in shame for your misprision. Cherish one another and console one another and make one tribe: and praise me as I am to be praised, both as the one and as the many. But know you both that to praise the sun as the purest manifestation of the act—either as the one or the many—is to praise cold ashes for the heat given by a roaring fire in winter, for such is the sun to the act within the womb of god. And know you both that to praise the stars as the purest manifestation of the act—either as the one or the many—is to praise the dried pits of cherries in autumn for the sweetness, richness, and healthfulness of the apple, the pear, and the peach in spring, for such are the stars to the act within the womb of god. Know you both that the act is more than and other than any of these. Praise the sun's warmth on the water in summer and the cold frost on the stones in winter and the difference between them, and you will praise the act, for the act may only be praised through difference. Praise the dry seeds of the pomegranate and the stars scattered on the night and the difference between them, and you will praise the act, for the act may only be praised through diversity. Praise the dark hard rock and the soft red fruit and the difference between them, and you will praise the act, for the act may only be praised through distinction.'

"And Jevim went out into the world, a contrite and wiser woman, to adore her god and praise the act as she had been bid. And Eif'h went after her, a contrite and wiser 'man, to assist her in adoration and praise. And they cherished and consoled one another and made one tribe. And again the daughters of Jevim and Eif'h prospered and praised among the works of god in her diversity. And that is the tale of our world's making." Raven folded her arms.

In the silence, one sailor snatched two fish from the grill. Glancing about, another placed down two more.

"So, now, Heathen Woman—" Raven laughed—"I have told you the tale of how god made the world, and its works, and women and 'men."

"It's certainly a good story," Norema said.

Bayle, watching them, had felt a tightening in his

belly that had begun at the flaying of Eif'h; the tale's sense of attack had centered in a knot of muscle just behind his testicles.

"But mark my word, woman," Raven went on, "the men in this strange and terrible land will try to take even this tale and turn it to their own, distorted purposes, be it Eif'h's name or Jevim's apple, or the privileged beasts themselves—even as Eif'h once turned the eagle and the worm to her purpose. For truly, 'men are the same all over, whether in your land or mine, however different the customs of each." She looked around. "Well, the rest of you 'men, the pretty ones and the not so pretty, have you overheard the tale you wished to hear? Come, which one of you will serve me some fish, for we are all daughters of Jevim and Eif'h, are we not?"

One sailor laughed; then another. (Bayle thought it an uncomfortable and embarrassed laugh.) Someone handed a roasted fish up to Raven; moments later, other fish went to Norema and Bayle; and the sailor's attention had moved to some other sailor's tale.

At one point, Bayle, standing at Norema's shoulder, greasy fingers picking at a comb of fishbones, said: "What a strange tale that woman told. It made me very uncomfortable."

Norema turned to him sharply. "It was awful!" she whispered. "It made my flesh crawl." Her face, in the quarter-light from the lantern, became for a moment shockingly ugly.

In his surprise, Bayle realized his own discomfort was now all mental: somehow the tenseness the tale had produced in him had settled his whole insides, and all the ghosts of incipient seasickness, plaguing him since they had launched, had mysteriously, if not magically, vanished—as though the tale had been a healing spell!

The spring night turned chill, and naked sailors sat or strolled the deck as though there had been no drop in temperature. And however awful Norema thought Raven's tale, Bayle, as he joked and grew more easy with the sailors, saw she certainly spent more time talking with the Western woman than with him. "But what must a story like that do to your men?" Bayle overheard Norema ask. "Making god a woman, making men into broken women, it seems as if it tries to cut them down at every turn."

"But there *are* no men in the story," Raven said. "Except Eif'h. And besides, it is *only* a story. I like it —it is a good story for me. As for 'men—well, it explains to 'men why they are weak and ignorant, instead of setting up for them—as so many of the tales do in this strange and terrible land—impossible goals that no man could rise to and which must make all your 'men feel guilty when they fail. Believe me, our 'men are much happier with our stories than your 'men are with yours. But then, our way is the natural way ordained by god herself, whereas I have no idea whose set of social accidents and economic anomalies have contoured the ways of your odd and awkward land."

"I can't believe that your men are happier," Norema said.

"But it's true," said Raven. "The story of Eif'h is very healing and healthful and reassuring for men. It teaches them their place in society and why they have it. It helps soothe the wounds god has inflicted them with." And Bayle, uneasily, remembered his own strangely alleviated seasickness and went off to wander among the other sailors. Their comments and jokes about the Western woman's odd cosmogeny were, anyway, not the sort you'd want women present for. Late in the darkness (it was perhaps eight o'clock), when all were exhausted, Bayle found the masked woman standing beside him. She put her hand on his shoulder and (surprising him) whispered: "So, not only are we all going to Garth, but we are all going to see Lord Aldamir. My island friend, there—" She nodded toward Norema—"has at last figured out that you and she are in competition." Raven laughed, again and too loudly. "Well I'm glad I'm not. Do you want my cabin for the night, pretty man? I'm going to sleep on deck in a blanket. Oh, don't worry, I shall not set on you in the night and besmirch your honor. But you have a berth on this ship with a space only half again the size of some eastern coffin and no doubt less than half as comfortable, whereas I have the royal favor of Krodar, of whom you have probably never heard, and I would spend my night in the clear air. Come, I'll show you . . ."

The lantern high in the companionway stained the boards an oily gold. "There," said the masked woman (whose breath, next to him, smelled of fish and fennel stalks—which the sailors had passed around to chew); she pushed open a door.

The dozen clay lamps suspended from the ceiling beams by myriad brass chains glimmered through a cabin half again the size of Norema's. Mumbling thanks, the potter's boy stepped within: and, when the door had been closed behind him for three minutes, went running out to retrieve his bundle from the forepeak locker. He returned with the strap in his hand and the bundle banging from ankle to ankle. Inside again, he found two of the beds too soft (this cabin had *three* beds!), the other too lumpy; finally he unrolled his blankets and slept on the floor, wedged into the corner, as he would have were he sleeping in the storage loft at Old Zwon's; as he would have were he sleeping in the forepeak locker; as he would have were he sleeping in the room with his brothers and sisters at home. Somehow, though, he was aware that *this* floor, that to be wedged into *this* corner, was luxury—which made him as uncomfortable, in its way, as the masked woman's tale.

3

Three days later, standing at the rail in indigo dawn, Bayle watched the first mate walk away. The mate had just delivered a message from the Captain, apologizing that he would not see them before they docked, less than an hour hence. Bayle turned to watch the drifting mists along the shore and thought: In three days we have eaten with this Captain four times, talked with him about navigation, his three families, his collection of miniature clay idols, and have all decided he is a deep and impressive, if somewhat absentminded, man. Yet, save I take this same ship returning, I may never see him again. Strange are the ways of travel.

Beyond mists, trees fell away with coming light. On the hills, cuprous ribbons slashed the slopes; rocky scarps rose toward jungle. The boat's shadow shook on the water. Bayle had just made out where, in that dim green, his own shadow was (head, bunched shoulders, arm jackknifed on the rail), when another shadow joined his.

"Well," said Raven, "your little competitor—" for in three days it had finally come out in ways restrained and civilized, which, while they had taken much energy and concern from both boy and woman, would also not make fit subject for a tale of civilization's economic origins, that Bayle and Norema were truly economic antagonists. "She is very worried about your feelings for her," Raven went on, for Bayle's feelings were clearly a combination of sexual attraction and social resentment over a business situation in which he thought right was on his side. After all, his master was a poor potter whom Lord Aldamir had petitioned for a franchise. Norema's mistress was a rich merchant who had chosen, just now, to petition Lord Aldamir for the same franchise.

"Ah-ha!" Bayle laughed. "She probably lusts after me and feels guilty at the same time that she must still fight with me over money," for these were barbaric times and certain distinctions between self and other had not yet become common.

Raven's masked smile, as she turned to watch the shore, suggested a more barbaric interpretation. Behind them, a sail collapsed; ropes ran on squealing pulleys; another sail clapped full. The boat turned, gently and inexorably, around a land spit which revealed—after six breaths—the dock.

Dawn activity in this southern port was minimal. As

the hull heaved against sagging pilings, Bayle saw that what life there was on the boards centered in one corner. ("All right, men, catch those ropes," shouted the first mate, standing at the far rail beside a sailor playing out a hawser.) On dock the few dockworkers scurried away from a short woman wearing a green shift and a complex headdress of thin, black braids. The heavy man beside her, from the satchels around his shoulders, was apparently her servant.

Brown men hauled in ropes. A hump-back with a gaff hooked in some hempen loop on the hull and was nearly tugged off his feet till three men joined him and together they hauled the boat back in.

Bayle glanced around at the deck to see Norema walking up among sailors. Somewhere, wooden wheels on a log crane lifted a gangplank then lowered it; the wooden lip caught behind the deckgate. The boat listed, rose.

"My cartons," Norema said, stepping over Bayle's bag (it was wedged against the lower-rail). "I suppose they'll get them all off."

Raven grinned below her mask.

The woman on the dock folded her hands and looked long and seriously the length of the railing till she apparently saw the passenger trio: her hands came apart, and she lifted her chin, smiling.

Bayle, bewildered but smiling back, waved, as the woman, followed by her turbaned servant, strode to the gangplank's foot, from where she beckoned them down.

Norema (following a sailor whom the mate had peremptorily ordered to take her crates) and Bayle (wondering whether Raven might not choose that moment to prick him jokingly from behind with her two-pronged blade) came down the limber plank.

"Well," said the woman, her hands folded again on the lap of her dress, "you must be the party Lord Aldamir is expecting. So pleased. His Lordship detailed me to come along, meet you and make excuses for his absence. But, then, I know you'll understand." Her hand went out to Norema, who tentatively extended her own to take it.

"Actually," Norema said, with a composure Bayle by now knew masked rank embarrassment, "I don't think his Lordship was expecting me . . ." She glanced at Bayle, even moved back a little for him (and Bayle felt a sudden surge of embarrassment at the prospect of stepping forward). "It's Bayle, I think. Bayle's the one who has corresponded with Lord Aldamir."

Bayle quickly dropped his bag and wiped his hand against his hip (breakfast had been fruit and fish, eaten with the sailors and no utensils; he had not yet thought to wash). "Yes," he said, shaking the old woman's hand. "Lord Aldamir sent us a message when I was back in . . ." He stepped from the plank's end.

From somewhere behind and further up than he would have expected, came Raven's bark: "His Lordship is certainly not expecting me!"

"But I'm sure he is!" insisted the woman. "Lord Aldamir expects everyone. Now there, my dear." She released Bayle's hand to take Norema's again and pat it. "You must be the secretary of my old girlhood friend from Sellese, Madame Keyne. Am I right?"

"Why, yes . . . ?" Norema actually stammered.

"And Krodar had aprized me of *your* coming . . ." The woman bowed a little toward the masked Raven, who sauntered down the ribbed boards. (This rather astonished Bayle, who had, by now, decided the woman was noble, whereas Raven still seemed some barbaric, or near barbaric, ruffian.) "I'm Myrgot," the woman added matter of factly like someone either used to being known about before being met, or who simply did not care whether she was known or not. "Allow me to make up for his Lordship's inconveniencing you by seeing you to the Vygernangx monastery." To her servant: "Jahor?" who turned and shouted an order off the dock. A large wagon, pulled by three oxen, rolled out on the dock's creaking boards. The driver, brown, barefoot, and bandanaed about the neck, leaped from the seat and started hoisting up Norema's crates and carrier bags. Bayle stepped back as his own strapped roll was heaved up; then the driver was then off haranguing sailors (obviously a practiced hand at receiving tourists) to make sure the ladies' and gentleman's luggage was all accounted for.

It was.

Jahor reached into the cart, pulled out a ladder that hooked over the sideboard. Myrgot smiled about her, then mounted; she offered Norema her arm when she climbed up next. Raven, with the strangest smile below her mask (thought Bayle), stepped back for Bayle to climb in, just as Bayle had stepped back for Norema. Then Bayle, boxes, Raven, and Jahor were all in place. The cart trundled up the dock road (dawn light as they rounded a turn laid bronze palms on Myrgot's, Norema's, Raven's, then the driver's shoulders) between the men, women, and children coming down to load from, or simply to gawk at, the boat.

"Certainly this has got to be——" said Myrgot (the cart bounced), folding her hands and looking beyond the rim——"the most beautiful countryside in all Nevèrÿon."

"It certainly——" Norema began (the cart hit another pothole)——"is very lovely."

Raven spread her arms out behind her, gripping the plank left and right, grinning with her tiny teeth. "How long will it take us to get to his Lordship's castle?"

"But there." Myrgot's face creased with an elderly grin. "I have not even told you of the greatest inconvenience his Lordship will subject you to. For you see, Lord Aldamir is not here——in Garth. At his castle. Today. Something has come up. He's had to go south ——quite suddenly. Just three days ago he left with a very impressive retinue from his court, leaving only guards, servants——a skeletal staff . . . really, you know these ancient piles, half fortress, half dungeon, with their open roofs and fetid cells. Most of them are not fit to live in anyway." She looked around brightly. "This is why Lord Aldamir has requested that I house you in the Vygernangx Monastery——which, believe me, is a lot more comfortable. And he begs you not to take offense because he does not have you chambered in his home."

"When will Lord Aldamir be back?" Norema asked.

And Bayle relaxed just a little because she had asked before he had.

"My dear, we don't know. His departure was very sudden. It was an emergency of some kind. And one just doesn't question a man like that."

"When did he leave?" Bayle asked.

"Oh, just before I got here. That's been, now—let me see: well, I said before—at least three days."

From her side of the cart, Raven suddenly barked above the creaking axle: "You mean I've come all this way to kill a man, and you tell me he's gone?"

"I'm afraid—" the cart jounced again—"I do, my dear." Myrgot's face held as tenaciously to its faint smile as Raven's held to its gross one; Norema's look went strangely blank. Bayle felt his features tugged around on the bone, seeking for the proper expression of surprise.

Myrgot folded her hands in the lap of her shift as if nothing of any seriousness had been said. "His Lordship hopes the three of you will be comfortable with the priests. They are a provincial lot—I know them of old. But they are always anxious to hear the tales from distant travelers. I know you don't feel as if you are, but all three of you are distant travelers now, strange and exotic to the likes of the locals. And the priests have their share of ancient stories—if you are interested in ancient stories."

Bayle was staring at a patch of straw where a length of Myrgot's hem lay: bent straws and straw ends made tents and puckers in the stuff; one, leaning, shook a filament of shadow over the cloth as the cart shook— he watched it all as if this play of detail might obliterate what seemed like the all too miserable form of the journey so far.

Myrgot was saying: "The valley you can see to your left is known as the Pit, where General Babàra made his famous stand a hundred and twenty years ago, at the behest of a dream in which his aunt, Queen Olin —my great, great grandaunt, by the bye—warned him to be on the lookout for a green bird flying between two branches of a sacred pecan tree . . ."

*   *   *

Carved in the lental stones, one section on each arm-long block, a dragon spread wings and beak. From the tiny doorway beneath, a robed figure bustled forward; the design on his hem and sleeves (the cloth blotched with food stains) Bayle remembered once having seen on some southern pottery that had briefly come through old Zwon's shop.

"Well, Feyer Senth," said Myrgot (Bayle recalled that Feyer was a southern form of address that meant both "maternal uncle" and "priest"), "I have done as Lord Aldamir wished. Here are your guests."

"Delightful!" announced the little priest, who had large, freckled hands, and a boney, freckled face. "Delightful! Now for news! Gossip! Tales of travel! Romance!" (Another and another priest emerged from the door. The youngest was probably Bayle's junior by five years; the oldest, who, with the youngest, hung back near the shrubs, could have been old Zwon's father.) "We will have tall tales and religious chatter, and—who knows—perhaps some deep and lasting insight into the workings of the soul." He lowered his freckled eyelids, narrowing the yellow pupils. "It happens here, you know. Come, let us help you down."

Bayle climbed out to the pine-needled ground as priests hurried up to take down Norema's bags and crates. At Feyer Senth's orders, they carried and scurried in and out of the low stone walls, all hung about with ivy hanks. Bayle's bedroll got handed down; and Raven, for all her sumptuous cabin back on the ship, seemed to have no baggage save the sword and purse at her hip. The priests clustered about Bayle now, to help the women down. Norema, helped by three eager feyers, climbed out—more hindered, really, than aided. Raven, seeing, vaulted off on her own.

Myrgot made small, dismissive gestures; feyers fell back. (Bayle's own discomfort grew; he tried to help the priests, who kept snatching boxes and bags out of his hands with solicitous grins and hurrying off. Should he offer to help Myrgot?) "There," the noble woman said from her seat in the wagon. "That's everything. I have done as Lord Aldamir wished and will be on my way."

"But Vizerine Myrgot," cajoled Feyer Senth, "won't you stay for the evening and enjoy our hospitality?"

Myrgot's face lined with unexpected intensity. She said: "I have spent too much time as your guest already . . . dirty little priest!" this last as if noticing an offensive smear on a child's face. With a wave of her hand, servant and driver were in their place and the cart trundled away.

Feyer Senth laughed. "Wonderful woman! What a wonderful woman! Completely open and forthright! A fine quality in a noble lady! A fine quality . . . indeed!" He turned among feyers and guests. "And she is among the noblest. But come in! Come in, all of you. And let us make you at home here for the length of your stay."

Hooking big, freckled fingers over Bayle's and Norema's shoulders, Feyer Senth guided them to the dark door and through it, the last priest preceding them with the last of Norema's boxes. Shadow and the dank smell of monastery walls closed over. Bayle heard the shrill laugh bark ahead in the passageway: Raven had already gone into the lowering pile.

Bayle found his expected confusion, as well as his own natural friendliness, both in a kind of suspension (and he was a young man who, when he became confused, tended to become over-friendly); but the chapels, storage cells, common rooms, and what have you that Feyer Senth busily pointed out as they walked did not so much confuse him as simply slip off across his memory without ever gaining traction. While the little priest babbled and pointed, Bayle wondered what his red-headed competitor was thinking. Then the wall flares' oily light fell before a wing of dawn, patterned with leaf-shadow.

They came out on a stone porch—perhaps it was a porch. At any rate, one wall was down—rather raggedly, as if it had been knocked in, or perhaps out, with violence and, over years, vague efforts made to straighten the debris and change the chamber into a patio.

Feyer Senth turned, chuckling. "We can sit here and relax a while. That, incidentally—you can just see it if you squint, out there between those two hills—is Lord Aldimir's castle. The Dragon Castle, we call it here."

"Where?" asked Raven, coming back across the moss-webbed flags.

Feyer Senth took the masked woman's shoulder (he and Raven were the same height, which surprised Bayle because he still thought of the Western Woman as tall while the priest was indeed quite short) and pointed up between the spotilly forested hills. "You should be able to get a glimpse right through there. Sometimes, though, the elm leaves are so thick this time of year you can't make out a thing. Here, sit down. We'll have some wine, some food."

Wooden legs scraped stone as one priest pulled a bench out from the wall. Another stepped up between Norema and Bayle with a basket of glossy-rinded fruits.

Two priests were already sitting on the floor, backs to the wall and arms around their shins.

"Sit down! Please sit down."

The seat edge bumped the backs of Bayle's knees as another priest smiled suddenly over his shoulder.

"Please, sit and be comfortable, here where we can look through the forests of Garth, out at the lovely Vygernangx morning."

"Feyer Senth!"

They looked at Raven—indeed, half the feyers stopped bustling.

"Feyer Senth, I will decline your hospitality." The masked woman stood with one foot on the ragged wall edging the porch. "My god is not your god. My habits are not your habits. I have a mission to complete now which cannot be completed. I must return to my employer and so inform him." The glazed smile took on the brilliance of ice smashed in the sun. Raven climbed up, jumped, and, to the sound of thrashing leaves, moved away.

Norema, sitting on one of the proffered chairs, looked at Bayle.

Feyer Senth laughed. "Such a fascinating girl, too. It's sad she didn't choose to stay. But here, have some

wine. Lord Aldamir wishes us to do well by all his
visitors. His family is illustrious and his history, which
does honor to all Nevèrÿon, is intimately connected
with these border territories. You, of course, would
be too young to remember, but it was a branch of
Lord Aldamir's family who sat on the High Throne of
Eagles, in the city then called Neveryòna, before the
current Child Empress—whose reign has, at times,
been both wrathful and rapacious, though I gather one
would never dare say such a thing were we fifty miles
closer to Kolhari. The Aldamirs have supported the
Empress since her coming to power. But we here have
always known—known since the time of Babàra's in-
vasions of the Garth—that such a relation between the
dragon and the eagle would never be truly easy. Well,
his Lordship is of course concerned with maintaining
the freest commerce back and forth with that city
(called, under his unfortunate cousin's reign, Neveryòna). That is no doubt why he has called you down
to negotiate with him for the franchise of children's
rubber balls; and no doubt that also explains why he
is so anxious that we entertain you as grandly as we
can here during his unexpected absence. You have no
idea how mortified he was that he had to leave. His
messenger came down from the castle to me in person
and conveyed his Lordship's most sincere regrets and
apologies," and, without punctuation, turned to Norema: "the presence of that Western Woman must have
made you feel terribly upset. I mean, for a woman used
to the place of women in this society." Recalling her
expostulation when he had asked for her reaction to
Raven's creation tale, Bayle expected some similar
restrained outburst now. But Norema returned that
silent, serious look across the rim of her wine cup (and
what cups they were! Metal creations of leaves and
flowers in which were set ceramic plates so thin the
light passed through, stained crimson with the wine!
What sort of potters threw cups like this here in the
south, wondered Bayle, as the glitter from his own
deviled his vision from below), which said that though
she of course would not say it, she felt no such thing.
   What Bayle found himself thinking, as conversation,

wine, and food drifted on their various ways through the morning (and what food they ate! Crisp, roasted birds stuffed with fruit and nuts! Pastries filled with spicy meats! Puddings that combined terrifying bitternesses and sweetnesses!), was just how present Raven, now she was gone, seemed. The conversation somehow managed to return to her at least once every hour. In between, it was almost as if she were lurking just outside, or spying from the dark niches behind them, or hiding in some chapel near them, observing and overhearing every inane and innocuous word or gesture made or uttered.

"So, you have made up your mind, my dear?" Feyer Senth's voice was nearly lost among the crickets'.

"Lord Aldamir has gone to the south. No one knows when he'll return. But you suspect it may be quite a while. It is silly to come all this way and give up just like that. I can hire people to carry my packages and guide me after him. I shall leave in the morning. After all, I have money."

"But you must remember," Feyer Senth said, "as one goes further and further south, money means something very different from what it does in the city once called Neveryòna."

"You have money." Bayle, a little drunkenly, swirled wine in the bottom of his goblet. "And I do not. At least not very much money. So tomorrow morning I shall get a ship back to Kolhari—" For an hour, following Norema, he too had been saying 'the city once called Neveryòna,' as the priests did; but as the sky had gone salmon outside the porch, then indigo, and the wax had been pried from the mouth of yet another jug, he had gone back to the 'Kolhari' he had used all his life.

"If I find his Lordship, I shall tell him you answered his messenger!" Norema said with an intensity that probably came from the wine they had been drinking all day on the porch, or in the chapels near it, or about the grounds just in front of it. "I will! I promise you, Bayle!"

Bayle said nothing—though he smiled—and swirled

his dregs. His feelings had alternated between a very real desire to accompany this city merchant's bold little red-haired secretary and a very real apprehension: he was only eighteen, this was the first time he had been away from the city; things had not gone according to plan: best return and leave heroics to a later year.

"I have money," Norema repeated. "Now if I only knew *where,* to the south, Lord Aldamir had gone. But you say I should not have any trouble finding him . . . ?"

Bayle stood up; the flares, in metal holders bolted to the stone, wavered and flapped uncertain light about the porch. "I must go to bed," he said thickly. "Good night, and thank you for a wonderful day . . ." Two feyers, who either had not drunk such amounts as he, or who were used to imbibing such amounts, were instantly at his side, leading him toward his cell somewhere off in the wobbling dark.

4

"I too should retire." Norema rose. She was by no means as drunk as the boy. Still, the last hour's drinking, with only the smokey flares to keep away night bugs, had left her quite tired. And her thoughts and feelings over the day of priestly entertainment had been much closer to what yours and mine would have been: between polite interest and polite boredom, she too had wondered what part the ritual realities of actual religion played in the lives of these rather indolent feyers. The decision to continue her journey had been sudden, and the thought she had given to it since was the sort one lavishes on an onerous but inescapable obligation. Now she wanted to retire early enough for the coming travail of tomorrow's tasks: the collecting

of guides, barers, tents, and provisions by the waterfront at dawn—a service she had performed several
times for Madame Keyne before at Kolhari and whose
difficulties she therefore knew. "No, I can find my own
way," she said, taking the flare from the priest who
started forward to guide her.

Some "Good-night's" chorused beyond the flare's
glow. An arch, and she entered it. Smoke trickled from
the brand to lick back on the ceiling, already ribboned
with soot from how many years' sleepy travelers' light-
ing their way to bed. A stone doorway inches lower
than the top of her head, and she ducked through.

The cell seemed much higher than she remembered;
but it *was* the right one: there, in brand light, were her
boxes and sacks. Through a window high in one corner
she could see brand-lit leaves and beyond them faint
stars. A bed; a metal wall-holder for the flare; a three-
legged amphora of water, a standing basin for washing.

She put the brand in its holder.

When—after washing, after plunging the brand in
the washed-in water, after dripping water on the tops
of her bare feet in the dark while she tried to get the
extinguished brand back in its brace, after turning
once and then turning again on the fragrant bed—
sleep came, she was not sure.

She woke at a strangled gasp, not hers; something
fell down to hit the bed's edge, thudded to the floor.
Blinking, she pushed herself up, started to swing her
feet to the stone—

"Don't, or your toes will be a-wash in blood," followed by a barking laugh above her—but a soft bark.

Norema looked down: someone lay with arms and
legs at awkward angles, while wetness crawled out
across the flags. She looked up: blocking moonlight,
Raven squatted in the window. She put one leg in and
let it hang.

With a shudder, Norema curled her feet up under
her—and Raven dropped down onto the bed's foot.

"What's *happened* . . . ?" Norema whispered hoarsely.

"Well, Heathen Woman," Raven whispered back,
squatting on the rumpled blanket and folding her arms,

"someone was going to kill you. So I killed her—or him, as the case may be." She bent forward, rolled the body back—"Him . . . but I should have expected that by now in your strange and terrible land—" and pulled something from the flank. An arm flopped on the floor; blood welled. Raven turned her two pronged sword, examining it, wiped it on the bed, examined it again.

"Kill me?" Norema demanded, trying to match Raven's whisper. "Why on earth . . . ?"

"Most probably—" Raven, still sitting, managed to get the sword, after several plunges, into its shaggy sheath—"because you were going to go on looking for Lord Aldamir and they don't want you to find him— or rather they don't want you to find out something about him once you start looking."

In the silvered dark, Norema squinted: "But how did you know I was going to go on? You'd already left before—"

Raven laughed again. "After I left, I doubled back. Oh, I stayed around, lurking outside, spying from dark niches, even got in and hid in one of the chapels. I must have heard everything the bunch of you said this afternoon."

"You did?"

"And you know what *they* did, these wine-bibing feyers? Sent a little herd of men out after me, very much of the cut of this one here. With orders to do me in."

"What did you do?"

"Pretty much what I did to this one. Snuck up behind, got one, then another. Quick and silent." Raven put her feet on what was presumably drier stone and stood.

"Bayle," Norema said suddenly. "What about Bayle?"

"Well, I couldn't keep guard on *both* your cells at once. When this one here climbed up into your window with a knife in her—in *his* teeth and a garrote cord knotted around his wrist, I was up behind and—" Raven made the jabbing motion Norema supposed would sink a sword in a kidney. "Fell in down across your bed and onto the floor there. Are you ready to get out of here?"

Norema looked for a place to stand, saw it, stood on it. "Don't you think we should check to see if Bayle's alive or dead?"

"Now why should these priests want to kill some poor, pudgy daughter of Eif'h? He was going home in the morning, and unless I miss my guess, if you'd volunteered to do the same, no one would have wanted to kill you either. But then, *you* had money. Look, if he's alive, there's nothing we have to do about it. If he's dead, there's nothing we can do. Get into your pants."

"I still don't—"

"Come, Eastern Heathen." Raven turned, stepped back on the bed, leaped for the window, and scrabbled up the wall; a moment later she was again perched in the moonlight. Turning, she reached down her hand. "Come on."

Somehow, pants and sandals were gotten into.

Norema had to jump three times before Raven's rough hand grappled hers. With her toes in the wall's deep mortices she scrambled up to crowd beside the small masked woman on the sill. "Where are we going?" Norema asked of the frayed black rag, inches from her face and punctured by eyes still indigo in the moon.

"To visit Lord Aldamir's great rubber orchards. And his magnificent castle," and she was off the sill onto a branch, climbing down. Norema was after her —it was longer down to the ground than it had been up from the bed. As Norema's sandals hit the pine needles—Raven had already taken several loping steps down the slope—there was a crashing in the brush beside them, and a creature jumped out, to land in a crouch, knuckles on the ground: "Raven, the coast is clear!"

"Ha, ha!" said Raven. "But we're not going to the coast. It's inland for us right now, back toward the castle."

Norema took her hand from her mouth and asked, with thudding heart: "Who's she?"

Raven said: "It is very hard in this strange and terrible land to be a true daughter of Jevim and not pick up little girls—like honey picks up flies—who desperately want to help." She reached down and tousled the curly hair of the crouching youngster. "Some of them are pretty plucky too. This one is even useful."

The girl, who was clearly local, grubby, and about twelve, stood up and said: "Who's she? The lady we're saving?"

"Lo," said Raven, "she is already saved, Juni. Norema, that's Juni. And she's smart," though Norema was not sure which of them the last sentence referred to. "Hurry up, both of you."

They followed the masked woman down the tangled slope, minutes at a time scrambling by vine-laced trees that, for all the moon, were lightless.

The two women and the girl, now grunting, now whispering for one or the other to step this way rather than that, leaves a-whisper about them, small branches a-crackle under foot, made their way, now down, now up.

"What's that?" Norema asked, as they reached fallen stones, those stones still standing covered with ivy.

A wing of moonlight flapped on Raven's face. (A branch among blowy leaves above them bent and bent again, revealing that grin below the mask.) Raven chuckled.

Juni said: "This is the wall around the Dragon Castle's parks and orchards."

"Lord Aldamir's castle?" Norema asked.

Juni blinked.

Raven nodded. "Let us examine them." She swung her leg over the lowest rock.

Juni vaulted over, then turned back to give Norema a hand. Norema grabbed among the leaves either side of the fissure—one hand closed on stone, the other, just on leaves—and pulled herself through.

They stood at the edge of a brambley field in moonlight. There were only one, two—no, three trees. One leaned almost to the ground, half its branches bare as pikes.

On the other side of the field, looking like a small

mountain, parts of which had been quarried vertical, other parts of which sloped irregularly, was a castle.

Norema said: "This orchard—or park—doesn't seem to be in use right now."

Juni looked at Raven and said: "You're right. She doesn't know."

Raven said: "All the grounds within the walls look like this. Or worse."

"Then perhaps the orchards that give the sap that makes the balls are outside the walled grounds—" She frowned. "Raven, are you trying to tell me there *aren't* any orchards?"

"Come. Let's go across into the castle."

Norema frowned again: "Won't some of the guards or servants . . . ?"

Raven said: "They didn't when I was here earlier today."

Juni said: "There are no guards. Or servants," then looked quickly back and forth between the two women.

"Come," Raven said again and started through the brush.

Once Norema nearly tripped over some fallen piece of statuary, then again over a plow-head on cracked shafts. A ditch wormed through the meadow with silver trickling its bottom. Norema, Juni, then Raven leaped it, Norema's sandals and Raven and Juni's bare feet sinking in the soft black bank.

A balustrade rose, cleaving the moon.

"That door's open." Juni pointed.

"How do you know?" Norema squinted at shadowed stone.

Juni said: "My cousin says it's been open since before I was born. I live with my cousin up on the hill," said this ragged little thing who *had* to be at least twelve. Again they were both off after Raven.

It was attached only by the top hinge and leaned askew, its gray planks scratched and carved at. The steps behind it were a-crunch with leaves; and the crunches echoed ahead of them up the stone corridor.

"Won't somebody . . . *hear* us?" Norema asked once more, with failing conviction.

Neither Raven nor Juni answered. Norema hurried

up behind them. They ducked through another arch: more moonlight, leaves, stone. They stood in some roofless hall, its pavings webbed with grass. Here and there the flooring was pushed aside by some growing bush. Broad steps near them went up to what may once have been—yes, that was certainly some ivy-grown dragon, carved and coiled about some giant seat.

"Now," said Raven, "doesn't this look exactly like what you'd expect of the castle of a great southern lord who had just taken a trip south only three days ago on an unexpected mission?"

"No one has stayed in this castle for years!" Norema said.

"My cousin stayed here once. For a night. With two of his friends—five years ago. They dared each other to sleep here. Only just before sunrise, they got scared and all ran away, back to their homes. That was when they were as old as I am now. But nobody lives in Lord Aldamir's castle."

"You mean there *is* no Lord Aldamir?" Norema asked. "But what's happened to him? And how did he send Bayle's master a message to come?"

Raven's laughter cackled in the hall. "The balance between the various aristocratic factions in your strange and terrible country is far too complex for the likes of me or you ever to unravel. Clearly it suits someone to have various factions in Kolhari—probably factions beneath the Eagle—think that there is still some heat left to the dragon in the south. Perhaps they pay our little feyers there to dispatch the occasional messenger to Nevèrÿon with an invitation to join in some profitable scheme with the great southern Lord. A naïve child like Bayle journeys down to the Garth, and here is told that his Lordship was unexpectedly called away; and the youngster returns by the next boat with tales of the absent Lord's might, given over to him throughout a day of entertainment by a host of drunken, garrulous priests."

"But thcy *didn't* expect me," said Norema.

"Nor me," said Raven. "Unless, as the lady said, Lord Aldamir expects everyone."

"Now Bayle will carry the tale of Lord Aldamir back to Kolhari—"

"—where no doubt," said Raven, "rumor will wind its way, up from the ports to the High Court of Eagles itself, that various business operations have been briefly delayed between Lord Aldamir and a waterfront potter. And for business relations to be delayed, there must be businessmen to begin with. The one thing that the rumor will not make them doubt is Lord Aldamir's existence."

"But what do we do with this information now we have it?" Norema asked. "Wouldn't it be dangerous to carry it back to Kolhari?"

"Ours is a very strange kind of information." Raven went over to the wall, folded her arms, and leaned there. "It is far easier to argue that something nobody believes in actually exists than it is to argue that something everybody believes in is unreal. And the general consensus in Nevèrÿon is that there *is* a Lord Aldamir. *I* would not want to be the one to have to return to Krodar and tell him that the man he sent me to assassinate is a figment of his imagination. And if you tell your mistress that, you just see what happens: first, she will say you had the wrong castle, then the wrong seaport, or even the wrong boat. I'd say, rather, stick to the tale we were told to tell—that Lord Aldamir was suddenly called away and we could gain no audience. Now come and let us wander these deserted halls, these abandoned stairs, these cramped and damp cells and high chambers where history has left off happening. I want to explore this absent aristocrat from every side—in case I ever *do* meet him and need to jab a blade into his absent gut." Raven uncrossed her arms and started off across the littered floor.

Juni and Norema looked at each other. The little girl darted forward after the masked assassin. Norema, chills prickling thigh and shoulder, followed.

For the next several hours they wandered into this room and that one, nearly silent the time. In one cell Juni accidentally kicked up an old tinder box; in another, Norema recognized an oil jar, still sealed with wax. So they made brands and carried them, flickering and smoking, through the darker chains of chambers.

In a kitchen midden they saw old pots and knives. Minutes later, Raven, standing in the small kitchen garden (a few vegetables were still recognizable in the moonlight despite the weeds), announced she was hungry, pulled out her sword, and turned to hack the head from a rather large hare that had leaped onto the stone wall to watch them.

"Juni," Norema said, astonishing herself with the authority she mustered, "run back inside and get that pan I was just examining. Here, no, give me your torch," and, with two torches in one hand, she bent to yank up some tubers whose taste she knew. "Those rocks will make a fireplace—and Juni, bring back a jar for water. I'm sure that stream down there is fresh . . ."

Raven sat down on a flat rock to watch, her hands on her knees, while Norema, in a panic of relief, now that she had something to take charge of, to organize, to *do,* began concocting an ersatz meal of rabbit, parsnips, and kale.

"Throw me the guts," Raven said suddenly, while Norema, with a knife whose handle was as ornate as the feyer's cups that afternoon, was busy sawing joints.

Juni, returning with the water jar on her hip, asked: "Can you read the future in the guts of hares?" Water sloshed from the brim, wetting the girl's thin, knobby wrist in moonlight.

Raven said: "I am going to make a length of cord. There's no need in letting such things waste in this strange and terrible land," and she fell to work over the bloody offal, milking out chyme, plucking away vein-webbed peritoneum, and stretching out the wet intestinal tract, thinner and thinner—which made Norema busy herself the more intently with the stew.

Juni, after watching Raven and ignoring Norema for fifteen minutes, said: "You have hands like a man."

Raven's bloody knuckles slipped one on another as she stretched and flexed and stretched. "No. In this strange and terrible land, most men have hands like women." A masked monkey, she squatted, pulling and pulling, the thinned gut growing in a coil on the stone between her feet.

In Norema's pan, oil sputtered and frothed as handfuls of cubed meat went in; bubbles sped to the copper rim and burst. Norema put in a handful each of white and green vegetables that had been cut up on the flat rock by the fire, which left a large spot of darker gray than the rock around, irregular as a mapped island.

Grayed in moonlight, with a few orange tongues chattering over the pan's edge, the food went golden.

Raven laid one stained hand on her cabled thigh; with the other she picked up the coil to examine it.

Juni said: "My mother, when she was alive, said girl children were a curse and a burden to a poor widow." Then she asked; "Did your mother weep and curse at your birth because she wanted a boy?"

The dark lips and chin—all that was visible under the fraying rag—turned to the girl, looking far more serious than eyes alone. The nostril edges, with threads hanging beside them, flared; the lips pulled back from stained teeth, and laughter suddenly barked. "My mother, when I was born and she saw I was a woman-child, got up still dangling the bloody rope between her legs—which could not have been easy, as I am supposed to have come out sideways—took up her ceremonial plow blade (and those things are heavy) and beat twelve times on the bronze gong that hangs on the wall. (We only beat it once if it's a boy.) Then she went back to her pallet, cooing and cuddling and proud as a tiger. Outside in the hall, her men ceased their chanting and gave a yowl of joy, and for the next three days walked around clicking their long nails on every pot and pan in the place. They'd yowl for a boy, too. But they *wouldn't* click their nails!"

"Then why," asked Juni, as if it followed logically, "do you wear that mask?"

"Oh." Raven turned the coil of string in her hands, then put it down. "I suppose because I grew up short and scrawny, like the smallest and thinnest of my mother's men. Ah, yes. I remember that man, too. He was a shy, tiny, beautiful man. He tried to teach me to be an acrobat. Almost succeeded, too. Oh, I loved him, and he was always kind to me. Sideways . . . that's probably why I've never wanted a baby. It's a hard way to do it and they say such things are passed down among women."

"They are not," said Norema, stirring faster. "Don't fill the child's head with nonsense." Then she asked Juni: "Did your mother weep and curse over you?"

"I don't have a mother," Juni said patly. "I told you, I live with my cousin. But she has two girls of her own. That's what she says," and then back to Raven: "How do you keep from having children?"

Raven laughed. "When do you pass your blood? At the full moon, like me?" She glanced up (Norema noticed the ivory orb was gibbous): "Well, then, you count off from the eleventh to the sixteenth day after that: and during those five days you refrain from tackling little boys in the fields and bringing them down in the furrows. Besides, despite what we are always saying in the women's barracks, little boys actually appreciate being left alone from time to time."

"What about," said Norema, prying up something from the bottom of the pan that had started to stick, "the big boys here who tackle you?"

"Well, yes, this part of the world has some very strange men in it who do things like that. I suppose a quick—" and here Raven rose in a single motion and brought her knee sharply up. "If you do that to them, right to the tender scars of Eif'h, they'll think twice, believe me, before tackling again. Really, this strange and terrible land is quite unbelievable to me." Once more she sat.

"Why do women pass blood?" the little girl asked.

Norema pushed the pan to a slightly cooler spot and wondered if they would get a recounting of Jevim's perils. But Raven said:

"The three or four days you pass blood are to get rid of the nonsense one picks up in the five days of heavy responsibility between moons."

Norema, at the fire, laughed. "There are times, Raven, you make me wonder if the women in this country don't have an awful lot of nonsense to get rid of."

"We always used to say, in the barracks," said Raven, a perfectly incomprehensible leer beneath her mask: "Save that blood for the boys. They can only take it in. They can never give it out. And that's why 'men have so much more nonsense about them than women."

Which made Norema open her mouth, nearly drop her knife into her stew, then close it again. "And do you have to repeat your . . . barrack-room talk in front of a child! Really . . ." She took a breath; and then found herself smiling behind and through the frown. "I've noticed something about you, Raven. Whenever you talk and there aren't men around, you get down to the body very quickly. I think that's because you are a barbarian."

"But you are the barbarian. Besides, in your country here, barbarians come from even further south than we are. At any rate, there *is* no civilization where the men cannot grow their nails. I am the civilized one." And brought her hand up to her mouth to bite at one of hers.

"I don't . . ." Juni paused, blinked—". . . pass blood . . . yet."

Raven (and Norema at the fire) grinned. Raven lifted her bloody fingers from her thigh and laid two against the girl's cheek. "Well, you will."

Norema said from the fire: "If you were from my part of the world, when you were old enough to bear children, your parents would go down to the beach and have a big party. You'd get presents, people would make speeches, and then you'd have to take a big shell full of water and throw it over your head—then you and all the other children who had reached their majority, boys and girls, for we give parties for both, would run and hide and the younger children would all have to go and find them."

"Humph," said Raven or something like it. "Both? I bet, knowing your part of the world, the boy's presents were bigger."

Which was true. Norema pushed the pot back to the hotter part of the fire.

"What do they do where you come from?" Juni asked. "I mean, when a girl first passes blood."

Raven said: "Your mother's men cut their nails and put them in a special bag that you have sewn with specially painted pieces of bark; you take the bag and a new sword deep in the jungle under the half moon. You bury the bag. You sing certain songs, and you eat certain plants that can only be picked with the left hand. And you kill something."

"Is that all?" Juni asked.

"No," said Raven.

"Then what?"

"You go to sleep on the forest floor with your face looking into the dead eyes of your kill, and in the morning you go back and tell your mother's oldest sister what it was you dreamed. She arranges stones and bones and dried flowers into an appropriate pattern and together you work out your future life by seeing what the dream and the stones say about each other. *Then* there is a party." And with great grin of her small teeth, Raven stood up and walked through the weeds to the stream where she squatted to wash her hands.

Juni watched a moment and then came over to the fire by Norema. "My aunt says that a woman can only wait for a man to take her—and no one will ever take me, because I am an orphan. She says that if a girl goes out from under her father's roof for more than a week, you can just bet slavers will take her."

"Well, I have been out from under my father's roof *quite* a bit more than a week. Several years more. And certainly one must look out for oneself. But I think that's just more nonsense to get rid of."

Juni looked suddenly to her right. A flash had deviled the edge of vision. Raven walking back from the stream, had removed her sword from its hairy sheath and was examining it again. Juni said: "Why is your sword like that? It's split in two and it looks funny."

"Does it now?" asked the masked woman as she

turned the blade around: moonlight ran down one side, firelight slid up the other. "Usually, in this strange and terrible land, all you see are single blades. But that's a puny, man's weapon. This—look, I'll show you." Raven squatted beside the girl. "It's sharp on the outside here and sharp on the outside there. That means it can cut either left or right." The blade swung one way, then the other. "And it also has this slit down the center—just like the line between the folds of your vagina. And the inside edges are just as sharp as the outside edges, all the way down and around the fork. So, if something gets between them that you don't like, you can—" Here Raven jammed the blade straight up in the moonlight—"cut it off!"

At the fire Norema again felt chills about her. She started to open her mouth, then clamped it very tight. As she looked about the clearing, she had the distinct feeling that something inside her, even as she stirred the stew, had gotten up, turned completely around, and then settled back down inside so that she did not quite feel she was the same person.

"I've seen slaves—women, and men—brought up from the jungles in the south. I think if I were taken by slavers I'd—"

Norema, at the fire, thought: This little girl and I were born hundreds of miles apart and I can complete her sentence just as easily as if she were my little sister: *I think I'd kill myself.* Norema ran the knife through the bubbling juices in the copper pan. "If I were taken by slavers," Norema said, "I think I would kill them. Now why don't you both come around here and eat your supper."

"A very good thought that is," said Raven.

"Go get those knives where I found this one, Juni, if you want something to eat with. Oh, you already have one. And Raven, while we eat, while we all eat, why don't you tell us the story of how your god made the world and men and—women and men. I think I want to hear it again. And I'm sure Juni would like it."

"Is it an exciting story?" Juni asked, squatting down by the fire. "That smells very good."

"Listen, little Heathen Woman, and decide yourself," said Raven, reaching with her sword point into the stew to spear the smallest piece of rabbit and raising it, still bubbling, through firelight, toward her small, stained teeth. "In the beginning was the act . . ."

5
_____

Blue and the chime of metal jewelry filled the sunshot door. Blue and green swished in by the jambs. Madame Keyne ducked her head beneath the slanted lintel. "Anyone in? Say, is anyone in. I want to buy a pot."

"A moment! A moment, gracious lady! Just a moment!" Old Zwon, who was slapping a flank of clay against a slate slab again and again to get the bubbles out so that, when molded and fired, it would not explode in the kiln, took a dripping rag from the jar on the ground and laid it over the moist chunk, then stepped around the bench, wiping his stone-colored fingers on his smirched tunic. "Now, what kind of pot would you like? If you'll step through here, I have on display some of my finer—"

"I want a pot that you do not have. I . . . excuse me, but this, well, dim and smelly shop. It's such a fine day outside, sunny and mild. And it won't be for long. Let's step into the sun and talk."

"Madame, for a single pot—?"

"I want a single *kind* of pot. It you can make it for me, I will want you to make a hundred of them."

"A *hundred* pots? By all means, madame, let us step outside into the sun where we can take a breath of air. Please, this way," and Old Zwon moved to the side of the door to follow the blue veils and jingling bangles outside.

". . . for all my lady's *warning!*" shouted a child, somewhere off in the sun, while a ball *popped* against a salt-stained wall; children ran shrieking down an alley.

"Now, my good friend," and Madame Keyne took the potter's wrinkled arm with a natural friendliness that, while warming, was just as disconcerting as her former disparagement of his close little place of business. "You know that for generations now, the people of Kolhari and the surrounding suburbs have cooked their meals in three-legged pots. You can put coals under them, move the heat about with a stick, move them about the heat—"

"Ah, yes! My mother made a boiled cherry pudding in those pots that I never remember without closing my eyes and tasting in the corner of my mouth for some remnant of—"

"So did mine. But that's—"

"Three-legged pots? Gracious lady, I can supply you with twenty-five of them right this day from my store. And decorated with the finest glazes in designs appropriate for common use or more refined—"

"I don't want three-legged pots." Madame Keyne pressed her beringed and bony hand to the back of Old Zwon's clay-ey knuckles. "You see I have recently walked through the Spur and seen the wives of the barbarians, newly moved to our city, cooking on their open fires in their little street camps, at the doors of their shacks. A dozen of their husbands work for me as the cheapest of loaders in my warehouses—when they deign to work at all. And I have seen pots overturned by careless-handed barbarian girls and women, by screaming barbarian children running at their games, by drunken barbarian men staggering in the street. And once, shame to say, when I was pursuing a lout who had stolen some coins from my warehouse, in a rage I knocked his woman's supper pot out on the ground when the man dared lie to me—but such are the shames that come with power. The point is, I have heard women curse the three-legged pot as an invention of a malicious god, made by no true craftsman—for these women were not brought up to use them and have not been instructed in their workings since childhood as our women have. No, they are not easy with them in the least."

"Brutish women, most of them," Old Zwon agreed. "No grace about them at all. Uncivilized and nasty-tongued to boot—those you can understand for the accent. Really, I don't know which are worse, the men or the—"

"I want you to make me a *four*-legged pot. And when you have made it, I shall examine it and see if it suits the conditions I think it shall likely have to endure. And if it endures them, I shall have you make me ninety-nine others like it."

"*A four*-legged pot?" Old Zwon's bushy eyebrows lowered in the sun to drop ragged shadows across his high, thin cheekbones. "Who ever heard of a four-legged pot?"

"A four-legged pot will be sturdier, potter, less likely to tip over. You do not have to be so careful in the cooking. Believe me, it fills a need and will sell—first to the barbarians. And who knows, the adventurous among our own women will find a spot for it in their kitchens."

"I *went* out *to* Babàra's *Pit*

"At the *crescent moon's* first *dawn*ing—
     [bounce!]—

"But the *Thanes* of *Garth* had *co*—Oh!"

"You missed! You missed! My turn! You missed!"

"Now with a three-legged pot," Old Zwon continued, as children's running shadows mingled with the two strolling oldsters' on the bright film of a puddle, then pulled away to merge with the whole shadowed side of the street, "you don't have to worry about getting leg-lengths exact: any three legs will always all touch the ground. With a four-legged pot, however, if one leg is shorter than the others . . . of course, there *are* ways to get around that with molds, especially if you're making a hundred. Still—"

"You will be making a hundred and no doubt another hundred. *And* you will be making money! These women need four-legged pots, believe me. And it will only be a matter of months, if not weeks, before our own women have taken them over. *We* need them as well. Or are you one of these men who has no sense of women's condition in our society?"

"Ah, yes. Money, madame. Well, I can certainly do what you ask, gracious lady. But, frankly speaking, I don't know that I am so well disposed toward money-making schemes this autumn as I was at the beginning of spring. Or, indeed, how well set up I am to under-take the making of a hundred pots. You do not know the sad tale of my assistant, madame—he was a fine young man, of whom I was as fond as if he were my own son."

"What has he got to do with the pots you make for me?"

"Oh, he was a fine young man, madame. Friendly, hard-working, eager to do well—responsible as they come. I took him from his family into my shop here and I would even say I loved him as much as they. More than they, perhaps. For he was a good boy, madame. A truly fine boy."

"Pots are what we're discussing, potter. Pots and money."

"And money is precisely what I am discussing, madame. At the beginning of this past spring, a mes-senger came from a southern lord, for whom I had done work—oh, years ago, from before the reign of our gracious Child Empress (whose reign is righteous and rich)—and he requested I send him someone I could trust in order that we might set up a franchise, from his orchards, to import—"

"For *all* my *la*dy's *warn*ing—Oh, look! It's gone into the cistern! We've lost another one!" Juvenile exclamations and groans chorused from the alley's end.

"—those pesky little balls, made from the southern saps, that, even now as we move into autumn are dis-appearing from our streets and avenues. Madame, I sent my assistant, on a boat, to the south—with *very* little money, madame; certainly not what anyone would call a great deal. And certainly—I thought—nowhere near enough to tempt such a good-hearted and re-sponsible lad to the sort of act for which you had to discipline your barbarian worker. But madame, he *was*

tempted. He was to be away for a week. And I have
not seen him now for three months. And that, madame,
is money for you!" The old man gave a bitter chuckle.
"Oh, first I feared that something had happened. I
sent a message, finally, to the south, asking my Lord
Aldamir if my boy Bayle had ever reached him; I was
blunt. I told him in my message I was afraid the youth
had absconded with my meager funds. I sent it by the
captain of the very boat on which the boy had
traveled south. I received a very kind and considerate
answer from some priests at a monastery where, apparently, Bayle had briefly stopped off. It was written
elegantly and feelingly, in three languages—in case
my reading skills were better in one than another,
though I had to comb the waterfront bars for two
nights before I found a prostitute who could read the
third . . . only to find what I had suspected all along:
it said the same as the first two. They said, in three
languages, that my worst fears were realized; that, indeed, a Kolhari youth named Bayle had stayed with
them at their monastery, the Vygernangx, for a day on
his way to Lord Aldamir's castle, and that during his
stay he talked of nothing but running away with his
master's funds, of how easy it would be, there in the
barbaric south, with no supervision and no constraints.
And then, they said, the next morning he was gone from
his room, they knew not where. But they sent a man to
the castle to see if he had arrived. He had not. Peasants,
they said, had seen him walking along a southern road,
early that morning." Old Zwon's hand moved and
knotted and released under the woman's. "Madame,
I have come seriously to question the whole concept
of money, and the system of profit and wages by
which it works. After all, under the old system, when
we paid in kind, if you took a poor apprentice into
your house and rewarded him with a meal from your
table, a bed in your store, the shelter of your own
roof, and the tutelage of your craft, then your apprentice was essentially as rich as you were, having his
share of all that supplied the quality of your life. But
if you take the same poor apprentice and pay him
with money—pay him with the pittance of money one

pays an apprentice—all you do is emphasize his poverty by your riches. How can one expect even a good boy to remain honest under such abuse and insult?"

But Madame Keyne's brow knit, and her hand left Old Zwon's to tickle her bony chin. "Feyers of the Vygernangx monastery in the Garth peninsula, you say?"

"The very ones, madame."

"Because I too have received a missive from them recently, old man. About a secretary of mine who also stopped there—also on a mission to Lord Aldamir. Also—may I tell you?—she was inquiring about those . . . but the what and why of my petition is not important. Suffice it to say that I too had sent her to petition his Lordship for an import franchise—"

"Had you, now?"

"I had. I dispatched my secretary—like you, at the beginning of spring—to the south. Like you, I waited for word, expecting it within the week. When, after three weeks, my fears began to grow, I can honestly say it was not toward absconsion that my thoughts turned. Though I had sent her with a goodly sum and gifts and presents to boot, I suppose I just assumed that I had provided for her so well that for her to escape that provision would be for her to doom herself—especially in the south—to a condition that no one could reasonably desire. You must understand that my secretary was a woman—I felt then and still feel—of privileged intelligence and uncommon sensibility. *My* thoughts ran rather to brigands or disease —for the south can be as pestilential as the alleys of the Spur. I too dispatched a message to that southern lord, outlining my fears. And by return boat I received a message—written only in one language, but perhaps they perceived that, as a merchant, I would have greater access to a translator than you would should their language prove to be not my most facile —from one Feyer Senth of the Vygernangx. It said that things had gone exactly as I feared; upon Norema's debarking from the boat at Garth, she was set upon by bandits. These evil men, sensing the weakness of a woman, had endeavored to rob her of all her possessions, but at last they were repelled by the good and loyal workmen on the dock. Norema sustained only a wound on her leg. She was taken to the monastery of these most hospitable southern feyers—no doubt the very ones that housed your knavish lout—where her wound became septic, her condition feverish. Three days later, they said, she was dead." Madame Keyne shook her head. "Those kind priests, by the same boat, returned me all the crates and bags which Norema had taken with her—by their account, everything save the clothes in which her body was buried. Even the bag of coins I had sent with her came back to me apparently untouched. Ah, I cannot tell you how I have smarted since over my stupidity for sending such a fine and fearless woman into such barbarous dangers."

Zwon's head, before Madame Keyne's had stilled, began to shake in sympathy. "Truly the south is a strange and terrible land, where every evil we here in civilized Kolhari can imagine of it comes reflected back to us with an accuracy as perfect as the image in the belly-mirrors that the young men of the Ulveyn from time to time wear on our docks . . . Yes, it must be a terrible place. No wonder its natives would rather starve here in our slums than brave its uncivilized horrors of bodily disease and moral degeneracy . . . though of course they end up bringing both with them to sicken our civilized streets. Madame—?" for here an oblique thought clearly startled the old man and from his feature's agitation he was clearly struggling to give it voice: "But tell me . . . how . . . *what* was the mission, the goal, the object of your secretary's visit? To Lord Aldamir, I mean?"

"But does it matter?" Madame Keyne's hand again clove to the back of the potter's. "I have practically forgotten. What must be foremost in our mind is that we shall be henceforth joined in a money-making scheme all in the glorious and innocent here and now —not in the errors of a disastrous past. Money, old potter, money—believe me, *I* am convinced that it is the greatest invention in the history of mankind and, for all your doubts, an entirely good thing. Get yourself another assistant. Get two. Get ten. Believe me, there will be work enough for them. Certainly there are youths a-plenty idling away their time on New Pavē that would be well-served by honest work. Why need we dwell on the schemes of the past that, with all their pain, have come to nothing, when glory lies in the schemes of the present? Four-legged pots, well-formed and cheaply made, that is where I want you to put all your thoughts and energies, old man!"

Away in another alley, children's shouts pummeled and tumbled in the autumn sun, though they were too far off to distinguish any one word amidst their childish gamings.

V

THE TALE OF
DRAGONS AND DREAMERS

But there is a negative work to be carried out
first: we must rid ourselves of a whole mass
of notions, each of which, in its own way,
diversifies the theme of continuity. They may
not have a very rigorous conceptual structure,
but they have a very precise function. Take
the notion of tradition: it is intended to give
a special temporal status to a group of phenomena that are both successive and identical
(or at least similar); it makes it possible to
rethink the dispersion of history in the form
of the same; it allows a reduction of the difference proper to every beginning, in order to
pursue without discontinuity the endless
search for origin . . .
—Michel Foucault
The Archeology of Knowledge

1

Wide wings dragged on stone, scales a polychrome glister with seven greens. The bony gum yawned above the iron rail. The left eye, fist-sized and packed with stained foils, did not blink its transverse lid. A stench of halides; a bilious hiss.

"But why have you penned it up in here?"

"Do you think the creature unhappy, my Vizerine? Ill-fed, perhaps? Poorly exercised—less well cared for than it would be at Ellamon?"

"How could anyone know?" But Myrgot's chin was down, her lower lip out, and her thin hands joined tightly before the lap of her shift.

"I know *you,* my dear. You hold it against me that I should want some of the 'fable' that has accrued to these beasts to redound on me. But you know; I went to great expense (and I don't just mean the bribes, the gifts, the money) to bring it here . . . Do you know what a dragon is? For me? Let me tell you, dear Myrgot: it is an expression of some natural sensibility that cannot be explained by pragmatics, that cannot survive unless someone is hugely generous before it. These beasts are a sport. If Olin—yes, Mad Olin, and it may have been the highest manifestation of her madness—had not decided, on a tour through the mountain holds, the creatures were beautiful, we wouldn't have them today. You know the story? She came upon a bunch of brigands slaughtering a nest of them and sent her troops to slaughter the brigands. Everyone in the mountains had seen the wings, but no one was sure the creatures could actually fly till two years after Olin put them under her protection, and the grooms devised their special training programs that allowed the beasts to soar. And their flights, though lovely, are short and rare. The creatures are not survival oriented—unless you want to see them as part of a survival relationship with the vicious little harridans who are condemned to be their riders: another of your crazed great aunt's more inane institutions. Look at that skylight. The moon outside illumines it now. But the expense I have gone to in order to arrive at those precise green panes! Full sunlight causes the creature's eyes to enflame, putting it in great discomfort. They can only fly a few hundred yards or so, perhaps a mile with the most propitious drafts, and unless they land on the most propitious ledge, they cannot take off again. Since they cannot elevate from flat land, once set down in an ordinary forest, say, they are doomed. In the wild, many live their entire lives without flying, which, given how easily their wing membrane's tear through or become injured, is understandable. They are egg-laying creatures who know nothing of physical intimacy. Indeed, they are much more tractable when kept from their fellows. This one is bigger, stronger, and generally healthier than any you'll find in the Falthas—in or out of the Ellamon corals. Listen to her trumpet her joy over her present state!"

Obligingly, the lizard turned on her splay claws, dragging the chain from her iron collar, threw back her bony head beneath the tower's many lamps, and hissed—not a trumpet, the Vizerine reflected, whatever young Strethi might think. "My dear, why don't you just turn it loose?"

"Why don't *you* just have me turn loose the poor wretch chained in the dungeon?" At the Vizerine's bitter glance, the Suzeraine chuckled. "No, dear Myrgot. True, I could haul on those chains there, which would pull back the wood and copper partitions you see on the other side of the pen. My beast could then waddle to the ledge and soar out from our tower here, onto the night. (Note the scenes of hunting I have had the finest craftsmen beat into the metal work. Myself, I think they're stunning.) But such a creature as this in a landscape like the one about here could take only a single flight—for, really, without a rider they're simply too stupid to turn around and come back to where they took off. And I am not a twelve year old girl; what's more, I couldn't bear to have one about the castle who could ride the creature aloft when I am too old and too heavy." (The dragon was still hissing.) "No, I could only conceive of turning it loose if my whole world were destroyed and—indeed —my next act would be to cast myself down from that same ledge to the stones!"

"My Suzeraine, I much preferred you as a wild-haired, horse-proud seventeen-year-old. You were beautiful and heartless . . . in some ways rather a bore. But you have grown up into another over-refined soul of the sort our aristocracy is so good at producing and which produces so little itself save ways to spend unconscionable amounts on castles, clothes, and complex towers to keep comfortable impossible beasts. You remind me of a cousin of mine—the Baron Inige? Yet what I loved about you, when you were a wholly ungracious provincial heir whom I had just brought to court, was simply that *that* was what I could never imagine you."

"Oh, I remember what you loved about me! And I remember your cousin too—though it's been years since I've seen him. Among those pompous and self-important dukes and earls, though I doubt he liked me any better than the rest did, I recall a few times when he went out of his way to be kind . . . I'm sure I didn't deserve it. How is Curly?"

"Killed himself three years ago." The Vizerine shook her head. "*His* passion, you may recall, was flowers—which I'm afraid totally took over in the last years. As I understand the story—for I wasn't there when it happened—he'd been putting together another collection of particularly rare weeds. One he was after apparently turned out to be the wrong color, or couldn't be found, or didn't exist. The next day his servants discovered him in the arboretum, his mouth crammed with the white blossoms of some deadly mountain flower." Myrgot shuddered. "Which I've always suspected is where such passions as his—and yours—are too likely to lead, given the flow of our lives, the tenor of our times."

The Suzeraine laughed, adjusting the collar of his rich robe with his forefinger. (The Vizerine noted that the blue eyes were much paler in the prematurely lined face than she remembered; and the boyish nail-biting had passed on, in the man, to such grotesque extents that each of his bony fingers now ended in a perfect pitted wound.) Two slaves at the door, their own collars covered with heavily jeweled neckpieces, stepped forward to help him, as they had long since been instructed, when the Suzeraine's hand fell again into the robe's folds, the adjustment completed. The slaves stepped back. The Suzeraine, oblivious, and the Vizerine, feigning obliviousness and wondering if the Suzeraine's obliviousness were feigned or real, strolled through the low stone arch between them to the uneven steps circling down the tower.

"Well," said the blond lord, stepping back to let his lover of twenty years ago precede, "now we return to the less pleasant aspect of your stay here. You know, I sometimes find myself dreading any visit from the aristocracy. Just last week two common women stopped at my castle—one was a redhaired island woman, the other a small creature in a mask who hailed from the Western Crevasse. They were traveling together, seeking adventure and fortune. The Western Woman had once for a time worked in the Falthas, training the winged beasts and the little girls who ride them. The conversation was choice! The island woman could tell incredible tales, and was even using skins and inks to mark down her adventures. And the masked one's observations were very sharp. It was a fine evening we passed. I fed them and housed them. They entertained me munificently. I gave them useful gifts, saw them depart, and would be delighted to see either return. Now, were the stars in a different configuration, I'm sure that the poor wretch that we've got strapped in the dungeon and his little friend who escaped might have come wondering by in the same wize. But no, we have to bind one to the plank in the cellar and stake a guard out for the other . . . You really wish me to keep up the pretence to that poor mule that it is Krodar, rather than you, who directs his interrogation?"

"You object?" Myrgot's hand, out to touch the damp stones at the stair's turning, came back to brush at the black braids that looped her forehead. "Once or twice I have seen you enjoy such an inquisition session with an avidity that verged on the unsettling."

"Inquisition? But this is merely questioning. The pain—at your own orders, my dear—is being kept to a minimum." (Strethi's laugh echoed down over Myrgot's shoulder, recalling for her the enthusiasm of the boy she could no longer find when she gazed full at the man.) "I have neither objection nor approbation, my Vizerine. We have him; we do with him as we will . . . Now, I can't help seeing how you gaze about at my walls, Myrgot! I must tell you, ten years ago when I had this castle built over the ruins of my parents' farm, I really thought the simple fact that all my halls had rooves would bring the aristocracy of Nevèrÿon flocking to my court. Do you know, you are my only regular visitor—at least the only one who comes out of anything other than formal necessity. And I do believe you would come to see me even if I lived in the same droughty farmhouse I did when you first met me. Amazing what we'll do out of friendship . . . The other one, Myrgot; I wonder what happened to our prisoner's little friend. They both fought like devils. Too bad the boy got away."

"We have the one I want," Myrgot said.

"At any rate, you have your reasons—your passion, for politics and intrigue. That's what comes of living most of your life in Kolhari. Here in Avila, it's—well, it's not that different for me. You have your criticism of my passions—and I have mine of yours. Certainly I should like to be much more straight forward with the dog: make my demand and chop his head off if he didn't meet it. This endless play is not really my style. Yet I am perfectly happy to assist you in your desires. And however disparaging you are of my little pet, whose welfare is my life, I am sure there will come a time when one or another of your messengers will arrive at my walls bearing some ornate lizard harness of exquisite workmanship you have either discovered in some old storeroom or—who knows—have had specially commissioned for me by the latest and finest artist. When it happens, I shall be immensely pleased."

And as the steps took them around and down the damp tower, the Suzeraine of Strethi slipped up beside the Vizerine to take her aging arm.

2

And again Small Sarg ran.

He struck back low twigs, side-stepped a wet branch clawed with moonlight, and leaped a boggy puddle. With one hand he shoved away a curtain of leaves, splattering himself face to foot with night-dew, to reveal the moonlight castle. (How many other castles had he so revealed . . .) Branches chattered to behind him.

Panting, he ducked behind a boulder. His muddy hand pawed beneath the curls like scrap brass at his neck. The hinged iron was there; and locked tight—a droplet trickled under the metal. He swatted at his hip to find his sword: the hilt was still tacky under his palm where he had not had time to clean it. The gaze with which he took in the pile of stone was not a halt in his headlong dash so much as a continuation of it, the energy propelling arms and legs momentarily diverted into eyes, ears, and all inside and behind them;

then it was back on his feet; his feet pounded the shaley slope so that each footfall, even on his calloused soles, was a constellation of small pains; it was back in his arms; his arms pumped by his flanks so that his fists, brushing his sides as he jogged, heated his knuckles by friction.

A balustrade rose, blotting stars.

There would be the unlocked door (as he ran, he clawed over memories of the seven castles he had already run up to; seven side doors, all unlocked . . .); and the young barbarian, muddy to the knees and elbows, his hair at head and chest and groin matted with leaf-bits and worse, naked save the sword thonged about his hips and the slave collar locked about his neck, dashed across moonlit stubble and gravel into a tower's shadow, toward the door . . . and slowed, pulling in cool breaths of autumn air that grew hot inside him and ran from his nostrils; more air ran in.

"Halt!" from the brand that flared high in the doorframe.

Sarg, in one of those swipes at his hip, had moved the scabbard around behind his buttock; it was possible, if the guard had not really been looking at Sarg's dash through the moonlight, for the boy to have seemed simply a naked slave. Sarg's hand was ready to grab at the hilt.

"Who's there?"

Small Sarg raised his chin, so that the iron would show. "I've come back," and thought of seven castles. "I got lost from the others, this morning. When they were out."

"Come now, say your name and rank."

"It's only Small Sarg, master—one of the slaves in the Suzeraine's labor pen. I was lost this morning—"

"Likely story!"

"—and I've just found my way back." With his chin high, Sarg walked slowly and thought: I am running, I am running . . .

"See here, boy—" The brand came forward, fifteen feet, ten, five, three . . .

I am running. And Small Sarg, looking like a filthy field slave with some thong at his waist, jerked his sword up from the scabbard (which bounced on his buttock) and with a grunt sank it into the abdomen of the guard a-glow beneath the high-held flare. The guard's mouth opened. The flare fell, rolled in the mud so that it burned now only on one side. Small Sarg leaned on the hilt, twisting—somewhere inside the guard the blade sheered upward, parting diaphragm, belly, lungs. The guard closed his eyes, drooled blood, and toppled. Small Sarg almost fell on him—till the blade sucked free. And Sarg was running again, blade out for the second guard (in four castles before there had been a second guard), who was, it seemed as Sarg swung around the stone newel and into the stairwell where his own breath was a roaring echo, not there.

He hurried up and turned into a side corridor that would take him down to the labor pen. (Seven castles, now. Were all of them designed by one architect?) He ran through the low hall, guided by that glowing spot in his mind where memory was flush with desire; around a little curve, down the steps—

"What the—?"

—and jabbed his sword into the shoulder of the guard who'd started forward (already hearing the murmur behind the wooden slats), yanking it free of flesh, the motion carrying it up and across the throat of the second guard (here there was always a second guard) who had turned, surprised; the second guard released his sword (it had only been half drawn), which fell back into its scabbard. Small Sarg hacked at the first again (who was screaming): the man fell, and Small Sarg leaped over him, while the man gurgled and flopped. But Sarg was pulling at the boards, cutting at the rope. Behind the boards and under the screams, like murmuring flies, hands and faces rustled about one another. (Seven times now they had seemed like murmuring flies.) And rope was always harder hacking than flesh. The wood, in at least two other castles, had simply splintered under his hands (under his hands, wood splintered) so that, later, he had wondered if the slaughter and the terror was really necessary.

Rope fell away.

Sarg yanked again.

The splintered gate scraped out on stone.

"You're free!" Sarg hissed into the mumbling; mumblings silenced at the word. "Go on, get out of here now!" (How many faces above their collars were clearly barbarian like his own? Memory of other labor pens, rather than what shifted and murmured before him, told him most were.) He turned and leaped bodies, took stairs at double step—while memory told him that only a handful would flee at once; another handful would take three, four, or five minutes to talk themselves into fleeing; and another would simply sit, terrified in the foul straw, and would be sitting there when the siege was over.

He dashed up stairs in the dark. (Dark stairs fell down beneath dashing feet . . .) He flung himself against the wooden door with the strip of light beneath and above it. (In two other castles the door had been locked); it fell open. (In one castle the kitchen midden had been deserted, the fire dead.) He staggered in, blinking in firelight.

The big man in the stained apron stood up from over the cauldron, turned, frowning. Two women carrying pots stopped and stared. In the bunk beds along the midden's far wall, a red-headed kitchen boy raised himself up on one arm, blinking. Small Sarg tried to see only the collars around each neck. But what he saw as well (he had seen it before . . .) was that even here, in a lord's kitchen, where slavery was already involved with the acquisition of the most rudimentary crafts and skills, most of the faces were darker, the hair was coarser, and only the shorter of the women was clearly a barbarian like himself.

"You are free . . . !" Small Sarg said, drawing himself up, dirty, blood splattered. He took a gulping breath. "The guards are gone below. The labor pens have already been turned loose. You are free . . . !"

The big cook said: "What . . . ?" and a smile, with worry flickering through, slowly overtook his face. (This one's mother, thought Small Sarg, was a barbarian: he had no doubt been gotten on her by some free northern dog.) "What are you talking about, boy? Better put that shoat-sticker down or you'll get yourself in trouble."

Small Sarg stepped forward, hands out from his sides. He glanced left at his sword. Blood trailed a line of drops on the stone below it.

Another slave with a big pot of peeled turnips in his hands strode into the room through the far archway, started for the fire rumbling behind the pot hooks, grilling spits, and chained pulleys. He glanced at Sarg, looked about at the others, stopped.

"Put it down now," the big cook repeated, coaxingly. (The slave who'd just come in, wet from perspiration, with a puzzled look started to put his turnip pot down on the stones—then gulped and hefted it back against his chest.) "Come on—"

"What do you think, I'm some berserk madman, a slave gone off my head with the pressure of the iron at my neck?" With his free hand, he thumbed toward his collar. "I've fought my way in here, freed the laborers below you; you have only to go now yourselves. You're free, do you understand?"

"Now wait, boy," said the cook, his smile wary. "Freedom is not so simple a thing as that. Even if you're telling the truth, just what do you propose we're free to do? Where do you expect us to go? If we leave here, what do you expect will happen to us? We'll be taken by slavers before dawn tomorrow, more than likely. Do you want us to get lost in the swamps to the south? Or would you rather we starve to death in the mountains to the north? Put down your sword—just for a minute—and be reasonable."

The barbarian woman said, with her eyes wide and no barbarian accent at all: "Are you well, boy? Are you hungry? We can give you food: you can lie down and sleep a while if you—"

"I don't want sleep. I don't want food. I want you to understand that you're free and I want you to move. Fools, fools, don't you know that to stay slaves is to stay fools?"

"Now that sword, boy—" The big slave moved.

Small Sarg raised his blade.

The big slave stopped. "Look, youth. Use your head. We can't just—"

Footsteps; armor rattled in another room—clearly guards' sounds. (How many times now—four out of the seven?— had he heard those sounds?) What happened (again) was:

"Here, boy—!" from the woman who had till now not spoken. She shifted her bowl under one arm and pointed toward the bunks.

Small Sarg sprinted toward them, sprang—into the one below the kitchen boy's. As he sprang, his sword point caught the wooden support beam, jarred his arm full hard; the sword fell clanking to the stone floor. As Sarg turned to see it, the kitchen boy in the bunk above flung down a blanket. Sarg collapsed in the straw, kicked rough cloth (it was stiff at one end as though something had spilled on it and dried) down over his leg, and pulled it up over his head at the same time. Just before the blanket edge cut away the firelit chamber, Sarg saw the big slave pull off his stained apron (underneath the man was naked as Sarg) to fling it across the floor to where it settled, like a stained sail, over Sarg's fallen weapon. (And the other slave had somehow managed to set his turnip pot down directly over those blood drops.) Under the blanket dark, he heard the guard rush in.

"All right, you! A hoard of bandits—probably escaped slaves—have stormed the lower floors. They've already taken the labor pen—turned loose every cursed dog in them." (Small Sarg shivered and grinned: how many times now, three, or seven, or seventeen, had he watched slaves suddenly think with one mind, move together like the leaves on a branch before a single breeze!) More footsteps. Beneath the blanket, Small Sarg envisioned a second guard running in to collide with the first, shouting (over the first's shoulder?): "Any of you kitchen scum caught aiding and abetting these invading lizards will be hung up by the heels and whipped till the flesh falls from your backs—and you know we mean it. There must be fifty of them or more to have gotten in like that! And don't think they won't slaughter *you* as soon as they would *us!*"

The pair of footsteps retreated; there was silence for a drawn breath.

Then bare feet were rushing quickly toward his bunk.

Small Sarg pushed back the blanket. The big slave was just snatching up his apron. The woman picked up the sword and thrust it at Sarg.

"All right," said the big slave, "we're running."

"Take your sword," the woman said. "And good luck to you, boy."

They ran—the redheaded kitchen boy dropped down before Small Sarg's bunk and took off around the kitchen table after them. Sarg vaulted now, and landed (running), his feet continuing the dash that had brought him into the castle. The slaves crowded out the wooden door through which Small Sarg had entered. Small Sarg ran out through the arch by which the guards had most probably left.

Three guards stood in the anteroom, conferring. One looked around and said, "Hey, what are—"

A second one who turned and just happened to be a little nearer took Small Sarg's sword in his belly; it tore loose out his side, so that the guard, surprised, fell in the pile of his splatting innards. Sarg struck another's bare thigh—cutting deep—and then the arm of still another (his blade grated bone). The other ran, trailing a bass howl: "They've come! They're coming in here, now! Help! They're breaking in—" breaking to tenor in some other corridor.

Small Sarg ran, and a woman, starting into the hallway from the right, saw him and darted back. But there was a stairwell to his left; he ran up it. He ran, up the cleanly hewn stone, thinking of a tower with spiral steps, that went on and on and on, opening on some high, moonlit parapet. After one turn, the stairs stopped. Light glimmered from dozens of lamps, some on ornate stands, some hanging from intricate chains.

A thick, patterned carpet cushioned the one muddy foot he had put across the sill. Sarg crouched, his sword out from his hip, and brought his other foot away from the cool stone behind.

The man at the great table looked up, frowned—
a slave, but his collar was covered by a wide neckpiece
of heavy white cloth sewn about with chunks of tour-
maline and jade. He was very thin, very lined, and
bald. (In how many castles had Sarg seen slaves who
wore their collars covered so? Six, now? All seven?)
"What are you doing here, boy . . . ?" The slave
pushed his chair back, the metal balls on the forelegs
furrowing the rug.

Small Sarg said: "You're free."

Another slave in a similar collar-cover turned on
the ladder where she was replacing piles of parchment
on a high shelf stuffed with manuscripts. She took a
step down the ladder, halted. Another youth (same
covered collar), with double pointers against a great
globe in the corner, looked perfectly terrified—and
was probably the younger brother of the kitchen boy,
from his bright hair. (See only the collars, Small Sarg
thought. But with the jeweled and damasked neckpieces, it was hard, very hard.) The bald slave at the
table, with the look of a tired man, said: "You don't
belong here, you know. And you are in great danger."
The slave, a wrinkled forty, had the fallen pectorals
of the quickly aging.

"You're free!" Small Sarg croaked.

"And you are a very naïve and presumptuous little
barbarian. How many times have I had this conversation—four? Five? At least six? You are here to free
us of the iron collars." The man dug a forefinger
beneath the silk and stones to drag up, on his bony
neck, the iron band beneath. "Just so you'll see it's
there. Did you know that *our* collars are much heavier
than yours?" He released the iron; the same brown
forefinger hooked up the jeweled neckpiece—almost
a bib—which sagged and wrinkled up, once pulled
from its carefully arranged position. "These add far
more weight to the neck than the circle of iron they
cover." (Small Sarg thought: Though I stand here,
still as stone, I am running, running . . .) "We make
this castle function, boy—at a level of efficiency that,
believe me, is felt in the labor pens as much as in the
audience chambers where our lord and owner enter-

tains fellow nobles. You think you are rampaging
through the castle, effecting your own eleemosynary
manumissions. What you are doing is killing free men
and making the lives of slaves more miserable than,
of necessity, they already are. If slavery is a disease
and a rash on the flesh of Nevèrÿon—" (I am running,
like an eagle caught up in the wind, like a snake sliding down a gravel slope . . .) "—your own actions
turn an ugly eruption into a fatal infection. You free
the labor pens into a world where, at least in the cities
and the larger towns, a wage-earning populace, many
of them, is worse off than here. And an urban merchant class can only absorb a fraction of the skills of
the middle level slaves you turn loose from the mid-
dens and smithies. The Child Empress herself has
many times declared that she is opposed to the institution of bondage, and the natural drift of our nation
is away from slave labor anyway—so that all your
efforts do is cause restrictions to become tighter in
those areas where the institution would naturally die
out of its own accord in a decade or so. Have you
considered: your efforts may even be prolonging the
institution you would abolish." (Running, Small Sarg
thought, rushing, fleeing, dashing . . .) "But the simple
truth is that the particular skills *we*—the ones who
must cover our collars in jewels—master to run such
a complex house as an aristocrat's castle are just not
needed by the growing urban class. Come around here,
boy, and look for yourself." The bald slave pushed
his chair back even further and gestured for Small
Sarg to approach. "Yes. Come, see."

Small Sarg stepped, slowly and carefully, across the
carpet. (I am running, he thought; flesh tingled at the
backs of his knees, the small of his back. Every muscle,
in its attenuated motion, was geared to some coherent
end that, in the pursuit of it, had become almost invisible within its own glare and nimbus.) Sarg walked
around the table's edge.

From a series of holes in the downward lip hung
a number of heavy cords, each with a metal loop at
the end. (Small Sarg thought: In one castle they had
simple handles of wood tied to them; in another the

handles were cast from bright metal set with red and green gems, more ornate than the jeweled collars of the slaves who worked them.) "From this room," explained the slave, "we can control the entire castle— really, it represents far more control, even, than that of the Suzeraine who owns all you see, including us. If I pulled this cord here, a bell would ring in the linen room and summon the slave working there; if I pulled it twice, that slave would come with linen for his lordship's chamber, which we would then inspect before sending it on to be spread. Three rings, and the slave would come bearing the sheets and hangings for the guests' chambers. Four rings, and we would receive the sheets for our own use—and they are every bit as elegant, believe me, as the ones for his lordship. One tug on this cord here and wine and food would be brought for his lordship . . . at least if the kitchen staff is still functioning. Three rings, and a feast can be brought for us, here in these very rooms, that would rival any indulged by his Lordship. A bright lad like you, I'm sure, could learn the strings to pull very easily. Here, watch out for your blade and come stand beside me. That's right. Now give that cord there a quick, firm tug and just see what happens. No, don't be afraid. Just reach out and pull it. Once, mind you —not twice or three times. That means something else entirely. Go ahead . . ."

Sarg moved his hand out slowly, looking at his muddy, bloody fingers. (Small Sarg thought: Though it may be a different cord in each castle, it is *always* a single tug! My hand, with each airy inch, feels like it is running, running to hook the ring . . .)

". . . with only a little training," went on the bald slave, smiling, "a smart and ambitious boy like you could easily become one of us. From here, you would wield more power within these walls than the Suzeraine himself. And such power as that is not to be—"

Then Small Sarg whirled (no, he had never released his sword) to shove his steel into the loose belly. The man half-stood, with open mouth, then fell back, gargling. Blood spurted, hit the table, ran down the cords. "You fool . . . !" the bald man managed, trying now to grasp one handle.

Small Sarg, with his dirty hand, knocked the bald man's clean one away. The chair overturned and the bald man curled and uncurled on the darkening carpet. There was blood on his collar piece now.

"You think I am such a fool that I don't know you can call guards in here as easily as food-bearers and house-cleaners?" Small Sarg looked at the woman on the ladder, the boy at the globe. "I do not like to kill slaves. But I do not like people who plot to kill me —especially such a foolish plot. Now: are the rest of you such fools that you cannot understand what it means when I say, 'You're free'?"

Parchments slipped from the shelf, unrolling on the floor, as the woman scurried down the ladder. The boy fled across the room, leaving a slowly turning globe. Then both were into the arched stairwell from which Small Sarg had come. Sarg hopped over the fallen slave and ran into the doorway through which (in two other castles) guards, at the (single) tug of a cord, had once come swarming: a short hall, more steps, another chamber. Long and short swords hung on the wooden wall. Leather shields with colored fringes leaned against the stone one. A helmet lay on the floor in the corner near a stack of grieves. But there were no guards. (Till now, in the second castle only, there had been no guards.) I am free, thought Small Sarg, once again I am free, running, running through stone arches, down tapestried stairs, across dripping halls, up narrow corridors, a-dash through time and possibility. (Somewhere in the castle people were screaming.) Now I am free to free my master!

Somewhere, doors clashed. Other doors, nearer, clashed. Then the chamber doors swung back in fire-light. The Suzeraine strode through, tugging them to behind him. "Very well—" (Clash!)—"we can get on with our little session." He reached up to adjust his collar and two slaves in jeweled collar pieces by the door (they were oiled, pale, strong men with little wires sewn around the backs of their ears; besides the collar pieces

they wore only leather clouts) stepped forward to take
his cloak. "Has he been given any food or drink?"

The torturer snored on the bench, knees wide, one
hand hanging, calloused knuckles the color of stone,
one on his knee, the smeared red here and there dried
to brown; his head lolled on the wall.

"I asked: Has he had anything to—Bah!" This to
the slave folding his cloak by the door: "That man is
fine for stripping the flesh from the backs of your dis-
obedient brothers. But for anything more subtle . . .
well, we'll let him sleep." The Suzeraine, who now
wore only a leather kilt and very thick-soled sandals
(the floor of this chamber sometimes became very
messy), walked to the slant board from which hung
chains and ropes and against which leaned pokers
and pincers. On a table beside the plank were several
basins—in one lay a rag which had already turned
the water pink. Within the furnace, which took up most
of one wall (a ragged canvas curtain hung beside it)
a log broke; on the opposite wall the shadow of the
grate momentarily darkened and flickered. "How are
you feeling?" the Suzeraine asked perfunctorily. "A
little better? That's good. Perhaps you enjoy the return
of even that bit of good feeling enough to answer my
questions accurately and properly. I can't really im-
press upon you enough how concerned my master is
for the answers. He is a very hard taskman, you know
—that is, if you know him at all. Krodar wants—but
then, we need not sully such an august name with the
fetid vapors of this place. The stink of the iron that
binds you to that board—I remember a poor, guilty
soul lying on the plank as you lie now, demanding of
me: 'Don't you even wash the bits of flesh from the
last victim off the chains and manacles before you
bind up the new one?' " The Suzeraine chuckled.
" 'Why should I?' was my answer. True, it makes the
place reek. But that stench is a very good reminder—
don't you feel it?—of the mortality that is, after all,
our only real playing piece in this game of time and
pain." The Suzeraine looked up from the bloody basin:
a heavy arm, a blocky bicep, corded with high veins,
banned at the joint with thin ligament; a jaw in which

a muscle quivered under a snarl of patchy beard, here gray, there black, at another place ripped from reddened skin, at still another cut by an old scar; a massive thigh down which sweat trickled, upsetting a dozen other droplets caught in that thigh's coarse hairs, till here a link, there a cord, and elsewhere a rope, dammed it. Sweat crawled under, or overflowed the dams. "Tell me, Gorgik, have you ever been employed by a certain southern lord, a Lord Aldamir, whose hold is in the Garth Peninsula, only a stone's throw from the Vygernangx Monastery, to act as a messenger between his Lordship and certain weavers, jewelers, potters, and iron mongers in port Kolhari?"

"I have . . . have never . . ." The chest tried to rise under a metal band that would have cramped the breath of a smaller man than Gorgik. ". . . never set foot within the precinct of Garth. Never, I tell you . . . I have told you. . . ."

"And yet—" The Suzeraine, pulling the wet rag from its bowl where it dripped a cherry smeer on the table, and turned to the furnace. He wound the rag about one hand, picked up one of the irons sticking from the furnace rack, and drew it out to examine its tip: an ashen rose. "—for reasons you still have not explained to my satisfaction, you wear, on a chain around your neck—" The rose, already dimmer, lowered over Gorgik's chest; the chest hair had been singed in places, adding to the room's stink. "—that." The rose clicked the metal disk that lay on Gorgik's sternum. "These navigational scales, the map etched there, the grid of stars that turns over it and the designs etched around it all speak of its origin in—"

The chest suddenly heaved; Gorgik gave up some sound that tore in the cartilages of his throat.

"Is that getting warm?" The Suzeraine lifted the poker tip. An off-center scorch-mark marred the astrolabe's verdigris. "I was saying: the workmanship is clearly from the south. If you haven't spent time there, why else would you be wearing it?" Then the Suzeraine pressed the poker tip to Gorgik's thigh; Gorgik screamed. The Suzeraine, after a second or two, removed the poker from the blistering mark (amidst the cluster of marks, bubbled, yellow, some crusted over by now). "Let me repeat something to you, Gorgik, about the rules of the game we're playing: the game of time and pain. I said this to you before we began. I say it to you again, but the context of several hour's experience may reweight its meaning for you —and before I repeat it, let me tell you that I shall, as I told you before, eventually repeat it yet again: When the pains are small, in this game, then we make the time very, very long. Little pains, spaced out over the seconds, the minutes—no more than a minute between each—for days on end. Days and days. You have no idea how much I enjoy the prospect. The timing, the ingenuity, the silent comparisons between your responses and the responses of the many, many others I have had the pleasure to work with—that is all my satisfaction. Remember this: on the simplest and most basic level, the infliction of these little torments gives me far more pleasure than would your revealing the information that is their occasion. So if you want to get back at me, to thwart me in some way, to cut short my real pleasure in all of this, perhaps you had best—"

"I told you! I've answered your questions! I've answered them and answered them truthfully! I have never set foot on the Garth! The astrolabe was a gift to me when I was practically a child. I cannot even recall the circumstances under which I received it. Some noble man or woman presented it to me on a whim at some castle or other that I stayed at." (The Suzeraine replaced the poker on the furnace rack and turned to a case, hanging on the stone wall, of small polished knives.) "I am a man who has stayed in many castles, many hovels; I have slept under bridges in the cities, in fine inns and old alleys. I have rested for the night in fields and forests. And I do not mark my history the way you do, cataloguing the gifts and graces I have been lucky enough to—" Gorgik drew a sharp breath.

"The flesh between the fingers—terribly sensitive." The Suzeraine lifted the tiny knife, where a blood drop crawled along the cutting edge. "As is the skin between the toes, on even the most calloused feet. I've known men—not to mention women—who remained staunch under hot pokers and burning pincers who, as soon as I started to make the few, smallest cuts in the flesh between the fingers and toes (really, no more than a dozen or so) became astonishingly cooperative. I'm quite serious." He put down the blade on the table edge, picked up the towel from the basin and squeezed; reddened water rilled between his fingers into the bowl. The Suzeraine swabbed at the narrow tongue of blood that moved down the plank below Gorgik's massive (twitching a little now) hand. "The thing wrong with having you slanted like this, head up and feet down, is that even the most conscientious of us finds himself concentrating more on your face, chest, and stomach than, say, on your feet, ankles, and knees. Some exquisite feelings may be produced in the knee: a tiny nail, a small mallet . . . First I shall make a few more cuts. Then I shall wake our friend snoring against the wall. (You scream and he still sleeps! Isn't it amazing? But then, he's had so much of this!) We shall reverse the direction of the slant —head down, feet up—so that we can spread our efforts out more evenly over the arena of your flesh." In another basin, of yellow liquid, another cloth was submerged. The Suzeraine pulled the cloth out and spread it, dripping. "A little vinegar . . ."

Gorgik's head twisted in the clamp across his forehead that had already rubbed to blood at both temples as the Suzeraine laid the cloth across his face.

"A little salt. (Myself, I've always felt that four or five small pains, each of which alone would be no more than a nuisance, when applied all together can be far more effective than a single great one.)" The Suzeraine took up the sponge from the coarse crystals heaped in a third basin (crystals clung, glittering, to the brain-shape) and pressed it against Gorgik's scorched and fresh-blistered thigh. "Now the knife again . . ."

Somewhere, doors clashed.

Gorgik coughed hoarsely and repeatedly under the cloth. Frayed threads dribbled vinegar down his chest.

The cough broke into another scream, as another bloody tongue licked over the first.

Other doors, nearer, clashed.

One of the slaves with the wire sewn in his ears turned to look over his shoulder.

The Suzeraine paused in sponging off the knife.

On his bench, without ceasing his snore, the torturer knuckled clumsily at his nose.

The chamber door swung back, grating. Small Sarg ran in, leaped on the wooden top of a cage bolted to the wall (that could only have held a human being squeezed in a very unnatural position), and shouted: "All who are slaves here are now free!"

The Suzeraine turned around with an odd expression. He said: "Oh, not again! Really, this is the *last* time!" He stepped from the table, his shadow momentarily falling across the vinegar rag twisting on Gorgik's face. He moved the canvas hanging aside (furnace light lit faint stairs rising), stepped behind it; the ragged canvas swung to—there was a small, final clash of bolt and hasp.

Small Sarg was about to leap after him, but the torturer suddenly opened his bloodshot eyes, the forehead below his bald skull wrinkled; he lumbered up, roaring.

"Are you free or slave?" Small Sarg shrieked, sword out.

The torturer wore a wide leather neck collar, set about with studs of rough metal, a sign (Small Sarg thought; and he had thought it before) that, if any sign could or should indicate a state somewhere between slavery and freedom, would be it. "Tell me," Small Sarg shrieked again, as the man, eyes bright with apprehension, body sluggish with sleep, lurched forward, "are you slave or free?" (In three castles the studded leather had hidden the bare neck of a free man; in two, the iron collar.) When the torturer seized the edge of the plank where Gorgik was bound—only to steady himself, and yet . . .—Sarg leaped, bringing his sword down. Studded leather cuffing the torturer's forearm deflected the blade; but the same sleepy lurch threw the hulking barbarian (for despite his shaved head, the torturer's heavy features and gold skin spoke as pure a southern origin as Sarg's own) to the right; the blade, aimed only to wound a shoulder, plunged into flesh at the bronze haired solar plexus.

The man's fleshy arms locked around the boy's hard shoulders, joining them in an embrace lubricated with blood. The torturer's face, an inch before Sarg's, seemed to explode in rage, pain, and astonishment. Then the head fell back, eyes opened, mouth gaping. (The torturer's teeth and breath were bad, very bad: this was the first time Small Sarg had ever actually killed a torturer.) The grip relaxed around Sarg's back; the man fell; Sarg staggered, his sword still gripped in one hand, wiping at the blood that spurted high as his chin with the other. "You're free . . . !" Sarg called over his shoulder; the sword came loose from the corpse.

The door slaves, however, were gone. (In two castles, they had gone seeking their own escape; in one, they had come back with guards . . .) Small Sarg turned toward the slanted plank, pulled the rag away from Gorgik's rough beard, flung it to the floor. "Master . . . !"

"So, you are . . . here—again—to . . . free me!"

"I have followed your orders, Master; I have freed every slave I encountered on my way . . ." Suddenly Small Sarg turned back to the corpse. On the torturer's hand-wide belt, among the gnarled studs, was a hook and from the hook hung a clutch of small instruments. Small Sarg searched for the key among them, came up with it. It was simply a metal bar with a handle on one end and a flat side at the other. Sarg ducked behind the board and began twisting the key in locks. On the upper side of the plank, chains fell away and clamps bounced loose. Planks squeaked beneath flexing muscles.

Sarg came up as the last leg clamp swung away from Gorgik's ankle (leaving it red indentations) and the man's great foot hit the floor. Gorgik stood, kneeding one shoulder; he pushed again and again at his flank with the heel of one hand. A grin broke his beard. "It's good to see you, boy. For a while I didn't know if I would or not. The talk was all of small pains and long times."

"What did they want from you—this time?" Sarg took the key and reached around behind his own neck, fitted the key in the lock, turned it (for these were barbaric times; the mountain man, named Belham, who had invented the lock and key, had only made one, and no one had yet thought to vary them: different keys for different locks was a refinement not to come for a thousand years), unhinged his collar, and stood, holding it in his soiled hands.

"This time it was some nonsense about working as a messenger in the south—your part of the country." Gorgik took the collar, raised it to his own neck, closed it with a clink. "When you're under the hands of a torturer, with all the names and days and questions, you lose your grip on your own memory. Everything he says sounds vaguely familiar, as if something like it might have once occurred. And even the things you once were sure of lose their patina of reality." A bit of Gorgik's hair had caught in the lock. With a finger, he yanked it loose—at a lull in the furnace's crackling, you could hear hair tear. "Why should I ever go to the Garth? I've avoided it so long I can no longer remember my reasons." Gorgik lifted the bronze disk from his chest and frowned at it. "Because of this, he assumed I must have been there. Some noble gave this to me, how many years ago now? I don't even recall if it was a man or a woman, or what the occasion was." He snorted and let the disk fall. "For a moment I thought they'd melt it into my chest with their cursed pokers." Gorgik looked around, stepped across gory stone. "Well, little master, you've proved yourself once more; and yet once more I suppose it's time to go." He picked up a broad sword leaning against the wall among a pile of weapons, frowned at the edge, scraped at it with the blunt of his thumb. "This will do."

Sarg, stepping over the torturer's body, suddenly bent, hooked a finger under the studded collar, and pulled it down. "Just checking on this one, hey, Gorgik?" The neck, beneath the leather, was iron bound.

"Checking what, little master?" Gorgik looked up from his blade.

"Nothing. Come on, Gorgik."

The big man's step held the ghost of a limp; Small Sarg noted it and beat the worry from his mind. The walk would grow steadier and steadier. (It had before.) "Now we must fight our way out of here and flee this crumbling pile."

"I'm ready for it, little master."

"Gorgik?"

"Yes, master?"

"The one who got away . . . ?"

"The one who was torturing me with his stupid questions?" Gorgik stepped to the furnace's edge, pulled aside the hanging. The door behind it, when he jiggled its rope handle, was immobile and looked to be of plank too thick to batter in. He let the curtain fall again. And the other doors, anyway, stood open.

"Who was he, Gorgik?"

The bearded man made a snorting sound. "We have our campaign, master—to free slaves and end the institution's inequities. The lords of Nevèrÿon have their campaign, their intrigues, their schemes and whims. What you and I know, or should know by now, is how little our and their campaigns actually touch . . . though in place after place they come close enough so that no man or woman can slip between without encounter, if not injury."

"I do not understand . . . ?"

Gorgik laughed, loud as the fire. "That's because I am the slave that I am and you are the master you are." And he was beside Sarg and past him; Small Sarg, behind him, ran.

3

The women shrieked—most of them. Gorgik, below swinging lamps, turned with raised sword to see one of the silent ones crouching against the wall beside a stool—an old woman, most certainly used to the jeweled collar cover, though hers had come off somewhere. There was only iron at her neck now. Her hair was in thin black braids, clearly dyed, and looping her brown forehead. Her eyes caught Gorgik's and perched on his gaze like some terrified creature's, guarding infinite secrets. For a moment he felt an urge, though it did not quite rise clear enough to take words, to question them. Then, in the confusion, a lamp chain broke; burning oil spilled. Guards and slaves and servants ran through a growing welter of flame. The woman was gone. And Gorgik turned, flailing, taking with him only her image. Somehow the castle had (again) been unable to conceive of its own fall at the hands of a naked man—or boy—and had, between chaos and rumor, collapsed into mayhem before the ten, the fifty, the hundred-fifty brigands who had stormed her. Slaves with weapons, guards with pot-tops and farm implements, paid servants carrying mysterious packages either for safety or looting, dashed there and here, all seeming as likely to be taken for foe as friend. Gorgik shouldered against one door; it splintered, swung out, and he was through—smoke trickled after him. He ducked across littered stone, following his shadow flickering with back light, darted through another door that was open

Silver splattered his eyes. He was outside; moonlight splintered through the low leaves of the catalpa above him. He turned, both to see where he'd been and if he were followed, when a figure already clear in the moon, hissed, "Gorgik!" above the screaming inside.

"Hey, little master!" Gorgik laughed and jogged across the rock.

Small Sarg seized Gorgik's arm. "Come on, Gorgik! Let's get out of here. We've done what we can, haven't we?"

Gorgik nodded and, together, they turned to plunge into the swampy forests of Strethi.

Making their way beneath branches and over mud, with silver spills shafting the mists, Small Sarg and Gorgik came, in the humid autumn night, to a stream, a clearing, a scarp—where two women sat at the white ashes of a recent fire, talking softly. And because these were primitive times when certain conversational formalities had not yet grown up to contour discourse among strangers, certain subjects that more civilized times might have banished from the evening were here brought quickly to the fore.

"I see a bruised and tired slave of middle age," said the woman who wore a mask and who had given her name as Raven. With ankles crossed before the moon-lit ash, she sat with her arms folded on her raised knees. "From that, one assumes that the youngster is the owner."

"But the boy," added the redhead kneeling beside her, who had given her name as Norema, "is a barbarian, and in this time and place it is the southern barbarians who, when they come this far north, usually end up slaves. The older, for all his bruises, has the bearing of a Kolhari man, whom you'd expect to be the owner."

Gorgik, sitting with one arm over one knee, said: "We are both free men. For the boy the collar is symbolic—of our mutual affection, our mutual protection. For myself, it is sexual—a necessary part in the pattern that allows both action and orgasm to manifest themselves within the single circle of desire. For neither of us is its meaning social, save that it shocks, offends, or deceives."

Small Sarg, also crosslegged but with his shoulders

hunched, his elbows pressed to his sides, and his fists on the ground, added, "My master and I are free."

The masked Raven gave a shrill bark that it took seconds to recognize as laughter: "You both claim to be free, yet one of you bears the title 'master' and wears a slave collar at the same time? Surely you are two jesters, for I have seen nothing like this in the length and breadth of this strange and terrible land."

"We are lovers," said Gorgik, "and for one of us the symbolic distinction between slave and master is necessary to desire's consummation."

"We are avengers who fight the institution of slavery wherever we find it," said Small Sarg, "in whatever way we can, and for both of us it is symbolic of our time in servitude and our bond to all men and women still so bound."

"If we have not pledged ourselves to death before capture, it is only because we both know that a living slave can rebel and a dead slave cannot," said Gorgik.

"We have sieged more than seven castles now, releasing the workers locked in the laboring pens, the kitchen and house slaves, and the administrative slaves alike. As well, we have set upon those men who roam through the land capturing and selling men and women as if they were property. Between castles and countless brigands, we have freed many who had only to find a key for their collars. And in these strange and barbaric times, any key will do."

The redheaded Norema said: "You love as master and slave and you fight the institution of slavery? The contradiction seems as sad to me as it seemed amusing to my friend."

"As one word uttered in three different situations may mean three entirely different things, so the collar worn in three different situations may mean three different things. They are not the same: sex, affection, and society," said Gorgik. "Sex and society relate like an object and its image in a reflecting glass. One reverses the other—are you familiar with the phenomenon, for these *are* primitive times, and mirrors are rare—"

"I am familiar with it," said Norema and gave him a long, considered look.

Raven said: "We are two women who have befriended each other in this strange and terrible land, and we have no love for slavers. We've killed three now in the two years we've traveled together—slavers who've thought to take us as property. It is easy, really, here where the men expect the women to scream and kick and bite and slap, but not to plan and place blades in their gut."

Norema said: "Once we passed a gang of slavers with a herd of ten women in collars and chains, camped for the night. We descended on them—from their shouts they seemed to think they'd been set on by a hundred fighting men."

Sarg and Gorgik laughed; Norema and Raven laughed—all recognizing a phenomenon.

"You know," mused Norema, when the laughter was done, "the only thing that allows you and ourselves to pursue our liberations with any success is that the official policy of Nevèrÿon goes against slavery under the edict of the Child Empress."

"Whose reign," said Gorgik, absently, "is just and generous."

"Whose reign," grunted the masked woman, "is a sun-dried dragon turd."

"Whose reign—" Gorgik smiled—"is currently insufferable, if not insecure."

Norema said: "To mouth those conservative formulas and actively oppose slavery seems to me the same sort of contradiction as the one you first presented us with." She took a reflective breath. "A day ago we stopped near here at the castle of the Suzeraine of Strethi. He was amused by us and entertained us most pleasantly. But we could not help notice that his whole castle was run by slaves, men and women. But we smiled, and ate slave-prepared food—and were entertaining back."

Gorgik said: "It was the Suzeraine's castle that we last sieged."

Small Sarg said: "And the kitchen slaves, who probably prepared your meal, are now free."

The two women, masked and unmasked, smiled at each other, smiles within which were inscribed both satisfaction and embarrassment.

"How do you accomplish these sieges?" Raven asked.

"One of the other of us, in the guise of a free man without collar, approaches a castle where we have heard there are many slaves and delivers an ultimatum." Gorgik grinned. "Free your slaves or . . ."

"Or what?" asked Raven.

"To find an answer to that question, they usually cast the one of us who came into the torture chamber. At which point the other of us, decked in the collar —it practically guarantees one entrance if one knows which doors to come in by—lays siege to the hold."

"Only," Small Sarg said, "this time it didn't work like that. We were together, planning our initial strategy, when suddenly the Suzeraine's guards attacked us. They seemed to know who Gorgik was. They called him by name and almost captured us both."

"Did they, now?" asked Norema.

"They seemed already to have their questions for me. At first I thought they knew what we had been doing. But these are strange and barbaric times; and information travels slowly here."

"What did they question you about?" Raven wanted to know.

"Strange and barbaric things," said Gorgik. "Whether I had worked as a messenger for some southern lord, carrying tales of children's bouncing balls and other trivial imports. Many of their questions centered about . . ." He looked down, fingering the metal disk hanging against his chest. As he gazed, you could see, from his tensing cheek muscle, a thought assail him.

Small Sarg watched Gorgik. "What is it . . . ?"

Slowly Gorgik's brutish features formed a frown. "When we were fighting our way out of the castle, there was a woman . . . a slave. I'm sure she was a slave. She wore the collar . . . But she reminded me of another woman, a noble woman, a woman I knew a long time ago . . ." Suddenly he smiled. "Though she too wore the collar from time to time, much for the same reasons as I."

The matted haired barbarian, the western woman in her mask, the island woman with her cropped hair sat about the silvered ash and watched the big man turn the disk. "When I was in the torture chamber, my thoughts were fixed on my own campaign for liberation and not on what to me seemed the idiotic fixations of my oppressor. Thus all their questions and comments are obscure to me now. By the same token, the man I am today obscures my memories of the youthful slave released from the bondage of the mines by this noble woman's whim. Yet, prompted by that face this evening, vague memories of then and now emerge and confuse themselves without clarifying. They turn about this instrument, for measuring time and space . . . they have to do with the name Krodar . . ."

The redhead said: "I have heard that name, Krodar . . ."

Within the frayed eyeholes, the night-blue eyes narrowed; Raven glanced at her companion.

Gorgik said: "There was something about a monastery in the south, called something like the Vygernangx . . . ?"

The masked woman said: "Yes, I know of the Vygernangx . . ."

The redhead glanced back at her friend with a look set between complete blankness and deep knowingness.

Gorgik said: "And there was something about the balls, the toys we played with as children . . . or perhaps the rhyme we played to . . . ?"

Small Sarg said: "When I was a child in the jungles of the south, we would harvest the little modules of sap that seeped from the scars in certain broadleafed palms and save them up for the traders who would come every spring for them . . ."

Both women looked at each other now, then at the men, and remained silent.

"It is as though—" Gorgik held up the verdigrised disk with its barbarous chasings—"all these things would come together in a logical pattern, immensely complex and greatly beautiful, tieing together slave and empress, commoner and lord—even gods and demons—to show how all are related in a negotiable pattern, like some sailors knot, not yet pulled taut, but laid out on the dock in loose loops, so that simply to see it in such form were to comprehend it even when yanked tight. And yet . . ." He turned the astrolabe over. ". . . they will *not* clear in my mind to any such pattern!"

Raven said: "The lords of this strange and terrible land indeed live lives within such complex and murderous knots. We have all seen them whether one has sieged a castle or been seduced by the hospitality of one; we have all had a finger through at least a loop in such a knot. You've talked of mirrors, pretty man, and of their strange reversal effect. I've wondered if our ignorance isn't simply a reversed image of their knowledge."

"And I've wondered—" Gorgik said, "slave, free-commoner, lord—if each isn't somehow a reflection of the other; or a reflection of a reflection."

"They are not," said Norema with intense conviction. *"That* is the most horrendous notion I've ever heard." But her beating lids, her astonished expression as she looked about in the moonlight, might have suggested to a sophisticated enough observer a conversation somewhere in her past of which this was the reflection.

Gorgik observed her, and waited.

After a while Norema picked up a stick, poked in the ashes with it: a single coal turned up ruby in the silver scatter and blinked.

After a few moments, Norema said: "Those balls . . . that the children play with in summer on the streets of Kolhari . . . Myself, I've always wondered where they came from—I mean I know about the orchards in the south. But I mean *how* do they get to the city every year."

"You don't know that?" Raven turned, quite astonished, to her redheaded companion. "You mean to tell me, island woman, that you and I have traveled together for over a year and a half, seeking fortune and adventure, and you have never asked me this nor have I ever told you?"

Norema shook her head.

Again Raven loosed her barking laughter. "Really, what is most strange and terrible about this strange and terrible land is how two women can be blood friends, chattering away for days at each other, saving one another's lives half a dozen times running and yet somehow never really talk! Let me tell you: the Western Crevasse, from which I hail, has, running along its bottom, a river that leads to the Eastern Ocean. My people live the whole length of the river, and those living at the estuary are fine, seafaring women. It is our boats, crewed by these sailing women of the Western Crevasse, who each year have sailed to the south in our red ships and brought back these toys to Kolhari, as indeed they also trade them up and down the river." A small laugh now, a sort of stifled snorting. "I was twenty and had already left my home before I came to one of your ports and the idea struck me that a man could actually *do* the work required on a boat."

"Aye," said Gorgik, "I saw those boats in my youth —but we were always scared to talk with anyone working on them. The captain was always a man; and we assumed, I suppose, that he must be a very evil person to have so many women within his power. Some proud, swaggering fellow—as frequently a foreigner as one of your own men—"

"Yes," said Norema. "I remember such a boat. The crew was all women and the captain was a great, black-skinned fellow who terrified everyone in my island village—"

"The captain a man?" The masked woman frowned beneath her mask's ragged hem. "I know there are boats from your Ulvayn islands on which men and women work together. But a man for a captain on a boat of my people . . . ? It is so unlikely that I am quite prepared to dismiss it as an outright imposs—" She stopped; then she barked, "Of course. The man on the boat! Oh, yes, my silly heathen woman, of course there is a man on the boat. There's always a man on the boat. But he's certainly *not* the Captain. Believe me, my friend, even though I have seen men fulfil it, Captain is a woman's job: and in our land it is usually the eldest sailor on the boat who takes the job done by your captain."

"If it wasn't the captain, then," asked Norema, "who was he?"

"How can I explain it to you . . . ?" Raven said. "There is always a man in a group of laboring women in my country. But he is more like a talisman, or a good-luck piece the women take with them, than a working sailor—much less an officer. He is a figure of prestige, yes, which explains his fancy dress; but he is not a figure of power. Indeed, do you know the wooden women who are so frequently carved on the prow of your man-sailored ships? Well he fulfils a part among our sailors much as that wooden woman does among yours. I suppose to you it seems strange. But in our land, a single woman lives with a harem of men; and in our land, any group of women at work always keeps a single man. Perhaps it is simply another of your reflections? But you, in your strange and terrible land, can see nothing *but* men at the heads of things. The captain indeed! A pampered pet who does his exercises every morning on the deck, who preens and is praised and shown off at every port —that is what men are for. And, believe me, they love it, no matter what they say. But a man . . . a *man* with power and authority and the right to make decisions? You must excuse me, for though I have been in your strange and terrible land for years and know such things exist here, I still cannot think of such things among my own people without laughing." And here she gave her awkward laugh, while with her palm she beat her bony knee. "Seriously," she said when her laugh was done, "such a pattern for work seems so natural to me that I cannot really believe you've never encountered anything like it before—" she was talking to Norema now—"even here."

Norema smiled, a little strangely. "Yes, I . . . I have heard of something like it before."

Gorgik again examined the redhead's face, as if he

might discern, inscribed by eye-curve and cheek-bone and forehead-line and lip-shape what among her memories reflected this discussion.

Something covered the moon.

First masked Raven, then the other three, looked up. Wide wings labored off the light.

"What is such a mountain beast doing in such a flat and swampy land?" asked Small Sarg.

"It must be the Suzeraine's pet," Norema said. "But why should he have let it go?"

"So," said Raven, "once again tonight we are presented with a mysterious sign and no way to know whether it completes a pattern or destroys one." The laugh this time was something that only went on behind her closed lips. "They cannot fly very far. There is no ledge for her to perch on. And once she lands, in this swampy morass, she won't be able to regain flight. Her wings will tear in the brambles and she will never fly again."

But almost as if presenting the image of some ironic answer, the wings flapped against a sudden, high, unfelt breeze, and the beast, here shorn of all fables, rose and rose—for a while—under the night.

—New York
Oct. '76—July '78

APPENDIX

Some Informal Remarks
Toward the Modular Calculus,
Part Three

When, in the spring of 1947, Muhammed the Wolf
flung his stone into the cave near Ain Feshkla, breaking open the jar containing the first of the Dead Sea
Scrolls, or, indeed, when, eighty years before, the
Turkish archeologist Rassam and the Englishmen Lay-
ard and Smith shoveled through into the Temple
Library at Nineveh, giving the world the Gilgamesh
epic, both provided steps in a clarification that had
been progressing apace even among the discoveries
made as Schliemann's workers sunk their pickaxes at
Hissàrlik.

The fragment known as the Culhar' (or sometimes
the Kolharē) Text—and more recently as the Missolonghi Codex (from the Greek town where the volumes, now on store in the basement of the Istanbul
Archeological Museum, were purchased in the nine-
teenth century, and which contain what is now considered to be one of the two oldest versions of the
text known) not only has a strange history, but a
strangely disseminated history. The most recent stage
of that dissemination has joined it with an abstruse
mathematical theory and the creative mind of a fascinating young scholar.

The Culhar' Text itself, a narrative fragment of ap-
proximately nine hundred words, has been known and
noted in many languages for centuries, among them

Sanskrit, Aramaic, Persian, Arabic, and Proto-Latin.
From time to time, claims of great antiquity have been
made for it—4,500 B.C., or even 5,000 B.C., which
would put it practically inside the muzzy boundaries
of the neolithic revolution. But such claims, at least
until recently, have been dismissed by serious scholars
as fanciful.

Still, the fact that versions of the text have been
found in so many languages suggests that at one time
it was considered a text of great importance in the
ancient world. But the reasons why the text was considered so important have only recently come to light.

The only ancient people who did not, apparently,
know of the Culhar' fragment were, oddly, the Attic
Greeks—though their ignorance of it no doubt goes
a long way to explain the length of time it has taken for
modern speculation to reach any productive level.

In 1896, four years after Haupt published the second of his two-volume edition of the then extant
cuneiform tablets, by chance a scholar of ancient Persian, visiting Peter Jensen in Germany when the latter
was engaged in his German translations which were to
appear in 1900 and 1901, recognized one of the fragmentary tablets that had been clearly excluded from
the Gilgamesh tale as a Babylonian version of the
Culhar', which till then had more or less generally
been thought to have originated in ancient Persia
many years later.

The establishment of the Culhar' Text's composition
at a date notably before Homer was a highly significant
discovery. Indeed, had the Nineveh tablets been found
to contain, say, a Babylonian translation of one of
the Homeric hymns, scholarly circles would no doubt
have been thrown into a turmoil that would still be
reflected today in every introduction to the Illiad or
the Odyssey and every popularized account of modern
archeological investigations. As it was, however, the
notice taken of that discovery seems to have been restricted to mentions only by three German orientalists.
And two of those mentions were in footnotes. Still,
at least one of the footnotes made the point that a
question—which apparently had last vexed a whole

monastery full of ninth-century Rumanian monks—
had once again come to the fore: In just what language
did the Culhar' fragment originate?

Schliemann's successor at Hissàrlik, Carl William
Blegan, discovered a Greek version of the text in the
fourth down of the nine cities built one a-top the other
at the site of Troy. Did even older versions exist in
level VIIa, the level now believed to be historical
Illium? If so, it was apparently not among the booty
Agamemnon brought back to the Argolis.

We have mentioned the Dead Sea Scrolls already:
what was found in '47, among the sewn-together parchments in their wrappings of linen and pitch among
the jars and copper scrolls from the caves on the
Dead Sea Shore, was one parchment fragment, clearly
not among the major scrolls and not clearly related to
the Essene protocols as were the interesting majority
of the others, containing an ancient Hebrew text that
seemed to be nothing less than a fragmentary vocabulary in which hieroglyphiclike markings were equated
with ancient Hebrew words and phrases. It was ini-
tially assumed, by Khun, Baker and others, that this
was a lexicon to facilitate the study of some lost
Egyptian text. But either because of the political situation existing between Egypt and Israel, or because the
Hebrew words were not part of the vocabulary associated with the Exodus, interest was more or less deferred in this particular parchment. (Edmund Wilson
in his book on the Dead Sea Scrolls does not even
mention its existence.) And the judgment that the
language was actually Egyptian was, itself, disputed
on so many counts that the question finally vanished
with the excitement over the contents of other texts
from other jars, other sites.

At any rate, it was not until 1971 that a young
American scholar, K. Leslie Steiner, who had been
given an informal account of this parchment by a
friend at the University of Tel Aviv, realized that most
of the Hebrew words seemed to be translations of
words that appeared in that at-one-time most ubiquitous of ancient texts: the Culhar' fragment.

K. Leslie Steiner was born in Cuba in 1945. Her mother was a black American from Alabama; her father was an Austrian Jew. From 1951 on, Steiner grew up in Ann Arbor, where both her parents taught at the University of Michigan, and where Steiner now holds joint tenure in the German, Comparative Literature, and Mathematics departments.

Steiner's mathematical work has mostly been done in an obscure spin-off of a branch of category theory called "naming, listing, and counting theory." By the time she was twenty-two, her work had established her as one of America's three leading experts in the field. This was the work that she was shortly to bring to bear on the problem of this ancient text in such a novel and ingenius way. When she was twenty-four, Steiner published a book called *The Edge of Language* with Bowling Green University Press—not, as one might imagine from our account so far, a treatise on ancient scripts, but rather a study of linguistic patterns common to comic books, pornography, contemporary poetry, and science fiction,* one of the decade's more daunting volumes in the field of popular and cross-cultural studies. Steiner's linguistic/archeological interests, nevertheless, have been a consuming amateur hobby—the tradition, apparently, with so many who have made the greatest contributions to the field, from Heinrich Schliemann himself to Michael Ventris, both of whom were basically brilliant amateurs.

Steiner's recognition of the scroll as a lexicon meant to facilitate the study of the Culhar' Text in some

* Steiner has written numerous personable and insightful reviews of science fiction novels that have appeared in several Midwestern science fiction "fanzines," many of whose readers are probably unaware of her scholarly accomplishments.

long-lost language would be notable enough. But
Steiner also went on to establish that the language
was *not* Egyptian, at least not any variety we possess.
Eighteen months of followup seemed to suggest, from
the appearance of the lost script, that, if anything, it
was a variety of writing related to the cuneiform
ideograms of the Mesopotamian and Indus Valley re-
gions. Her subsequent efforts to locate exactly *which*
form of cuneiform it might be (during which she herself distinguished three distinct forms among the numerous untranslatable tablets that still exist) will no doubt
someday make a fascinating book. Suffice it to say,
however, that in 1977, one Yavus Ahmed Bey, a
24-year-old research assistant in the Istanbul Archeological Museum, directed Steiner to a codex of un-
translated (and presumably untranslatable) texts on
store in the library archives.

The codex, a set of loose parchments and vela, had
been purchased in Missolonghi in the late summer of
1824, a city and a year that readers of Romantic poetry
will immediately associate with the death of Byron—
though from all accounts, the sale of the codex, some
four months after the poet's death in the war-ravaged
town, had nothing to do with Byron *per se*. Indeed the
36-year-old poet, who, by the cruel April of his demise,
had become obese, drunken, and drug besotted, has
the dubious distinction of more than likely knowing
nothing at all of the valuable collection of texts that
shared the village with him in a basement storage chest
a kilometer and a half up the road. The private col-
lector who bought the codex immediately spirited it
away to Ankara.

Shortly after World War I, the codex came to the
Istanbul museum, where apparently it remained, all
but unexamined by any save the odd research assistant. It took Steiner only an afternoon's search through
the contents of the codex to locate the short, five-page
text, clearly in the same script as the parchment un-
earthed thirty years before by a Bedouin youth. Between the Ancient Hebrew lexicon and what is known
of other translations of the Culhar' fragment, it was
comparatively simple to establish that here was, in-

deed, a parchment copy of still another version of the Culhar', this time in an unknown cuneiform-style language. But the significant point here was a note, in yet *another* language, written at the end of this parchment; we must point out again that this codex was purchased in 1824 and all but ignored till 1977. But since the late 1950's, practically any amateur concerned with ancient scripts would have recognized the script of the appended note: it was the ancient Greek syllabary writing from Crete, deciphered by the young engineer Michael Ventris in 1954, known as Linear-B.

The parchment itself, from the evidence of other markings, most probably dates from the third century A.D., but it is also most probably a copy made from a much older source,* very possibly by someone who did not know the meaning of the letters put down. Indeed, it is the only fragment of Linear-B ever to be found outside of Crete. And it is a language that, as far as we know, no one has known how to read for something in the neighborhood of five to six thousand years. The Linear-B fragment, which was soon translated, reads:

> Above these words are written the oldest writing known to wise men by a human hand. It is said that they were written in the language of the country called by our grandparents Transpoté.

Here, in this fragment, we most certainly have the explanation for why the Culhar' was so widespread during ancient times and the nature of its importance: apparently, over a good deal of Europe and Asia Minor, during ancient times, the Culhar' Text was thought to be the origin of writing, or the archetrace.

Where Transpoté might be is a complete mystery still, though from internal evidence one would assume it was on a coast somewhere, of a body of water large enough to have islands more than a day's sail from land. In Greek, "Transpoté" would seem to be pos-

---

* Other parchments in the codex, written in the same ink and presumed to come from the same time, are transcriptions of block-letter Greek inscriptions, that sculptural language written on stone in upper case letters without word-breaks, dating from pre-classic times.

sibly a play on the words "across never." The Homeric meaning includes the possibility of "across when" or "a distant once." There is also, of course, a more prosaic reading possible, that reads "pote-" as some sort of apocopation of "potamos" meaning *river,* so that the translation may simply be "across the river." Other translations possible are "far never" and "far when"—none of which, alas, helps us locate the actual country.

But if the Linear-B fragment is authentic, then it establishes with high probability the neolithic origins of the Culhar' text—and probably the language transcribed in the Missolonghi Codex—since Linear-B was in use only in the very early stages of the history of the neolithic palaces at Cnossos, Phaistos, and Malliá.

3

But to explain the nature of Steiner's major contribution, we must leave the Culhar' fragment itself for a page or so and speak about the origins of writing; and about Steiner's mathematical work.

The currently reigning archeological theory holds that writing as we know it began not as marks made on paper or skins, or even impressions made on soft clay with pointed sticks, but rather as a set of clay tokens in the shapes of spheres, half spheres, cones, tetrahedrons, and—at a later date—doublecones (or biconoids), as well as other shapes, some with holes or lines inscribed on them, some without. For some five thousand years at least (*c.* 7,000 B.C. to *c.* 2,000 B.C.) these tokens in various parts of the Middle East formed a system of account keeping, the various tokens representing animals, foods, jars; and the numbers of them corresponding to given amounts of these goods. The tokens have been found in numerous archeological sites from numerous periods. Until recently archeologists tended to assume they were beads, gaming pieces, children's toys, or even religious objects. The consistency in the shapes from site to site, however, has only recently been noted. And it was practically at the same time as Steiner was making her discoveries in Istanbul that Denise Schmandt-Besserat realized that a number of the cuneiform signs in the clay tablets associated with Uruk and Nineveh were simply two-dimensional representations of these three-dimensional shapes, complete with their added incisions, holes, and decorations.

Thus "the violence of the letter" (a phrase given currency by Jacques Derrida in his book on the metaphor of "speech vs. writing" in Western thought, *Of Grammatology* [Paris: 1967]) may very well have begun, to use Schmandt-Besserat's words, with the clay ". . . rolled between the palms of the hand or the lumps pinched between the fingertips . . . incised and punched." Indeed, Derrida's "double writing," or "writing within writing," seems to be intriguingly dramatized by the most recent archeological findings.

In Mesopotamian contractual situations, so runs the theory, these clay tokens were used to make up various bills of lading, with given numbers of tokens standing for corresponding amounts of grain, fabric, or animals. The tokens were then sealed in clay "bullae," which served as envelopes for transmitting the contracts. The envelopes presumably had to arrive unbroken. In order to facilitate the dealings, so that one would know, as it were, what the contract was about (in the sense of around . . . ?), the tokens were first pressed into the curved outer surface of the still-pliable clay bulla, before they were put inside and the bulla was sealed. Thus the surface of the bulla was inscribed with a *list* of the tokens it contained. In a legal debate, the bulla could be broken open before judges and the true "word" within revealed.

The writing that *we* know as writing, in Babylonia at any rate, came about from situations in which such double writing-within-writing was not considered necessary. Curved clay tablets (and the reason for those curves has been hugely wondered at. Storage is the usual explanation. Schmandt-Besserat's theory: they aped the curve of the bullarum surfaces, from which they were derived) were inscribed with *pictures* of the impressions formerly made by the tokens. These pictures of the token impressions developed into the more than 1,500 ideograms that compose the range of cuneiform writing.

Bear in mind the *list* of tokens impressed on the bulla surface; and we are ready for a brief rundown of Steiner's most exciting contribution, in many people's opinion, to the matter. Steiner herself has written in a popular article: "Briefly, what I was able to do was simply to bring my mathematical work in Naming, Listing, and Counting Theory to bear on my archeological hobby. N/L/C theory deals with various kinds of order, the distinctions between them, and also with ways of combining them. In a 'naming' (that is, a collection of designated, i.e., named, objects), basically all you can do—assuming that's the only kind of order you possess—is be sure that one object is not any of the others. When you have this much order, there are certain things you can do and certain things you can't do. Now let's go on and suppose you have a 'list' of objects. In a 'list,' you not only know each object's name, but you know its relation to two other objects, the one 'above' it in the list and the one 'below' it in the list. Again, with this much order, and no more, you can do certain things and cannot do certain others. And in a 'count,' you have a collection of objects correlated with what is known as a 'proper list.' (Sometimes it's called a 'full list.') A 'count' allows you to specify many, many complicated relationships between one object and the others—all this, of course, is detailed in rigorous terms when you work with the theory." For the last dozen years or so N/L/C theoreticians have been interested in what used to be called "third level order." More recently, this level of order has been nicknamed "language," because it shares a surprising number of properties with language as we know it.

"Language" is defined by something called a "noncommutative substitution matrix." As Steiner explains it, a noncommutative substitution matrix is ". . . a collection of rules that allows unidirectional substitutions of listable subsets of a collection of names. For example, suppose we have the collection of names A, B, C, D, and E. Such a matrix of rules might begin by saying: Wherever we find AB, we can substitute CDE (though it does not necessarily work the other way around). Whenever we find DE, we can substitute ACD. Whenever we find any term following ECB we can substitute AC for that term. And so forth." Steiner goes on to explain that these rules will sometimes make complete loops of substitution. Such a loop is called, by N/L/C theoreticians, a "discourse." "When we have enough discursive (i.e., looping) and nondiscursive sets of rules, the whole following a fairly complicated set of criteria, then we have what's known as a *proper* noncommutative substitution matrix, or a full grammar, or a 'language.' Or, if you will, an example of third level order."

N/L/C theory got its start as an attempt to generate the rules for each higher level of order by combining the rules for the lower levels in various recursive ways. Its first big problem was the discovery that while it is fairly easy to generate the rules for a "language" by combining the rules for a "naming" and a "list," it is impossible to generate the rules for a "count" *just* from a "naming" and a "list," without generating a proper "language" first—which is why a "language," and not a "count," is the third level of order. A "count," which is what most of mathematics up through calculus is based on in one form or another, is really a *degenerate* form of language. " 'Counting,' as it were, presupposes 'language,' and not the other way around." Not only is most mathematics based on the rules governing the "count," so is most extant hard computer circuitry. Trying to develop a real language from these "count" rules is rather difficult; whereas if one starts only with the rules governing a "naming" and a "list" to get straight to the more complicated third-level order known as "language," then the "language" can include its own degenerate form of the "count."

To relate all this to the archeology of ancient languages, we must go back to the fact that we asked you not to forget. Inside the bulla we have a collection of tokens, or a "naming." On the outside of the bulla, we have the impressions of the tokens, or a "list."

How does this relate to the Culhar' Text? Soon after Steiner made her discovery in the Istanbul Museum, a bulla was discovered by Pierre Amiet at the great Susa excavation at Ellimite, containing a collection of tokens that, at least in x-ray, may well represent a goodly portion of the words of the ubiquitous Culhar' fragment; the bulla probably dates, by all consensus, from *c.* 7,000 B.C. Is this, perhaps, the oldest version of the Culhar'? What basically leaves us unsure is simply that the surface of this bulla is blank. Either it was not a contract (and thus never inscribed); or it was eroded by time and the elements.

What Steiner has done is assume that the Missolonghi Codex is the "list" that should be inscribed on the bulla surface. She then takes her substitution patterns from the numerous versions in other languages. There is a high correlation between the contained tokens and the inscriptions on the parchment discovered in Istanbul.

Using some of the more arcane substitution theory of N/L/C, coupled with what is known of other translations, Steiner has been able to offer a number of highly probable (and in some cases highly imaginative) revisions of existing translations based on the theoretical mechanics of various discursive loopings.

Steiner herself points out that an argument can be made that the tokens inside the Susa bulla may just happen to include many of the words in the Culhar' simply by chance. And even if it is not chance, says Steiner, ". . . the assignments are highly problematic at a number of points; they may just be dead wrong. Still, the results are intriguing, and the process itself is fun."

4

Whatever other claims can be made for the Culhar', it is almost certainly among our oldest narrative texts. It clearly predates Homer and most probably Gilgamesh—conceivably by as much as four thousand years.

The classic text in Western society comes with a history of anterior recitation which, after a timeless period, passed from teller to teller, is at last committed to a writing that both privileges it and contaminates it. This is, if only by tradition, both the text of Homer and the text of the Eddas. And we treat the text of Gilgamesh in the same way, though there is no positive evidence it did not begin as a written composition.

The Culhar' clearly and almost inarguably begins as a written text—or at least the product of a mind clearly familiar with the reality of writing.

The opening metaphor, of the towers of the sunken buildings inscribing their tale on the undersurface of the sea so that it may be read by passing sailors looking over the rail of their boats, is truly an astonishing moment in the history of Western imagination. One of Steiner's most interesting emendations, though it is the one least supported by the mathematics, is that the image itself is a metaphor for what might be translated: ". . . the irregular roofing stones of the sunken buildings mold the waves from below into tokens [of the sunken buildings' existence] so that passing sailors looking over their boat rails can read their presence (and presumably steer clear of them)." In some forms of the token-writing, Steiner also points out, the token for "bulla" and the token for "sea" are close enough to cause confusion. Steiner suggests this might be another pun.

But if this reference to token-writing *is* correct, it poses what may be a problem later on in the Culhar': at almost the exact center of the fragment there is a reference Steiner herself admits translates as "an old woman on the island, putting colored 'memory marks' on unrolled reeds" These, incidentally, are among the tokens "reed," "old woman," "island" that show up most clearly inside the bulla, though of course we have no way to be sure—from the bulla—what their order is supposed to be. Were there at one time two forms of writing? Or perhaps, as Steiner suggests, there actually was ". . . a 'natural' writing, that came as an amalgam of vegetable and mineral pigments and vegetable or animal parchments, anterior to this Mesopotamian ceramic violence-within-a-violence, a writing in which the Culhar' begins, a writing later surpressed along with '. . . the three-legged pots and the weak flights of the storied serpents [dragons?] . . .' that the Culhar' mentions both towards its beginning and its end."

Here are some further examples of traditional versions of the Culhar' with Steiner's mathematically inspired emendations:

"I walk with a woman who carries two thin knives," reads the second sentence of most versions of the text in at least half the languages it has shown up in. Previous commentators have taken this to refer to some kind of priestess or religious ritual. Steiner reads this (at one of the two places where her reading makes the text more, instead of less, confusing): "I travel (or journey) with a hero (feminine) carrying a double blade (or twin-blades)." One has to admit that, weapon-wise, this is a bit odd.

The emotional center of the Culhar', for most modern readers at any rate, is the narrator's confession that he (Steiner, for reasons that must finally be attributed to a quaintly feminist aberration, insists on referring to the narrator as *she*) is exiled from the city of Culhar', the city that names the text, and is doomed to spend his (her?) life traveling from the "large old roofless greathouses" to the "large new roofed greathouses" and "begging gifts from hereditary nobles."

Steiner's comment about the sex of the narrator is illuminating about her mathematics, however: "The highest probability my equations yield for my suggested translations is fifty percent—which, as anyone who has worked in the field of ancient translation knows, is a lot higher than many versions that are passed off as gospel (with both a small, *and* capital, 'g'). Since the sex of the narrator of a sexually unspecified text is always a fifty-fifty possibility, I simply take my choice, which is consistent with the rest of my work."

A phrase that has puzzled commentators for a long time reads, in some versions: "the love of the small outlander for the big slave from Culharē." Although here Steiner's equations did not settle anything, they generated a list of equally weighted possibilities (Steiner prefers the word *"barbarian"* to "outlander," and argues for it well):

1) "the love of the small barbarian slave for the tall man from Culharē"

2) "the love of the tall slave from Culharē for the small barbarian"

3) "the small love of the barbarian and the tall man for slavery"

"It is even possible," writes Steiner, "that the phrase is a complex pun in which all these meanings could be read from it." Just how this might actually function in the narrative of which the Culhar' fragment is a part, however, she doesn't say.

Here are some other emendations that Steiner's matrix equations have yielded *vis-à-vis* some of the more traditional versions that have come from other translations:

"For a long time they starved in the greathouse after the women had eaten their sons," runs the consensus version from Sanskrit to Arabic.

Steiner's emendation: "He starved in the greathouse many years after she had eaten her own twin sons." Moreover, says Steiner, the antecedent of *He* is none other than our tall friend from Culharē.

At least five traditional versions have some form of the sentence: "The merchant trades four-legged pots for three-legged pots," which is usually taken to be a proverb that, because we are not sure exactly what the pots were used for, we do not quite understand.

Steiner: "The merchant [female] ceases to deal in three-legged pots and now deals in four-legged pots."

The traditional translation: "Dragons fly in the northern mountains of El' Hamon. The Dragon Lord rules over the south, and the southern priests, and the children's high bouncing balls."

Steiner: "Dragons fly in the northern mountains at Ellamon. But the Dragon Lord vanishes in the south among the southern priests and the children's high bouncing balls." Though precisely *what* the Dragon Lord is doing with the children's bouncing balls is a question that has puzzled everyone from those Rumanian monks to Steiner herself; it is finally anybody's guess.

Steiner's translation of the closing of the Culhar' pretty well agrees with most traditional versions, though some of her "fifty percent possibility" alternates are a bit disconcerting, if not disingenuous:

". . . the polished metal mirror [or "stomach" suggests Steiner without comment; or "genitals"] destroys [or "distorts," or "reverses"] all I see before me and behind me."

Whatever one may say, most of Steiner's suggestions make the text a lot more coherent than it appears in most versions. Problems remain, however, such as the vanishing Dragon Lord or the twin blades. Some of Steiner's suggestions (for instance, that the "child ruler Inel'ko" referred to in the text is really a girl) should probably be taken with the same grain of salt with which we take her suggestion that the author is a woman. One recalls the eccentric theories of Samuel Butler and Robert Graves on the feminine authorship of the Odyssey; and one smiles with the same intrigued indulgence.

But whichever of Steiner's readings one accepts or rejects, it is impossible not to find one's imagination plunging into the images thrown up by this archeological oddity, this writing on and around and within writing, and not come up with myriad narrative possibilities that might meet, or even cross, in this ancient fragment. If some writer were to actually put down these stories, just what sort of reflection might they constitute, either of the modern world or of our own past history?

Could one perhaps consider such an imaginative expansion simply another translation, another reading of the text, another layer of the palimpsest?

It is difficult here not to recall Lèvi-Straus's suggestion that all versions of a myth must be studied together in order to complete the picture—ancient versions and modern alike—and that Freud's "Oedipus Complex" is simply the most modern version of the Oedipus myth and should be taken as part of it. Yet by the same token (as it were) one must yet again recall Derrida's *Of Grammatology,* whose first half is such a crushing critique of Lèvi-Straus's nostalgia for "primitive presence" in matters anthropological. The question must finally be: Are Steiner's equations the expressions of a conservative collective speech, which would certainly seem to be the case with any probability work concerning myth or language; or, are they the expression of a radical individualistic authority—which seems, at any rate, to be the collective view of mathematical creativity, if not authorship/authority itself.

But the recall of *Of Grammatology* is itself appropriately double. Let us consider Derrida's reminder that the basic structure of written signification is not, as it is in speech, the signifier of the signified, but rather the signifier of the signfier, a model of a model, an image of an image, the trace of an endlessly deferred signification.

Just what would the value of such an imaginative narrative experiment, as we spoke of, be? Exactly what sort of imaginative act would constitute, as it were, the mirror of Steiner's own? Our answer must be deferred, however, since such a tale, or set of tales, written in reflection of the extant versions of the Culhar' Text has not been written. And the Culhar' Text itself seems to play through the spectrum of Eastern and Western languages as translations of translations, some older, some newer, but finally with no locable origin.

—S. L. Kermit
January, 1981

ABOUT THE AUTHOR

SAMUEL R. DELANY, born April Fool's Day, 1942, grew up in New York City's Harlem. His novels *Babel-17* and *The Einstein Intersection* both won Nebula Awards from the Science Fiction Writers of America, as have his short fictions *Aye, and Gomorrah* and *Time Considered as a Helix of Semi-Precious Stones* (which also took a Hugo Award during the World Science Fiction Convention at Heidelberg). His books include *The Jewels of Aptor, The Fall of the Towers, Nova, Driftglass* (short stories), *Dhalgren, Triton, Heavenly Breakfast* (nonfiction) and *Tales of Nevèrÿon*. With his wife, National Book Award-winning poet Marilyn Hacker, he co-edited the speculative fiction quarterly *Quark*. He also wrote, directed and edited the half-hour film *The Orchid*. In 1975 he was visiting Butler Chair Professor of English at the State University of New York at Buffalo. For the last half dozen years Delany and Hacker have lived between New York, San Francisco and London. They have one daughter.

THE IMAGINATIVE WORLDS OF
SAMUEL R. DELANY

NOVA

A passion for vengeance drives Capt. Lorq von Ray to dare
what no mortal has ever done—to sail through the splintering core of a disintegrating sun. His obsession draws aim-
less souls into the vortex of his madness—wandering
adventurers who would plug into any ship that promises
escape.

DHALGREN

The sun has grown deadly The world has gone mad,
society has perished and savagery rules. All that was
known is over, all that was familiar is strange and terrible.
In these dying days of earth a nameless young drifter enters
the city—to influence the lives of those around him.

TRITON

The human race has colonized Triton, moon of Neptune,
where the ideals of universal prosperity are possible. Within this strange climate of complete utopia and certain
doom, Bron Helstrom seeks passion and purpose from a
gypsy woman whose wisdom and power will forever reverse his life.

TALES OF NEVÈRŸON

The world of a barbarous alien empire ruled by primal
brutality, intrigue and fear. A world of bizarre paradoxes,
powerful mysteries and sexual abandon. The world of
Gorgik, thick-hewn mine slave whose prowess defies the
mighty.

HEAVENLY BREAKFAST

A long, searching personal look back at the scenes of
Samuel Delany's youthful adventures—the launching pad
for the psychedelic voyages that shapes his phenomenal
science fiction.

These books by Samuel Delany are all Bantam Books,
available wherever paperbacks are sold.